PRAISE FOR *GHOSTS OF GLENCOE*

"The Adirondacks are magical, but also more complicated than many visitors ever realize. This book helps capture the majesty and the complexity of one of the world's great places."—**Bill McKibben, author of** *Radio Free Vermont*

"*Ghosts of Glencoe* combines a gripping narrative with a lush and lyrical description of the landscapes they are set within. Mountains and characters come alive in this work that has the finest elements of expedition story, coming-of-age novel, and thrilling adventure."—**Julia Goren, Adirondack Mountain Club education director, contributing author to** *Adirondack Archangels*, **and board president of Northern Lights School**

"Suspenseful, gripping, and fast paced, with adept scene-shifting—some unlikely ninth graders from an unusual school collide in a deadly encounter with two escaped convicts in the winter-deep Adirondack woods. Safeguarded secrets clamor to spring loose, challenging the head of school to come to terms with his own shameful past."—**Laura Waterman, author of** *Starvation Shore*

"Riveting and wise, a page-turner with ratcheting suspense, stunning mountains, and a big heart; characters with painful secrets and self-doubts find their own strength as they push the limits of physical endurance. Chilling bad guys, pathless woods, and extreme winter conditions threaten three teens from an Adirondack school and challenge its headmaster in an edge-of-the-cliff adventure that changes lives."—**Susan Strehle, Distinguished Service Professor of English at Binghamton University**

"*Ghosts of Glencoe* is a gripping tale with its roots in the Adirondacks that the writer knows so well. The plot begins with many descriptive and disparate strands that the author weaves expertly into a fascinating tale of challenge and growth. A thoroughly entertaining read!"—**Philip**

Corell, treasurer of Adirondack Forty-Sixers and contributing author to *Adirondack Archangels* and *Heaven Up'Histedness*

"*Ghosts of Glencoe* is a truly authentic adventure story set in the wilderness of the Adirondack mountains, a place where I spent countless hours as a kid and camp counselor. Readers will enjoy the suspenseful outcome of the main protagonists: a sixty-three-year-old headmaster and a fifteen-year-old ninthth grader who struggle with personal accountability for shadows they themselves created. This compelling tale is set at a unique boarding school where children are key contributors to its operation, where experiential education is paramount, and where the utilization of technology is healthy and suitably limited."—**James Steyer, founder of Common Sense Media, civil rights attorney, professor, and author**

"*Ghosts of Glencoe* is a thrillingly plotted, utterly authentic coming-of-age story of what we can all learn from wilderness, at any age. I cared what happened to these characters and couldn't stop reading until its most satisfying conclusion."—**Marion Nestle, professor of nutrition, food studies, and public health, emerita, New York University, and author of books about food politics**

GHOSTS OF GLENCOE

CHUCK SCHWERIN

BOOKS

NORTH COUNTRY BOOKS

North Country Books
An imprint of Globe Pequot, the trade division of The Rowman & Littlefield Publishing Group, Inc.
4501 Forbes Blvd., Ste. 200
Lanham, MD 20706
www.rowman.com

Distributed by NATIONAL BOOK NETWORK

British Library Cataloguing in Publication Information Available

Library of Congress Cataloging-in-Publication Data
Names: Schwerin, Chuck, 1950– author.
Title: Ghosts of Glencoe / Chuck Schwerin.
Description: Lanham, MD : North Country Books, an imprint of Globe Pequot, the trade division of The Rowman & Littlefield Publishing Group, Inc., 2024. | Summary: "In the fall of 2002, dramatic events engulf three ninth graders (not the best of friends), their passionate Scottish headmaster, and an unlikely pair of desperate escapees from a nearby prison. The inevitable collision of these forces demonstrates that age and experience has no monopoly on bravery or vulnerability"— Provided by publisher.
Identifiers: LCCN 2024000199 (print) | LCCN 2024000200 (ebook) | ISBN 9781493085088 (paperback) | ISBN 9781493087693 (epub)
Subjects: LCGFT: Novels.
Classification: LCC PS3619.C495 G48 2024 (print) | LCC PS3619.C495 (ebook) | DDC 813/.6—dc23/eng/20240122
LC record available at https://lccn.loc.gov/2024000199
LC ebook record available at https://lccn.loc.gov/2024000200

♾️ The paper used in this publication meets the minimum requirements of American National Standard for Information Sciences—Permanence of Paper for Printed Library Materials, ANSI/NISO Z39.48-1992

PROLOGUE

Hamish MacLean paused behind a boulder to shelter from the wind, his breath steaming in the glow of his headlamp. He fished a small flask from inside his parka, thoughtfully stowed near his chest to prevent it from freezing. He checked his watch; it was nearly one. *Probably still a mile or so to the CIC hut*, he thought, referring to the rustic shelter at the base of Ben Nevis, a Scottish Highlands magnet for hikers and climbers of every stripe, and the highest point in the British Isles. Hamish flicked off his headlamp for a moment to take in the extraordinary moonless sky, the firmament seemingly twinkling just for him. It was as spiritual a feeling as his twenty-year-old sensibility could conjure.

Once his heart rate had settled, he returned the flask to his parka, switched his headlamp back on, and picked his way carefully along the steepening path, the snow hard-packed by the day's previous climbers. With no trees on the barren landscape, the February wind howled. He readjusted the balaclava to cover his nose and mouth and tightened his parka hood. His boots crackled on the frozen path.

There was little difference in temperature as he entered the darkened hut after the testing two-hour hike from the North Face trailhead near the town of Torlundy. The tidy shelter was quiet, save for gentle snores from perhaps two dozen sleeping bodies arrayed before him. He wiped icicles from his scraggly beard as he swung his headlamp around the main room of the Spartan hut, searching for the empty bed he had reserved. But all bunks were taken. Swearing under his breath, Hamish unshouldered his pack, heavy with climbing gear, unrolled a foam pad and sleeping bag, and found a spot on the stone floor in front of the fireplace, a few embers still giving off a modicum of warmth. *Some crummy bastard is sleeping in the bed I paid for*, he thought. Soon, his own snores blended in with all the others.

Five hours earlier he had departed Edinburgh. Driving up the A9, with a stop in Glencoe for supper, gave him ample time to consider the challenge for which he had so meticulously prepared—the second recorded winter ascent of the mountain via a route called Zero Gully. At an elevation of 4,413 feet, Ben Nevis is not particularly tall, but the latitude at which it sits, roughly at Scotland's waist, is well north of Moscow; the winters in the Scottish Highlands are brutal. Technical climbs to the summit of the Ben are not long by Alpine standards, but scaling precipitous routes on the north side, especially during winter months, is serious business.

Hamish was wrestling his way through college in Edinburgh, uncertain where his degree in education would lead. If teaching, it would probably be in outdoor education. His passion was mountaineering. To that end, he spent many weekends honing his skills in preparation for classic climbs in the Alps, which he had only read about. This trip would be the culmination of all that work. The plan was to meet up with a climbing buddy from Glasgow to tackle a snow and ice route up a gully that had only been climbed once before, two years earlier in the winter of 1957. If he and Robbie McNulty could summit Zero Gully, Hamish was convinced he could then tackle the hardest routes in the Alps—the Grandes Jorasses, the Petit Dru, the Matterhorn, and the prize of them all, the north face of the Eiger.

While dining earlier that evening at the Clachaig Inn, a spot Hamish always favored on his trips to the Scottish Highlands, he wondered if some of the legends in climbing might already be at the hut tonight. Men like Patey, Nicol, and MacInnes, who had cracked the Zero Gully puzzle with an audacious five-hour assault. Hamish read every account of their exploits he could find, and dreamed of climbing with them one day. He hoped Robbie was already there, imagined him coaxing those icons to share every iota of information about the technical nuances of Zero Gully.

What Hamish did know was intimidating. There were few opportunities to place protection against a fall and poor locations from which to safely belay one's climbing partner. In April of the previous year, three experienced climbers had died on the route, due, it was believed, to an ice axe belay that had failed. That episode fresh in his mind, Hamish knew it would be a delicate dance, and success would depend on favorable snow and ice conditions as much as nerve and skill. *Thank God Robbie's my mate on this one*, he thought, recalling how his friend had dragged him up many climbs when Hamish was still learning the craft as a teenager. Now, he was every bit as strong as Robbie. Of modest height at five-seven, Hamish was built like a bullet, all muscle, sinew, and brains. Together, he and Robbie had blitzed climbs in times so fast they bordered on the absurd. But Robbie was also a flake. Hamish often teased his friend that he'd be late for his own wedding. Or funeral. Mastering Zero Gully was more important than either of those life events, in Hamish's eyes, and he knew Robbie shared his fervor.

When Hamish emerged from his sleeping bag the next morning all the climbers had left. Only the caretaker was still in the hut, quietly sweeping up. Hamish checked the logbook, half expecting to see Robbie had hooked up with some other climbers. But his name was absent. *Why do I hitch my wagon to such a wingding,* he thought. *Because he's the best damn climber I know. That's why.* Hamish felt confident in his abilities, and well prepared for the hardest effort he'd ever faced on a winter climb. But there was no way he could solo the route without a rope or a partner to hang on to the other end. That was a death wish. A thought crept into his head, an explanation for Robbie's absence. *Maybe this was too much for him and he couldn't bring himself to tell me.*

Between oversleeping and a no-show climbing partner, Hamish's plans to tackle Zero Gully were shot. He lit his cookstove and went outside to fill a pot with water from the standpipe. The weather was ideal; sunny and crisp. *I bet the ice conditions in the gully are prime*, he thought, feeling sorry for himself that it was not to be. *Christ, what a waste, after all this anticipation.* Hamish began to think how he could salvage the weekend when a tall young man strode up to the hut, nodding to him as he passed, and entered the hut. Hamish followed him in and set about preparing his breakfast of oatmeal and tea. The blond newcomer was deep in conversation with the caretaker, who had stopped sweeping and leaned on his broom.

"I don't think it wise to try Number 5 Gully yourself," the caretaker said. "It's gnarly and you've not got a partner, have ye? Do ye know much about the climbs on this side of the Ben?"

"No, I'm not that familiar with the area. But I didn't come all this way to spend the day in a hut. It was sort of a last-minute thing," the newcomer said, towering over the diminutive caretaker. He spoke the most proper English with no hint of a Scottish accent.

"The routes in this valley are not for the faint of heart. Ye got to know what yer about," the caretaker advised. "But if ye think ye have the stuff, talk to the laddie over there," he said, gesturing in Hamish's direction. "He's on his own as well. Maybe you two can pair up and find a route ye can handle while we still got some sun on us."

The young man walked over to the table where Hamish was spooning honey into his mug of hot cereal and stuck out a hand. "Hi there. My name is Andy Boarder. Would you be interested in climbing together today?"

Hamish stood up and shook hands with the newcomer, taller by a good six inches. "Hamish MacLean," he said. "I might well do so," he said. "My buddy never showed, so if you'd like to try your hand on one of the gullies on the Ben, maybe we can make a day of it."

Andy Boarder took off his pack and sat down on a bench across from Hamish. "I'm not familiar with routes on the north side," he said, "but I've always wanted to see what the fuss was about. I'd hate to waste the hike all the way up here on such a beautiful day. Can you lead routes of this quality? I can follow most anything."

"With my eyes closed," Hamish lied.

"You're on. Do you have a route in mind?"

"I do, as a matter of fact," Hamish replied.

Although Andy was not as experienced as was Hamish at high-angled mixed routes of rock, snow, and ice, he was twenty-six, had been climbing longer than Hamish, and could be the second man on difficult climbs as long as a rope and a skilled person above was there to support him. Medical studies had eliminated most of his leisure activities, but this February weekend offered a rare opportunity to steal a day for himself. Andy hoped to make the most of it.

"I'd avoid anything ambitious today, given your late start," the caretaker said as Hamish and Andy sorted out the climbing equipment they would need, leaving a pile of personal gear in a corner of the hut. "And keep an eye on the sky. Looks nice now, but it wouldn't surprise me if we get a blow through here later."

"Noted," Hamish said.

"Don't be a hero," the caretaker added, concerned he was not being taken seriously. "We lose a few every year, and it puts us all at risk to chase after ye." He did not know either climber; experience had taught him to be skeptical of strangers attempting anything on the North Face of Ben Nevis, especially in winter.

"We'll be careful," Hamish said as they exited the hut. A brilliant sun reflecting off the snow made them squint and they both donned glacier glasses. Hamish worried it was already ten thirty; sunset would come around five. The bottom of Zero Gully was not far, and the approach to the gully over ice-glazed rocky ground was easy, but in the back of his mind, Hamish knew their chances of success were slim given the intricacies of the route and how relatively little daylight they had left. The best in the world had managed to climb it once, a five-hour triumph. Today's late start was a handicap, but Hamish was determined to try.

The two men encountered few difficulties over the lower approach, during which they got to know each other a little. With no need for roping up, they climbed side-by-side, chatting about their respective experiences in the mountains and their career aspirations—Andy in medicine, Hamish in education. Their progress slowed when they reached the first ice-choked chimney and surveyed the route ahead.

"I guess here's where we find out what we're made of," Andy said, watching Hamish prepare to lead the first pitch.

"Aye. I've been looking forward to this moment for quite some time. Just wish we had a bit more daylight to work with. But I'll get us up there, one way or another, Doc." For such a youthful climber, Hamish was bursting with confidence. He led carefully, working his way up the narrow chasm, noting with alarm there were few possible points to pound a piton into a crack in the rock or a screw into the ice. Ice screws had just been invented the previous year. Hamish carried a few, but used them sparingly as he was still uncertain as to whether he could trust his life to them. Andy remained below, slowly giving Hamish slack on the rope as the Scotsman climbed up the chimney. The farther he climbed between protection points the more vulnerable Hamish felt. Hamish hoped Andy's own stance was secure enough to hold him, should he slip.

When Hamish reached the top of the chimney, he tied himself into the rock and shouted down for Andy to follow. Slowly, Andy tried to duplicate where Hamish had placed his own hands and feet while the young Scotsman belayed his English companion, keeping a tight leash.

The next pitch was vastly harder, requiring a delicate traverse over steep rock thinly covered with ice. Hamish took an inordinate amount of time getting back to the main gully while Andy waited, growing colder as the wind picked up. He stamped his feet to keep the blood circulating but he could not get them warm.

Finally, Hamish completed the pitch, found a stance to belay Andy, and called for his partner to climb up. It took the Englishman more than an hour, relying mostly on his arms. As Andy stumbled up to the small perch, Hamish could see how his partner's technique had deteriorated. The man looked exhausted.

They had completed four of the seven pitches with the crux of the climb behind them now. Hamish decided it was safer to press on to the summit and descend an easier way. *Down-climbing this damn thing with Andy will be a nightmare*, he thought. There was no discussion about their options between the two men, who were little more than strangers. Had Robbie been on the climb instead, he and Hamish would have debated and argued and cajoled every step of the way. Andy was suffering, but to this point had said nothing. There was a formality between them that reflected their inexperience as partners. Hamish prepared to push on and coiled the rope for Andy to hold. *If he can get himself up to the summit, somehow, I'll get him down*, he convinced himself.

A frighteningly steep icefall was the next challenge. "I can't go on," Andy pleaded, as Hamish turned to leave their narrow ledge. He was freezing and would not move. "I'm done."

Hamish knew that above this pitch, a much less steep snowfield was all that lay between them and the summit. But that snowfield would require them to climb simultaneously, without protection. If they were roped up and one of them fell, the other would have no chance to hold his partner. There was no way, Hamish was certain, that Andy could muster the confidence, strength, or the technique, to continue. The game was up; there was only one choice—retreat. But Hamish could not shake the allure of success, so tantalizingly close. He could not let go of his dream.

Until that moment, Hamish had been so focused on the technical problem of the climb he had failed to note that the caretaker's prediction was coming to pass. Wisps of cloud enveloped them. He looked past Andy, down toward the valley. It was now lost in the mist. He felt the wind pick up, a sure sign a front was coming through.

To reach the summit now meant they would have to climb in the dark. He and Robbie had trained on all kinds of terrain but never had they attempted such a difficult route with only a headlamp to guide them. If he continued on his own, there would be no one to hold the other end of the rope. A small voice in his head screamed, *This is madness. You do not leave your climbing partner. You do not betray the fellowship of the rope.* Yet he forced that better angel to the background. His hubris would not allow him to abandon Zero Gully.

"I'll give you my extra sweater," Hamish said, lamely. "And tie you into the ledge. Finish this thermos. I'll be back with help soon." Andy couldn't speak. He just shivered. After securing him into the wall as best he could, Hamish turned his back and climbed off the ledge. He concentrated only on the ice and rock above him, convincing himself that speeding to the top was the best way to save Andy.

It was nearly midnight as Hamish negotiated the last problems of the icefall and pulled himself onto the final snow slope. With ice axe jammed ahead of him as his only point of safety, Hamish gingerly took each step with extreme caution as the storm hit full force. Icy needles drove into his face, which was only partially protected by the hood of his parka. He focused only on the next step. And the next. And the next.

Finally, his headlamp could not reveal anything higher than where he now stood. He had summited Ben Nevis via Zero Gully. After indulging himself in the slightest moment of self-satisfaction, Hamish realized there was no time to descend the easy way and organize a rescue that could reach Andy at night. The Englishman would never last that long. It was solely up to him to get Andy down. That meant retracing his steps with no one to provide a protecting belay.

Far below, clinging to the narrow ledge, Andy suffered through his own private purgatory. As his body chilled, it directed as much blood as possible to maintain his core temperature, sacrificing his extremities. For a time, he stamped his feet to increase circulation but inevitably the painful chill turned to numbness. There was no way he could extricate himself from this ledge. Unable to unscrew the thermos Hamish had left him, Andy shook one mitten shell off. It dangled from a cord that threaded through his parka sleeve, around his neck, and down to the companion mitten shell on the other hand. He removed the wool Dachstein mitten in order to grip the top of the thermos and shoved it under his other armpit. As he poured lukewarm tea into the cup that doubled as thermos top the loose mitten came free. It landed on the ledge by his feet. Andy shuffled his stonelike feet to retrieve it, inadvertently kicking the mitten away and dropping the thermos. Both fell into a black void. There was nothing left to do but slip his now-vulnerable left hand, still clad in a thin glove, back into the dangling mitten shell and try to keep it warmed against his chest. His anguish was beyond measure.

Hamish had not eaten nor drunk for hours. He was dehydrated, weak, all adrenaline spent. Down-climbing in the midst of a ferocious storm was nightmarish. His headlamp's failing batteries finally illuminated the ledge that still held Andy's body in lemony light. *He hasn't blown off! Amazing! How the fuck do I get him down?* It seemed unimaginable. Fighting exhaustion as well as enormous guilt, thinking of the time Andy had had to spend, so exposed, while he, Hamish, fulfilled his dream, he wondered if Andy might well be dead. *Somebody can retrieve him tomorrow,* he thought, morbidly. He touched his back tentatively. Andy shivered the slightest bit.

"I'm here, Andy. It's Hamish. I'm going to get you down." But he had no idea how to achieve such a thing.

"Is my mum coming?" Andy whispered in delirium.

The thermos was gone. "I've got to make this right," Hamish swore under his breath.

Andy could do nothing to help. His legs were completely useless, and he kept muttering nonsense. Carefully, Hamish lowered him half a rope length, then found some rock to loop the rope around or a minuscule crack that would take a piton. Hamish used Andy as a counterweight while he rappelled down to the level to which he had been lowered. Then Hamish tied him into the mountain to prevent a slip, re-climbed to the top of the rope, collected the anchor he had left, and down-climbed back to him. He had so few pieces of protection he could not afford to simply leave them in place or he would have run out, making a rappel impossible. Time after time he repeated these moves, each round trip excruciatingly slow and precarious. While contorting himself to retrieve a piton, Hamish ripped a muscle in his back, the pain tearing across his torso like the snap of a horsewhip.

Hours passed as Hamish agonizingly lowered his companion. At first light they reached the relatively gentle slope at the base of the climb. The storm had blown through, leaving a fresh coating of snow with hints of pink coloring the gray morning sky. Hamish slung the comatose climber over his shoulder and staggered down the slippery scree slope in the direction of the hut, the pain in his back beyond description. When he was close enough to see smoke curling up from the CIC hut and smell burning wood, Hamish gently laid his companion down, removed his own parka and tucked it around Andy, carefully cushioned his head with Andy's backpack, and stumbled the remaining yards to the hut. He threw open the door and fell to his knees. It took his eyes a moment to adjust to the dim light within. The caretaker was adding logs to the fire; a few climbers were huddled around a wooden table, their cookstoves purring. Hamish had only energy to tell those who could hear his weary whisper where the body could be found. Then he collapsed, comatose, onto an empty bunk.

PART I

Taking a new step, uttering a new word, is what people fear most.
—FYODOR DOSTOYEVSKY

I

Promise of a New Year

HERO TO ZERO. THE DETAILS OF BENEDICT ARNOLD'S PRECIPITOUS FALL from grace are known by every child who grows up by the shores of Lake Champlain, site of the first naval battle of the Revolutionary War. Tracy Barcomb was about five when his dad told him the story of the Battle of Valcour Island. Young Arnold, freshly promoted to brigadier general, had been recruited to build a pesky little navy and given an outrageous task—to stall a large fleet of British warships intent upon sailing down from Canada to capture the lake and separate New England from the rest of the colonies. The inquisitive little boy was not so interested in the traitor Benedict Arnold became only four years later. There was no magic for him in that part of the story.

"Tell me again, Daddy," six-year-old Tracy pleaded as their chartered catamaran sailed into the narrow strait between Valcour Island's western shore and the New York side of the lake, where Arnold's small fleet had lain in wait to spring their surprise on the night of October 11, 1776. "How did they get past the British in the dark, through the mist?" Tracy knew every detail, how Arnold ordered their oars covered with cloth to dampen the sound as they rowed past enemy warships so close their onboard conversations could be heard; how they dodged and burned their way down the lake, losing most of the fleet along the way. Tracy requested the saga again and again. There was comfort in the repetition. He was plying the same waters as those Continental Navy boys, feeling their fright, coasting on their bravery. He imagined himself on their desperate retreat south to Fort Ticonderoga after a day of brutal bombardment, eighty fewer sailors than when they'd first engaged the British that morning. For a youngster thrilled by fantasies, the Battle of Valcour was his lodestone, Lake Champlain his center of gravity.

Tracy loved the lake for its history and its mystery but as he grew, Champlain took on new meaning, as the gateway to his growing passion for exploring the deep woods and airy ridges of the Adirondacks on the New York side. He had taken the ferry between Burlingtn and Port Kent numerous times, first on hiking trips with his parents, and now nine years later in the fall of 2002, to begin his last year at Glencoe School, a junior boarding school situated a few miles outside of Lake Placid. It never failed to stir his sense of awe as the view of the mountains grew more dramatic on the east-to-west crossing. This was the last time the Barcomb family would be making the pilgrimage to Glencoe, for Tracy was slated to graduate in June, moving on to tenth grade somewhere else.

Even with a stiff breeze in their faces, the warm September sun enabled Tracy, Wendell, and Emily Barcomb to stand comfortably on the top deck in shirtsleeves, watching the most prominent peaks sharpen against a cerulean sky. Tracy knew the names of all the mountains visible to him from the ferry, and had been on most of their summits at least once during his previous two years at Glencoe. He planned to climb the few he'd not visited during the upcoming year.

"Make the most of it, honey," Emily said, hugging her son. The top of her head brushed up against his chin, which was a good five inches higher than it had been when school let out in June. Tracy was nearly six feet, only a couple of inches shorter than his dad, and just as lean. "What happened to that little sprout who used to run between my legs?" Emily asked wistfully.

"You keep feeding me," Tracy grinned. "These things happen."

"I imagine you're thinking about all those delicious hikes to come. There's more to your ninth-grade year than just becoming a 46er," she said, referring to the club that honored those who managed to scale the collection of Adirondack mountains at least four thousand feet in height. "I hope you do some more theater, too. And study a bit." She rumpled his shaggy red hair. How he had changed since that first trip across the lake when her nervous thirteen-year-old threw up on the ferry, overcome with anxiety about going away to a strange school. Now a handsome young man, his social skills still had a ways to go to catch up to his height. If there was one area his parents hoped to see improvement in this final year at Glencoe, it was maturity. The letter they'd received from school the previous June spelled that out in no uncertain terms. Tracy was a jewel in so many ways, but for ninth grade to be a success, the letter stipulated, he needed to grow up emotionally. Tracy's devil-may-care attitude toward academics and social norms, especially when girls were concerned, was getting in the way.

"I'll be fine, Mom," Tracy smiled. He didn't mind her affections. They were a comfort his emerging adolescence still permitted.

"We expect you to focus on studies if you have any hopes of getting into Exeter next year," Wendell Barcomb interjected. "The mountains will always be there."

"Don't put added pressure on our son," Emily cautioned. "Exeter is not the only place where he can thrive. I don't want to write off Putney. It's a lot closer to us, physically as well as philosophically," she said.

This was a recurring conversation between his parents, and Tracy preferred to stay out of it. He had given very little thought to what came next after Glencoe and, like many other hard choices, the decision about where to go to high school was one of many he could still kick down the road a bit. Procrastination was a skill he had mastered. Tracy worried he didn't have the academic chops to succeed at a place like Exeter. Though he had never expressed this to his parents, and had yet to see either school in person, deep down he thought Putney would be a better fit; more like Glencoe with its small classes, intimate residences, and a vibrant outdoors program. If you had to go to school, you could do a lot worse than Glencoe, Tracy fervently believed. He was not ready to decide where to embark upon the next phase of his life.

"He's fifteen years old now, Emily. About the age I started working nearly full-time on my dad's spread. If he wants to run the farm when I'm too old to do it he can just as well go to Burlington High. Help me out in the afternoons and save us a ton of dough," Wendell said.

"I see," she said, chuckling. "You presume our son has no other professional aspirations beyond taking over the family business? Not college material?" she said, with a mischievous twinkle.

"Now, don't put words in my mouth, Emily," Wendell said. Tracy knew what was coming next. It was a familiar dance. "Farming has been in this family for generations, and I've been proud to carry it on. College isn't the only path to happiness and success."

"Mmhmm. Words to live by Mr. I-got-my-degree-in-plant-science-at-an-Ivy-League-school-but-let's-pretend-I'm-a-redneck-farmer-who's-got-but-two-pairs-of-overalls," Emily jibed, referring to her husband's undergraduate work at Cornell's renowned College of Agriculture and Life Sciences.

Wendell looked from wife to son, unable to hide his giggle. "I'm just saying. The family business doesn't require him to get a lot of letters after his name." This was a gentle tease at his wife, who was currently at the all-but-dissertation stage in her PhD studies at the University of Vermont. Tracy knew this faux argument was of no real import. His parents wanted his future to be his to decide, and to give him the tools to make wise choices. They were both immensely inquisitive and valued education highly. They had also worked hard to instill in their only child a passion for wilderness, a respect for the environment, and the skills to move respectfully and safely in that world.

"And that's why you're pushing Exeter?" Emily said. "To make him a smarter farmer?"

Wendell threw up his hands in defeat, clapped his son on the shoulder. "I give up. Let me see if they sell healthy snacks on this tugboat," he said, stalking off.

Tracy had no intention of following in the footsteps of his forebears. As fond as he was of living on a farm, taking the reins from his dad was not his vision of the future. Mountain climbing and cycling were more important to him than which high school or college he attended. What he hadn't figured out yet was how to make a living pursuing either passion.

A few minutes later, Wendell rejoined his family, waving three granola bars in the air triumphantly. "Peace offering?" he asked, handing a snack to each of them.

"Will you come on my finishing climb?" Tracy asked, unwrapping the bar, which reminded him he had not had much lunch and would no longer be able to raid the kitchen at any hour once he was back at boarding school. "I've only got nine left."

"Now that depends on how miserable it is," his dad said. "Hamish may still be foolish enough to bushwhack those trailless peaks at his age. But we're not that crazy," he said, referring to Hamish MacLean, who, at sixty-three, was in his third decade as headmaster. "Can you save an easy one for us?"

"Easy for some ain't easy for all," Tracy teased. "Hamish promised he'd be there for me, regardless of which one was last. It would be great to have you guys join us." He knew his dad was still fit enough, but worried his mom's balky knees would give her trouble. For that reason, he had decided Whiteface would be best, for it offered a paved road she could drive up to meet him at the summit.

"We'll make every effort to share it with you, darling," Emily said. "Either in person or in spirit. We know how important this is to you. But you know my limitations."

That's got to be the one, Tracy thought, gazing at Whiteface, looming ever larger in the distance as the ferry plowed on toward the New York side. His parents stepped away from him and took seats on a nearby bench, munching on their granola bars and chatting about a journal article Emily was working on that she hoped would be worthy of publication. Her husband was her best editor and supremely proud of her academic pursuits, his earlier comments about his son's education notwithstanding.

Tracy clung to the railing, the afternoon sun warm on his tanned face. He snugged his ball cap securely down around his ears to keep the wind from tearing it off and let his mind return to a familiar daydream about that final climb, the culmination of so many hours of pleasure and hard work. Whiteface would be perfect, he decided, so his friends at school, even the ones who didn't enjoy hiking that much, could join him for the party. And the toll road solved the problem for his mom.

Aside from Hamish, he also counted on the presence of Pete Hedges, Head of English and, more importantly, the guy in charge of the outdoor program. Tracy was confident that if he could reach forty-five peaks, Pete would find a way to schedule a Whiteface trip before the end of school, even if the only option was the day before graduation.

Many nights before sleep overcame him, Tracy fantasized about his finishing trip and the joy of celebrating with the people who meant the most to him. Gazing at the mountain of his desire, golden in the western sky, that image returned in vivid detail. Pete Hedges would watch the weather like a hawk, ideally picking a Saturday in early June when the last snows would be gone and the trails sufficiently free of mud. Tracy imagined a perfect mountain day, fair weather clouds with a gentle breeze from the north, just enough to keep the hiking party cool and the blackflies from feasting upon their heads. His parents would come over the day before, maybe find a bed-and-breakfast near the mountain. Wendell would meet the Glencoe van at the Whiteface trailhead, the one at the base of the old Marble Mountain ski lift—the shortest route to the top. It would be fun to have his dad hike with them. Get to know his mentors, Hamish and Pete, a little bit. His mom would have time to kill before driving the toll road up to the summit. She could bring the cake! And Hamish would show him the coveted 46er patch, to be sewn upon his frayed ball cap that had accompanied him on so many climbs. But Hamish wouldn't give it to him. He would say something like, "You earned this, Tracy. And you learned a bit along the way. This patch, signifying you summited each of the Adirondack High Peaks, shall be yours . . . as soon as you fill out the club's paperwork and pay their dues!" That was his headmaster. A character.

Tracy recalled a trip Hamish had orchestrated for an ex-student the previous year. Marie *Something* had graduated from Glencoe years earlier and had managed to chip away at her list of unclimbed peaks. When one remained, she wrote to Hamish, asking him to join her on a hike up Big Slide for old time's sake. Hamish agreed, but to make it as memorable as possible, he insisted she should not take the normal trail, but must bush-whack the mountain directly from school. "I'm told it's how they used to climb it back in the 1940s when gas was rationed during the war, Marie. Let's make it an adventure you'll remember."

Hamish had an ulterior motive, which was to provide cover for caterers to take the trail and set up a surprise party atop Big Slide. Honored to have been included in the climbing party, Tracy recalled Marie's frustration as the difficulties increased; she fretted they might run out of time. What she expected—an easy, triumphant day—had become a serious struggle. Hour upon hour they battled a steepening pitch and thick undergrowth. Finally, they burst out of the brush to meet the state trail. From there it was an easy walk along the ridge to the summit, where grinning servers in bow ties and tuxedos waited with trays of food and bottles of champagne. Marie was blown away. Tracy watched in awe at Hamish's thoughtfulness to create a total experience for his former student. Standing atop Whiteface with friends and family by his side one day next spring would be the perfect conclusion to his Glencoe years, he imagined.

Tracy's reverie suddenly shattered as Whiteface became a blur. A blue-black curtain of countless birds descended a few yards off the starboard side blocking his view. "Will you look at that!" Emily marveled, now at his side, her arm linked through his. She did not have to explain; all eyes were trained on an exquisite choreography overhead as a murmuration of starlings confronted the ferry. Uncountable in number, vigorously vocalizing, back and forth they swooped and swerved as if but one organism, reversing direction every few seconds in perfect harmony, creating fleeting shadows on the deck.

"Wow!" Tracy exclaimed, as he fixed upon the fluttering mass seemingly following some mysterious calling. "That's so cool!" How was leadership determined, passed, and accepted, he wondered. Instantaneous consensus. No dissent. How would they decide when it was time to settle? Who would be responsible for that choice? Was it a choice? He thought of the Tour de France bike race, recently completed, and of its peloton, the homogeneous clutch of elite cyclists that navigate country roads much like this mass of birds; each racer a leader, each a follower, the speed of the whole dependent upon tacit agreement that individual leadership is temporary and ephemeral. A marriage of cooperation and competition. *Coopetition*, he decided.

"Incredible show," Wendell said. "Do you know how those starlings manage to coordinate?"

"No. Do you, big shot?" Emily asked.

"Lucky for you I get to show off my birding expertise," he boasted. "It works like this: each individual starling registers the movements of seven others nearby."

"Nearby?" Tracy exclaimed. "They're all nearby. They're within inches of each other."

"True enough. What you're seeing is a collection of intersecting groups of eight. It's extraordinary how all these groups make instantaneous decisions about speed and direction with the result being total cohesiveness. It's been reduced to a mathematical algorithm, details of which I cannot reveal," he said, smiling. The ferry slowed, aiming for the wharf. "We're nearly there. I'll go start the car."

"We'll be down in a moment," Emily said. She lingered with Tracy at the rail, watching the other passengers scurry to the lower deck. "It's never easy for me, sweetie. Saying goodbye." She continued to hug him. "I feel like I'm missing out on a huge part of your upbringing."

"It's not like I'm in another country," Tracy said. "I'm just across the lake."

The incessant chirruping had suddenly disappeared, replaced by a few uncoordinated squawks. Tracy looked up. The starlings had moved on, seeking a new audience, or perhaps driven away by the next act—sensible gulls—who now circled purposefully above. Having cleared the skies of their gymnastic cousins, these newcomers hovered nearly motionless, their flapping wings mitigating the breeze. The effect was calm compared to the recent aerial frenzy, but with no less urgency. With laser focus, gull eyes searched for any scrap of food that might be left on deck by the departing bipeds. The flight algorithm for these folks, Tracy decided, was first-come, first-served.

The captain blew a foghorn as the bow nestled into the slip, the ferry jostling gently to a stop. "I've got to visit prep schools soon, Mom. You'll drive me, right?"

"Of course."

"Or, maybe I should just go to school in Burlington," he teased, playing on the mixed feelings he knew she had about his going away. "Then you won't have to miss me at all."

"You and your dad deserve each other," she said, playfully punching his arm. "Glencoe has been such a good place for you. I'd hate to deny you the chance to build upon all you've learned there. I'm torn. When you're a parent you'll understand," she sighed. "Okay, let's get to the car. We can talk about it later in the fall, honey."

The drive from the ferry landing to the Glencoe School took about an hour. In early September, forests of birch, maple, beech, and oak, just beginning to change color, rose in waves from the road to distant ridgelines—Jay Range to the east, and the Whiteface Mountain massif to the west. Though this was old hat for him now, Tracy still felt a pang of anxiety. School was school, expectations for him were high, and he knew the attention deficit disorder that had challenged his ability to succeed in each of his two previous years at Glencoe had not magically disappeared. Mixed with anxiety was the anticipation of seeing the object of his summer obsession—Libby Goldman. A mailing from school had informed him that Libby would also be living in Phelps House. The residences at Glencoe were all coed, Swiss chalet in style, and designed for only eight students plus two teachers doubling as houseparents. He hoped she would see that his adolescent goofiness, which had not worn well with her in eighth grade, had gotten washed out over the summer.

Since they had started carrying him on their hikes as a three-year-old and allowing their insistent son to walk on his own a year later, Wendell and Emily had instilled in Tracy a love of the wilderness and the importance of its stewardship. Tracy shared all the insecurities adolescents face wrestling with maturation from child to adult, but in the woods, he was already an old soul, supremely confident in his abilities, knew his limits, and enjoyed helping others not so secure. He had become a valued member of the Glencoe outdoor education program even as his immaturity in other areas of school life frustrated its headmaster as well as its faculty.

On many a staff meeting the previous two years, Hamish would verbalize some version of: *The lad has such potential. Why does he make it so hard on the rest of us to help him realize that promise?* During staff orientation the week before students arrived some time had been spent discussing how to help Tracy to be a leader in his senior year, in all areas of school life, not just in the mountains.

It was just past five as the Barcomb car turned onto the Glencoe campus, sheltered from the highway by a wall of interwoven evergreen, planted intentionally for that purpose a half century earlier. It passed the MacLean farmhouse, a stone's throw from two modest barns housing a small menagerie of farm animals. Farm staff and a couple of early-arriving students were walking up the gravel road to the barnyard to perform afternoon chores. Though Tracy chose to avoid most barn activities—he had enough of that at home—he felt immediately at ease, eager to find friends at his home away from home.

A quarter mile farther on, around a gentle curve, stood Dewey Hall, the two-story academic hub. "Should be harvesting soon," Wendell said, as they drove slowly past flower and vegetable gardens in their final stages of annual growth. "Root crops now," he said, mostly to himself. As a farmer himself, Wendell appreciated the emphasis Glencoe placed on the farm experience, working it into the curriculum wherever possible.

Glencoe educated roughly seventy kids from fifth through ninth grades. It could not have differed more starkly from a traditional prep school. There were no broad lawns ringed by brick-and-clapboard dorms, nor a multi-columned library lording over a geometrically perfect quadrangle. Dewey Hall and an adjacent performance center—Marcy Hall—housed all of the academic and administrative activities. A short walk up a gentle grade stood eight chalet-style residences, tucked unobtrusively into the woods and interconnected by grassy paths. Walking west from Dewey along a trail covered in pine needles brought one to a fenced riding ring and athletic field more akin to a pasture for grazing than, say, a manicured soccer pitch. Just over a rise beyond the field, a private spring-fed lake rippled in the predominant westerly breezes, waiting for students to sail, kayak, or skate come the dead of winter.

They drove past Dewey at the heart of the campus and turned up the short drive to the "dorms," nestled in a horseshoe arc against a wooded slope rising gently to a rocky ridgeline high above the campus. Wendell parked near the front door to Phelps House, whose houseparents, Jane and Payton Henderson, were on their hands and knees planting mums.

"Welcome, pilgrim," Payton beamed, getting to his feet and giving Tracy a bear hug, which he enthusiastically returned. "Excuse the dirty hands." Tracy was overjoyed to have learned, via mail, that he had been granted his first choice of residence, as well as roommate—Jake Thompson. "You let your parents drive, eh?" Payton joked.

"They only let me drive their tractor," Tracy grinned.

"Nice to see you again, Payton," Emily said, hugging her son's new house-dad. Glencoe faculty all answered to their given names, from the headmaster on down. Respect was earned by one's contributions, not artificially bestowed by a surname or job title.

Jane wiped her hands on a rag and gave each Barcomb a warm embrace as well. "We're thrilled to have Tracy with us this year," she said. "Don't tell anyone," she whispered to Tracy conspiratorially, "but we've got the best group of kids in Phelps. I can't wait to get started."

Their four-year-old son, Nicky, sat in the dirt engrossed with earthworms. He looked up, seemed to recognize Tracy, waved weakly, and returned to the serious business of excavating a home for the wiggly things.

"How was your summer? Get some climbing in?" Payton asked, his arm lingering on Tracy's shoulders.

"Some. Mostly helping Dad on the farm," Tracy said. "We did a good part of the Long Trail in Vermont," he continued, giving his parents an appreciative look. "Next year, they promised me we could get up into the Mahoosics," he said, referring to one of the wilder stretches of the Appalachian Trail that straddles the New Hampshire and Maine border.

"That's one place I've always wanted to see," Payton said.

Wendell unstrapped a sleek road bike from the roof rack and lowered it to the ground.

"Wow. You got new wheels!" Payton exclaimed.

"Bought it myself with summer work money," Tracy said, proudly. "Maybe we can go touring together sometime? I'm hoping the school will let me do some racing this year."

"If there's interest, maybe we can start a team," Payton offered. "Did you watch the Tour this summer?" he asked, knowing Tracy would understand his shorthand reference.

"Didn't miss a day," Tracy said. "Though I had to catch it in the evenings. And I want to take French this year, so when I am interviewed by the press after winning a stage in the Tour, I can speak their language."

"First I've heard of that!" Wendell laughed. "But I support anything that stretches your brain and expands your cultural sensitivity. Who teaches French at his level?"

"Ron Handy," Payton said. "Same guy that turned Tracy into such a thespian last year. Ron will be tickled to hear he has such a motivated student. I guess you were pleased Lance Armstrong made it four in a row."

"The guy destroyed the field," Tracy said. "I think he won by over seven minutes."

"I don't believe the guy raced clean," Payton said. "But we'll see."

"Do you think we might take a cycling trip up the Whiteface toll road this year?" Tracy asked, referring to the five-mile twisting route that rises more than 2,300 feet to just below the summit, which one can then reach via elevator. It is a tourist mecca and the only peak where uber-fit hikers and couch potatoes who drove up the mountain can mingle, each eyeing the other like visitors and resident animals at the zoo. Tracy considered his mother an exception to the couch potato, confident she would not wear pink pants or high heels if she had to take that route to the summit for his finishing trip party.

"You think you're ready to tackle the toll road? That's a pretty ambitious goal," Payton said. "If you're a fan of the Tour you may know, and I have no idea why I am aware of this fact, the grade up Whiteface is about the same as the toughest mountain stage at the Tour you watched this summer. You think you can handle that?"

"Really? Whiteface is as steep as the Col de Tourmalet? That's crazy," Tracy said, eyes widening. If he could ascend the Whiteface road, maybe he was nearly ready to tackle the actual Tour de France.

"I said the grade is equivalent," Payton chuckled, appreciating how he had set Tracy up. "But only half as far. You'd have to do Whiteface twice with no descent to match that climb in the Pyrenees."

"Oh," Tracy said, deflated.

"Why don't you park that puppy in our garage? I bet you'd rather not keep it with the beat-up rock bikes we have at this place."

"Thank you. I was hoping to keep it inside someplace safe."

"We've got all year to debate Tracy's cycling future, Payton," Jane said. "Why don't you guys get Tracy's luggage up to his room?"

"Merci beaucoup," Wendell laughed, clapping his son on the back. Tracy and the two men lugged his suitcases and a huge backpack crammed full of climbing gear up to the second floor. From his window, Tracy could see the summit of Algonquin, the second-highest peak in the Adirondacks, soaring above adjacent ridgelines, creating a dramatic skyline in the distance. He was in his element now, content to let his parents finish their pleasantries and depart.

Though unique in many ways, Glencoe was not a new-age, modern educational experiment. It had sprung from a chance romantic alliance formed decades earlier. In 1928, two idealistic master's students, Glenn Stallings and Susan Coe, met while pursuing their degrees at Teachers College, part of Columbia University, in New York. Each registered for a class taught by John Dewey, a titan in the world of progressive education, then in his last years as a professor. You could draw a straight line between the imprint that class had on the young couple and their later decision to purchase land in the Adirondacks. They chose to label their institution in a manner that merged their names, Glenn and Coe, and honored a shared hiking destination in Scotland. *Glencoe* became the embodiment of the learn-through-doing theme Professor Dewey hammered home to them. The school became a model for children to blossom through free, unstructured play, and experiential education. Academics were rigorous, with the great outdoors of the Adirondacks deployed as an extraordinary laboratory for adolescents coming of age.

Glenn and Susan prevailed upon her brother, a budding architect, to implement some of his ideas on the three-hundred-acre Glencoe campus. From its classrooms, one could gaze upon mountain views in one direction, a small duck pond in another, deep forest that cloaked the campus in a third. Smooth wooden slides snaked next to stairways, a tempting alternative for students to descend from floor to floor. Every consideration was given to maximizing natural light and energy efficiency, unique priorities for buildings constructed in the mid-twentieth century.

Glenn and Susan created a school where students were partners in its operation, not simply the focus of all attention. Farm animals were fed, by students, before humans got their meals; staff weren't solely responsible for sweeping classrooms each morning, or splitting wood for the maple sugar operation, or starting the vegetable garden in the greenhouses, or transferring those pots to the fields when weather permitted, or harvesting the potatoes and other root vegetables in the fall, or setting tables for each meal, or waiting on those tables once the food was served. Students participated in all of those chores, rotating each week to new ones. Some came from families with untold wealth who had never been asked to handle a chore, or had even been inside a kitchen. Many came with some level of financial aid. All arrived with a unique story, for it is rare that a family chooses to send their child away to a junior-level boarding school, one that is not specifically designed for students with learning disabilities. Glenn and Susan's bottom line was this: education at Glencoe happened *with* children, not *for* children.

Extending from the main axis of Dewey Hall, a gymnasium had been constructed using semicircular sheets of corrugated steel and internally paneled with honey-colored maple. The horizontal half cylinder replicated a design by a World War I British major named Nissen. At Glencoe, the unique gym thus carried his name. By the double doors that opened into the gym stood a twenty-foot climbing wall sporting a spray of multihued nylon ropes affixed to the ceiling. This was where students received their initiation to rock climbing, before graduating to cliffs beyond a small ski hill, a short walk through the woods behind Dewey.

"You can go now," Tracy said to his parents, once his clothes were safely tucked away and his bed made by his doting mother. "Do you know where Jake might be?" Tracy asked Payton, noting that his roommate's things were already unpacked.

"I bet he's shooting hoops in Nissen," Payton said. "Do yourself a favor, Tracy. Change out of those flip-flops so you don't bust an ankle your first day back."

"Good call," Tracy smiled. "That's something I would do, isn't it?"

Wendell and Emily exchanged a knowing look and each offered him a final embrace. "Give us a call after you've settled in," his dad said. "Love you, son. We'll see you later." Emily said nothing, biting her lip to hold back her tears.

Once he heard them on the stairs Tracy walked down the hall to see if Libby Goldman or her roommate, Tina Sherman, had arrived. Although he felt much more comfortable with the free-spirited Tina, with whom he'd gotten close in eighth grade, the real object of his desire was her mysterious roommate. If this was Day One, how was he going to get through a whole year living with two goddesses under one roof? *This will be sweet, if I don't screw it up*, Tracy vowed.

2

Troubling News from Home

LESS THAN FIFTEEN MILES FROM GLENCOE SCHOOL, BUT A WORLD apart, stood the Adirondack Correctional Facility, a state-run medium-security prison for men. Until 1920, the institution was a sanatorium for tuberculosis patients who had been sent to the small community of Ray Brook, largely because of the cool, clear mountain air that was thought to be beneficial for sufferers of that lung disease. It was later reimagined as a treatment center plus prison for drug addicts, and then dormitory space for state police and border patrol personnel during the 1980 Winter Olympics. Now the facility, commonly referred to as the ACF, held nearly six hundred male inmates.

In the sixteen months since he had been incarcerated, Ramon Ortiz tried to maintain a low profile behind bars, but it had proven nearly impossible. Confrontations had a way of finding him whether or not he sought them out, and generally it was due to pigmentation. Being born Hispanic was something he wore on his face, and there was no way to change that fact.

The ACF at Ray Brook was a cakewalk compared to the other prisons where he had served time and, with only two months remaining before his first parole board hearing, Ramon desperately hoped his nightmare was coming to an end. A favorable decision by the board would permit him finally to get back to the city, to turn his life around, and make up for all that lost time when he should have been helping his mother, Eva, raise the family. Yet Ramon worried that the difficulties he had encountered at the Comstock maximum-security prison where he had begun his sentence stood like a giant fence between him and a thumbs-up from the parole board. Those troubles, though not of his own making, meant that chances were good he'd be ordered to complete the remaining eighteen months of his sentence. Parole boards weren't in the habit of cutting inmates much slack.

On the evening of September 20th Ramon had just returned to his cell from the library where he had been reviewing material on the Building Maintenance program he was attending when he noticed an envelope on the floor. The handwriting was unfamiliar, and a bit childlike. Normally, his mom addressed all letters from home, regardless of who authored the missive. He tore it open and as he read the single line his face fell. *Hey bro, call home as soon as you get this. Pablo.* Ramon checked his watch; there was still time before the phones got shut off.

After a brief wait for a free phone, Ramon began the humiliating process of dialing his family's number, the only one he was authorized to contact. Anxiously he waited for someone to pick up. Hopefully not his little sister, who would be clueless about agreeing to take responsibility for a collect call from a prison. It was yet another reminder that his life was not his own. After a few anxious moments the familiar voice of his younger brother came on.

"Pablo. Hey. It's Ramon! I got your letter. What's up? Everything okay?" It was unusual for anyone other than his mother to pick up at this time of night. Red flags.

"Hey. Thanks, bro. You got my letter? I tried to call you a few days ago."

"You can't call me, Pablo. Don't you know that after all this time? It's not allowed. I've got to call you!" Ramon had a routine that he'd maintained for as long as he had been incarcerated. He would make a call home at the same time every Tuesday evening. There seemed to be less competition for the phones then, and he could count on being able to talk briefly with his mom and his three siblings. Inmates were not permitted to receive incoming calls, which made it challenging for a family to proactively contact their incarcerated loved one.

"I needed to talk to you, man," Pablo said. "I didn't want to wait for your Tuesday call."

"Okay, you got me now. Everything okay? Where's mama?"

"No, man, Everything's not so great," his younger brother said. Ramon could hear a sniffle.

"Shit, man. Speak to me. I ain't got all night."

"It's Miguel . . . and mama. They're both in Bellevue."

It was like pulling teeth to get the details out of his brother while keeping his emotions in check and willing his brain to remember and process what he was hearing. It was obvious to anyone watching the slight, wiry inmate trembling by the phone, and there *was* someone watching, that bad news was being received. Pablo reported that Miguel, fifteen, the youngest of the three Ortiz boys, had gotten into a fight with a group of Eastern European kids in Tompkins Square Park, a few blocks from a clutch of high-rise public housing apartments on Avenue D in Manhattan. There had been a dispute during a pickup basketball game in the park. The argument had escalated; one of the European teens had pulled a knife, and Miguel had taken it in his gut.

"Mama was screaming when the police came to the door and told her about Miggy, man. Then she collapsed and they had to get an ambulance for her, too. She's in the ER. I just got back," Pablo choked. "Mama had a cardiac something," Pablo sniffled. "They gotta check that none of Miguel's organs got messed up. When you coming home, Ramon? I can't do this by myself, bro."

"I ain't on vacation," Ramon muttered. "If I'm lucky they'll let me go in two months. Otherwise, it's another fourteen."

"That's too long. They might be gone. Get out of there, Ramon. We need you, man."

"Sure. I'll be home tomorrow," Ramon muttered. "I'm doing my best, Pablo. This is not where I want to be any longer than I have to. Where's Consuela?" Ramon asked, referring to their aunt, Eva Ortiz's sister.

"She came over to look after Marianna," the seven-year-old baby of the family. "Aunt Consuela is swearing and shouting. She's crying. We don't know what to do, man."

"And you expect me to fix this?" Ramon muttered. "Lemme talk to Consuela."

After a few seconds his aunt picked up the phone. He heard her sniffling. "Ramon, honey. It's so good to hear your voice."

"I haven't said anything yet," Ramon snapped. "Are they going to die, Aunt Consuela? What did the docs say? I can't understand what Pablo's telling me."

His aunt began a rapid-fire stream of details Ramon had difficulty following. *This is going nowhere,* he thought. *One's worse than the other.*

As Ramon struggled to comfort his distraught family, he felt the presence of another inmate eavesdropping on his call. Garth LeGrange, a mountain of a man, leaned against the wall no more than ten feet from the phone booth, listening intently. He absently traced a finger over a raised scar that dominated his left cheek, just above a jet-black beard. The towering lumberjack was the last man in the prison that Ramon wanted to attract, and he struggled to concentrate on the words his aunt was saying. He cupped his hand over the receiver to increase his privacy. "Stop crying," Ramon urged. "Take a breath and put Pablo back on." He could hear the phone on the other end banging against a wall.

"Hey, bro. It's crazy here."

"Consuela wasn't too clear, Pablo. Slowly, tell me what's wrong with them?"

Pablo went through the events again while his brother could see a line forming to use the phones before they were turned off for the night. "Pablo . . . Pablo," he interrupted. "I'm outta time. Gotta go. I'll call you again soon." *How am I supposed to do anything from up here?* Ramon said to himself as he hung up the phone, feeling scared, impotent, and not much better informed as to the condition of his mom and brother than when he had first called. *They are shitty communicators.*

Growing up on the corner of Avenue D and 6th Street in Manhattan's vibrant, diverse East Village, Ramon cherished the oasis of his relatively spacious four-room apartment on the twelfth floor of their building, one of several identical-looking brick edifices. The tenuous balance of ethnicities competing for space and attention made for a neighborhood on edge, a dangerous place for a growing boy facing, too soon, the obligations of being the man in the family.

Many of his childhood friends were either dead or behind bars, victims of drugs, gang wars, and the cycle of poverty. Adolescence had taught Ramon how to be nimble, how to avoid trouble before it found him. He had learned to survive. Born in San Juan, he had come to New York with Eva, baby sister, and two younger brothers when he was thirteen. His father made the choice to remain in Puerto Rico to care for his ailing parents. He promised to join his family as soon as possible and sent them all the money he could spare from his work on a tobacco plantation.

One night, only a year after the family had emigrated to New York, Ramon came home late to find Eva and her sister, Consuela sitting together at the kitchen table. Their eyes were red from crying. Ramon reflexively thought it was something he must have done to disappoint them. They had such high standards for the children, and it was rare that he didn't feel shame for failing to live up to their expectations. But that wasn't it. With Consuela clinging to her, Eva called the children together and informed them that a tractor had tipped and crushed their father that morning in a freak accident. Ramon felt numb but could not summon tears. He knew it was on his shoulders now to keep the family together.

Money was scarce, certainly insufficient to attend the funeral in Puerto Rico, but its lack was rarely discussed. Pride would not permit Eva Ortiz to share her sorrows with her four youngsters. She augmented her earnings as a housekeeper for wealthy folks uptown with food stamps and, between the two sources, there was almost always something hot and healthy on the table each night. Ramon was keenly aware how hard his mom labored and it frustrated him that he could not contribute. It was time to stop wasting hours staring at the classroom ceiling. He couldn't understand how taking up space in a chaotic, overcrowded schoolroom would ever help him feed his family. Mrs. Robertson was a nice enough, well-meaning teacher but she might as well have been a member of the policemen's union rather than the teacher's union for all the educating she was able to do. One day, in the spring of his fifteenth year, without a word to the mother he revered above all else, who would have screamed at him had she known his intentions, he stopped going to school.

Each morning he gathered his books, kissed his mom goodbye, and walked to the nearest stop for the 8th Street crosstown bus that would transport him to the West Village, a new world where shopkeepers would not recognize him. To his disappointment, Ramon discovered that finding an honest job was more difficult than he imagined. "Why aren't you in school?" "You old enough to work, kid?" "Where's your permit?" The quest lasted only two weeks. Dismayed, Ramon cast about for other ways to earn a living.

Drugs of every kind flooded the neighborhood. Dealing was like turning on a faucet and watching the money pour out, or so it seemed to an impressionable young man who envied the clothes and the cars that seemed so tied to drugs. Ramon was an ideal foot soldier for pushers looking for help, inexpensive to hire and, as a minor, someone who wouldn't face severe punishment if caught.

His mother may have suspected where the money was coming from, but she never asked. From the look on her face, however, Ramon knew she was worried about him. The first time he handed over his earnings, announcing he had found an afterschool job at a butcher shop, his mom chose to accept the help without asking for details.

It was so easy making money as a drug courier that Ramon couldn't imagine quitting. The older guys in the gang would package the coke for him, tell him where to make the sales, and give him a cut of the action. It wasn't much, not like the bundle they reserved for themselves, but it helped the Ortiz family pay the rent. One thing Ramon promised himself—he would try very hard never to consume the drugs himself because he saw the effect it had on his customers.

Street smarts usually kept Ramon out of trouble. One day, however, when he was negotiating a deal with three men from New Jersey, he allowed himself to be transported by them in the back seat of their Escalade to a lonely pier near the Hudson River where he was stripped of his cocaine, cash, and clothes to prevent him from any thoughts of pursuit. It was a lesson nowhere to be found in any of Mrs. Robertson's homework assignments.

Ramon never thought of himself as a delinquent, nor headed for a life of crime. He saw the devastation drugs caused. The awful sight of junkies sprawled in doorways throughout the neighborhood was grim evidence of that fact. But, he rationalized, if others wanted to abuse themselves, that was their cross to bear. And if making drugs available to those who could afford it put food on his mother's table, so be it. Ramon drew the line at selling to children, a prohibition he did not discuss with his "employers" but one he scrupulously followed.

He was fourteen the first time he was arrested, standing stoically as a juvenile court judge wagged a finger at him and told him sternly that he would come to no good if he didn't associate with a better class of people. He was nearly sixteen when Mrs. Ortiz, weeping quietly in the back of the courtroom, heard the judge sentence her eldest child to one year at an upstate reform school.

Ramon returned to the city starved for family togetherness, chastened by twelve months of harsh discipline. He felt the absence of his father more keenly than ever. Though memories of life in Puerto Rico were dimming, Ramon carried with him a vision of life in a warm, caring environment, with two devoted parents, ever present. No one asked or expected him to assume the role of father and provider, but as he grew, he felt the need to step up to that responsibility, especially as he saw how his year away had afflicted his mother. The fatigue lines in her face, the loss of merriment in her eyes, were indisputable signs of how life now weighed her down.

For several weeks Ramon tried going straight. He bagged groceries at the local supermarket, washed dishes at a corner bistro, and even hooked up with a production company shooting a commercial in Tompkins Square Park. It was all honest work, but temporary, and paid next to nothing. His brothers needed new sneakers; his sister suffered constantly from ear infections. There was just not enough money to keep the family going. It destroyed him to see his mother so exhausted from her house-cleaning jobs, so desperately unhappy.

As a child, Ramon would fall asleep to his mother's favorite big-band sound. She must have had every record the Mambo Kings ever released. Often, she and Consuela would dance the merengue or the rumba with each other, heads thrown back, laughing, as they tried to persuade the children to join them. It was the most joy he ever saw on those two adult faces. As he grew and developed his own taste for music, the fresh sound of Cubop, a cross between the brass of bebop and a style of percussion with Afro-Cuban origins, drew him in. Late one Friday night, six months after his release from reform school, he decided to take in a set of Cubop at a nightclub near Harlem.

At the 66th Street subway station, he noticed a young couple get on the train. From his vantage point near the rear of the car he stared at them as if observing the mating habits of another species at the zoo. Ramon didn't need to hear what they were saying; their body language told him everything. The young man looked like a model out of a Brooks Brothers catalog—loafers (no socks), beige slacks, a white, V-necked burgundy sweater layered over a blue, button-down, Oxford shirt, a pair of expensive-looking leather gloves stuffed carelessly in the pockets of his dark wool Burberry overcoat. His date nodded and smiled in all the appropriate places, adding a few words here and there to hold up her end of the conversation.

Their subway car was at least half-full as it rocketed through the grimy tunnel beneath Broadway. Mugging them initially crossed his mind as an innocent abstraction. It would be so easy to shake them down. Nothing to split with the boys on the corner. Pure gravy. He knew how to do it. Neighborhood kids bragged about it all the time. *Make sure they're white*, they counseled, *and off their own turf. They'll scare easy.*

He watched the couple, playing out the steps in his head, ashamed to even be fantasizing about such an act. In his eyes, selling dope didn't carry the same stigma as did mugging. In fact, he considered selling drugs even less of a crime than jamming vending machines or breaking into pay phones. Where were the victims in a drug deal? Nowhere, if you only sold to those who wanted to buy. Nobody got hurt, nobody got mad. Of course, that was not what his mother and Aunt Consuela preached to the Ortiz children, night and day, it seemed, yammering all the time about the horrible effects addiction wreaked on millions of people unable to resist temptation and the shameful people who made the drugs so available. What if Eva could see what he was contemplating now? It might kill her on the spot, Ramon suspected.

At 79th Street he dismissed the idea of robbing the couple, worried others in the car would block his escape, though he continued to envision what it would feel like. By the 96th Street station he had himself convinced that if he timed it right, doing the deed just as the train pulled into the next station, he could jump out before anyone stirred up enough courage to stop him. *Probably Columbia students,* Ramon thought. He started to feel angry and bitter. *Why do these two deserve a college education when I can't even finish high school and keep food on the table? Maybe they ought to make me a personal donation.*

The young couple seemed oblivious to his presence and that only heightened his resentment. Ramon stood by the door next to the young man's seat, listening to their meaningless conversation. *Reggie,* she called him, fawning over him as if he were some rock star. Ramon played out in his head how the next few minutes would go, for he had to execute the plan before the train rolled into the next station. As he thought through the steps, Ramon felt adrenaline pulsing through his body, generating instant energy and courage. *Empty your pockets into this hat real quick and nothin' happens to your girlfriend,* he would demand. Reggie would flinch, edge closer to his petrified date. The aggression in his own head shocked him but that's what was necessary to make the bluff work. If the guy chose to fight, Ramon was ready to run. *Reggie, give him what he wants,* the woman would plead, pulling on his coat so hard that the neck would ride up to his ear on the other side. Ramon chuckled at how ridiculous the man would look. *Okay, okay,* Reggie would stutter, stalling for time as he glanced down the train looking for help. Seeing none, he would start negotiating while trying to realign his clothing and his respectability. *I'm sure we can work something out,* he would say, stalling for time. In his head, the whole event played out like a movie.

Ramon knew there were precious few seconds remaining before they pulled into the next station. He had to act now or all was lost. In his pocket Ramon felt the pocketknife that had never been used for anything but cleaning his nails and opening packages. Did he have the nerve to use it to commit this crime? Would the threat of a brandished weapon be enough to cause Reggie to cave in without a fight? The two continued to chatter innocently as the train screeched to a halt. The doors opened, and a flood of people surged in. With a mix of relief and frustration Ramon dashed out onto the platform, took the stairs to the street three at a time, and didn't stop running until he had reached the shadows of Riverside Park. He was angry with himself and disgusted at the same time. Catching his breath, Ramon realized the sober truth. He didn't have the nerve to go through with it. Did that make him a coward? In the eyes of some of his buddies on the street, perhaps; but they didn't count. Not really. His mom and Consuela, they were the ones whose judgment he valued. At the end of the day, he had to admit to himself, mugging people was not who he was, who he was brought up to be. As long as he sold drugs, society would look at him as a criminal, but in his own heart there was a difference. Though the line he tiptoed might be thin, it was a line he apparently was not prepared to cross.

It was now close to midnight. The lure of Cubop no longer held much appeal. He headed back to the subway to retrace his route downtown. During the long ride he contemplated how it felt to have come so close to compromising the moral code his mother had strived to imprint upon each of her children. He knew she would be disappointed in him if she learned he was selling drugs, even if it was only to help out the family, but it would break her heart if she thought he assaulted and stole from people. Ramon resolved never to give in to that temptation.

When he got home the apartment was quiet, save for the even breathing of his mother asleep on the couch in the living room, and her sister on the cot reserved for occasional visitors. He undressed quickly and slid beneath the blanket on the bed he shared with Miguel, gently nudging his sleeping brother to make room for himself at the edge of the mattress.

3

A New Student Makes an Impression

MALCOLM DANDRIDGE HUNCHED OVER A LUMP OF WET CLAY THAT spun precariously upon the potter's wheel before him, his face obscured by a thick shank of blond hair that fell unevenly over his eyes. He sat uncomfortably atop the tractor-style metal seat that faced the wheel, oblivious to the brilliant sunshine bathing the Glencoe School art room in warmth that belied the crisp Adirondack air outside. His right foot pumped steadily on the circular cement base to maintain the wheel's velocity, then withdrew his uncertain hands from the slick gray mass. Beads of sweat dampened the faint peach fuzz on his upper lip and darkened the Led Zeppelin T-shirt he wore. He eyed the clay warily, an adversary to be cajoled and coerced into shape. He tensed his arms tightly to his sides in an attempt to steady them. There was no joy, rather an ominous anticipation of failure. His mutterings attracted the attention of his ninth-grade classmate Libby Goldman and the ceramics teacher, Christine Mason, who was critiquing a watercolor the willowy girl was painting. Christine stepped over to the wheel and leaned in by Malcolm's shoulder to help him center it. Almost instantly, the wobbly column obeyed the pressure of her relaxed, experienced hands, dutifully finding its place in the center of the wheel. Libby felt mild resentment that she had lost the attention of her favorite teacher, but she marveled at how easily Christine could move from one art medium to the next, providing gentle encouragement to a new student who was already proving to be a handful. Anticipation there might be drama, Libby set down her paint-brush to watch.

The heavyset boy grudgingly nodded in admiration, inhaling the perfume from Christine's hair. Libby could not help noticing how Malcolm seemed to relish the art teacher's closeness. He leaned imperceptibly toward her, and Libby saw Christine stiffen.

Two younger students were collaborating on a woolen tapestry across the spacious, well-appointed art room. Marnie Marks and Sarah Welliver were nearly done with the weaving they hoped would grace a prominent wall in the school's dining room, and proudly touted their effort to all within earshot. As they wove the final rows on one of three large wooden floor looms, they giggled at Malcolm's amateurish attempts to master the clay.

"Okay, Mal. Your turn," Christine urged, stepping away from the now perfectly symmetrical cylinder. Malcolm glanced at the girls, distracted by their whispers.

"Will you two shut up? I'm trying to work here," he growled.

"Ignore them, Malcolm," Christine soothed. "You need to concentrate. Transform it into something beautiful."

"Yeah, a horse's dick."

Marnie and Sarah howled with laughter. Christine blanched. Libby had already seen Malcolm had a short fuse in the two weeks since school had begun and she worried about what might happen next. All eyes in the room were now on Christine to see how she would deal with him. This was the one aspect of teaching—the discipline part—that she detested.

"How'm I supposed to do this with those assholes over there?" Malcolm implored.

"Don't use that language in here, please," Christine ordered.

"Anger management, Malcolmmm," Sarah chorused.

Libby wished she could defuse the growing tempest. About to turn fifteen, but looking several years older, the stunningly attractive girl from Manhattan's Upper West Side was in her second year at Glencoe. Libby admired the magic Christine Mason was able to generate from students who had never considered themselves "artistic." She gravitated to Christine's art room, spending as many afternoons as her schedule would allow, learning from her favorite adult on campus, and mentoring the younger students. Libby glanced up at Christine, sensing she was losing the battle, and decided to help change the mood in the room before it exploded.

"Forget it, Malcolm," Libby encouraged. "Don't listen to those idiots." Christine threw her a grateful glance. If any of the school's male teachers were in this room, Libby thought, Malcolm would never speak that way. It irritated her that the newbie from Ohio took such liberties.

"Stay focused, Mal, or you'll lose it," Christine cautioned. "Now that we've gotten it centered, press your thumbs together down into the middle like this." She stepped toward him again, accepting the brush of his T-shirt against her. As her thumbs dove into the middle of the spinning slickness the clay parted obediently, creating a well surrounded by thick walls. Malcolm stared, momentarily mesmerized. She withdrew her hands carefully, dipped a sponge into a bowl of muddy water, and gently squeezed drops into the well and along the lip.

"No, keep going," Malcolm said softly. "What's next?"

Libby was struck by his sudden gentleness. Christine seemed to be, too. Malcolm appeared absorbed by the creative process. Perhaps, Libby hoped, that was all it took to forget the taunting from the girls across the room. She recalled what Hamish MacLean had told her one time about how Glencoe's uniqueness could help students whose adolescent insecurity masqueraded as indifference. More often than not, a student struggling in one area experienced a complete turnaround thanks to some positive event in a completely different aspect of Glencoe life. *Give them a way to find success. That's what we aim to do*, he said. *Light a fire under them and it'll spread like kudzu.* Libby was not familiar with kudzu, the fast-growing plant that resisted human control, but she thought she grasped the message. Libby had arrived at Glencoe the previous year with a real chip on her shoulder. She did not want to go away to school, and she resisted all efforts from the staff to encourage her to embrace the opportunities Glencoe offered. It was not until she had taken to horseback riding and found she had an innate ability to communicate with the animal beneath her that her attitude toward school began to evolve. By the time afternoon rides were suspended for the winter Libby could canter with ease and coax her favorite steed, Prince, over three-foot jumps with confidence. Her schoolwork soared simultaneously.

At every annual staff orientation before the students arrived, Hamish would trot out the story of Ricky Woodward, who, some years prior, had arrived at Glencoe as a cocky seventh grader, fresh off the rough-and-tumble playgrounds in Bronx, New York. His confidence dominated on the basketball court, but only there. That first semester in the classroom he was a lost soul, though not due to a lack of ability. Woodward's folks hoped Glencoe would open Ricky's eyes to a broader world beyond an inflated leather ball, the only object he felt he could control.

Like every other student, Ricky was assigned a weekly chore. His assignment the last week of a snowy February was tending chickens. As with all the kids doing barn chores, Ricky had to wake up thirty minutes earlier than his peers with work jobs in the school buildings. He braved the morning chill on the quarter-mile walk to the barn, fed and watered the two dozen or so hens that crowded about his ankles, and gathered all the eggs those hens had laid. He toted the basket back to the school kitchen, noting on a clipboard how many eggs he had delivered. It was a brutal way to start each day, and Ricky could not wait for the week to end.

During remarks after lunch on Saturday, what Glencoe referred to as Council, following his usual review of that afternoon's activities, Hamish walked to Ricky's table and placed his hands on Ricky's shoulders. Unused to being the focus of anyone's attention beyond the confines of a basketball court, Ricky squirmed. The other kids around the table giggled in anticipation of some mortal embarrassment about to take place.

"I want to take a moment before we go off to our afternoon activities," Hamish announced, tapping his hands gently upon Ricky's shoulders. "We owe our friend, here, a hearty congratulations. As far back as we've kept records, no one has ever . . . ever . . . coaxed so many eggs out of our dear chickens as has Ricky Woodward this past week. They're going to miss you." He clapped Ricky on the back. "Well done, son! Please share your secrets."

Ricky kept his head lowered, eyes on his plate. But there was no hiding the prideful grin, nor the extraordinary turnaround that followed in his classwork the rest of the semester. That was Hamish's kudzu at work.

As Malcolm pumped away with his foot to maintain speed, Christine again bent close to him, shoulder to shoulder. Libby knew the teacher was struggling not to move away. Placing two fingers of one hand within the well, two fingers from the other hand on the outside wall, Christine began to raise them while imparting firm, gentle pressure to the clay spinning in between. Responding to her touch, the walls thinned and rose gracefully, transforming the gray mass into a handsome bowl.

. . .

"Awesome!" Malcolm exclaimed. Christine stood up to admire her work, carefully brushing a wayward hair out of her eyes with her forearm. From across the room the two girls regarded the elegant piece.

"Hey, Malcolm, did you do that?" Marnie Marks asked with genuine surprise.

"Better than that piece of trash you're weaving," Malcolm retorted.

"Malcolm is off his meds again," she teased. Sarah snickered.

"Shut up, you guys!" Libby interjected, abandoning her fanciful painting. She stood up and positioned herself between Malcolm and the weavers so they could no longer follow his progress.

"Malcolm! Please pay attention," Christine warned. Libby could see he was again distracted, his fuse about to blow. "It's a little too wet," Christine warned. "Take the sponge and hold it down in the bottom to soak up the excess."

"Okay, okay" he muttered, throwing a withering glare in the direction of his tormentors. He pressed the sponge against the clay bottom as Christine had suggested but glanced up to see if the girls were still watching. As Malcolm's head lifted, his hands followed. Before Christine could intervene, his fingers had jammed into the delicate walls of the bowl. Critically out of balance, it wobbled and then collapsed in on itself.

"Shit!" Malcolm hissed.

"Another masterpiece down the drain," whispered Marnie, just loud enough to be heard by her target.

Malcolm exploded. "That's it! I've had it with those bitches."

He pushed away from the wheel, wiped his muddy hands on a sweater Libby had left draped over a nearby chair, threw it to the ground and slammed the art room door behind him. Distraught, Christine glared at Marnie and Sarah, both abashed at the results of their teasing, and hurried upstairs to quell any more destruction he might leave in his wake.

School had not even been in session a month, yet Malcolm Dandridge had already made an indelible impression upon students and teachers alike. Libby felt terrible for Christine and anticipated the guy was going to be a challenging addition to her senior class.

There was no sign of Malcolm in the long hallway that bisected Dewey Hall. It was in Nissen where Christine found Malcolm shooting baskets and talking trash with several boys, the unpleasant incident in the art room seemingly forgotten. She closed the door quietly, turning to find Libby, muddied sweater in hand.

"Drives you crazy, doesn't he?" Libby asked.

"Sorry about your sweater, sweetie. He didn't think."

Libby shrugged. "Seems to be a pattern. You tried."

"It might have worked if those two hadn't provoked him. I just hope he lets it go," Christine sighed.

After dinner, Malcolm sat by his cubby in the large mudroom of Dewey Hall, waiting for students and faculty to depart for their residences, a hundred yards up the gravel road. When he felt alone, he slipped downstairs to the art room. He groped along the darkened walls in the classroom in search of the supply closet, his penlight guiding his way. Encountering a padlock on the closet door he pointed his light on the counters that ringed the room and scanned the bare tables. The student cleanup crew had done a good job. Malcolm was about to admit defeat when a glint of light reflecting off metal caught his eye. Focusing the beam beneath a chair in the corner of the room he saw a forgotten pair of scissors.

Tracy Barcomb had also not yet left Dewey to join his housemates in Phelps House, where they were already preparing for reading period in the cozy living room, Glencoe's version of "study hall." Having just finished his evening work job, which meant helping the kitchen staff process the dinner plates and utensils through the Hobart industrial dishwasher, his excuse was understandable. All bones, freckles, perpetually ruddy cheeks beneath a thatch of unruly red hair, the lanky ninth-grader from Vermont was popular and perplexing, his affability blemished only by a maddening proclivity to become distracted by whatever crossed his line of sight. His mom presumed it was undiagnosed attention deficit hyperactivity disorder. His dad chalked it up to laziness and immaturity. Tracy could lead schoolmates with ease through dense cripplebrush and blowdown hour upon hour to reach some remote Adirondack mountaintop. And he had an uncanny talent for memorization, especially useful in the school theatrical productions.

As bees to watermelon, Tracy was drawn to Malcolm. The Ohio boy's mysterious past and defiant persona initially intrigued Tracy, whose easygoing, "life's-a-dance, everybody's my friend" attitude drove Malcolm nuts. The more Tracy poked innocent fun at the ungainly newcomer, the more committed Malcolm became to making the redhead's life miserable.

When everything had been washed, dried, and shelved for the night, Tracy toted a bucket of food scraps earmarked for the pigs down to the root cellar below the kitchen. At first light, those pigs would patiently line up against the calloused boards of their pen, awaiting sleepy-headed students off to their morning chores. Tracy waved goodnight to the head cook who was already preparing the next day's menu, threw on his coat, jammed a Pawtucket Red Sox baseball cap over his shaggy hair, collected his books from a nearby locker in the circular mudroom that adjoined the kitchen, and headed out into the evening chill.

He skirted the rear of Dewey Hall on his way up the hill to Phelps House. Paused for a moment. Even for a self-absorbed, hormone-driven adolescent it was impossible not to stand in awe of the astonishing starry display above the darkened ridgelines of the peaks that surrounded the Glencoe campus, most of which he had scaled several times. As he stared at the twinkling light of infinity, a breath of wind the only sound in that remote corner of the world, his peripheral vision caught an unexpected glimmer through the art room windows. He walked over to a door that led directly into the room for a better look. Oblivious to the audience outside, Malcolm was systematically scissoring a nearly finished weaving into worthless scraps of wool.

"Holy shit! You out of your mind?" Tracy sputtered as he burst into the room. Malcolm looked up in shock, instinctively snapping the flashlight off as though he could still avoid being recognized.

"Just getting even," he sneered, gripping the scissors ever more tightly in the dark. "It's not your fight so stay the hell out of it."

Tracy stepped to the wall and clicked on the lights. "How could you ruin someone's work like that? That's sick." For what seemed like minutes, the two boys faced each other in awkward, tense silence. Each could feel a fight was possible and neither welcomed it. At five-foot-ten, Tracy had a good four inches on Malcolm, but was easily outweighed by twenty pounds.

"They had it coming," Malcolm shrugged with indifference. "And I don't want those lights on, okay?"

Tracy glanced at the scissors. He clicked the overhead lights off again. In the faint moonlight filtering in through the picture windows he could barely see Malcolm approach him. "When Hamish hears about this your ass will be outta here," Tracy said, backing toward the door.

"And you plan to rat me out?"

"I won't have to. You're going to admit to Hamish what you did and take the consequences," Tracy warned. He reached for the door and shoved it open. "Let me tell you something," Tracy continued. "This place has been pretty good to me. Why don't you just go back wherever it is you came from and screw up some other school? This one's just fine without you."

"I ain't got nothing to say to Hamish," Malcolm disgustedly tossed the scissors across the floor. "And you better not neither."

The two boys left the art room and walked uncomfortably together up the gravel road to their houses on the hill where the rest of the student body was already halfway through reading period. From a spot under trees outside Marshall House they saw Pete Hedges, English teacher and co-houseparent with Christine Mason, check his watch and walk to the window. He cupped his hands to his eyes and peered out into the darkness, looking for the missing person from his household.

"What are you going to do?" Malcolm challenged.

Tracy kicked idly at a stone. "I dunno. What you did tonight was way out of line. You've been here like a minute, and already everybody hates you. I don't care how rotten your life has been. There's no excuse for that shit."

"Those girls deserved it. If I get kicked out that's the way it goes. Maybe everybody will quit trying to find the perfect place for me. If someone crosses me, they'll wish they hadn't. Don't believe me? I'll give you some names to talk to," Malcolm called as he headed up the front steps to Marshall House.

Tracy muttered a curse under his breath and turned toward Phelps House, perhaps thirty yards farther along the gravel path on the semicircle of residences sitting at the edge of the darkened woods behind. As he opened the front door quietly, several housemates filed past him on their way upstairs, trailed by Jane Henderson, holding little Nicky's hand. Tracy was fuming and trying to hide it.

"Something important keep you from reading period?" she asked, giving him the benefit of the doubt.

"Sorry, Jane. Kitchen cleanup took longer than usual. I'll make up the study hall time now."

"Okay. Grab your book and come down to the living room so you're not distracted by all the shenanigans upstairs."

In one of four rooms reserved for Glencoe students in Phelps, Tina Sherman sat cross-legged on her bed, reciting a letter from her parents to her roommate, Libby Goldman.

"*You wouldn't believe the flora and fauna of suspicious origin floating in the tea we were served by our Nepalese porters this morning,*" Tina read, absently twisting the braids of her long, blonde hair. "*The food is unusual, to say the least, a bit thin nutritionally. We are trying mightily to avoid dysentery, which is rampant in these parts. We are looking forward to sharing that wonderful Glencoe Thanksgiving meal with you, darling.*" Tina looked up and noticed her roommate's distress. "And so on and so forth . . . blah, blah, blah."

Libby's emerald eyes filled. "I'm sorry, Tina. Whenever you get a letter from your folks it just makes me feel like crap. I can't remember the last time I heard from my parents. You'd think I had some contagious disease, or something. And whenever I call, there's always some strange voice at the other end telling me they'll take a message. It's like they're parking me here so I won't get in their way." She sat up, wiped her eyes with a tissue and blew her nose.

Tina groped for sympathetic words to mollify her friend. Prior to becoming Tina's roommate in Phelps House, Libby had been merely a casual acquaintance the previous school year but now, thrown together in the same room as seniors, the two ninth graders had quickly become fast friends, nearly inseparable. They were excited to be in Phelps House, presided over by Jane and Payton Henderson. As graduating Glencoe seniors looking ahead to tenth grade somewhere else, Tina and Libby appreciated having each other to enjoy their last year at Glencoe and to help each other navigate the shoals of high school applications, interviews, and the possibility of rejection.

Both girls had something in common that immediately drew them together and provided fodder for hours of conversation. Neither had spent more than two years in any one school, but the reasons for their constant movement as well as the impact of those disruptions on their psyches were starkly different.

Glencoe was just the most recent stop on Tina's educational journey, not from a lack of love, but rather due to her parents' nomadic lifestyle. Her father, a city planner, worked in many nations and had always brought his family with him. For two years, he designed sewer systems in the Peruvian highlands; for three, he struggled with the insoluble problem of moving India's untouchable caste off the streets of Calcutta and into subsistence housing. Currently, a visiting professorship had taken them to Kathmandu University in Nepal. The itinerant lifestyle meant Tina was forever leaving her friends and starting anew whenever Dad's assignment changed. At last, her parents decided a little continuity was needed in Tina's life, so they applied to Glencoe and reluctantly sent her away to the school in upstate New York.

The previous year, Tina's first at a boarding school, had been a difficult one. She didn't blame her parents for their decision, but for most of the year she suffered deeply with homesickness. This fall, however, fresh from a glorious summer sailing with her family in the South Pacific, Tina felt more settled as she returned to the familiar confines of Glencoe for her final year. Rooming with Libby proved therapeutic, as well.

"I guess my story is quite different," Tina said. "I've always taken my family's closeness for granted, which is interesting since we are not usually close . . . geographically."

"You get a regular stream of letters and care packages," Libby said. "I get zilch. I wonder what it's like to have a family who lets you know they care." Libby paused. Her roommate looked uncomfortable. "I'm sorry. I'm whining," Libby grumped.

As Tina reflected the light side, Libby mirrored the dark. Tall, slim and physically mature for someone just turned fifteen, Libby's mystique both bewitched and intimidated other students, her enigmatic personality often misinterpreted as standoffishness. She gravitated more toward the adults on campus rather than her fellow students. She had good reason to appear independent and self-possessed. Glencoe was the third school Libby had attended in the past four years.

Home was a spacious, stark, triplex apartment on the Upper West Side of Manhattan. Her parents, both educators, ran an elementary school based upon Waldorf education, adhering to a philosophy that children who are encouraged to think, feel, and do, through a curriculum that emphasizes the arts as strongly as traditional academic coursework, become more well-rounded adults. The school was called "Austro-Lab," honoring the Austrian heritage of Rudolf Steiner, the patron saint of the Waldorf Education method. Adam and Shelley Goldman deployed the considerable wealth he had inherited from his mother to purchase the building, which housed the school, a beautiful brownstone, adjacent to their own apartment building.

"I didn't mean to bum you out," Tina said, returning the letter to its envelope and filing it away in the lacquered box her parents had sent from Nepal. "I do wish I could see my parents more," she said, her throat constricting. Students at Glencoe rarely received letters; telephone and email had all but eliminated that mode of communication. Most parents called once a week, but those calls were, by necessity, to the landline in each of the student residences. To prevent classroom distractions and to avoid the constant reliance on an electronic device, or complaints about its inevitable misplacement, no student was permitted a cell phone. Text messaging via computers was permitted, but a constant topic of debate at faculty meetings.

Tina's parents preferred old-fashioned letter-writing as their method of communicating with their daughter, and the fact that Kathmandu was so many time zones away made calls both expensive and challenging to schedule. Letters from her parents were a tenuous link to that distant world, and Tina cherished the simple act of opening the envelope, quickly scanning the contents to see how long a "visit" she had in store, then reading it over and over until she had it memorized.

Libby so envied the obvious love in the letter Tina had just read, and felt a deep vacancy in her heart. Her sadness seemed to fill the room. "Tina, I know it's tough having your folks be so far away and you can't just see each other whenever you want. My parents only live a few hours from here, but they seem perfectly happy to ignore me until winter break. Maybe if I ran away, they'd notice me for a change."

"That's ridiculous, Libby. I know they're busy people, and they probably just assume you're happy here and don't need for them to pop in here every other weekend."

"They don't need you to make excuses for them. No offense," Libby responded. "Maybe I just get in the way. Maybe I'm too demanding or something. Don't you think I could get a call once in a while like everyone else in this house? Except you, of course. I understand you've got a different situation, and those letters are . . . sweet," she said, stifling a sob.

"I wish I could make you feel better, Libs. You've got so much going for you. You're smart, gorgeous . . ."

"Yeah, right," Libby interrupted, half-hoping Tina would contradict her and toss more flattery her way.

"I'm serious. My God, I would kill for your looks."

"You're full of crap, Tina. Everybody loves blondes. You look like you just fell off a surfboard."

"That's overrated. You've got that dark, mysterious look that drives boys nuts. Me, they treat like their best friend or kid sister. Don't tell me you never noticed how they just sit around the pool when we go swimming in Placid. Who do you think they're looking at?"

"You're crazy."

"No, just observant. Especially when you wear that black and white thing you got in Miami. Guys start walking around with towels in front of them they're so embarrassed. It's goofy."

Libby laughed, tossing a pillow at her roommate.

"Tell me again why your folks sent you here," Tina said.

"Well . . . you know they are *educators*, right?" Libby said, making air quotes with her fingers. "You ever hear of the Waldorf Education?"

"Doesn't ring a bell," Tina said.

"It's a way of teaching kids that's got some things in common with Glencoe. It's based on this guy Rudolf Steiner who believed kids should get a lot of art and music and, I don't know how to explain it exactly. But my folks think Glencoe has a lot of similar philosophies about learning. The school they run, Austro-Lab, uses those methods, and it's pretty cool, actually. But I couldn't stay there. That would be too easy. My folks wanted to see how other schools do things, so they ship me around every year or so, like an experiment. If they weren't school heads themselves, I doubt I'd have gotten in anywhere. The competition in New York is ridiculous.

"I hated it. I was always the new kid. Then they got it into their heads a boarding school like this, in the country, would somehow be better for my *well-rounded education*," she said, making the air quotes again. "And that the city is maybe too dangerous; or too many temptations for a teenager. Who the hell knows what my parents think?"

Tina placed her arm around her friend's shoulder, uncertain how to make her friend feel better.

"They're so absorbed in that damn school they never seem to have time for me when I am home," Libby continued. Tears were now welling up, but she had a head of steam and license from her friend to vent, so out it came. "Once I hid my mom's phone. Because I wanted her to go shopping with me?" she said, her voice rising on the last syllable. "She went absolutely ballistic, tore the house apart and accused everybody except me of taking it. Since no one confessed, she fired the housekeeper. I was so embarrassed I couldn't tell her I did it. Maybe I'm better off here." Libby reached for a tissue and dried her eyes.

"Somehow you turned out okay," Tina said.

"Because I'm not a serial killer yet? I'm still a kid. When I grow up, you'll probably read about me. Yeah, I can just see it now," Libby said with a wry smile, forming a picture frame with her hands. "There you'll be, on line at the checkout counter with an infant screaming at you from the grocery cart and look who's staring at you next to the picture of the alien, your best friend from ninth grade, Libby Goldman, on trial for slaughtering her parents."

There was a soft knock on their door. "May I interrupt?" asked Jane Henderson. Now in their early thirties, Jane and Payton had met at Glencoe as twenty-five-year-old interns, stayed on as full-fledged teachers, she in English, he in Spanish, and married after three years of living in separate residences and spending far too many nights sneaking up and down icy fire escapes to spend time together without alerting the community. After seven years at Glencoe, they were considered lifers, ensconced in a modest apartment with their four-year-old son, Nicky, adjacent to the student section of Phelps House.

"Sure, Jane," Tina said, waving her in. "We're just talkin' about stuff."

"What kind of *stuff*? Or am I prying?" Jane challenged, with a smile.

"Family stuff," Libby offered. "You know, why I'm such a freak." Though they'd shared Phelps House only briefly since the beginning of school, Jane knew exactly what Libby meant. She and Payton had already devoted many hours commiserating with Libby about her unusual situation and the seemingly callous way Adam and Shelley Goldman handled their daughter.

"I hope my Nicky grows up to be as nice a freak as you," Jane comforted. "Listen guys," she continued, changing the subject. "Payton and I have to run over to the MacLeans'. We should be back within the hour. Will you watch the little one? He fell asleep on the couch," she asked.

"No problem," Tina said. "We'll bring Nicky in with us if he wakes up." She turned to Libby and whispered, "He goes in your bed, not mine."

"Tina! I heard that!"

"Oops. Sorry, Jane," Tina said, abashed.

"If you want to talk privately, please wait until I've left the room. Can I count on you or not?"

"Yes, ma'am."

"Thank you, young lady."

"Why did you do that, Tina?" Libby asked after they heard Jane's footsteps on the stairs.

"It came out without my even realizing it. I love that little kid, but I don't want him mucking up my sheets," she giggled.

"Fine, Tina. I'll take Nicky in with me if he wakes up."

"I know someone who'd be pretty jealous if he knew someone else was sharing your sheets," teased Tina.

"And who would that be?"

"Your boyfriend down the hall. The one I hear you whispering to in your sleep."

"Tracy? Don't make me vomit! And I don't talk in my sleep."

"How would you know? You're asleep," Tina said. "You'd be amazed what comes out of your mouth at three in the morning."

4

Headmaster's Challenge

CHRISTINE MASON DISCOVERED THE DAMAGED WEAVING BEFORE breakfast while preparing materials for the day's art classes. Barely able to control her tears, she made a beeline for Hamish's office, catching him with his first cup of coffee and a stack of welcome letters to parents. She tossed the julienned strips of cloth on his desk and slumped down into a chair across from him. "Marnie Marks and Sarah Welliver were hoping to present you with this, Hamish," she said, choking the sobs in the back of her throat. "Why would anyone want to do this to them?"

"Not what I hope to see first thing in the morn," Hamish sighed, fingering the pieces gingerly, as though they might disintegrate. Devastated, Christine recounted the events of the previous afternoon, describing how excited and enthusiastic Malcolm was as he watched his clay bowl take shape, then how upset he became as Marnie and Sarah taunted him.

"Aye, but no proof the boy's responsible?"

Christine shook her head. "No. But it explains why he didn't come home until reading period was nearly over. Pete and I talked to him when he showed up, but he seemed to have an alibi that he'd been talking to Tracy and lost track of the time," she said. "He's still getting accustomed to the routines here, and I don't know that he's been held accountable for his whereabouts in the past. But Tracy ought to know better. It didn't all fit, but we let it go." The bell signaling breakfast brought an end to the conversation. Hamish set his unfinished paperwork aside and rose to accompany her to the dining hall.

Hamish MacLean, only the third Head in the school's history, had directed Glencoe for twenty-five years. Under his guidance, the school had flourished as a unique and innovative educational experience. Imbued with the teachings of Outward Bound, an adventure program of human interdependence originally forged among the lakes and crags around the tiny Welsh town of Aberdyfi, Hamish first learned of Glencoe through an academic journal. He was struck by the name, wondering why an American school should be named after a tiny Scottish town, and he was stirred, too, by the aerial photo of the wooded Glencoe campus, nestled within a horseshoe of mountains. The accompanying article that profiled this unusual American boarding school based upon the teachings of John Dewey, of whom Hamish had become acquainted while pursuing a master's in Education at the University of Aberdeen, touched a nerve, but it wasn't until he reread it months later that the urge to learn more took hold and would not let go. The piece described a school for children in the fifth through ninth grades that combined the rigors of a working farm with a traditional academic curriculum, a place where a child could muck out a horse's stall before breakfast, study French and algebra before lunch, ski-jump all afternoon, and attend a violin recital after dinner. It seemed a definitively more exciting place to be than the traditional English school he had been running, devoid of passion.

A year later, Hamish learned by chance that Glencoe was seeking a new headmaster. Almost as a lark, he submitted his name. After a series of letters and telephone calls from trustees and prominent alums, he accepted an invitation to come for an interview. It was Hamish's first trip to America. He nearly abandoned it just outside Kennedy Airport after having to joust for roadway in his rented car with seemingly crazed taxicab and truck drivers, all driving on the wrong side of the road. His stomach in knots, he finally escaped the chaotic metropolitan highways. Five hours later as he neared school property, negotiating the final miles of winding blacktop beneath precipitous, ice-caked cliffs, his spirits lifted. He felt oddly that he was coming home. Though the heavily wooded slopes did not resemble the heathery landscape of Scotland, there was a familiarity to the ancient terrain that resonated. At the base of those formidable cliffs, he discovered a place of uncommon beauty, a polyglot community of boys and girls from some of the world's most illustrious families as well as its most desperately poor neighborhoods. The rugged Scotsman with a rough-hewn manner and lyrical brogue felt immediately welcome.

The school had undergone inevitable modifications during his tenure, a natural maturation and recognition that an institution could not stand still while the society it served evolved. Hamish prided himself that his stewardship had not caused deterioration in the ideals and philosophies that the founders had imprinted upon the place nearly seventy years prior. Glencoe remained true to the precepts of Dewey, perhaps even more so now than was the case in the early days of the school. A hefty percentage of the food eaten in the dining room was directly attributable to children's hands planting, weeding, and harvesting. Maple syrup on the breakfast table was there thanks to afternoon chores carried out by children chopping and splitting wood, hammering taps into maple trees, and hauling buckets of sap to collection tanks. Maintenance staff weren't the only ones pitching hay bales into the barn's loft; students did their share. The woods and lake on campus were ideal laboratories. The best-learned lessons often were those taught outside. A prime example was Pete Hedges, who, aside from his classroom duties as Head of English, was also a competitive orienteerer, cartographer, and student of Adirondack geology. Pete drew exquisitely detailed maps of the place, laid out courses for his students to follow, and sometimes, instead of using the traditional red and white nylon flags known around the world to mark orienteering targets, he would embed pictures of plants on the maps his students carried as they raced across campus. When they discovered a flag, they were to identify the correct plant by which it had been hung; one of innumerable examples of experiential learning to engage and stimulate Glencoe students.

It had not taken Hamish long to discover that Glencoe did not magically eliminate all mischief in every student, nor mold each student in one image. In the early years of his directorship, there had been precious few incidents that had required serious disciplinary action. But in recent times, mirroring the increase in social permissiveness, the school had admitted more children willing to "push the envelope." It confounded the faculty that their Spartan headmaster could be so disciplined personally, could demand so much of himself and his staff, while demonstrating unexpected leniency with students who didn't buy in to the philosophy.

While contemplating his bowl of strawberry rhubarb compote, Hamish considered how best to confront Malcolm, the obvious suspect. Making a mental note to speak to Geraldine, the head cook, about more liberal use of honey in the rhubarb to coax finicky eaters to give it a try, he made his way to Pete Hedges's table, thinking about whether this vandalism rose to the level that demanded separation from the school.

"Someone took scissors to a loom in the art room last night," Hamish whispered to Pete beyond earshot of the children. "Christine tells me you and she spoke to Malcolm about missing reading period."

"I was afraid there was more to Malcolm's absence last night than he would own up to. He said he was studying late in the building with Tracy."

"That's a bit o' malarkey. Tracy wouldn't give the time of day to that boy."

"That was his story," Pete shrugged. "Chris and I wondered if there was something else going on. I guess now we know what that may have been."

"No proof yet, but surely stinks. How much more rope can I give that lad?" Hamish sighed. He glanced over at his own table to see if calm still prevailed, then made his way to Malcolm's table on the other side of the dining room.

"Excuse me," Hamish said to Ron Handy, who was heading the table of five students that included Malcolm. Ron was the school's most senior faculty member. A master music and French teacher, Ron had earned a reputation as a consummate rock climber, pioneering many first ascents in Yosemite back in the day. Diminutive in stature at a mere five-foot-five, Ron towered above the other faculty in terms of the respect he had earned over thirty-five years at Glencoe. He was the only teacher remaining who'd been hired by the founders, and he proudly carried the mantle of their philosophy. In deference to his longevity, he no longer was expected to function as houseparent as well as teacher, though he often subbed in the residences for others on their nights off, in order for all the students to get to know him, not just the ones in his classes.

Apart from his wife, Bonnie, Hamish relied upon Ron as confidant and sounding board. Since his arrival at Glencoe, Hamish had frequently leaned upon Ron for his institutional knowledge and breadth of experience. Ron's genius as lyricist and composer should have foretold a life creating Broadway musicals. His PhD from Berkeley in religious studies and theology certainly prepared him for a career in higher education. Hamish once asked Ron why he had chosen Berkeley, to which he replied, "Spitting distance from the big walls at Yosemite. That's where my passion lay, but not a good career move." And to the question why he ended up teaching music and French to schoolchildren? "They listen better. The older they get, the harder it is to convince them they don't know everything yet. When you get to our age," Ron winked, "you realize you don't know a damn thing about anything." Nearing seventy-five, Ron could still be the sanity check Hamish needed from time to time.

"May I have a word with Malcolm?" Hamish asked. Ron nodded and immediately diverted the attention of the others around the table with a brainteaser about a man who went crazy after eating albatross soup.

"Please come down to my office after you're done eating, Mr. Dandridge," Hamish said brusquely.

"Uh oh," interjected a ruddy-faced seventh grader sitting across from Malcolm.

Malcolm delivered the boy a swift kick under the table without taking his eyes off Hamish.

"Jesus! What did you kick me for?"

"I've got Spanish first period," Malcolm said, ignoring the boy.

"Skip it," said Hamish.

"Sounds good to me."

Fuming, Hamish returned to his own table, sat down long enough to hand a steaming plate of cinnamon-laced French toast to the student on his left, then excused himself once again, leaving the table in the charge of a ninth grade girl who was only too happy to slide into his chair at the head of the table and begin giving orders. Hamish walked back to his office at the east end of the building. He asked Cathy Swenson, the school secretary, to check the Albany-to-Columbus, Ohio airline sched-ule and was in the midst of thinking how he would explain the expulsion to Mathilda Graham, Malcolm's guardian, when the door opened.

"Malcolm is here to see you," said Cathy.

"Show him in," growled Hamish. Malcolm walked in and stood before the desk. "Sit down, sit down. Let me get right to the point." The headmaster wheeled his chair tightly into the desk. He leaned forward aggressively, the sudden move sending a familiar searing pain down his back. He grimaced and reached reflexively for a pill bottle in his desk. Holding the bottle beneath the level of the desk for privacy, he shook out two tablets, then another two for good measure. He tossed them down with a swig of coffee as Malcolm sat down warily.

"There is strong evidence that, sometime yesterday evening, you destroyed a weaving in the art room. Though you've just barely arrived at this school and we're still getting to know you, I must tell you I am up to here with your shenanigans, Mr. Dandridge." He watched Malcolm's eyes for a reaction but got none. The boy was either innocent or incredibly practiced at deception.

"What makes you think it was me?"

"I'm told you were extremely angry at the girls whose work was ruined," charged Hamish, a flush rising in his cheeks. "You stormed out of the art room making threats, then were absent without leave after dinner."

"That's it?" Malcolm asked.

"What do you mean *That's it?*"

"Because I had an argument with a couple of . . . girls . . . over the bowl I was working on, you think that proves I'm guilty?"

"Well, this is your chance to give me your side of the story."

"Sure, I was angry with the girls. I don't deny it. Huge pains in the . . . uh . . . You can ask Christine. But that doesn't mean I cut the loom. That's heresy."

"You mean 'hearsay,'" Hamish corrected, realizing Malcolm had a point. "Why did you miss reading period?"

Malcolm looked down at his feet, paused for a moment, and looked straight at Hamish. "I was with Tracy. He has kitchen duty, and I waited for him after dinner. I wanted to ask him about a history assignment. Then we got to talking and lost track of time. Sorry."

"I'm hard-pressed to believe you," Hamish said sternly. He sat back in his chair, steepled his fingers together beneath his chin and stared at the boy. Malcolm shrugged as if there was nothing more he could say. "If I find out through other sources that you were responsible for this, you will be out of here so fast it'll make your head spin."

"Yes, sir."

"I've no tolerance for people who care so little for the rights of others in this community!" Hamish continued, his voice rising in anger. "This is not New Winds," he said, referring to the nearby alternative school for juvenile delinquents that Glencoe sometimes played in soccer and basketball. Those were always nerve-racking afternoons for the staff who watched the Glencoe athletes get physically mauled and were reminded how different their lives would be teaching at that school. "We expect our students to respect each other's space and property as if it's their own," Hamish fumed. "Otherwise, we've got chaos, and a very unpleasant place this would be."

He probably thinks I'm way overreacting, Hamish thought. It was probably a bad analogy to mention New Winds. Scissoring a weaving would not raise too many eyebrows at that place.

"That's all for now, Malcolm. Please get yourself to class."

Malcolm backed out of the office, walked halfway down the hall, ducked into a small bathroom and closed the door almost all the way, leaving open a crack through which he could see who else might be called to the headmaster's office. Sure enough, Cathy Swenson strode past the bathroom, then returned several minutes later with Tracy in tow.

Hamish looked up from his desk when Tracy walked in and motioned him to sit down. From the boy's hangdog look the headmaster was convinced Tracy was not surprised to have been summoned. *He has to assume Malcolm has already been grilled*, Hamish thought. By the answers Tracy gave, Hamish would see how defensive he was, and whether he expected Malcolm had laid the blame on him. It pained Hamish to think Tracy could ever do such a thing, given how diligently Tracy had worked during his three years at Glencoe to earn the respect of the Scotsman. It didn't add up.

"We have a problem, Tracy. I'm hoping you can shed some light on it for me."

"I'll try."

"Are you aware of some vandalism in the art room?"

"I dunno," Tracy stammered, squirming in his chair. "I, uh, worked late in the kitchen last night."

Hamish arched an eyebrow. "Who said anything about last night?"

"Uh . . . nobody . . . I just assumed . . ." Tracy cursed himself for his blunder.

"I've been told you missed reading period. Where were you?"

"I was, like, talking to, uh, Malcolm . . . and we didn't realize how late it was."

"That's odd. I don't think I've ever seen you spend more than ten seconds talking to that boy if you didn't have to. What was so important about your conversation that would cause you to skip reading period?"

Hamish could sense Tracy's disgust with Malcolm, yet the lad would not throw him under the bus—a stupid code of honor among students. It made it very difficult to get to the bottom of the thing.

"I don't remember exactly what we talked about. We just lost track of the time."

Hamish stared at Tracy. "Did anyone tell you a weaving was destroyed?"

"I guess somebody may have mentioned it." Tracy chewed on his lip.

"It wasn't discovered until this morning. When did you hear of it?"

"Umm, I'm not sure. After breakfast, I think." It was lame and they both knew it.

"Tracy, this doesn't sit right with me. Has Christine spoken with you about it?"

"Uh . . . no sir . . . I mean . . . maybe," he stumbled uncomfortably.

"You're not being honest with me, are you?"

Hamish thought he saw trickles of sweat on Tracy's temple and imagined the boy must be furious to have Malcolm put him in this noose.

"Well, maybe I do have an idea but I'm not sure . . . and I shouldn't say something I'm not sure about."

"Let's cut to the chase," Hamish said sharply, banging the desk with an open palm. "Did you destroy that weaving?"

"Of course not, sir," Tracy said, aghast.

Hamish believed the reaction was honest, but had to test him. "Do you know who did?"

"I can't say for sure, sir."

"You mean you won't say."

Tracy looked like he was struggling to breathe, and Hamish felt maybe he had gone too far with his interrogation. But he wanted the truth. He wanted no lingering doubt that could color an entire year for both boys. Tracy was clearly furious. That's not how a guilty person acts. Hamish resisted the urge to probe further, to push Tracy harder. He sat back in his chair and waited. The silence in the room begged to be filled, but Hamish decided he would not be the next one to speak.

"You've put me in a tough spot," Tracy said, finally.

"How so?"

"I don't owe that punk anything," Tracy muttered. "But I can't stand a snitch. It's a code. Maybe a stupid thing."

"You can get yourself out of that spot right now, Tracy. Seems to me you've got a case of misplaced loyalty. The way it looks to me, son, if you are willing to stand by and let others destroy the fabric that makes Glencoe special, you're guilty, too. Tracy, do you approve of what's happened here?"

"No, sir."

Hamish stood and began to pace around the office, hands clenched behind his back. "If you won't corroborate other information that places the blame where it belongs, then he'll get away with it. Do you think that's fair to the girls who worked so hard on that weaving? Or to the rest of us who have to deal with this sort of garbage?"

Tracy just shook his head.

"But you're not going to tell me, are you?"

Tracy sat silently, then inexplicably, began to giggle. Hamish was stunned. Did he not make it explicitly clear to the boy how serious this was?

"Hal, if I tell thee a lie, spit in my face, call me horse," Tracy said, a twinkle in his eye. The headmaster immediately recognized the line from a school play the previous year. It cut the tension that had become unbearable for both of them.

"It's Hamish . . . not Hal . . . smarty-pants," MacLean smiled, shaking his head in wonder at Tracy's talent for dialogue. It was a phrase the director, Ron Handy, had stolen from *Henry IV*, deploying it in an original spoof, staged for the parents at Thanksgiving. Tracy had spoken those words as Falstaff. Hal was the name Falstaff used for King Henry, and the fact he could pull that arrow out of his quiver at a time like this tickled Hamish to no end. Tracy was a curiously multifaceted young man, a diamond clearly worth polishing.

"Did he threaten you?" Hamish asked, softening. He regretted putting Tracy in such a bind. "I need the truth." Without Tracy's help there would be no way to implicate Malcolm, no trip to the Albany airport to send the boy back to his guardian aunt.

Tracy's eyes fixed on an old coffee stain on the rug. His shoulders slumped. Hamish waited. "I'm sorry about all this, Hamish. I got there too late to stop it," Tracy said, almost in a whisper. His eyes never left the floor. "Snipping a weaving is minor league compared to the things he told me he'd done in the past."

"That most likely is a lot of talk, not who he really is," Hamish said, relieved they were finally making progress. "He's trying to make his way here and, I'm afraid, he's not picked a good way to make friends."

"Maybe so. But I don't want him coming after me all year because I gave him up."

"That's not something you need to worry about. I'll take it from here. Thank you, Tracy. I appreciate how difficult this was for you."

This was not the first time Hamish had had to confront this silly anti-snitch honor code among his students. Though he knew Tracy detested his classmate, not betraying the code was a stronger impulse.

He saw so much of himself in Tracy—the brash, faux confidence, earnest concern for the natural world, affinity for theater. A sad, sweet fantasy of a son he and Bonnie would never have. Hamish imagined a leisurely discussion at home around his kitchen table, the two of them helping Tracy reconcile this misplaced adolescent loyalty with the intimate informality only parents can provide. That would have been nice.

5

Consequences of Youthful Indiscretion

SPRINGTIME IN MANHATTAN IS GLORIOUS. PILES OF SOOTY, ROTTING snow that glutted the wintry streets are long gone. Warm zephyrs blow off the Hudson River onto a city eager for annual rebirth. Budding trees promise that shade is near, in time to combat the coming summer swelter. It was Ramon Ortiz's favorite time of year.

It was nearly dusk on a Saturday in May 2001. Drenched in sweat, Ramon walked gingerly through Tompkins Square Park. His feet ached from blisters coming on from two heated hours of full-court basketball with no socks. *Idiot*, he thought. *I'll be paying for those two hours for days.* The near-mugging in the subway was still on his mind as he chugged icy malt liquor from the forty-ounce Colt 45 his buddy had slipped him out the back door of the supermarket on Avenue C. He was eighteen, able to vote and legally kill people in the service, but not old enough to legitimately buy a bottle of beer without a fake ID.

At that moment, a 911 operator was taking a call from a corner bodega on 12th Street.

"Again, they're stealing my stuff! Again! What are you people going to do about it? I'm trying to run a business here!" the owner shouted. According to the caller, a young Hispanic man had shoplifted several forty-ounce bottles of Bud Light, the third time that month it had happened. "Why they steal from their own people?" he complained to the operator. "Shame on them!"

As Ramon crossed Avenue B, his Colt 45 snugly hidden in a paper bag, a cruiser rolling down 10th Street spotted him and flipped on its lights. It mattered little that the shoplifted brew did not exit the store in a paper bag. Nor that Ramon's cold one was the wrong brand. The cops saw a young Hispanic toting an oversized bottle of something from somewhere and that was enough. Trained in the way of the streets, in a nanosecond Ramon realized that any interrogation would reveal a small amount of cocaine in his possession from an earlier drug transaction that day. He panicked, dropped the bottle but not the backpack with the drugs, and ran. Backups were radioed and three hours later, a distraught Eva arrived at the station house to bail him out, her eyes bloodshot from crying. She composed herself in front of the officers, a proud and resolute woman come to protect her little boy, no matter what the circumstances.

But now the rules of the game had changed. As an 18-year-old he was subject to a different and harsher legal world. Simple probation or detention in a relatively benign juvenile facility was no longer an option. He was given a choice. Help the cops, wear a wire, finger at least two other drug dealers or face real jail time for possession of a controlled substance.

Ramon shared the terms of the deal in a tense family meeting. His court-appointed lawyer recommended he turn it down. What should he do? Real prison was no joke. Pablo, Miguel and Marianna sat close together on their couch, watching their mother.

"Maybe it's best?" she said, looking to Consuela whose face was tight with worry.

"Over my dead body," Consuela hissed. "Do you know what happens to PIs?"

"What's a P-I, Auntie C?" Marianna asked.

"Police informant," Consuela said, softening her tone for the little girl. "Someone who secretly works for the police, Marianna." She turned to stare at Ramon, forcing him to meet her gaze. "I've had the pleasure of serving on one jury in my life," she said, "and it taught me everything I need to know about PIs.

"It was a murder trial. I never in a million years expected I'd be selected for that jury. There were, like, three hundred people called up, and by the end of that first afternoon there, I was being questioned by both attorneys and no one felt I was a bad risk for their case. The judge told me I was good to go and, boom, I'm on the jury. I was shocked."

"Who was on trial? A police informant?" Pablo asked.

"Jesus, no," she sighed, clearly reliving the experience. "The PI was the one murdered," she said, eyes boring into Ramon. "The young man, I don't remember any names, was just a passenger in a car, the two of them going fishing one morning. Cops pulled over the car for speeding, they's both black kids so, of course, the cops got to search them, and the car. They find drugs in the glove compartment, arrest 'em both. Poor kid, the passenger, never had a run-in with the police in his life. He had no idea who he was riding with that day. He's offered a shit deal—give us the names of three dealers and we'll wipe this off your sheet—or you go to trial with your buddy, who turned out to be a small-time dealer himself. The kid gets the same advice you're getting, Ramon. He takes the deal, worms his way into the drug scene, gets three names including one big shot, and turns them over. Whole thing supposed to be secret. His name supposed to never get out. But some stupid cop includes his name in some police report or something, the big shot's attorney gets a'hold of it and now the game's changed. If this kid can't testify, the drug dealers go free 'cuz there's no evidence. So, the dealers hire a hit man and take out the innocent young man. End of story. That's what can happen to a PI."

"Wow," Miguel said. "Who was on trial?"

"Oh, some poor idiot who was told to get a gun to give the hit man and make sure he had a good time the night before, him being a stranger in this little town upstate where it happened and all. They moved the trial down here for fairness, they said."

"Your guy on trial didn't kill anyone?" Ramon asked, shaken.

"Nope. Doesn't matter. If you help get a police informer killed, you get the same charge as the one pulling the trigger. Ramon, honey, you take that deal and I will personally kill you myself!"

Eva sobbed silently. She would not lose a son that way. He must turn it down, period.

One to three years, the judge decreed, and not to be served in some country club detention center for celebrities. Ramon heard the judge intone "Comstock" as his destination but it might as well have been Siberia as far as he knew.

Following his sentencing, Ramon was held overnight at Rikers Island in the middle of the East River, his first taste of what real prisons were like, with real prisoners, and real guards to whom he was nothing but a piece of worthless human garbage. He asked a few fellow inmates what they knew of Comstock and thus learned there were, in fact, two prisons loosely referred to by that name. *Pray to God you get sent to Washington Correctional,* a knowing inmate advised him. *If they send you to Great Meadow, that's maximum security, you might as well kiss your ass goodbye.* After only one sleepless night, spent warily eyeing his cellmate, ears attuned to the unfamiliar and frightening sounds of a big grown-up prison, he was relieved when the guards came to lead him to a corrections van that headed upstate with its cargo of transferring prisoners.

Five hours north of the city Ramon caught his first glimpse of the Comstock prison complex set back against the hillside, ringed by high-voltage razor wire glistening in the morning sun. He thought about the deal he had declined. That would have been a roll of the dice. Was this any better? He looked around at the other inmates, like him, staring out at their future. So many trees. Such an alien place. How could he survive? He felt his chest tighten and his breaths came shallow and quick. He felt beads of sweat roll down his armpits. This was raw fear; he felt his heart pounding in his chest and worried he might pass out.

"Hey, bussy," one inmate yelled to the driver of the van. "Take your next left to Washington Correctional. My plane leaves from there! Drop the rest of these assholes at Terminal 2," he smirked, gesturing toward the massive structure of Great Meadow ahead of them.

As if following orders, the driver took the turn onto Lock 11 Road and made for the front gate of Washington Correctional. An officer at the front of the van stood up, consulted a clipboard and called out the names of those inmates assigned to the medium-security prison. Ramon gripped the seat in front of him, willing the officer to call out his name. All he wanted now was to blend into the woodwork, keep to himself, and pay his debt to society in anonymity. Until his siblings grew older, he was still the main provider and as long as he stayed in jail, he was doing his family no good at all. Fortunately, Eva had just landed a new part-time position as a housekeeper for a well-to-do family uptown. Aunt Consuela would watch the children when she could, but there were many days when Eva was uptown and Ramon had to look after his siblings, making sure they were fed and put to bed at a decent time. To rid himself of the awful guilt he felt at not being there for her, he resolved to do anything that would shorten his incarceration.

When the last name was called panic welled in Ramon's chest. "Sir?" Ramon called softly to the corrections officer with the clipboard. "You sure there's no mistake? My name is Ramon Ortiz and my sentence is a lot shorter than what some of those guys got," he said, gesturing to the now-empty rows in the van. The officer quickly scanned the sheet of paper again and shook his head.

"There's a shortage of beds at Washington," he said. "Some of you got assigned to Great Meadow until things open up. Sorry, buddy."

By the third day of his captivity at the maximum-security facility, the enormity of Ramon's misfortune hit home with disastrous consequences. He seemed to have been singled out by a prisoner of Mexican descent who occupied another cell in his block. Hector Mercado controlled the local chapter of the feared Mexican Mafia, one of the six major gangs that operate freely within American prisons. Mercado's allegiance could not be missed; the telltale eagle standing atop the letters EME emblazoned in black ink across his neck branded him a sworn member. Although their main enemies were African American or other Mexican gangs, Mercado was particularly interested in subduing any other Hispanic gangs at Great Meadow, including the Neta Association, made up of Puerto Rican inmates. When Hector learned fresh meat had joined their community, he wasted no time trying to intimidate the new prisoner, making it brutally clear that if Ramon associated with the Netas, Mercado would personally make his life a living hell. During the exercise period, Hector would hang on the chain-link fence, challenging and threatening Ramon. Though it took all of his self-discipline, Ramon tried to ignore the assaults, which served only to further inflame Mercado.

The pot finally boiled over late one afternoon as the prisoners in Ramon's block took their exercise in the yard. Hector approached, as always surrounded by at least five other gang members.

"Lost my boots, man," Hector jeered.

"Who the hell cares," Ramon answered, eyeing a basketball hoop.

"Know where I lost 'em?"

"Just shut up and leave me alone, okay?" Ramon snapped.

"Under yo mama's bed, man," Hector sniggered. "Where I left 'em last time I jammed up your mama. Tell her to mail 'em back to me when she's done lickin' 'em off, maricón."

Reacting instinctively, Ramon whirled and slammed the basketball he was holding up against the bottom of Mercado's chin in a blind attempt to shut the man's mouth. Hector's jaws snapped down hard against his tongue. At the searing pain and taste of blood, Hector roared in anger and barreled into Ramon, pitching him into a cinder block wall. Ramon felt his kidneys scream at the impact but he bounced off the wall and instinctively went into a defensive crouch. As Hector spat out a mouthful of blood, Ramon sensed an opening and rolled into the Mexican, snapping Hector's knees sideways. Mercado bellowed, finally drawing the attention of several guards nearby, and began kicking wildly at Ramon, who curled into a ball to protect his head. Wondering, through the pain, how long he could withstand this relentless attack, Ramon then heard Mercado curse as a guard bludgeoned him with his nightstick. Quickly, the guards pulled both men to their feet, cuffed their arms behind their backs, and led them back toward their cells.

"Watch it, man. You sleep, you're fuckin' dead," Mercado hissed, spitting at Ramon as they parted.

Ramon lay down on his bunk, his ribs aflame, despairing that his chances of surviving in this godforsaken place were next to nil.

As punishment for the disruptive behavior the warden assigned Ramon to three weeks in SHU, the "special housing unit," otherwise known as "the box." Ramon had no idea what had become of Mercado but was grateful for the isolation, a period of calm where he was protected from Hector or any other Mexican gang members. Other members of the Neta Association had kept their distance, letting Ramon twist in the wind, unwilling to come to the defense of one of their own. Ramon assumed that was because he had spurned their offers to join the gang but Mercado hadn't seemed to care. He was apparently making an example of Ramon for all the Neta members to see.

One hour a day he was allowed to exercise alone in a small caged yard reserved for prisoners in solitary confinement. His amenities included a single iron bunk, stainless steel seatless toilet, and a small sink. A series of similarly outfitted "boxes" was situated on one side of a long hall. No prisoner could see into any other cell but they could communicate with each other by shouting through the small opening in the cell door. As they were led out for their daily exercise, each to his own private caged yard, Ramon noticed that the others in this unit were sizing him up. Even without Mercado, there would be no relaxing, he realized. New prisoners were scrutinized very closely, for they represented value of some kind, some because of their physical prowess; others, their ability to provide contraband from the outside. The barter economy that flourishes in even the most rigid penal institutions is a testament to human ingenuity.

His three-week punishment passed uneventfully and Ramon was moved once again into general population. He still had a cell to himself, but he was now in a different block, on a tier with dozens of other inmates with no particular vendetta against him. Each morning before breakfast the corrections officers "cracked" the cells, allowing the men to pursue a semblance of normal existence, to eat together in the main mess hall, to work, and to mingle freely in the recreation yards. As he went about his duties in the prison kitchen and when he chose his seat during meals, Ramon sought anonymity. With each passing day Ramon awoke hoping against hope that this day would see him move over to Washington, the medium-security prison at the Comstock complex. With each day of peace, he began to lower his guard and to worry less about survival.

Late one chilly afternoon as shadows crept across the yard, Ramon lay flat on his back, working on his bench press. As usual, he lifted alone, with no spotter to catch the weights. With eyes squeezed shut to focus his entire strength on the iron bar extended above his chest, the sudden pressure of a boot on his groin forced him to exhale in a loud gasp. Startled, Ramon opened his eyes, struggling not to let the weight collapse

63

on him, but the wintry sun over the man's shoulder prevented him from identifying his tormentor. Tensing the muscles of his midsection, Ramon carefully replaced the barbell on its stand, squirmed off the bench, and struggled to his knees. Now he could see the eagle tattoo perched atop the thick, block letters EME. There was no mistaking the brutal grin and the picket fence of stained, broken teeth.

"Mercado!"

"Shut the fuck up, mariçon!" Hector rasped in Spanish. A knot of fellow Mexican prisoners surrounded them, blocking the view of several COs who stood at the other end of the yard. "I'm going to fuck you up, gusano."

"Leave me alone, man, I ain't got nothing against you." Ramon tried to stand but was pushed roughly back to his knees by one of Mercado's henchmen. "Yo! Officer!" Ramon shouted, desperately trying to get someone's attention. The COs remained in conversation. Either they could not hear or they were intentionally ignoring him, for their backs remained turned. Either way, he was in trouble. Hector cut him off in mid-cry with a cuff across the face. "I told you, man, the day would come when we'd settle up."

"Why don't you just let me do my time?" Ramon pleaded, still on his knees. He could see no possible escape. "I'm not lookin' for trouble, man and I ain't joining no Netas."

Hector stepped closer to Ramon, cutting the distance between them to only a few inches. Ramon could feel the man's breath on his face and smell the stench of rotting teeth. "Nobody lays a hand on me and walks away, understand?"

"Look, Hector, I . . ." Before Ramon could react, an arm shot out, grabbed the back of his neck, and forced his face downward. His head met Hector's knee with a sickly thud, crumpling his nose. His mouth began to fill with blood, and he stumbled to the ground. Reflexively, his hands went to his face. With alarm, he felt cartilage floating where his nose used to be, and when he looked up, the Mexicans had dispersed and he was alone. At the far end of the yard, he saw them talking to the guards. They were all laughing.

The infirmary stay represented fourteen days of safety from the Mexican Mafia, three hundred thirty-six hours' grace period before a decision he would inevitably have to make. He had to join the Netas or his life was worth zero, thanks to the insane Mercado. However, when the morning came he was ordered to take leave of the infirmary and rejoin the general population, it was not to his old cell that Ramon was led but to a prison van. Although a free bed had not yet opened up at the Washington Correctional Facility next door, there was an opening upstate at a place called Adirondack, smaller and less imposing than the massive Comstock facility he watched disappear in the distance.

Adirondack Correctional Facility was located in the small town of Ray Brook, halfway between Lake Placid and Saranac Lake. He had just been given a new lease on life, a significant upgrade from his nightmare at Comstock. No gang pressure, he hoped, no violence, no time spent in the hole. Parole was right around the corner if he could stay out of trouble . . . until that fateful call with Pablo.

6

An Adirondack Classroom

SINCE HIS SECOND YEAR TEACHING AT GLENCOE, PETE HEDGES HAD introduced every new student to a geology orientation atop a nearby mountain. Though his area of expertise was English, the history of the Adirondacks, including its formation, was a passion and he persuaded Steve Jacobs, head of the science department, that he, Pete, should lead that class. He scheduled it early in the fall while the foliage was at peak and the trail dry. On the third Wednesday of the term nine new students, representing half of the newly matriculating group in 2002, departed Dewey Hall after classes were done.

Pete repeated this trip as many times as necessary for all new students to gain the experience of hiking to nearby Balanced Rocks, hearing how the Adirondack Park came to be, and witnessing for themselves the exquisite beauty of the region. For those traveling from distant countries, the three-hour hike-and-lecture provided a crash course on their new surroundings. But it was just as foreign to kids living in urban America, for the Adirondacks have a unique geologic story, and a prime example of how Glencoe put experiential learning into practice.

Pete brought along another staff person to ensure the group was properly covered in case of emergency, and always asked one of the returning students to join, as sort of a teacher's aide. Today that was Tracy, nearly a foot taller than some of the anxious new students for whom this was their first hiking experience. A trip up Balanced Rocks, a mere mile-and-a-half hike from school, was a chance for Tracy to break in new boots, get in a workout, and help out his favorite teacher. He made sure each new student was properly equipped with day pack, sweater, water bottle, sturdy shoes, and a wind jacket. The other staff person Pete invited was his co-houseparent, Christine Mason. Though they each had an apartment to themselves in Marshall House, it was an open secret that they were a couple looking for any excuse to spend time together.

In keeping with state regulations limiting group size on the trails, Pete scheduled multiple afternoon trips for this lecture. Delivering it outside the classroom was, in Pete's estimation, the best way to combine physical activity and a teachable moment. Glencoe sat in the middle of a living laboratory, perfect for the study of earth science. While most academic subjects were taught traditionally, the Glencoe science curriculum took advantage of the woods, streams, and hills right out the back door.

While only an hour's hike, the climb to Balanced Rocks was still demanding. Leaving the school property, Pete led the group past Marcy Hall into the woods following a soft trail bed covered in pine needles. The grade was easy as the pine grove gave way to deciduous hardwoods, multihued leaves rustling gently above. The line of students chatted easily. Maple dominated the lower slopes, flaming red as September came to a close. Soon, the trail reached a brook that once upon a time had supplied the school with drinking water, later replaced by more reliable deep wells. The trail paralleled the brook up a drainage, gradually becoming steeper as they neared the ridge toward Balanced Rocks. Though he had hiked this route countless times in the course of his three years at Glencoe, Tracy never failed to enjoy the simple pleasures of walking through a forest, listening to burbling brooks and songbirds.

For little Lauren Chang, a new sixth-grader who had grown up in Shenzhen, a vast economic powerhouse near Hong Kong, the effort began to take its toll with the steepening trail and a gap widened between her and the hiker ahead of her, who happened to be Malcolm Dandridge. Being overweight, Malcolm had not engaged in much of the easy banter; his breath came hard.

Christine, picking up the rear, noticed Lauren wheezing and whistled for Pete to stop.

"Hang on a moment," Christine called. "Lauren and I could use a break."

"I'm not used to this," Lauren said breathlessly, wiping sweat from her bangs. "I'm a little asthmatic. But I don't want to hold anyone back."

Christine reached for a water bottle in the side pocket of her pack. "Take a swig. You'll feel better in a moment."

"It's okay. I brought water, too."

"I'm happy to share mine. Yours is buried in your pack."

To get Lauren's mind off her difficulties, Christine asked questions about her life back home, empathizing how challenging it must be to leave the familiar for this new and daunting environment half a world away. Sure enough, once Lauren began to chatter about her family and friends, and how different Shenzhen was, she forgot her anxiety, her breathing returned to normal, and she resumed the climb. Soon the gap to Malcolm began to expand once again.

Their route left the main brook, following a tributary now dry, parched from a dearth of rain since early August. The hikers kicked up dust as they climbed. Conversation became more labored as the pitch grew steeper; each hiker focused on the steps ahead. Approaching a downed tree that blocked their path, everyone used a large rock conveniently situated to negotiate the fallen birch. The pressure and torque of each step caused that rock to wobble, forcing everyone to grab a branch from the tree for balance. As Malcolm negotiated the difficult spot, the rock came free after he had pushed off. Twenty yards below, head down, concentrating on the way ahead, Lauren failed to see the cantaloupe-sized stone bearing down on her. It nearly tumbled off the trail, hitting a beech beside the creek bed that caused it to ricochet back down the fall line toward Lauren. Watching disaster about to unfold, Christine lunged at the diminutive Chinese girl, shoving her into a bed of ferns. Christine's forearm took a glancing blow as the stone hurtled past. Though no one was below them to be warned, Christine instinctively shrieked "Rock!!" Momentum caused her to roll into the soft ferns next to the stunned Lauren.

Hearing the shout, Pete halted and looked back to see the two sprawled on the creek side of the trail. "Y'all okay?" he shouted.

"I think so," Christine called back, getting to her feet and rubbing her arm. "A big rock just missed us. Or almost missed us. I guess somebody loosened it and I saw it at the last second. Are you all right, sweetie?" she asked, looking at Lauren. She nodded and picked herself up.

Malcolm looked crestfallen. "I'm so sorry, Lauren," he said. "It felt wobbly when I stepped off it but I didn't know it had come out." Lauren shrugged her shoulders as if to say, *I have no idea what just happened.*

"Next time, pay attention," Tracy said to Malcolm, who bristled at the criticism. "Okay, okay," Pete said, trying to defuse a potential situation. "It was an accident waiting to happen. We all contributed. Everyone—pay attention to your surroundings. Branches can catch you in the eye, a falling rock can kill you. We have to look out for each other. Christine did what you're supposed to do when this happens. Shout out the warning. One word is all you need to say. We all know what it means."

Shaken and subdued, the group resumed their climb, carefully watching their steps until the steep region was behind them.

"Okay, this is it," Tracy announced as the Glencoe contingent emerged from the woods onto a flat plateau of open rock, about a thousand feet above the Cascade Lakes glistening in the afternoon sun. The panorama of mountains before them was stunning, especially for those in the group who had never been on a mountaintop of any reasonable size. Arrayed before them were the majority of the High Peaks, many whose flanks were striped with the scars of new and ancient rockslides. The tongue of the plateau, roughly a hundred yards long and forty yards across, came to a blunt point, beyond which cliffs descended to the forest and valley below. From their perch it was possible to pick out Dewey Hall, the barns, the lake beyond, and even the roofs of some of the residences. There was talk among the kids about who could spot their own house, "Find a comfortable spot and I'll tell you a tale," Pete said authoritatively.

"In the interest of time, since we want to be back for dinner," he began, "I'm going to skip the first few hundred million years of the story." He paused, hoping the audience would appreciate his attempt at comedy. They did not. "Believe me, this area was unrecognizable from what you see today; much of it was under water, and the rocks we are sitting on were once sand." You could see kids absently feeling the rock and struggling to imagine it being a sandy bottom. "The enormous pressure and heat that impacted those sands eventually transformed those sediments into an extremely hard rock, called anorthosite. Let's pick up the story more recently, about twenty million years ago," he said chuckling. "We—and by 'we' I mean geologists—do not have a clear understanding as to why the mountains you are looking at began to rise in the shape of a dome. It wasn't a large dome; maybe a hundred and fifty miles in diameter. Who can tell me what a diameter is?"

One of the students proudly supplied a reasonable answer and Pete moved on. "But rise it did, exposing the top surface to the erosive effects of wind and rain which carved away soil, leaving the bedrock on which you all are now sitting. Trees and shrubs grew back on the tops of most Adirondack mountains in recent centuries, but forest fires, rather than erosion, exposed many of the rocky summits you see in the distance.

"Those boulders in front of you we call the Balanced Rocks," he said, pointing to two enormous rocks poised at the edge of the plateau, about four feet apart, each the size of a small cabin. "Later, you may try leaping from one to the other if you have the nerve. How they got here is part of this remarkable geological story. There are some cool tunnels to explore in the rock below those babies, too." He had their attention now.

"These rocks you all are sitting on, if they could tell you their age, that number would have about ten digits in it. How old does that make them?"

"Ten would mean a billion, right?" Lauren piped up.

"That's right, Ms. Chang. But despite their old age, they are not done moving. This whole dome continues to rise, about twelve inches every hundred years. That's a bigger amount than the reduction that occurs from continuing erosion. Human tramping also erodes the trails but does not affect their height. One of the important lessons we will learn later this year is how humans should behave in these mountains to reduce the impact we cause. Those are wilderness ethics conversations, not geologic ones. Talk to Tracy about that. His mom is an expert in such things." Tracy beamed—he had no idea anyone outside his immediate family had any notion about his mom's knowledge of environmental policy.

"Nevertheless," Pete went on, "the summits continue to get higher, so you better climb them now." This weak joke, like the others, was lost on most of the students, still thinking about those tunnels and whether they had the stomach to try jumping from one boulder to the other.

"The next important event I want to tell you about occurred quite recently, less than two million years ago. That's when the so-called Ice Age occurred as a result of the earth entering a major cooling off period. How many know the geological name for that period, or epoch?"

No hands went up. "Okay, you will now learn a new word: Pleistocene. The Pleistocene Epoch caused glaciers to form over much of the North American continent. As you might expect, those glaciers crept southward from the North Pole, reaching its final destination in these parts as recently as 21,000 years ago and lasted about 10,000 years during a period called the Wisconsin Glaciation. Ice is powerful stuff. The ice that covered the Adirondacks was more than a mile thick. As it slowly flowed south it moved a lot of earth beneath it. That movement is what carved out the valleys between these peaks. And as that earth got churned up, boulders such as the ones in front of you got caught up in the ice. When the world began to warm again, glaciers retreated back north and debris got left behind in strange places, like right here. Those rocks are examples of what we call glacial erratics, because they were picked up and dumped erratically. The word 'erratic' comes from the Latin *errare,* which means 'astray.'"

Lauren raised her hand, hesitantly.

"Seems like Lauren is the only one contributing today," Pete said. "Dodging that rock must have really sharpened her thinking. What's your question?"

"I thought a stray was, like, a dog or cat or something. A rock can be a stray, too?"

"Lauren, you've put your finger on the difference between the written English word and the spoken one," Christine chuckled. "A missing animal is 'a stray'—two words," she said, exaggerating the pause between the two. "Astray—one word—means something has gone off its proper path. I'm sure that is confusing, especially for those of you now living in an English-speaking country for the first time."

Tracy, sitting next to Lauren, patted her on the back. "Good question, Lauren."

"I hope you all will take advantage of the hiking opportunities while you are here at Glencoe," Pete continued. "And I promise you will see many such boulders, in the middle of the woods, on top of summits like this, in lots of weird places. Now you know how these erratics got there.

"The melting ice also created huge lakes, some of which drained away, but some remain. The Cascade Lakes below us, for example, are quite deep as a result of the carving those glaciers did on their journey through these parts. It's a dramatic story whose ending has not yet been written.

"There's another beautiful peak I hope many of you will climb, called Giant. Sometimes we take trips up the slides on its west face, which has a distinct curve. That entire face was carved out by small glaciers that created steep walls, so steep that vegetation had a hard time staying put. They're called slides because the earth slides off from time to time, exposing the bedrock. Those curved walls are called cirques. When you have cirques on opposite sides of a mountain, the ridges in between can be sharp and narrow. Those are called arêtes. We don't have too many in these mountains; you're more likely to find them in the Alps or the Rockies. Probably the most famous mountain that is known for its sharp arêtes is the very pointy-topped Matterhorn, on the border of Switzerland and Italy."

"Is that the mountain on the Toblerone chocolate wrapper?" Malcolm asked.

"In fact, it is," Pete responded.

"I wish I had one of those right now," Malcolm said.

"I am about to distribute some treats before we head back to school. Sadly, chocolate isn't on the menu this afternoon," Pete replied. "Dried fruit and cheese will have to do.

"The last thing I want to tell you is that the rocks that formed the Adirondack mountains are quite good for climbing . . . at least those that don't tumble on us. If you haven't explored the campus yet, you should know that on the backside of our ski hill are some small cliffs, or crags as we call them, where you can learn technical rock climbing. If the weather's bad you can practice on the climbing wall by the gym, as well.

"Once you are sufficiently skilled, we'll get you out on longer, more challenging climbs on some of the peaks you're looking at. The anorthosite I mentioned earlier is ideal for climbing. No crumbling sandstone here.

"Okay, that does it for my lecture. Make sure to drink some of the water you carried up. Have fun on the Balanced Rocks and the tunnels beneath if you wish. Let's meet back here in ten or fifteen minutes and we'll head down."

"Come," Malcolm said to Lauren, extending a hand. "Let's explore together. I promise, I won't try to kill you again." She giggled and accepted his hand.

7

A Harsh Coming-of-Age

BAM! WENT THE SCREEN DOOR OF THEIR SINGLE-WIDE ON A HOT JULY evening in 1979. Twenty-two-year-old Sally LeGrange never looked back, leaving Frenchy, her drunken, abusive husband, comatose on the couch after another bender, and their six-year-old son, Garth, who should have been asleep at that hour, cowering in the corner, the unwanted result of poor judgment by two teenagers having sex in a backseat in the summer of 1972.

To say that Garth LeGrange grew up to be one of the most notorious men raised in the Adirondack village of Tupper Lake would be minimizing his reputation. At six-foot-three and 265 pounds, with a full black beard and piercing, deep-set eyes that missed nothing, Garth had already packed a lifetime of hard living into twenty-nine years that resulted in his current home address at the Adirondack Correctional Facility. From one look at his calloused hands, with fingers twisted at odd angles, it was clear Garth dealt with life roughly, and straight on. He favored plaid flannel shirts and long-sleeved thermal underwear regardless of the weather or the season. Neither heat nor crisis, it seemed, could make the man sweat.

It had been nineteen years since Garth had seen his father. As for his mother, her face was a memory even more vague. Rumor had it she moved down south and changed her name so they'd never find her. Garth spent most of his adolescence alone in the woods outside the town, watching lumber crews at work, eating whatever he could scrounge, and hiding from his father's drunken rampages. Only when the elder LeGrange was sleeping off his latest binge would Garth creep back to the trailer. Frenchy knew how ill-equipped he was to take care of his only child. This fact became painfully clear as soon as his disgruntled wife took off. He understood it fell to him to instill good habits in the boy but had no clue what those habits were. He would try to put food in front of the boy and make sure there were sheets on his cot but beyond that, well, his son would have to figure out the rest. There was one exception to his hands-off approach, one area of discipline that Frenchy insisted upon, the only relic from his departed wife's parenting. Though the boy's clothes might be skimpy and not necessarily clean, though his diet might be heavily weighted with junk food, Frenchy insisted that Garth not neglect his teeth. It didn't fit with anything else in his life, but there it was, the only semblance of parental interest. Every six months Frenchy would march his son down to the county clinic when the dental hygienist was in town. Every night, when he wasn't totally blotto from liquor, Frenchy would hover over his son at the bathroom sink, timing how long Garth brushed his teeth. Their fridge might be next to bare but there was always toothpaste and dental floss on the shelf above the toilet.

Complaints about the frequent rampages in the LeGrange trailer began to filter in to the Department of Social Services. The overworked, underfunded bureaucracy was slow to react. One night when Garth was seven, he returned after supper at a friend's house where he'd spent the afternoon playing. Garth stepped out of his friend's car, waved to them as they drove off, then listened for the sounds of his father before deciding whether or not to walk up the short gravel driveway to the trailer, its faded vinyl siding cracked and dented from years of neglect.

Sure enough, the slurred voice of Frenchy LeGrange could be heard as he lurched from one end of the cramped quarters to the other in search of a misplaced liquor bottle. Knowing his father would turn on him when he appeared, Garth cautiously turned away and crept quietly around the trailer to a familiar wooded area where he could wait safely for his father to sober up. He lay down in the tall grass, still warm from the long hours of absorbing sun, and nodded off to the sound of mating crickets and a father in full bellow.

Sometime after midnight an acrid smell woke him. He sat up and saw flames throwing shadows all about, dancing off the glade of trees where he had slept. Flashing red lights suggested others had smelled the burning trailer before him. Garth dashed toward his disintegrating home, now half-consumed with flames. His father lay on a stretcher in the grass, an oxygen mask over his face. One of the firemen saw Garth and intercepted him before he could reach Frenchy.

"You his son?"

Garth nodded, his eyes wide with fear.

"Don't worry. He's gonna make it. Just swallowed a lot of smoke."

Garth stared at the motionless figure, overwhelmed with conflicting feelings of fear, loss, anger and relief. It was all a-jumble in his seven-year-old heart. It was only a matter of luck that there was not a second stretcher in the grass holding his own body.

"Smoking in bed, best as we can figure it," the fireman continued. "How come you weren't in there, too?"

Garth hesitated. "I was campin'. Can I talk to him?"

"Not just yet. We're gonna take him in to the hospital for some treatment. You got friends or family around here that can bring you later?"

The frightened boy nodded again and pointed to another trailer perhaps a hundred yards down the road. "They'll take me, I guess."

"I'll walk you over there if that's okay, son." The fireman led the now-homeless child away from the burning trailer. Garth's fingers were lost in the fireman's big mitt. It had been a long time since anyone had held his hand and it was a comfort.

Frenchy LeGrange survived the fire but soon thereafter he was deemed unfit to care for his son. Eight-year-old Garth was sent to live with a family in the town of Blue Mountain Lake, the first of what would prove to be a series of well-intentioned but ultimately failed attempts, to place Garth with a foster family. He would never spend another night under his father's roof. No one bothered to ask Garth his opinion and it wouldn't have changed things if they had. Despite the wretchedness of sharing a trailer with his dad, Garth did not take the move well. In the next few years, it seemed he spent as much time running away as he did adjusting to new surroundings. Each set of foster parents did their best to make him feel a part of their home, but they had little notion of how to deal with the anger that burned in that boy. It seemed the only thing that would calm him down was a packet of dental floss.

Academically, school was a disaster. What kept Garth enrolled was the positive reinforcement he earned on the lacrosse field. Tupper Lake was the class of the public school lacrosse league in upstate New York during Garth's junior year. While he had yet to fill out to be the giant he became as an adult, the seventeen-year-old was feared for his strength and speed, and he led the league in scoring. When Garth carried the ball toward an opponent's goal it was the rare defenseman who could get close enough, or hit hard enough, to dislodge the ball from the webbing in his stick.

With state championships upcoming, the Tupper Lake coach decided the best preparation would be to schedule an exhibition match with an Akwesasne Reservation club team from the St. Regis Mohawks. Lacrosse originated with Native Americans and their skill remained legendary, even as the sport gained popularity in many parts of the country. While most lacrosse players were now using plastic sticks, Akwesasne was one of the few remaining places where fine wooden sticks were still being manufactured. Often, the first gift received by a St. Regis Mohawk baby was a miniature wooden lacrosse stick.

So it was that Garth found himself on a school bus headed for the reservation one dreary April afternoon to play the Akwesasne Attack. Sitting beside him was Blake Monroe, a teammate whose dad was a state trooper and often assigned to that part of northern New York that housed the American side of the St. Regis Mohawk reservation. Blake kept his teammates spellbound with stories his dad had told him about life on the reservation and he kept up a running commentary as the bus crossed into Mohawk territory. Garth noticed most of the homes were narrow trailers like the one he had grown up in before fire ended that part of his life. Curiously, in the small yards adjacent to many of those run-down trailers were roll-off containers, the type that eighteen-wheeled tractor-trailer trucks haul.

"See all those boxes?" Blake asked, jabbing a finger against the bus window, wet with spring rain.

"Yeah. What's the deal with that?" Garth asked. "Is everyone a trucker up here?"

"Nope. They're just for storage. My dad says most are filled with cigarettes and booze they smuggle across the border. They're worth about a quarter-million dollars each."

"If that's so, why are they living in trailers?"

"They park them there for the chiefs. Those guys live in mansions you can't see from the road and they don't want containers in their yards. My dad says the guys living here, the 'little fish' he calls them, take motorboats across the St. Lawrence River over to the part of the reservation that's on the Canadian side. They load up their boats and bring 'em back after dark. The Canadian Mohawks buy the stuff someplace cheap where there's no tax and shit. Then it gets sold here on the US side for a lot less than you can buy off the reservation."

"If your dad knows so much, why don't they stop it?"

"Tough to catch those guys after dark. Tough to prove. He says they could shut it down if they put enough police boats out there but the word from above is, ignore it because it's one of the only ways the Mohawks make any money. At least that's what he says."

"What do you know about the guys we're playing today?" Garth asked.

"As good as any we've seen this year," Blake replied. "They'll be in shape, for damn sure. I read someplace that one of their guys competed in this thing they call the Survival Race all by himself. Usually, it's a relay with one person for each event. Not this guy. He soloed it."

"Survival Race? Like a triathlon?"

"Two more legs than a tri. First you swim a bunch, then you canoe a ways, then you bike, then you run a mile with a freakin' 80-pound pack on your back, then you ditch the pack and run another six."

"Jesus," Garth exclaimed. "Which one is he?" he asked, scanning the competition already warming up as the Tupper Lake bus stopped at the edge of the already-drenched field on Cornwall Island, a bleak spot buffeted by stiff wind coming off the gray waters of the St. Lawrence River.

"Not sure. They all look ripped," said Blake. "This could be a long afternoon."

Before long it was clear who the superman was. He carried the longest lacrosse stick and played midfield, roaming back to help the defense when Tupper Lake had the ball, sprinting ahead to attack when his team controlled the action. As the so-called "long stick middie," the boy was clearly the class of the Attack team. He ran circles around everyone else, deftly intercepting pass after pass that was meant for Garth, who lingered in front of the Attack goal. During a timeout Garth asked one of the Tupper Lake coaches about the Mohawk star.

"Yeah, he's a handful," the coach chuckled. "Name's Berry. Ty Berry. He's torn up every scoring record in the Canadian league they play in. I'm not putting money on you outscoring that one, Garth." The last comment was intended to stir the competitive juices in the LeGrange boy and it hit the mark.

"We'll see," Garth said. "This afternoon will be a nightmare for the kid."

The cold April rain continued to pelt the players whose only means of staying warm was to run continuously. The Akwesasne Attack seemed to be toying with the Tupper Lake team, scoring as needed, playing keep-away for much of the first half. Garth scored a couple of goals when Ty Berry went to the bench for a breather but when the Survival Race kid was in the game it seemed as though he was playing by himself. No one could touch him or slow him down. At one point, as Garth was winding up for a shot just outside the opponent's crease, Ty closed from behind, snapped his stick across Garth's own, grabbed the ball in midair and set off down the field. Incensed, Garth swung his own stick blindly, catching Ty behind his knees. The Mohawk boy went down as if shot and the whistle blew for a slashing penalty. As Garth headed to the sideline to serve his penalty, Ty rose and winked at him, showing no sign of distress. Shaking off the injury, he then proceeded to score as if nothing had happened, freeing Garth to come back onto the field. "Thanks for the advantage," Ty said as the two passed at midfield. Garth sneered, looked down at Ty's leg and noticed a lump the size of a golf ball where Garth's stick had landed. It appeared to have had no effect.

Early in the fourth quarter the two boys came together again in front of the Attack goalie. Ty took a pass from a defenseman and while he could not see Garth charging from behind, he sensed an impending collision. With a deft juke, Ty faked left and turned right to go upfield. Sensing he was too late, a familiar rage overcame Garth, and the rules of the game went out the window. He hurled his body at the Mohawk player, spearing him in the back with his helmet. With a groan, Ty went to the ground, his face mask buried into the muddy turf. Garth stood over him, smirking.

"You again!" Ty winced.

"Bet your ass." Garth did not hear the ref's whistle, nor the call for a personal foul. He had to be led to the sidelines by a teammate, so locked in was his focus on retribution. Ty staggered to his feet, slugged down a sport drink offered by the water boy and huddled his team around him. His lecture was unmistakable. Fun and games were over. With water dripping off his helmet, the rain nearly horizontal blowing off the St. Lawrence River, Garth grimly watched as Ty led his team down the field on three consecutive drives, resulting in goals each trip. Unable to return to action due to his non-releasable personal foul, Garth had to observe the surgical demolition of his proud squad from the penalty box. By the time he had served the full time, it was clear the game was lost.

"Lemme give you some advice, Garth," the Tupper Lake coach said as the team headed for the bus. "Somehow you need to corral that anger. Your act is hurting the team. The boys may not have the guts to tell you to your face but they're better off with you on the bench. Get it together, son."

Garth's formal education ceased after that junior year. He chose to sign on with a French-Canadian lumbering operation and began to practice his father's craft. Soon his fists and fake ID saw him running with the same crowd as had Frenchy, men used to living hard, for whom a Saturday night without a barroom brawl was rare.

Alcoholism had a way of tickling Garth's hair-trigger temper and more than once those brawls took an ugly turn. One night, a couple of ironworkers from the St. Regis Mohawk tribe made the mistake of stopping in at PJ's Shamrock Tavern, Garth's favorite hangout, on their way home to the Akwesasne reservation. The men had finished a week-long stint building skyscrapers in New York City and were eager to leave some of their take-home pay behind in exchange for a few draft beers at the tavern. For more than a century, Mohawks had been prized for their nerveless ability to work on the naked girders of bridges and skyscrapers. Many insisted on being compensated in silver dollars, with which they paid for their drinks as they barhopped their way back to the reservation after tough weeks on high-risk, high-altitude construction sites in the big city.

PJ O'Callaghan had run the Shamrock Tavern for more than thirty years; he was used to the diverse collection of local loggers, visiting tourists, and transient ironworkers that frequented his watering hole. The soup was always fresh, the cheeseburgers thick and fashioned from ground sirloin, but the main attraction for most of his clientele was the longest list of draft beers in the North Country. And an owner who knew how to pour a proper Guinness Stout.

Hunched in a booth with three buddies, twenty-three-year-old Garth was well into his sixth cold one, regaling his companions with stories of high school lacrosse heroics when noise from the bar interrupted his storytelling. Two ironworkers were singing an ancient Mohawk chant at a level that drowned out the background country music and drew the attention of everyone in the bar. Knowing smiles came from most of the customers but not from Garth's booth. Though his buddies tried to defuse the situation, Garth was not to be deterred. He shouted for the two men to pipe down. When they ignored his suggestion, adding foot stamps to their boisterous chants, Garth strode to the bar and threw down a challenge—a hundred bucks to see if an Indian or a white man was more accurate throwing a hatchet. Spewing insults, the three men left the bar and stumbled into the woods, bottles of booze in hand and a small axe that Garth had pulled from the equipment box in his truck. A vision of Ty Berry flashed before his blurry eyes; he had never gotten over that particular humiliation. Thirty minutes later the bottles lay shattered on the ground, broken over the heads of the two Mohawks, who staggered away to escape further injury. Garth lay nearby, passed out near his vehicle. Sometime toward dawn, his slumber was interrupted by a smell of burning flesh and searing pain on the side of his face. As he came to, he felt his head immobilized between the knees of one Mohawk, his arms and legs pinned behind him like a hogtied rodeo calf. The second Mohawk straddled his torso, one end of a twisted coat hanger glowing red in his hand. "Something to remember us by, asshole," the man spat. Retaliation complete, the two men left him writhing in the weeds.

After the swelling on his cheek subsided, a scar in the shape of a hatchet remained, an angry welt for a few months before gradually fading to brown. Whenever something caused his blood to boil, the raised "brand" on his face would begin to quiver.

It was the last weekend in July 1997. Saranac Lake, a nearby town, was preparing to host their annual Can-Am rugby tournament that drew teams from all over. It was tough to find a room, even in Tupper Lake, miles away. Young men in full bloom of their athletic prowess, and middle-aged men refusing to admit their glory days were dim memories, gathered to play hard, bleed a little, and drink a lot. Games went on nonstop throughout the long weekend. While awaiting their next scheduled match, participants repaired to their favorite watering holes to swap war stories and nurse their wounds with pints of beer. Garth had adopted the sport after his high school lacrosse career came to an end. Rugby suited him. No pads to blunt the colliding bodies, loose refereeing that let most of the physical play go unchallenged. And the Shamrock Tavern was always hopping, country music blaring, tables and booths filled with testosterone-fueled tough guys looking to take home the trophy.

Garth's last game that Sunday had ended hours earlier. The long table his team had taken over near the front of the bar was littered with empty pitchers of beer and mountainous remains of chicken wings. During a brief lull in the music and general cacophony, Garth heard familiar voices coming from the rear of the tavern. The scar began to twitch and bile rose in his throat. A pair of Mohawks had entered via a door at the back of the room, which led out to a parking area and had taken a booth near the rest rooms. PJ O'Callaghan was taking drink orders as Garth approached the group.

"PJ, you can put your pen back in your pocket. These gentlemen won't be needing any drinks tonight," Garth snapped. The Mohawks shifted uneasily in their seats. They recognized the glowering lumberjack whose face they had branded and understood this was not a confrontation they could talk their way out of. As an experienced tavern owner who knew Garth's history as well as his drinking habits, PJ saw this confrontation would, at the very least, end with him sweeping broken glass and, maybe, calling the police.

"Now why don't you folks settle this out back so my other patrons will not be disturbed," PJ suggested, stepping between Garth and the Mohawks, who had risen from their seats to shorten the distance between themselves and the towering giant.

"Good idea. This won't take long," Garth said, waiting to see if his antagonists would accept the challenge or take a beating where they stood.

PJ opened the rear door, waiting for the three men to leave his premises. He locked it behind them. Whatever happened next would be someone else's problem. In the yellow glow of sodium vapor lights in the parking lot, the two Mohawks separated, moving in tandem to corner Garth against a nearby shed. Having spent the last three hours imbibing beer, Garth's reflexes were dulled, but the glint of sodium light on the knife one Mohawk pulled snapped him back to sobriety. Within seconds both adversaries lay dead in the tall grass behind the shed, slain with their own weapon. Bleeding from a gash on his arm, Garth stumbled to his truck and retrieved a shovel and a bag of quicklime left over from a concrete repair job earlier in the week. He buried the two together in a shallow grave between several junked automobiles and sprinkled the bodies with lime, hoping to remove odors that might attract police dogs. He managed to drive home without incident, immediately fell asleep on the couch, awakening the next morning more refreshed than he had ever felt since the branding.

Given the chilly relationship between the leaders of the Akwesasne reservation and the state police, it was not surprising that a report of two missing men got only cursory attention. But the Mohawk chiefs refused to give up. Two weeks after the skirmish, PJ O'Callaghan received a visit from two officers carrying photos of the missing men. PJ recognized them and recalled the incident. He advised the investigators to speak to Garth, the last person to have been seen with the two. With no clear evidence or bodies to examine, it was difficult for the troopers to challenge Garth's alibi that, yes, they had argued in the parking lot, a heavy downpour had cooled emotions, and the Indians had taken off with friends who Garth could not describe. The investigation soon lost steam, becoming just another cold case. The needle barely moved on Garth's moral compass. A white guy might have given him something to think about, but was the world any poorer for the loss of two Mohawks who stepped way over the line with him? Not hardly.

When he wasn't felling trees, draining liquor bottles, or feuding with Mohawks, Garth enjoyed fast automobiles, and it didn't matter whether they belonged to him or not. Many a weekend ended with his hotwiring somebody else's sports car, hard-driving it down backwoods roads, playing chicken with deer and fellow road-ragers. When the gas tank hit empty, he would douse the interior with kerosene, light a match, and walk away.

One night, the effects of another Saturday night six-pack dulling his brain, his wallet slipped out of his pocket as he pulled matches to destroy yet another fancy sports car. It was a simple matter for the police to track him down when they found his identification at the scene. There was no plea-bargaining. Garth received a sentence of up to fifteen years at the Adirondack Correctional Facility. At the sentencing, he reacted without emotion, never doubting for a moment that escape was simply a matter of time. It was his twenty-fourth birthday.

From his first day behind bars, Garth regarded prison as just a temporary inconvenience. When the moment presented itself, he would blend into the Adirondack wilderness until the authorities stopped looking, then head for Canada and a new life in some backwater lumber camp. During his months in captivity, Garth worked out the details of his escape. Portions of the plan beyond his control were to be executed by loyal buddies on the outside. The centerpiece of the strategy was to hole up in the deepest wilderness so long that the authorities would give up looking. But that required substantial resources, more than even he could carry. He needed a donkey, someone able to carry a heavy pack and easy to intimidate. Despite his reservations about the youthful Puerto Rican, Ramon looked strong enough to survive and scared enough to do as he was told.

8

Creative Solutions

As he grew, Malcolm Dandridge developed an unfortunate habit of confusing friendship with conspiracy. Where a common enemy could be found, he was adept at recruiting accomplices. Otherwise, he worked alone. His relationships were merely bonds of convenience, held together as long as an adversary remained active. His enemies tended to be the "All-American" types, boys with strong personalities, rule-followers, or those who found his being overweight an easy target for ridicule. Despite his heft, Malcolm was surprisingly strong, as those who tested him soon discovered.

He willingly told whoever would listen, and there hadn't been many, that Glencoe was just the most recent in a line of homes and boarding schools he had torn up like a hurricane. His last adventure had been at a military academy in Ohio, from which he had been asked to withdraw due to "numerous transgressions of its ethical and moral code," as the letter to Hamish had obtusely stated. The hazing and bullying he had suffered could have resulted in the expulsion of several others had Malcolm fingered the culprits, but in keeping with his own moral code, squealing was not an option; thus, he was the only student asked to leave.

Perhaps fearing she had nowhere else to turn, Malcolm's guardian aunt, Mathilda Graham, had come pleading for a place in the ninth-grade class at Glencoe a week after the school year had commenced. To Mathilda's relief, Hamish MacLean enthusiastically welcomed Malcolm into the community, a decision second-guessed by every member of the faculty, who wondered among themselves why their leader embraced a student with all the earmarks of a troublemaker. In fact, Hamish had struggled with the decision, seeking counsel from the one he often turned to—Ron Handy.

After reviewing the report sent by Malcolm's previous school, and interviewing Mathilda Graham to get the family side of the story, Hamish sought out Handy's familiar shock of white hair at his favorite haunt, a table near the fireplace in the empty dining hall, nursing a cup of coffee, chatting with Christine Mason.

"Got a minute for me, Ron?"

"What can I do for you?" Ron asked, curling his hands around the steaming cup. The heat helped ease arthritic pain in his knuckles, gnarled long ago from jamming them into cracks on hard rock routes on Half Dome and El Cap in Yosemite Valley.

"Is this a private conversation?" Christine asked. She was new enough at school to still feel she might be intruding when the old-timers got together.

"I don't think so," Hamish said. "In fact, given who you have in your house this year, the fellow who's making the hair I have left turn as white as this fellow's, maybe you should be part of this conversation."

"Malcolm got your panties in a twist again?" Ron asked.

"You know I hate to admit we've made a mistake with admissions. But I'm close to the end of my rope with that one. It's a shame. Mal could use what we have to offer, if he'd only let himself."

"Convinced this place can do miracles for anyone," Ron said.

"Pretty much, yes. But I always appreciate your judgment about these things. Like what we pulled off with Scotty Morrison, what was it? Six years ago? Way before your time, Christine. Ron helped me find a creative solution to keep a kid here that most folks would have let go. I'm sure we turned that boy's life around. I've got a hunch we can do something wonderful for this new fellow as well, if he'd give us half a chance."

"What happened to Scotty Morrison? Was he a bully like Malcolm?" Christine asked.

"Nothing like him," Ron said. "He was one of the leading lights here for a number of years. Really matured from his first year as a fifth grader. I mean, how many parents send their kids to boarding school in the fifth grade? There's always a story behind it and, usually, we're the ones to turn it into a positive."

Hamish then picked up the thread of the story. "Scotty was a ninth grader, like Malcolm, but with a strong record of success here. About a month before graduation, we discovered he had been sexually harassing several female students. Consensuality, if that is a word, was not a defense, though he trotted that out for size. We discovered mattresses in a corner of the furnace room in the basement of Dewey Hall that Scott had installed for his hoped-for conquests."

"He was quite the charismatic leader among the students," Ron added. "A bit like Tracy, but vastly more successful attracting female attention."

"How serious was it? Did he force them to go all the way?" Christine asked.

"We don't think it got that far. But it might have, had we not intervened," Ron said. "By all rights, Hamish ought to have put Scotty on the next bus home. The faculty supported that decision, swallowing their disappointment that one of the stars of the student body had flamed out."

"His expulsion would certainly have jeopardized his admission to the elite prep school he had his eye on and parental lawsuits could have shut this place down for good," Hamish added.

"I'm guessing that's not the solution you all came up with," Christine said.

"I was pretty close to pulling the trigger," Hamish admitted. "But sometimes a chat over a single malt can make one see things through a different lens, especially when that chat includes this character," Hamish said, tousling Ron's thick head of hair.

"As I recall, we had just finished one of those community morning projects," Ron said, "Maybe a chicken harvest? I always find those things morally repugnant. Anyway, your good wife invited me for tea because, I suspect, she wanted to orchestrate one of those kitchen cabinet summit meetings we've had over the years. You were unhappy with the consensus at the staff meeting the night before to expel Scotty, right?"

"Yes. I just couldn't bring myself to kick that boy out," Hamish agreed. "But I couldn't find an alternative I could live with, either. You earned your keep that day, old friend."

. . .

"Scotty's been here since the fifth grade, hasn't he?" Bonnie asked the two men as they sat around the MacLean kitchen table drinking tea, often the site of creative thinking among the three. It was May 1996. The Adirondacks were emerging from its annual winter hibernation. Pollen filled the air, trees were budding out, students bursting at the seams, much like the seedlings newly transferred from greenhouse pots to newly composted garden soil.

"Aye. He's grown up here. And now we're watching him disintegrate. How have we failed that boy?" Hamish sighed.

"There's no doubt he has to be held accountable," Ron said, weighing his words. "He has made this an unsafe place to be an adolescent girl. The freedom we give these children can cut both ways. We don't regiment every minute of their life. We don't oversee their every move like at most schools. So, we bear some responsibility when they don't exercise that freedom in positive ways. Everyone, children and adults alike, are watching to see how we handle this one, Hamish."

"It's an opportunity, Hamish," said Bonnie. "The easy answer is to put him out. No question. Every school head in the country would make that choice—the safe choice—a clear resolution that everyone would support. Especially the trustees," she added.

"Damn the trustees," he muttered. "They aren't worrying about how this could ruin the boy's life. Yes, he made a serious mistake. But we don't just kick him to the curb after trying to teach the boy how to be a responsible human being for the last four years."

"I have an alternative for you to consider," Ron said, draining his cup. Hamish reached to refill it from the teakettle on the stove, but Ron covered it with his hand. "I'll just have to pee again," he said, eyes twinkling.

"Will we all consider Scotty's experience at Glencoe to be a failure if we send him home?" Hamish asked, looking from Ron to Bonnie for a reaction. His wife seemed to have a strong opinion from the set of her jaw.

"He needs to be separated from the community. There's no doubt," she said, winding the string of her tea bag around the spoon to squeeze out every drop. "And he must think about how he has treated these girls and what standards he should live by."

Hamish refused to believe the Institute, as he sometimes called it, could not find a way to help Scotty salvage what had otherwise been an outstanding experience. Expulsion was the easy way out.

"I know you're ready to step out on a limb for Scotty," Bonnie continued. "And I suspect your partner in crime here might be incubating some unique solution. I'm confident he would not suggest something immoral, would you, dear?" she said.

Ron smiled. "Immoral? No. Whether it's legal is another question. I believe Scotty is a lot more fragile than he lets on. Expulsion may be the preferred solution through the administration's eyes. But I fear it will crush him. He needs to think hard about his behavior, his actions, the impact on other innocent people over whom he has power, whether he knows it or not. Problem is, we don't really build in a way for these kids to have much contemplative time around here. We have those kids on a merry-go-round nearly 24/7." Ron was silent for a prolonged period as he gathered his thoughts. No one else felt the need to fill that space and let him process his proposal.

"How do we get Scotty that gift of time? I'm thinking that after classes are over each day, he should pack up some clothes and his books and walk the backwoods road behind Glencoe to the McMahon farm."

"That's a seven-mile walk!" Bonnie exclaimed. "Alone?"

Behind the school, about a half-mile through the woods, ran an old tote road, never paved and now largely overgrown, that stretched down into a valley between steep, parallel ridges. The abandoned road was ideal for horseback trips in the fall and cross-country ski outings in the winter. It was to be avoided when mud season made the route nearly impassable. By May, however, the route was dry enough. At the end of that road lived Terry and Joanie McMahon. For decades, Terry directed maintenance at Glencoe while his wife supervised the housekeeping staff. They knew every student's name and most of their histories. The McMahons' impact on the place was legendary and it was a significant loss when they retired five years into Hamish's tenure. But retirement did not mean out of mind. Hamish was careful to keep them connected, inviting them to theater productions, musical performances, and each year's graduation. Horseback overnights in the fall usually ended up at the McMahons' farm. Students turned their horses out into the fields behind the barn, rolled their sleeping bags out in the hayloft, and munched on warm cookies that Joanie delivered after their cookout dinners.

"That'll give him time to think, to not participate in afternoon sports, to not be home with his peers, and to not have contact with these girls he has coerced," Ron continued. "If Terry and Joanie agree to take him in and drive him back to school each morning, it could be a real wake-up for Scotty. If he handles it like a mensch, let him graduate. What do you think?"

"What do I think?" Hamish asked. "I think you are a remarkably creative thinker who cares deeply for his students and is willing to put the whole place in jeopardy. Send him alone down that road for seven miles every day? With no supervision?"

"Let's not reject the idea out of hand, Hamish," Bonnie interjected. "At first blush it may sound crazy. But Scotty is nearly as comfortable in these woods as you are. That's a gift we've given him. Are you afraid he'll get lost, or run off, or get eaten by bears? The alone time might do him a world of good. And Terry and Joanie could be the perfect adults for him right now—nonjudgmental but firm. Ron, I like the idea very much."

"What if the Health Department found out? Or our insurance agent? They'd shut us down in an instant. Probably put me in jail for malpractice. Lord knows the trustees would never approve such a plan," Hamish countered.

"Nor his parents, most likely. Scotty must agree to keep this just between us," Ron said.

"Coconspirators," Bonnie said. "After all the positive he's done here, the boy will do anything not to throw it all away."

"It's a lot to ask," Hamish said, rubbing his chin. "And could be a ticket back to Scotland for us. But it's creative, I'll give ya that. Maybe brilliant," he said, "Now I just have to persuade Terry, Joanie . . . and Scotty."

"And get the faculty to not report you," Bonnie added. "It's ethically a bit questionable."

"Aye. That as well. Scotty and I need to have that chat and we'll see."

. . .

"How did he take it?" Christine asked, after hearing the story of Ron's proposal.

"The next afternoon, after class, I invited Scotty for a walk-and-talk around the lake. I did not berate him. I simply laid it out as an alternative to the nuclear option he was expecting. He saw it as an incredible lifeline, and I could practically see the weight lift off his shoulders," Hamish said. "Scotty embraced the idea just as Ron and Bonnie had predicted. It did not have to be hammered home to him how any misstep in this scenario would bring immediate dismissal. While he saw that he could not escape humiliation in the community, it was worth the pain to avoid expulsion as well as the certain rejection he would have received from the prep school he'd hoped to attend the following year."

"And he went off, on his own, every day?" Christine asked.

"For two weeks, no one saw Scotty from the end of classes until the following day's breakfast when Terry McMahon would drive him back to school. The solo seven-mile hike he took each afternoon had the desired effect of crystallizing what was most important to him. He apologized privately and profusely to the girls involved, and publicly participated in difficult discussions with students in the lower grades about sexual harassment. Scotty graduated with his class and has come back every year at spring break to help with the maple sugar harvest."

"Every situation demands a unique response in this business," Ron said. "I don't know Malcolm all that well but he's no Scotty Morrison. Nor is he Tracy Barcomb. But that's why you get the big bucks, Hamish. To compensate you for the wisdom to consult with the likes of me!"

"You egotistical son of a bitch," Hamish laughed. "Christine, I can't take any more of his bluster. See you all later."

This was Hamish at his best; having slowly learned over the years that trusting his gut was not leadership. Hubris and instinct were insufficient tools to lead a community. They may have gotten him up formidable mountains, both physically and metaphorically, when he was young and headstrong, but they were false flags for showing others the way. As many have found, it's lonely at the top. It's the rare bird who has the courage to tell the boss what is true and what is possible. Giving permission to those few to challenge you is a mark of generous leadership that is only possible when the leader has humility and trusts his advisors. It is a trait that rarely favors the young, and often evolves as a result of loss or shame. Hamish knew both.

Malcolm Dandridge did present a far different challenge. To Hamish's dismay, there seemed to be no reasonable intervention that would make a difference. The following week, Hamish nearly blew an artery in his neck so angry was he to discover Malcolm lobbing eggs against the MacLeans' cherished stained-glass window at their farmhouse beyond the barns. After the lecture, which included numerous words and phrases Malcolm must have thought could not really be English, Hamish was left wondering if it was Malcolm's disregard for the eggs, not the glass window, that bothered him the most.

With Tracy's confirmation that Malcolm had destroyed the weaving, the next step, by all rights, should have been dismissal. As with Scotty Morrison, however, Hamish was loath to admit failure. Needing to get away from the constant stream of demands at school, Hamish decided to spend an afternoon off campus, clearing his head.

"Cathy, I'm out 'til three," Hamish said to his secretary, throwing on his coat.

At that moment, Pete Hedges walked into the office. "Gee, I was hoping to catch you. Will you be gone long?"

"What's up, Pete?"

"Not a big deal. It's about a road cleanup I am organizing with the Lake Placid DPW, and I had a couple of things to run by you."

"Tell you what," Hamish said. "Let's discuss over a bout with some trout."

"Huh?"

"I need a couple of hours of away time to figure out what to do with this Dandridge fellow. Thought I would head down to the Ausable River for some fly-fishing. Join me. I could use a sounding board."

"I know as much about fly-fishing as I do about crocheting," Pete said. "I admire folks who can do it but I'm too ADD myself."

"You don't have to fish. You just have to listen."

"Well, It's my afternoon off. It's that or doing laundry with Christine. And it isn't going to do itself."

"Laundry can wait," Hamish said, oblivious to the real reason Pete wanted to spend time with the object of his obsession. "Meet me at the farmhouse, Pete. Ten minutes."

Pete Hedges had come to Glencoe as a teaching intern five years earlier following his graduation from Colby College in Maine. He proved so promising, both in the classroom, as part-time houseparent, and especially in the woods leading trips, that Hamish decided he should not be allowed to escape after his one-year appointment. Pete took about five minutes to accept the full-time teaching contract with summer incentives that Hamish offered. Over the ensuing years, Pete grew a beard, which made him look older than his years, and earned a leadership role despite his youth and relative inexperience. Hamish hoped he would become a "lifer," devoting his career to Glencoe. The headmaster went out of his way to include Pete on winter mountaineering trips, to tutor him on the most rugged outings. He paid for Pete to split his summers between workshops developing English curricula and wilderness education with the National Outdoor Leadership School.

Glencoe seemed a perfect fit for the young educator, except for one aspect; it offered few prospects to find a mate. Each spring, Pete wrestled with the reality that, if the past was prologue, he would likely retire from Glencoe as a single man. But in August of his fourth year Christine Mason showed up, wearing a Duke Blue Devil sweatshirt, and quickly stole his heart. While the two tried their best to be discreet about their budding relationship it was an open secret that they were mutually smitten. Students saw it and teased them both. Bonnie did everything she could to encourage it. So consumed was he with the day-to-day demands of running the Place, Hamish might have been the last to know that his protégé was overwhelmingly distracted.

The Ausable River is an exquisite, world-class trout stream. By no means a consummate fly fisherman, Hamish discovered that his emotional batteries could best be recharged while standing mid-thigh in the slow-moving waters, framed by distant mountain ridges glowing purple in the long rays of the afternoon sun. Pete sat on the warm, grassy bank watching Hamish whip his fly line over the gentle waters time, after time, after time, listening to his mentor's internal debate about what to do with Malcolm.

Though no fickle trout chose to gasp the rest of their short lives in Hamish's fern-lined wicker creel that afternoon, the outing still served its purpose, as Hamish walked through the options he had been incubating, seeking a solution that would afford Malcolm a bit more time to be exposed to the Glencoe way of life. Pete offered little, but his purpose was only to sit there on the bank and listen to the options as they were proposed. Once Hamish was satisfied with the formula, the fishing came to an end.

"Thank you for indulging me this afternoon, Mr. Hedges," Hamish said as they walked back to the car.

"Of course. I think we found a good solution," Pete laughed. "You couldn't have done it without me."

Between the main course and dessert that evening Hamish walked to the front of the dining hall and rang the little bell for silence. "Everyone, I'd like your attention for a moment. Malcolm, you have the floor."

With great flair, Malcolm arose from his seat and walked deliberately to the front of the room. On his walk he passed by the tables where Marnie Marks and Sarah Welliver were seated and handed each an envelope. Hamish noted with dismay how comfortable Malcolm appeared to be, delivering each girl his letter of apology, hastily written before dinner at Hamish's insistence.

"Uh, I, um . . . I made a mistake and I want to say 'Sorry' to everyone," Malcolm stammered, eyes glued to the floor. "Especially to Marnie and Sarah. Sorry about the weaving. They teased me about the pot I was throwing, but I got to control my temper better." As he went on, talking about how he felt when someone teased him, including a bizarre incident from his previous school, his eyes lifted from the floor and, Hamish thought, he appeared to almost enjoy sharing a past humiliation. "Guys," he said, looking from one girl to the other, "you can bust one of my pots if you like." There was a titter of laughter from the audience and Hamish decided the performance had gone on long enough.

"That will do," he said, stepping to the front, frustrated with the results of his plan. "You may sit down." Hamish devoted two solid afternoons walking with Malcolm in the woods behind the campus and clearing brush on the ski hill, trying to get inside the boy's head. He also scheduled him for weekly meetings with Elaine Foxworthy, the school psychologist. Hoping he had found a way to channel Malcolm's disruptive behavior in more positive ways, Hamish left for a weeklong fundraising junket to the West Coast, eager to add in a day or two climbing in Washington State's Cascades. Though he would not know it for some time, his bend-over-backward efforts to turn around Malcolm's rough start did not have the desired effect.

9

At the Boiling Point

AT SEVEN FIFTEEN ON A FRIDAY MORNING AS A SAFFRON SUN LIFTED over Pitchoff Mountain behind the Glencoe campus, Malcolm emerged from Marshall House, his breath generating steamy pulses as it hit the bracing Adirondack air. Oblivious to the riotous fall colors in the woods that encircled the campus, and with sullen demeanor firmly in place, he trudged off to feed the pigs, joining on the gravel road a small contingent of other children assigned to barn chores for the week.

As usual, he lingered on the road as long as possible, for he hated pigs. The others were well into their chores when Malcolm squeezed through the barnyard fence. He passed the hen house and the compost pile, steaming with decomposing barn waste, and walked reluctantly toward the pigpen. Suddenly, the idea came to him, and his scowl lifted. It was simple and elegant. If only he could be there to see the reaction. The pigs might have been puzzled as their usual tormentor sloshed a generous allotment of food scraps into their troughs. Absent were the normal curses and kicks he typically proffered.

At the conclusion of chores later that afternoon Malcolm slipped behind the hen house, waiting until the last person had left the barnyard. Armed with a plastic bag and small trowel he had borrowed from the garden shed, Malcolm ducked into the hen house. He held his breath against the acrid smell of ammonia as he waded through the sea of beaks and feathers, fending the poultry away with his boots to clear space on the floor where piles of excreta, a combination of feces and urine, were evident. After a few careful scoops, he was back on the road, a bulging packet held gingerly within his flannel-lined denim barn jacket. As the waiters' bell clanged, signaling to table setters it was time to head to the dining room, Malcolm picked up his pace.

It was six o'clock sharp as the Glencoe community headed in for dinner, but Malcolm was not among them. "Anybody home?" Malcolm bellowed from the mudroom at Phelps House. Hearing no reply, he bounded up the stairs and easily located Tracy's door by the poster of bikini-clad women skiing over a cliff at a Utah resort. Now he had to decide which closet held Tracy's clothes, which one Jake's. As much as Malcolm detested Tracy, he did not have any bone to pick with Jake, who was perhaps the only Glencoe student of whom Malcolm was wary.

One of only six Black students at Glencoe, Jake hailed from Brooklyn's Bedford Stuyvesant neighborhood. Ironically, his upbringing more closely matched Tracy's than did the experience of the other students of color, at least financially. The Barcombs had more assets than Jake's single mom, but neither family's resources came close to matching most of the Black students at Glencoe. Three were children of wealthy African diplomats and one was the daughter of a New York City Supreme Court judge. Other than skin color, there was not much Jake had in common with those kids. The sixth, who hailed from Ashview Heights, a downtrodden section of Atlanta, was just a fifth grader. As the eldest person of color at such a predominantly colorless school, Jake took responsibility for their welfare, and took it very seriously. But it was not just the Black students who regarded Jake with such respect. He was universally admired as the most mature, put-together boy in the school.

Malcolm wanted no part of Jake and was relieved to find Tracy's name stitched on the collar of a barn jacket, which made it easy to target the right closet, thus avoiding a mistake he might regret. Two minutes later he was on his way back to Dewey Hall, entering just as students and teachers were sitting down to baked spaghetti casserole, arugula salad and warm oatmeal bread.

"Didn't you hear the bell?" Payton Henderson asked as Malcolm slid into his chair.

"Sorry, Payton. I was finishing up a math assignment in the computer lab." Everyone at the table found him unusually merry that evening. "Man, this spaghetti is outta sight," he said, savoring each mouthful.

Weekends brought a welcome break from the normal schedule. With no mountain climbs offered by the staff on this particular Saturday, Tracy elected to join a lunchtime horseback riding trip along trails that ran for miles through the "sugar bush," the dense maple forest that surrounded the campus and provided sap the community boiled each spring in a rustic sugar house. It was not so much a love of horses that prompted Tracy to choose such an activity, but, rather, a love of the girls who loved horses and always signed up for these trips. Malcolm had seen Tracy's name on the bulletin board and, therefore, knew his victim would be reaching for his boots that Saturday morning.

While he much preferred basketball and mountain climbing to horseback riding, Tracy came to Glencoe with far more riding experience than most of the students. But for him it was a means to an end, spending fleeting moments of time with his workaholic father. Wendell Barcomb leased a small farm on a hillside above Mallet's Bay, just north of Burlington. On a clear day from a tractor or a horse the view across Lake Champlain to the Adirondack High Peaks was spectacular. It was that view that mesmerized Tracy when he and his dad would ride the fields below the house on the infrequent weekend day that Wendell allowed himself a bit of leisure time to spend with his overly energetic son. Following in the ancient footsteps of Jamie Barcomb, the first of his line to settle in the New World, Wendell Barcomb represented the sixth generation of family farming the stony fields of Vermont.

The Barcombs had worked the fields in Ireland's County Leitrim for generations before Jamie was called up to join the British army and fight Napoleon Bonaparte. While Jamie was away, the family came together to shoulder the extra work and, as experienced by countless other farmers on the Emerald Isle, they enjoyed unprecedented demand for their agricultural products. Irish beef and dairy kept British troops fed. Irish boys kept the British troops strong. But with peace in 1815 prosperity vanished; the British no longer needed such a huge fighting force nor as much produce to feed them. It did not take long, after Jamie Barcomb returned home, for him to realize that financial ruin was in the offing, a stunning realization that dawned on an entire nation.

Ten years of suffering followed. Ireland was devastated by economic depression and disease. Jamie decided his future lay elsewhere and, one drizzly October morning in 1825, he announced to his family that he had booked passage to Canada. He would establish a new home and send for the family as soon as he was settled. His true destination was Vermont, but sailing into Canada was less expensive and so he followed the path of so many others who had reached the same conclusion.

Two years earlier, the Champlain Canal had opened, a sixty-mile ribbon of water connecting the south portion of Lake Champlain to the Hudson River. Almost overnight, vast markets in Albany, New York City, and beyond opened up for Vermont goods. Labor was needed to farm, and to operate gristmills and sawmills. Word reached Ireland that extraordinary opportunities awaited. In the two centuries prior to the Napoleonic conflicts, perhaps a half-million Irish men and women had emigrated to America. In only three decades following the end of those wars, twice as many made that pilgrimage, including Jamie Barcomb.

During a summer visit to Burlington in 1832, Nathaniel Hawthorne noted the vibrancy of the once-sleepy community as well as the sheer number of Irish he found there. They manned the shops, they logged the woods, they crewed the sloops, schooners, and steamboats moving produce down the lake to the canal, from whence they made their way to the burgeoning populations to the south. Thirteen years later the terrible Potato Famine of 1845 brought thousands more across the Atlantic from Ireland. By that time, Jamie was well enough established to hire some of those immigrants himself.

It was Wendell Barcomb's misfortune to be the last of the Barcomb farmers, just after his father had lost the family spread to foreclosure. Too many years of substandard crops, plus some poor investments in new equipment, resulted in an upside-down economic picture that forced Tracy's grandfather to sell the homestead at a loss. Forced to start over, with no land of his own, Wendell agreed to work someone else's spread. He befriended an old friend of his dad's, Paul Miller, who was nearing the end of his own active farming life. With no offspring of his own to continue the family farm, Paul proposed to let Wendell work the land on a lease/buy basis. The Miller property was a mix of pasture and woodlot. The former supported a dairy operation and the latter, maple sugaring. The beautiful spread also came with a couple of ponies that needed caretaking.

Wendell and his first wife, a high school fling, divorced after eighteen months. A young woman he met contra dancing two years later, Emily Spitzer, proved to be an ideal mate. She shared her new husband's passion for the land and a career path of her own. Three years in toward her doctorate in the environment and natural resources at the University of Vermont, Emily was already juggling academic work and an internship with the Sierra Club when she became pregnant. She embraced the challenge of bringing Tracy up while trying to finish her dissertation on wilderness politics, a work that she hoped would result in an academic career, and a desperately needed second income. They were well-matched; he, the pragmatic farmer, hands in the soil, worrying about crop yields and weather; she, the one who fretted about the chemicals Wendell spread upon their land and, writ large, what those practices were doing to the world's water supplies. She often quoted her favorite author, Aldo Leopold, whose most renowned work, *A Sand County Almanac*, never left her bedside. Emily also developed a pen pal relationship with Laura Waterman, downstate Vermont neighbor and co-author with her late husband, Guy, of a seminal work on backwoods ethics. As Wendell taught their little boy to feel comfortable in the woods, to identify the flora and fauna he found there, to camp without leaving a trace, to deploy the rest step to conserve his strength on long hikes, Emily instilled in Tracy a strong sense of stewardship for the wilderness in their Green Mountain backyard.

Both parents agreed they should break the long tradition of Barcomb family farming that now threatened to drive them to bankruptcy despite Wendell's best efforts. The local public school lacked the underpinnings they felt their son would need to compete later in his educational career. Prep school, and the necessary scholarship to afford such a place, seemed out of the question unless Tracy's academic performance improved. Given his battles to pay attention, the chances of that happening looked slim.

Apart from occasional hikes within an hour's drive, horseback riding was a way for Wendell to spend quality time with his young son in a way that was least taxing. Tracy treasured those too-occasional hours of trailing his dad around the property, peppering him with questions in a generally unsuccessful attempt to earn his dad's attention. When Tracy reached the age of thirteen, Emily and Wendell decided to apply to Glencoe and hope that experience would prepare him for a ticket beyond the family farm. The hook they dangled was *mountains*. Tracy had already climbed all five four-thousand-foot peaks in Vermont and had begun to pester his dad about weekend trips across Lake Champlain to the Adirondacks. Glencoe's backyard was full of such challenges. There would be horses to ride, forty-six new peaks above 4,000 feet to conquer, and they could easily visit him on weekends, now and then. When the letter arrived offering admission and a healthy scholarship, Tracy decided he would try to make the most of it. He understood his parents' argument about giving him the tools he needed to succeed, but also saw that, with him away, his mom could focus on her dissertation and his dad on generating enough income to keep them afloat. But he wished it was harder for them to say goodbye.

In a hurry, as usual, dreaming of the afternoon's flirtations, Tracy raced out of Nissen following a heated one-on-one basketball game with Jake. He charged up the hill to Phelps House and took the stairs to his room two at a time. As he grabbed the boots from the back of his closet, he noticed a faint rancid smell. Making a quick mental note to send his barn jacket to the laundry, he jammed his feet into the boots and hustled downstairs, out the door, and down to the riding ring where the group was already sorting out who would ride which horse.

Seven girls were adjusting helmets and stirrups as Tracy approached his assigned horse, a bored bay mare cropping blades of grass at the perimeter of the ring.

"Yuck. Does Phelps House have a hot water problem?" Sally Goodwin wrinkled up her nose from atop a palomino.

"What's that supposed to mean?" Tracy asked, jerking at the bay's reins to interrupt her grazing.

"No offense, but you smell like you haven't had a shower since school opened." Sally shrugged her shoulders in a sorry-gotta-be-straight-with-you kind of look.

Tracy felt blood rush to his face. Mortified with embarrassment, he kicked the sides of the bay to get her moving and, as he did so, felt dampness between his toes. He pulled the horse to a halt, slipped one boot out of the stirrups and lifted his leg up across the horse's neck where it met the saddle. The aroma of ammonia, mistakenly attributed to his barn jacket, was there again. He dismounted and pulled off the offending boot. The stench of chicken excreta made him gag. Bewildered and humiliated, he grabbed the boot, jumped over the riding ring fence, and ran into the woods, trying to put as much distance as possible between himself and the group of girls convulsed with laughter. He circled through the woods, cursing every time his stocking feet landed on a pinecone, until he reached the toolshed by the flower garden. Opening a spigot, he spent the rest of the afternoon trying to rinse out the memory as well as the smell. Tracy left the boots to dry in the sun on the front porch of Phelps House and sought out his roommate to commiserate.

News of the prank had already reached Jake when Tracy found him in the library. "I think we should take a walk before you explode," Jake advised. He steered Tracy into the woods for a long walk. They chose a remote trail that wound through the sugar bush on the slopes at the edge of campus, which bordered state land, an area of the school where they could be assured of privacy. The trail took them past tree forts, rope swings, and gnome villages, encouraging the kind of unstructured free play with little or no adult supervision that could rarely be found outside of Glencoe. This helped students remember they were still children, encouraged to fantasize.

Tracy and Jake stopped at a lean-to in a clearing from which they could see much of the lake, a mirror of gold reflecting the sun dipping over Ampersand Mountain to the west. They sat on the wood floor of the lean-to, which was mostly used to familiarize the youngest students about the joys of an overnight camping trip, but not too far from their own beds. In a fury, Tracy recounted how embarrassed he was in the riding ring in front of all those girls. "I'm ready to rip someone a new one."

"And who would that be?"

"Three guesses." Tracy scowled. "This must be his way of getting back at me for squealing on him for the shitty thing he did to those girls' weaving. And that's another thing I'm steamed about, getting linked to him on that one. You have no idea how sick it made me feel to get interrogated by Hamish like I was the criminal."

"What are you going to do about it?" Jake asked. "I'm worried this thing between the two of you is getting out of control."

"Don't know what I'm going to do, but it'll be something he'll remember for a long time. I'd love to get his fat ass out of here. I'd be doing everyone a favor."

"Watch your step, dude, or it may be your name on the Trailways ticket."

"Will you help me, Jake?"

"Sorry. This is your fight, not mine. But let me know what you've got in mind, just in case."

10

The Truth about Zeus

IT WAS MID-OCTOBER; A FEW SHORT WEEKS REMAINED TO PULL THE Thanksgiving production together. Each year, Ron Handy created as original a theatrical experience as could be found at any school. *This time I've bitten off more than I can chew*, Ron thought as the kids filed in for another afternoon reading. Although everyone was confident that he had fashioned yet another blockbuster, Ron was inwardly petrified. His annual torment.

If there was one teacher who touched all the students and helped to bring them together as a community, it was Ron. His pied-piper mystique charmed the younger ones, and his stories about big wall climbs in California's Yosemite Valley enthralled the jocks. Long ago, he had climbed forty-five of the Adirondack 46ers, back when it took a serious knowledge of map and compass to climb many of the trailless peaks, yet he had purposely shunned climbing the last one. When asked why, he would laugh. "You'll just be one of thousands who can wear that 46er patch. You don't meet many 45ers, do you? I prefer it that way."

More than once during his tenure at Glencoe, Ron had been approached by school parents in the theater business who, in awe of his work, tried to persuade him he had a real shot to become a "show doctor," a niche profession of talented individuals who could parachute into a troubled production and make the necessary fixes under excruciating time pressure. Though flattered, Ron never seriously considered leaving the comfortable and low-risk world of Glencoe. He knew his constitution could never hold up under the strain of a professional production.

Just putting on these annual gems at Glencoe caused sleepless nights and gastrointestinal complications that plagued him each fall term.

Ron was content to direct amateur adolescents in plays and musicals he created, ironically funny parodies of the human condition. He took stock of the natural talent in each year's student body and, like a great coach, adapted his system to the existing talent pool. This year, the underlying theme was Greek myth, with a lot of choreography to suit the excellent dancers at his disposal. The show, titled *The Truth about Zeus*, was yet another brilliant Handy original, a lyrical and visual smorgasbord of deception and dalliance in the court of the shrewd, but vain, Zeus.

The popularity of his shows was so great that it attracted students to participate who would normally have had zero interest. Tracy Barcomb was not one of those hesitant thespians. His acting chops had been on full display the previous year as Falstaff in Ron Handy's take on Shakespeare's *Henry IV*. Despite the boy's mercurial emotions, Ron counted upon Tracy to be the steadying force. Sure enough, when Ron took down the sign-up sheet two weeks into the semester, Tracy's name was first on the list.

Unfortunately, success appeared to hinge on Tracy's hormones. If the boy quit his incessant preening and flirting with every female on the set and concentrated on his part, Ron believed the show would come together.

Much of Ron's summer vacation was devoted to writing the libretto, orchestrating the lyrics and music. His recollection of Broadway musical theater was encyclopedic. His familiarity with six musicals loosely based upon Greek or Roman mythology, which opened for at least a single performance on the Great White Way, became the basis for his newest venture. Ron truly believed that imitation was the finest form of flattery, so his productions reflected the shows he admired most. He did not plagiarize as much as pluck kernels of content from these shows. Truth be told, there were a few stanzas he "borrowed" word for word but not to steal; he used them as homage to the works he revered.

There was Rodgers and Hart's, *By Jupiter*, a 1942 musical about Amazonian women. And *One Touch of Venus*, a Kurt Weill/S. J. Perelman/Ogden Nash send-up of the famous Pygmalion myth, produced in 1943, which was later transformed into the blockbuster hit of the 1950s—*My Fair Lady*.

There was *The Golden Apple*, which opened on Broadway in 1954, based upon the epic poems *The Iliad* and *The Odyssey*. Though the show was not a huge success, Ron was drawn to its clever decision to set the story in a modern era using current events of those times.

When seeking a break from office work, Hamish would often sneak over to Marcy Hall to catch a rehearsal of *Zeus*. One evening, after the students had filtered out after another exhausting run-through, Hamish met him backstage.

"You've done it again, Ron. I hear kids walking past my office, singing your words, dancing in the hall, totally unprovoked. It's remarkable!"

"From your mouth to God's ears," Ron muttered, slumped over his piano. He pulled a pencil from behind his ear, licked it, and made some notes on a page of sheet music.

"I'd like to believe the good Lord listens to me," Hamish chuckled. "At least when I'm sober. So should you, once in a while."

"I do when you say something sensible," Ron said.

"If I'm not mistaken, I think it was, what, three years ago when you went down to New York City to see that show . . . what was it . . . some high-camp spoof . . ."

"*Xanadu.*"

"Right. *Xanadu*. I remember after you got back, all full of piss and vinegar, about how inspired that show made you to use myths as the foundation for one of ours."

"You are dead right, sir. I'm impressed. That became the basis for this one, with a little help from an old Cole Porter show I won't bore you with. Always thinking three years ahead. That's going to come to an end someday soon. Just warning you. I'm running out of ideas and steam. If you hang on here longer than me . . . Sorry, than I . . . you're not going to get much more than a Punch and Judy production from the next victim you hire to do my job, Mister Headmaster."

"I am well aware of that sad fact. Maybe we need to retire simultaneously."

The one musical from which Ron drew the most was *Out of This World*, a Cole Porter show that debuted in 1950, based upon *Amphitryon*, a comedy by the Roman playwright Plautus. Ron was taken by the concept of bored Roman gods looking for amusement by tormenting mere mortals. To Ron, Cole Porter was the standard by which all composers should be judged. While the show was not a huge critical success, it gave Ron the hook he was looking for, as well as a few Cole Porter excerpts he included as "Easter eggs," hidden gems only the most sophisticated audience member would recognize.

These theatrical vehicles were always multilayered, littered with double entendres. Out of the mouths of babes, the Glencoe student-actors, would come beautiful prose they thought they understood and struggled to memorize. The words they spoke, the songs they sang, had one meaning to them, literal and simple, defining a story arc they could appreciate and embrace. But on another level, Ron crafted completely different themes to tickle an audience of adults. As the production unfolded, you could see on the faces of parents their growing recognition that the author was weaving a sophisticated tapestry and playing with them. It was a private joke, not to be shared with the youngsters. The closer to the line of outrageous, bawdy, tawdry, subject matter he could get, couched in innocence, the more Ron seemed to enjoy it.

"If you're not too tired, you're welcome to come up to the farmhouse for a nightcap," Hamish offered.

"I'd love to," Ron answered. "But I've got to simplify some of these transitions. Sometimes I forget these kids are . . . kids."

"Rain check, then. How's the tummy holding up this year?" Hamish asked.

"As well as can be expected. I never thought a man could subsist on Tums, but I'm living proof." Ron sensed Hamish was dawdling, that he had come backstage for a purpose. "I'm sensing you're about to ask me to do something I will regret."

Hamish often turned to Ron for help with the prickly ones, students who for one reason or another could not find their way. The headmaster forever marveled at the unusual techniques Ron employed with these recalcitrant members of the community, challenging, goading them to perform beyond their expectations. It seemed to others on the faculty that Ron managed the children effortlessly, but they had no idea what physical exhaustion he battled until the Thanksgiving break.

"Malcolm?" Ron guessed.

"I'm at my wit's end," Hamish admitted.

Ron nodded knowingly. He had been at the forefront of those among the faculty who lobbied Hamish not to admit Malcolm in the first place.

"Don't give me that *I told you so* look, Ron. Is there anything you can do to help me bring him into the fold? I'd be grateful if you could spare me the anguish of calling his aunt and admitting you all were right about him."

Ron pursed his lips, calculating how many more antacid pills to buy on his next trip to Placid. "I'll try him backstage on the lighting crew. But I warn you, Hamish, I'll not sacrifice the success of the show to cater to that boy's pathology."

"Give him a try, Ron. I know deep down he wants to make it here."

The honeymoon lasted a week. Malcolm cooperated as long as Tracy was elsewhere. But when their paths crossed, the intersection of their personalities became explosive. Ron wasn't sure the production could survive their pyrotechnics, but it was too late to get rid of either one of them.

11

Soul-Searching

TINA SHERMAN'S PARTICIPATION IN THE MUSICAL WAS A GIVEN. HER dancing talent thrust her into the limelight of the play preparations, and she eagerly anticipated the Thanksgiving Day performance in front of all the parents as well as the entire school community. Her roommate, Libby, was one of the few ninth graders who passed on the opportunity. In fact, she resented Tina's absorption with *The Truth about Zeus* and the lack of time she had left for her friend. Though she hadn't exactly figured this out herself, Libby felt abandoned and groused at Tina over the slightest irritation—a misplaced bathrobe, a highlighter borrowed without permission. During objective moments, Libby recognized she was being unfair, and suspected Tina must be mystified by her roommate's moodiness. It just made Libby feel worse that she wasn't being a better friend.

One evening, as the girls walked up the path from the dining hall to Phelps House, Libby admitted to Tina how badly she was handling her friend's all-consuming involvement with the show. Libby tearfully let it all out to the one person who could take it. "I'm really ashamed of myself for the way I've been treating you," Libby sniffled. "I know I've been an ass and I'm sorry."

"I knew something was bothering you," said Tina. At least the issue was finally out in the open. "I guess I've been so busy I never thought to ask you about it. What did I do to get you so worked up?"

"It's not you, Tina. It's me. And I'm going to try to do something about it, because I hate myself."

Their reconciliation was interrupted as Tracy came up behind them. He aggressively wedged his way between the two girls, wrapping an arm around each in a way that made Libby squirm and Tina giggle.

"Hey roomies, what's shakin'?" he teased, flashing an impish grin and giving each of them a squeeze. Flirting was like breathing for the effervescent Barcomb.

"Get your grubby mitts off me, Tracy," Libby said, twisting out of his grasp. "And I'm not your *roomie*, thank God." More gently, Tina also extricated herself. Unperturbed, Tracy slowed his pace to match theirs as they continued up the path.

"Relax, girl. I don't have the plague."

"Too bad. Then they'd quarantine you and we'd get a little peace," Libby retorted.

"Lighten up, Libby," Tina said, smiling.

"You may tolerate this crap, but I don't have to," Libby snapped.

"Yeah, chill," Tracy said, sounding hurt. "Maybe the attention would do you some good. What's your problem?"

"Find someone else to harass," Libby said, quickening her step.

"The vibes don't lie, man. The vibes don't lie," he smiled as they entered Phelps House.

"Jesus Christ, I'd like to slaughter him," Libby muttered when she and Tina reached their room.

"He sure knows how to push your buttons, doesn't he?" Tina smiled.

"One of these days he's going to push it too far, Tina. Somebody needs to teach him some manners."

"Seems like someone tried," Tina said.

"You think Malcolm put the chicken shit in his boots?"

"Everyone seems to think so," Tina said.

"Maybe that's going too far. I don't know if anyone deserves that. Yuck."

"Why do you get so skeezed up over him, Libby? Tracy just needs to grow up a little. If you didn't let him get under your skin, I bet he'd tone it down. He likes getting those reactions from you. It means you're paying attention."

"You're not suggesting I have some subconscious crush on him, are you?" Libby asked archly.

"You said it, girl, not me."

"Don't be crazy. He makes me physically ill."

"Whatever's bumming you is not Tracy. He's harmless. And kind of cute," Tina smiled. "And I respect the hell out of his acting. He blew me away last year with that Falstaff bit. That's not easy."

Libby considered that. She respected Tina, and if her friend could see something in Tracy, could see through all that immature bluster, maybe the problem lay closer to home.

"Listen, I wish I had more time, but I promised Ron I would spend half an hour with the kids doing the swing dance after reading period. Maybe we can do this later?"

Libby nodded, deflated. There were so many things that set her off these days. The slightest remark caused anger to well up. If only she could understand where the fury came from, she'd deal with it, or so she tried to convince herself. It wasn't fun always being ready to boil over. Tina was the one person she could open up to, someone willing to hear her and help her sort the real from the imagined.

"Whatever. We'll discuss it when you have more time."

"Hey, I've got an idea. Why don't you give us a hand with the set design? Christine says you draw fantastic. If we don't get some help with the sets, the show's a disaster," she fibbed. "And it would be a lot more fun for me if you were around."

"I'll think about it," Libby answered as they walked downstairs together. Tina opened the door to leave. "I'm sorry, Tina." Her roommate smiled, waved goodbye, and dashed out the door and down the hill to Marcy Hall. Life wasn't easy for Libby now and it was increasingly more difficult to hide the sadness. Without knowing why, she was hurting the people for whom she cared the most.

As Tina left, Rambler, the MacLeans' twelve-year-old golden retriever/border collie mix, slipped into the Phelps House mudroom before the front door closed. She was making the rounds of the houses as she often did in the evening, seemingly bred to check on everyone's whereabouts. The MacLeans had rescued her as a puppy from a shelter in

Saranac Lake, and it didn't take long for the dog to figure out that *some-body* needed to look after all these children. On the first overnight trip that Hamish led after adopting Rambler, it became clear how at home their dog felt in the woods, and how responsibly she took her job as a trip leader. You could almost see her counting heads as the children hiked past, making sure all were accounted for. Once satisfied, she bounded back to the front, following the path unerringly on hikes that followed established trails, or picking out sensible routes on bushwhacks where no established trails existed. She was equally comfortable on winter trips, leaving the group occasionally to pursue unseen critters but always returning to make sure her charges were adequately supervised. Nearly every weekend a teacher would request that Rambler accompany them on a hiking trip. She became such a fixture that, by the age of ten, she had climbed all of the forty-six High Peaks in the Adirondacks. Bred to herd, Rambler was guide, chaperone, and companion, and she was more patient with children than typical border collies. Now semiretired, Rambler was less often permitted to participate in the hiking program. Though her eagerness was unflagging, Hamish saw with dismay that the closest thing he had to a child was finally slowing down as arthritis stole her ease of movement.

Libby sat down in the cubby meant for her coat and boots and scratched the aging dog behind her ears, down her back, to the base of her tail. That triggered Rambler's hind left leg to rhythmically rat-a-tat the linoleum. She cocked her cappuccino-colored head, accented by a splash of teardrop-shaped white fur that split her wise old face in two. She gazed into Libby's eyes with a look of unconditional affection. *Get a grip*, Libby scolded herself. *At least I'm not stuck in New York with those crazy parents of mine and their wacko friends. I've got a beautiful place to live, a roommate, and houseparents who try to keep me sane. Stop feeling so sorry for yourself and deal with it.* Rambler licked her hand as though trying to offer sympathy. Libby smiled at the concerned look on the dog's face, gently took each of her ears in her hands, knelt toward her, and rubbed noses. Rambler wagged her tail, sighed, made three circles around Libby's ankles in search of the precise place to settle and curled up contentedly at her feet. Libby patted Rambler one more time on the top of her head and silently apologized for removing herself just as the dog had found a comfortable place to lie. She stood and went to find Jane Henderson and, with any luck, some hot cocoa.

12

Art Room Confessions

At least the set design was going smoothly. After lengthy discussions with Ron regarding his vision of what the backdrops should look like, Christine directed various art students to sketch small renditions of each mural. Once they had been revised to her satisfaction, she then supervised the painting of full-scale versions depicting ancient Greece and the kingdom of Zeus.

Christine was grateful that Libby had volunteered to help; the art teacher saw quite a bit of herself in the beautiful girl from New York City and appreciated her company. Quiet afternoons in the art room painting murals of Greek columns, flying horses, and golden chalices were savored moments. Christine looked forward to spending those times with Libby, painting and gossiping, away from the maelstrom that swirled through the building after classes were over, getting to know each other. It was clear that Libby was struggling to dissipate some emotional cloud that seemed a permanent fixture. The references Libby made to her life at home, her parents' formal relationship with her, bubbled up in many of their afternoon conversations. Christine found herself acting as an amateur therapist, for which she felt unqualified but sympathetic, gradually sharing some of her own history.

The art room at Glencoe was a comfortable, peaceful space. In one corner sat a group of wooden floor looms, strung like horizontal harps with countless, multicolored threads. Intricately patterned cloth emerged from the looms as student weavers sent weft yarn across warp strings, back and forth, row after row, the click of the shuttles a mesmerizing mantra. The art room was a special place, an oasis from the incessant activity that permeated Dewey Hall on the floor above.

"This is my happy place," Libby once said to Christine. "It just calms me to come down here. It doesn't seem to matter if the room is full or not."

"I wish I could take credit for that," Christine said, obviously pleased.

"Of course, you can. You set the tone here. I admit there are exceptions," Libby said, shaking her head. "When you-know-who drops in to throw a pot."

Christine made a face and smiled. She gazed through the broad windows that flanked the south side of the room, at the still-emerald lower pasture, at the peak of one barn peeping above the trees, and in the distance, the rocky summit of Mt. Algonquin looming large and forbidding. It was a happy place for the most part, and she was glad she got to spend so many hours there.

"I can't believe you've never worked with pastels before," Christine said one afternoon, leaning over Libby's work. "Where did you learn that technique?"

"You're joking, right?"

"Not at all. You're really very good."

"Thanks. Maybe I've found my calling. My mom used to tell me if I didn't go to college, I could always make a career out of painting by numbers and doing dot-to-dot puzzles."

"Seriously, Libby, you should consider taking an art course over the summer. I think you'd lap it up. Want me to suggest it to your parents when they come for Thanksgiving?"

"If you have time," Libby said shyly. "What do you like to do best, Chris? Paint or ceramics?"

"Depends upon my mood, I guess. I go through stages where I prefer one or the other. Since I came to Glencoe, I've gotten interested in batik, actually. There's so much to learn, you never stop, even when you become a teacher."

"Did you like art when you were a kid?"

"I took courses after school in North Carolina until the beauty pageants began to take too much of my time," she said with some embarrassment.

"Are you serious? You were in beauty pageants? I thought that was, like, old school."

Christine feigned taking offense.

"Not that you couldn't," Libby added quickly. "You weren't Miss America, were you?"

Christine laughed. "Not hardly."

"Well, everyone thinks you're gorgeous. Especially Pete," Libby grinned, fishing for a reaction. "Who did you have to pay to end up covering the same house this year?"

"Now don't start with that," Christine said, blushing.

Libby resumed painting as Christine circled the tables, doling out equal doses of encouragement and constructive criticism to the attentive group of aspiring artists.

"I've always wondered what it's like being in a beauty pageant but never knew anyone to ask," Libby said when Christine had returned to sit by her.

Christine eased onto a stool, her gaze focused on a previous life. "I don't talk about it much. Frankly, I find it embarrassing. But in the interest of education, here goes. My sisters and I didn't have much choice growing up in North Carolina, at least not in my family. As long as you didn't have three legs you were expected to compete. You can't imagine how many young girls are shuttled from pageant to pageant during their adolescence until they feel their entire worth is dependent upon how some judges rate them. It's depressing for most of them because very few actually win anything. The main beneficiaries of the racket are the dressmakers and tap dance, voice, and piano teachers.

"When I finally decided to quit, my mother had a difficult time accepting my decision. I think she had stars in her eyes, imagining me winning the Miss America title or something. It was a great source of pride for her when I won something, and a personal tragedy when I didn't." Christine looked around to see if anyone was still listening, for she had dropped into a personal reverie, almost talking to herself.

"She lived for the reflected glory of my successes. I suppose it was something she wished she'd done herself, but it took its toll on all of us. It was especially difficult for my two older sisters, neither of whom had the stomach for it—no pun intended."

"They weren't as good-looking as you?" asked Libby.

"They were born with the same incredible bone structure as I have," Christine joked, "but they preferred spending weekends at NASCAR events rather than beauty pageants. Nonetheless, they resented all the attention Mom lavished on me."

"Your dad didn't approve?"

"My father was willing to invest in gowns and piano lessons as long as I was enthusiastic. But one time, I think it was at a pageant before the Bluebonnet Bowl, one of the contestants was found, umm," she hesitated, deciding how much to say. "Well, let me just say she took it really, really hard after failing to make the finals." Christine immediately regretted saying even that much and hoped Libby would let it pass. "My dad sat me down and asked me for the first time if I was participating for myself or for Mom. I admitted the life was not what I would have chosen, but I didn't want to disappoint them. He said that he didn't want me going into a tailspin on account of my mom's dreams, and that was the end of it for us."

Christine stood to check again on the other students and their projects, making it clear the peek through her personal window had come to an end.

"Thanks for sharing," Libby said, gratefully.

"Probably oversharing," Christine said, inwardly scolding herself.

"My turn, I guess," Libby said.

"Meaning what?"

"Can I trust you not to get me in trouble if I confess something? It's bothered me for a year and I need to get it off my chest," Libby said. "It's about Richard Hahnemann."

. . .

During the fall semester the previous year, a revered social studies teacher named Amy Tolliver had been stricken with ALS. Her eighth grade class, which included Libby, Tina, and Tracy, was devastated when she announced to them that she could no longer be a part of their community, let alone continue to teach their favorite class. Hamish scrambled to find a replacement who could start immediately.

Richard Hahnemann arrived a week later and proved to be the worst hire Hamish had ever made. He had no business running a classroom and quickly alienated students and faculty alike. Short and squat, with a round face and wire-rimmed glasses that gave him an owlish demeanor, Hahnemann arrived with a sterling set of references from a string of junior colleges but no experience teaching middle school children. His first act was to institute multiple-choice tests so difficult no one in Libby's class could earn even a B. Most failed.

Students complained to their houseparents, who pleaded with Hamish to intercede. Following the third test in a row where no one received a score above sixty, Hamish began fielding calls from distressed parents, demanding to know why their children had suddenly become so inept.

Hamish routinely granted each teacher a great deal of latitude in how they ran their classroom, and he resisted the urge to step in. But after learning of several incidents where Hahnemann had publicly embarrassed students for their supposed stupidity, Hamish decided to sit in to see for himself.

"I expect you found my talk illuminating," Hahnemann said after his students had filed out.

"We don't tend to lecture eighth graders," Hamish said evenly. There had been no discussion. Zero engagement. "You know your subject well. That is apparent. But I did expect more interactions. More discussion. A question or two. Perhaps their test performances are a reflection of the fact you are delivering the material in too sophisticated a manner."

"Coddling them will not prepare them for the next level. I challenge them, and that's what you pay me to do. Am I correct?"

It was obvious to Hamish that his new hire was uninterested in any advice or mentoring. A few days later, after more humiliations of his fellow students and the prospect of another impossible test the next morning, Tracy decided to take matters into his own hands. Following class, he waited for Hahnemann to head for the teacher's lounge to get coffee, as was his habit. Tracy grabbed a classmate who had been ridiculed and asked him to stand watch while Tracy slipped back into the room. Under the desk at the front of the class he found Hahnemann's briefcase. Inside was a grading book, a copy of the next day's test, and an answer sheet. Tracy ignored the test, inking the letter for each correct answer on his forearm. He replaced the papers into the briefcase and hurried out of the room just as his confederate warned him Hahnemann was coming. "Hi Richard," Tracy said nonchalantly as the man shuffled down the hall, a steaming mug in one hand, his head buried in a copy of *Foreign Affairs* magazine. "Great class, as always."

"Glad you were paying attention for a change, Barcomb. A bit more studying tonight and maybe you'll manage a D this time. That should raise your average."

Tracy felt bile start to rise from his stomach but resisted the urge to give a smartass response. "If I get an A, will you give us a week off from tests?" he challenged.

Hahnemann thought for a moment. "An A? All the way to an A? Tell you what. For every A the class earns I'll eliminate one test going forward. But for every D or below I'll add one more. Deal?"

"Deal!" Tracy said, instantly worried his classmates would kill him if he couldn't figure a way to get them the answers without *somebody* getting caught.

And then it came to him.

Down the stairs to the art room he bounded. Libby was in her usual seat, painting a watercolor and chatting with Tina Sherman.

"I need your help," Tracy whispered to Tina, pulling her out of her chair to be assured no one overheard their conversation. Libby was too absorbed in her work to notice. And she rarely noticed Tracy under any circumstance. Tina was one of the few girls at Glencoe who tolerated Tracy's style. She would help, Tracy was certain.

Tina's eyes widened as he explained the problem, furtively rolling up his sleeve to expose the series of blue letters on his arm. "Should we get Libby to help?" she asked.

Tracy shrugged. "She hates my guts. Not sure we can trust her."

Tina nodded in agreement. "Okay. I'll handle it. Get me some colored paper and scissors."

Over the next hour Tracy and Tina tried to puzzle out how to hide the test answers in plain sight. When they had finally decided what to do, they cut out letters in blue, red, green, and black paper, connecting them with string. The resulting banner described the challenge Hahnemann had proposed.

An A today subtracts one test
A D or F means another exam
So cram and study hard as you can
Be smart and always do your best

Libby finished her painting and noticed her roommate and their housemate huddled at a far table. It was unusual to see Tracy in the art room, so she walked over to satisfy her curiosity. "What is this bizarre thing?" The language was clumsy. Awful. What was the point?

Tracy looked at Tina with concern. *Do we dare tell her?* he tried to communicate telepathically. Both girls were suffering the same bad grades as Tracy in Hahnemann's class. *Maybe she'll be grateful I'm trying to do something to fix it*, he thought.

Tina made the decision for them. "Tracy has an idea how we can end Hahnemann's testing crap." She pointed to the red letters in their banner; all were either A, B, C, or D. There were 20 of them, interspersed among the other colored letters. Then she made Tracy roll up his sleeve to reveal the matching answers. Libby's eyes got wide.

"That's cheating! You both are okay with this?"

"You know the class is a disaster. He insults us and gives us college-level tests. We don't deserve to be treated like that," Tina said. "I'm good with this."

Tracy was grateful for her support. Contemplating cheating was not something he took lightly. After all, his mom was doing that wilderness ethics bit for her PhD. She had schooled him since he could talk on the importance of doing the right things for the right reasons, for the environment and in life. She would be disappointed in him, he was sure.

Libby chuckled. "Tracy, you must be the second coming of Till Eulenspiegel."

"Who?"

"Till Eulenspiegel. He was a fourteenth-century German jester who traveled around Europe making pompous people look foolish. Somebody wrote a children's book about him and my parents used to read it to me when I was little. It was actually clever. Look him up—I'll give you the spelling. This sounds like the kind of thing Till would do. He got run out of a lot of towns, so be careful you don't get caught."

They walked to Hahnemann's empty classroom and taped the banner next to the whiteboard. Before dinner, Tracy and Tina gave each class member a heads-up on how to beat the test and warned them not to divulge anything, for they were bound to be questioned later. Each student was assigned a number, which represented the red letter in the list that they should *not* answer correctly. Tracy explained that he wanted no perfect tests and no identical ones. There should be no evidence they were copying off each other's papers—which was technically true.

The following morning, after reading the poorly worded message, Hahnemann commented that whoever had made the silly sign ought to take English as a second language. Then he distributed the most difficult test he had yet designed, impatient to score the papers and prove to the class they had yet to hit rock bottom and needed to apply themselves more diligently.

After ten minutes, however, each student had answered the twenty questions, handed in the test, and walked out confidently. The next morning, Hahnemann, subdued and puzzled, distributed their papers without comment. Every result was a 95. Each had one wrong answer and no two papers had the same wrong answer.

"How'd we do?" Tracy crowed, unable to control himself. "I see a lot of 95s! That means no more tests for the rest of the semester, right Richard?" He could tell Hahnemann was seething, his eyes glued to his grade book. Tracy knew the man did not like to be called by his given name. Hahnemann had mentioned once that he considered it disrespectful, but he grudgingly accepted it as the norm at Glencoe.

"I congratulate all of you," Hahnemann mumbled. "Clearly, you did something different to earn these grades." Everyone understood this was not meant to be a compliment, that he meant they had managed something underhanded. As soon as class ended, Hahnemann marched down to Hamish's office and stood in the doorway.

"We've got a class full of cheaters, and I expect you to get to the bottom of it, sir."

"Oh? How do you know?"

Hahnemann explained that the results were all the evidence he needed. This was the first time in his long tenure that Hamish had to deal with a suspicion of widespread cheating. Had it happened to any other teacher Hamish would have been furious. But in this case his first thought was relief that such extraordinary grades meant a cessation of calls from irate parents. He was not enthusiastic about investigating the incident to a level that would satisfy Hahnemann but he did perfunctory interrogations with each member of the class and learned nothing.

Following winter break, Hamish revisited Hahnemann's past record and, after several pointed phone calls, determined that the glowing recommendations accompanying Hahnemann's application had been concocted by his previous employers to facilitate his departure from their schools. Hamish decided to cut his losses and let the man go after one semester. The cheating incident was never spoken of again.

. . .

"I've felt guilty about that ever since," Libby admitted after she had recounted the salient details to Christine. "It wasn't right, even if he was a bastard to us." She knew she should not use that kind of language with her teacher but somehow the past hour of sharing uncomfortable personal truths had made her feel a closeness that gave her license.

"He was not my favorite human being," Christine admitted. "And certainly wasn't a good fit here. I'm glad he left. But you're right. You did cross a line that should not be crossed." Then she smiled. "Pretty damn clever, though. Till Eulenspiegel, huh? I'll have to look that one up."

Dancing with the Devil

RAMON WAS CATALOGING AND SHELVING BOXES OF USED BOOKS THAT had been donated to the prison when he felt a huge paw clamp down on his shoulder. "Hey, bro. Sure is easy duty you're doing here. I was wondering if you could point me in the direction of a good book on prison escapes," Garth LeGrange said, deadpan.

"You want what?" Ramon asked, taking a step away. *Why*, he wondered, *do these monsters keep finding me?*

"You heard me. I'm fixin' to break out and wanted to get some pointers from an expert. Can you help me, or do I have to go talk to the librarian?"

"Why are you playin' with me?"

Garth sighed. "Entertainment. Don't you ever get bored with this place?"

"You know the answer to that," Ramon said. "I never see you in the library. You lookin' to me for somethin'?"

"My intentions are honorable," Garth said, stretching his arms out wide. "I heard you been having some tough calls with folks at home. I just wanted to see how you're doin' and if I can help."

"Thanks, but I got it under control," Ramon said, hoping to end the conversation. In truth, his recent calls back home had not provided any relief. Miguel was healing slowly but it was touch and go whether he would need to wear a colostomy bag for the rest of his life thanks to damaged intestines from the knife attack. At least his mother was home, though she hadn't been able to resume work for those rich folks uptown. "I don't need your help," Ramon added.

"The hell you don't," Garth said, both massive arms now resting on Ramon's shoulders like a pair of anvils. It was hard for Ramon to take his eyes off the ugly scar that dominated the man's face. It resembled an axe or hatchet, seemingly too distinct to be an accident. He realized to shrug off the man's arms was going to escalate things fast. He would have to talk his way out.

"Look, man. I got no trouble with you. I got a sick mom and an injured brother. I'll figure it out."

Ramon wanted to say *It's none of your business* but thought better of it. Garth turned his head and spat a load of tobacco juice onto the floor, just missing Ramon's face. *What is it about me,* Ramon wondered, *that attracts all these bullies?* It was clear that whatever insane idea Garth LeGrange might offer, Ramon knew he should avoid it. In two months he might be out of prison if the parole board gave him a break, legally back with his family.

"I'm just trying to help a brother out," Garth said. "We are both in here for shameful reasons, I bet," Garth added. "That makes us brothers in my eyes. If we don't help each other, who will?"

Help? Each other? Don't fall for this crap, Ramon thought. He had avoided Garth LeGrange during his time at the ACF after receiving a piece of advice from a sympathetic corrections officer the first week of his incarceration.

. . .

"Watch out for that one," the CO warned. "He's as rough as we get around here. I have a couple of false teeth to prove it. I went to high school with the bastard. Trust me, I know what I'm talking about."

"Why you telling me this?" Ramon asked.

"You look like a good kid. LeGrange chews your kind up and spits them out. Don't let him notice you if you know what's good for you."

. . .

"Tough being here when you're needed there, huh?" Garth commiserated.

Ramon sighed. "You got that right. It's frustrating. What am I gonna do? They don't give weekend passes, do they?"

"Maybe we should talk. I might have an idea or two, Jack," Garth said. "When you've enough of this shit come talk to me."

Ramon realized his fists were clenched. He thought again of Pablo's pleading voice, his aunt's hysteria. His family was in shambles. He knew in his heart the odds were good he'd be denied parole the first time. If it turned out he had to serve the remaining sixteen months what would even be left at home to return to? Maybe he owed it to his mother and Miguel to listen to what LeGrange had in mind, though every fiber told him not to.

Over the course of the next two weeks Ramon called home several more times, maxing out his monthly allotment of time. He became increasingly anxious there would not be food on the table if their mother didn't get better soon. The family was circling the drain while he was doing nothing to prevent it. Against his better judgment, he reluctantly sought out Garth at dinner one evening.

"Haven't seen too much of you lately. Where you been hiding, Jack?" Garth asked, sliding over to make room for Ramon at his table. In truth, Ramon had been studiously avoiding the man.

"Mostly studying in the library," Ramon offered.

"How's news from home?"

"Not a whole lot better. I thought maybe we could talk about that thing you mentioned the other week."

Garth's face creased a satisfied smile, revealing sparkling teeth, despite the chaw of tobacco. "Maybe we could. After this shitty meal come on back to my cell where we can talk."

With the memory of Pablo's shaky voice still lingering, Ramon warily sat down on Garth's bunk, the giant hovering above him. Instinct told Ramon this would not end well, but he was desperate to get back to the city before his family crumbled. Facing a set of bad choices, Ramon decided there was no harm in listening.

"What I'm about to tell you stays between us, right?" Garth asked sharply.

Ramon nodded. He did not need to be scared into keeping quiet. There were advantages to having Garth as an ally in this place. It meant protection from the Mercados of the world, though no one at ACF, save Garth himself, came close to instilling the kind of fear in Ramon that Hector Mercado had achieved.

"I've put in enough time at this place," Garth said quietly. "I don't see the value in sticking around as long as I'm supposed to. Got places to go, a life to lead that doesn't include bars and guards. I've fucking had it with this place, and I bet you've got better places to be, too."

"You seriously plan to break out?" Ramon said with sincere surprise. "How does that happen, exactly?"

"It's not as hard as they want you to believe, Jack. Look, this as a win-win deal for both of us. You get to spend a few less days in this hellhole and get home as quick as possible. The thing of it is, I get to split this country and make a new start someplace where they don't know every mistake I ever made. I figure you're the right guy to kick this thing into gear, eh?"

"Why is it you need me?"

"I got a foolproof plan. But I need another guy to make it work. I need somebody who's tough enough to hang in the woods with me for a time. The stupidest move is to get on the highway right off. They'll be blocking every route for miles. There's not a chance in hell we could avoid 'em all. No, the plan is to chill for a bit 'til they got better things to do. With all those troopers looking for us, speeding tickets don't get written, drunk drivers don't get stopped. It's a disaster for the villages around here. They count on the cash coming in from fines and penalties and shit. We tie up the state police for a few weeks, the politicians start feeling the pinch, then they get to whining. After a while, the cops write us off and then we waltz right outta here."

Ramon wasn't sure what all that meant but it sounded like Garth had thought this through. He was a woodsman, there was no doubt about that. And he was certainly familiar with the territory, having grown up locally. Ramon knew all about that from the CO who had warned him about Garth that first week.

"I got buddies on the outside happy to set this up when I say 'Jump.' I'm not going into all the details but if we're on the same page, Jack, I'll put this thing into gear. You ever been camping?"

Ramon thought back to a weekend or two he'd spent in the Catskills with other kids in his neighborhood who belonged to the Boys' Club. He remembered long bus rides, lousy food, chilly nights around a campfire listening to scary stories, and sleepless nights on cold ground in thin sleeping bags whose zippers didn't zip. The woods were foreign places to a boy from the Lower East Side.

"A couple times," Ramon said. "In the summer." He thought of the increasingly chilly evenings as fall deepened. "How long we gonna need to be out there? And why don't you just take off by yourself?"

"So many questions," Garth said. "That's okay. I need you to be all in or it'll just be a problem for both of us. The woods around here are home to me and I can make sure it's comfortable for you, too. I'll be honest. If we want the cops to lose interest we have to be prepared to hide out for a couple of weeks, anyways. And that means carrying more gear than even I can manage. Between the two of us we got this. They figure we dead or gone, they go back to normal policing, we head our own way. The trick is, knowing where to hide out and having the right stuff to do it. That's where I know how to make it work." Garth moved from the cell door and sat down beside Ramon on the bed. Ramon flinched as the lumberjack moved closer.

In low tones, Garth attempted to close the deal. "You and me, we can do this. I got the know-how. I'm betting you got the strength to keep up. You're small, but not a weenie. I seen you lifting weights, you're no pussy. Thing of it is, I could have left a long time ago, but the way I got it figured, it'll take two to make this work smooth. I just haven't found the right guy 'til now."

Against his better judgment, Ramon was warming to the idea. It was partly the adventure, but mostly his blind ambition to get home that made him keep asking questions instead of turning his back on the scheme. "You haven't said how we'd pull this off. We're not digging tunnels, are we?"

Garth laughed. "Not hardly. We'll practically walk right out of here. You'll see. And then we're in my backyard. I've spent my whole life in the woods around here. I'll find places in Canada like this, no problem. If I hadn't screwed everything up my whole life, I'd be happy just cutting logs in the Adirondack Park the rest of my days. Find some sweet young thing, maybe a schoolteacher or a nurse, settle down in one of these little mountain towns, raise a couple of brats and teach 'em what it takes to live off the land like I done. Not a bad life. Now I'll just have to do it a little farther north."

It struck Ramon that Garth had probably never voiced these regrets, hopes, or dreams to anyone. He had unwittingly unlocked a vault Garth had never opened.

"That's still how I hope my story ends," Garth continued. "But I guess it's gonna have to happen in Canada." He paused for a moment. It seemed to Ramon that his coconspirator was lost in the vision of what a future in a faraway place might really look like. "Here's what I need you to do, kid. You're still on library duty, right?"

"Uh huh."

"Get off it. Say you got some allergy to book dust or something. I dunno. Be creative. Tell 'em you'll do anything else. You need fresh air. You're willing to do the highway crew. That's hard work and they're always losing guys who get sick or blisters. Whatever. They'll be surprised you want to give up shelving books for clearing brush, but that's where I need you to be, okay?"

"That's how we get out of this place? Clearing brush?"

"Get yourself on that crew . . . and soon. We don't want to be hidin' out in the woods all winter. I'll take care of the rest."

14

A Director's Challenge

WHEN TRACY FOUND EVEN HIS DREAMS WERE BEING HIJACKED BY MAL-colm Dandridge, he decided it was time to take action. The chicken manure caper had already entered Glencoe lore, a tale to be handed down to each incoming class of students, right alongside the one where some-one had tied all the student doorknobs to each other so none could get out of their room, or the one where someone had led a goat up the stairs into a dorm room while the occupants slept, then pulled the fire alarm to freak out the animal. Rarely did a day pass that someone failed to remind Tracy of his humiliation.

Rehearsals of *The Truth about Zeus* were becoming increasingly stressful as Ron continued to tweak the script, forcing the kids to forget what they'd learned and memorize new revisions. Whenever it was Tra-cy's turn to speak, Malcolm stopped whatever he was doing backstage to pay attention in hopes his nemesis would forget the revisions, spout the older lines, and incur the wrath of the director. Each misstep was a precious needle Malcolm used to prick his classmate.

Instead of twenty-six children, Jake's Zeus had forty-six off-spring—not coincidentally equivalent to the number of High Peaks in the Adirondacks. One of his favorites, Hermes, became God of Purses. Helen of Troy became Helen of Albany, a neighboring town to Troy in upstate New York.

But those were all sidebars to the main theme, which involved one of Zeus's more inscrutable sexual conquests. When Zeus was informed that the most beautiful boy in the land lived in Albany (not Troy), he decided to kidnap Ganymede, played by Tracy. Disguised as an eagle, Zeus flew him to the summit of Mount Marcy, (not Olympus). There, he anointed Ganymede as Chief Maple Sap Bucket Supervisor, responsible for all the maple syrup production in the North Country. Zeus mesmerized the young lad, who is overwhelmed with the attention the king of the gods showered upon him.

The most blatant borrowing Ron did was to insert lyrics from the Cole Porter song *From This Moment On*, which had been created for the Broadway show *Out of This World*, but was dropped during rehearsals, only to become famous in the 1953 film, *Kiss Me Kate*. Part of the fun for Ron was listening to a modern-day teenager, playing an ancient God, mouth such unmodern lyrics. But in the end, recognizing his audience, he excised the third stanza as a bit too risqué, replacing it with more innocuous lines of his own making.

During one evening rehearsal, while Tracy was backstage preparing to make an entrance, he heard a shout, then watched Malcolm hurtle as if shot by a cannon from the equipment room where he had been untangling spotlight cables. Two members of the "Greek Chorus" snickered as Malcolm rushed past, eyes wide as high beams. Tracy collared the two sixth graders and led them to a quiet corner.

"What's up with Mal?"

"Guess he found 'em," shrugged one, winking at his friend.

"Found what?" Tracy pressed.

"Snakes," the second boy said simply.

"What snakes? There aren't any snakes in there."

"Whatever," smirked the first, poking his collaborator in the stomach.

"Give it up," Tracy demanded, squeezing the arm of one boy.

"Hey, cool it, Tracy, it was just a joke. Since when is he like your best friend?" Tracy squeezed harder. "Okay, okay. Ease up. They're just rubber pythons my cousin sent me. We wrapped 'em around the spotlights so Malcolm would find 'em. He's scared shitless of snakes." The boy squirmed out of Tracy's hold and ran to the adjoining room to collect his trophies. He returned in an instant, proudly displaying two very lifelike rubber snakes.

"How'd you know?"

"He won't go near the terrarium in the Science Room. He can't stand those garter snakes we captured near the duck pond. He acts big and all that, but he's such a weenie. Please don't tell him we did it!"

"Your secret's safe with me," Tracy assured them, his mind already hard at work crystallizing an idea that would even the score once and for all. Silently thanking the boys, he stepped confidently onstage to present his lines. Retribution was right around the corner.

"What's with the shit-eating grin?" Jake whispered, as Tracy entered stage left with a huge smile.

"Hello?!!" snapped Ron, staring stilettos at Tracy from behind his piano. "This is a dramatic scene, Ganymede. You're about to deliver the bad news the maple syrup has been poisoned, right? Zeus is about to chew you up and spit you out. Make you come back on your knees to apologize so he doesn't toss you to the wolves. This does not call for happy face."

"Sorry, Ron. I'm just in a good mood. I'll refocus," Tracy promised.

"You're weird," Jake muttered. "Let's do this."

"Okay. Try that entrance again, Tracy. Your face tells the story. Make it convincing. You want Zeus to continue to shower you with favors, not slings and arrows."

"Got it."

The rehearsal continued, but it was clear to the actors as well as to Ron that Tracy's head was elsewhere. He knew his lines; Tracy always knew his lines. As Hamish discovered earlier that fall, Tracy could recite lines from the previous year with no prompting. But as he ran through Ganymede's part that evening it was a perfunctory effort. It completely threw Jake off his game as well. Cues were missed and songs were sung in a lackadaisical manner. Finally, Ron called an early end to the misery, wolfing down several antacid tablets to calm his turbulent insides.

He found Tracy as the kids were exiting the auditorium. "Tomorrow after class I'd like us to take a walk and figure out where we're going with this show. I'll meet you at your locker and we'll spend the afternoon sorting this out, okay?"

"Umm. Steve asked me to help him with the orienteering course he is setting out for the sixth grade."

"Forget that. Steve's a big boy. He can handle it on his own. I'll speak to him later. At your locker tomorrow at three."

"Yes sir," Tracy said obediently.

Glencoe's three-hundred-acre campus was mostly wooded, criss-crossed with trails the faculty and maintenance crew had laid out over the years. Some were primarily for horseback rides, others to facilitate the placement of taps and tubes in hundreds of sugar maples.

Maple syrup production was a big deal at Glencoe, and it required hours of preparatory work from staff and students alike. Taps had to be in the trees before the ice was off the lake or precious sap would be lost as it coursed up the trunk from root to canopy. Trees needed to be felled, sawed, aged, and split to feed the wood-fired evaporator that produced the precious product. Much of the sap was collected without human intervention; it ran downhill through thin plastic tubes connecting taps to collection tanks near the sugarhouse. But the old-school method of hanging tin buckets from individual taps was still used to give students the experience of seeing clear sap dripping from the trunk, tasting its ever-so-faint sweetness, and marveling at the transformation of sap to syrup during the boiling process.

Only ninth graders were invited to stay up past bedtime with Steve Jacobs, the teacher who managed the sugaring operation, to make the finished product. Each night of boiling season a pair of students were invited to experience the ritual. During afternoon work jobs when Tracy and Jake were splitting logs, they often talked about what a kick it would be, to lounge in the ancient Adirondack chairs in front of the roaring fire beneath the labyrinthine tin evaporator, swapping stories by lantern light, waiting for the sap to boil. Tracy knew the basic process from the minor operation his dad had set up on their farm. But this was big-time compared to what they did at home:

1. Feed the beast with wood to keep the heat steady;

2. As the river of sap in the narrow metal channels of the evaporator bubbles up, threatening to overflow its banks, touch that flow with a bit of butter at the end of a stick to break up the surface foam;

3. Open the tap at the lowest channel of the evaporator when the liquid reaches its desired consistency, as measured by a hydrometer dropped into the fluid;

4. Pour a wee sample into a small glass vial;

5. Hold it up to the light and compare its hue to a palette of colors on a time-worn cardboard sheet to identify its proper grade;

6. Fill the pint, quart, and gallon jugs with the golden fluid and seal them tight;

7. Finally, mark the jugs with the proper grade and stack them in cardboard boxes;

8. Repeat the process with fresh sap.

For Tracy and Jake, it was a religious experience.

. . .

Peak foliage color generally graces the Adirondacks in early October. Thousands travel to the area to marvel at the symphony of change before the onset of winter. One of the factors keeping Ron Handy at Glencoe all those years was his love of taking walks on the lake trail during those few weeks when the display was most vivid. Though he favored taking those walks alone, the path also served a useful purpose for heart-to-hearts with students in need, as he was doing now with Tracy, as he had done with Scotty Morrison years before. Orchestrating so many young amateur actors and musicians to pull in the same direction was no easy task and such a walk seemed a useful prescription to get one of this year's stars back on track.

As Tracy and Ron topped the hill overlooking the lake, deserted save for two loons diving for supper in a sheltered cove, the brilliance of the view gave them pause. The sweep of color from woods in metamorphosis demanded acknowledgment.

"This never gets old for me. I'm inspired every year," Ron exclaimed. "Perhaps the most important lesson I've ever taught children here is to lift their eyes. We're generally so focused on our next steps we neglect to look up and see the beauty above us. You miss so much when you keep your head down. It's a simple thing."

They began to descend a grassy hill toward the water below, rippling in the soft breeze. In winter, it was a spectacular take-off point for sledding when the ice on the lake was thick. But that was still months off; this Indian summer afternoon was warm enough for shirtsleeves, and to keep native birds in the neighborhood a bit longer before their winter migration.

Tracy stopped in mid-stride at the call of a familiar bird. "That's gotta be a white-throated sparrow, right? That song is so distinctive. My first year here, when we took a house overnight to one of the lean-tos on the other side of the lake—it seemed so far away at the time—I remember hearing that when we went to sleep. It was really comforting to a kid with terrible homesickness. I'll always recognize it."

"You nailed the second most important lesson I teach at this place, Tracy. The first is to look up; the second is to listen. That birdsong, so clear, plaintive, is the sound I also associate with the Adirondacks. Some say it sounds like Old Sam Peabody, Peabody, Peabody," he crooned. "Others think it's more like My Sweet Canada, Canada, Canada. One of the great joys of springtime is to hear that pure tune again each year."

They had reached the shore and picked up the trail, coated with fallen pine needles in some places, soon to be fully covered in leaves after the next heavy rain. Even now, with each wind gust, a few early travelers fluttered down from the canopies about their heads.

Coming in the other direction was another student-teacher pair—Christine Mason and Libby Goldman—heads down, swiveling, looking for something.

"Looks like neither one of them has absorbed my Greatest Lesson Number One," Ron chuckled.

"Hi, Ron. Tracy," said Christine. "Putting in some extra rehearsal time?"

"Lord knows he needs it," Ron muttered.

"Whatcha looking for?" Tracy asked his housemate. Seeing her walk toward him on the trail made him feel something he couldn't put into words; a feeling of inadequacy and longing. "Mushrooms?"

"I'm trying to find the most beautiful, undamaged, leaves for an art project I'm doing. Christine was nice enough to help me on her afternoon off," Libby said, smiling at her teacher. The plastic bag Libby was carrying was already fairly bulging with iridescent yellow and burnt-orange leaves.

"Just two colors?" Tracy asked with true interest. "What's the project?"

"I'm trying to replicate something Andy Goldsworthy does," Libby said. "You probably have no idea who I'm talking about."

"He doesn't," Ron said with a twinkle. "But I do. Explain it to him. He can be stretched a little, culturally."

Libby patiently described how the British artist repurposed simple products of the natural world, like sticks, stones, and leaves, to make temporary works of art that would disintegrate soon after their creation, but not before he would take brilliant pictures of them. Their beauty was ephemeral, seen in the wild by a lucky few, but memorialized in coffee-table art books for the world to enjoy.

"I'm going to use water to 'glue' these leaves together in shapes and patterns that will make you ooh and ahh," Libby said, smiling. "I'll lay them out against a totally different background in the woods someplace, maybe by a stream, with no competing colors. Then take photos and make a display. I have to get the leaves while they still have lots of color."

"I'm sure it will be spectacular," Ron said. "Good luck!"

"I suppose I should know this, Ron," Tracy said a few minutes after parting ways with the other two. "When Libby was talking about her leaf project, I realized I've never understood what makes fall colors."

Ron was silent for a moment. He had purposely asked Tracy on this walk to change the boy's attitude about the musical, to persuade him to take it more seriously, to channel Tracy's natural charisma in a way that would positively impact the other actors. There had already been one distraction on this walk, and Ron realized there was yet another tangent to be tackled.

"I'm a music teacher, not a biologist," Ron said, with a chuckle. "But I know it's a matter of sunlight and sugar. As I understand it, and I may be giving you more information than you really want . . . but I *am* a teacher after all . . . as the nights get longer in the fall, chlorophyll gradually stops being produced in the leaves. That reduces sugar, which is what keeps the leaves green. Once that happens, the curtain is lifted, to use a theater analogy, and the true colors of the leaves are revealed."

"The leaves really are a different color to begin with? The green is just a mask?"

"I believe that's the case. The amount of color depends on how much sun and rain occur during the fall, too. But check with Steve Jacobs. He may have a much more accurate explanation."

Ron and Tracy traveled halfway around the lake before the music teacher got to the point of the walk. "It's a glorious place, Tracy; especially, this time of year. You may have noticed I get a bit anxious as show-time gets closer, and I know you can't be enjoying me snapping at you."

"I guess I deserve it sometimes."

"You and Jake are the anchors that hold this production together, and the reason I asked you to join me is to make sure you and I are on the same page. Tracy, I'm counting on you. Jake's not on this walk because he already gets it. He's really serious about his role in making this successful. To be frank, you need to be as committed as he is, or we're in trouble. And my stomach can't take that."

"I love doing your shows."

"And you're damn good in them, or I wouldn't keep casting you. But I'm getting too old to play mind games with my leading boys and girls. You'd be doing us all a favor if you could leave the potty mouthing you and Malcolm engage in at the stage door. I know you may feel it's innocent fun but it distracts everyone else and we don't have time for that anymore."

"It's not fun for me, Ron," Tracy said. "He just gets under my skin and I have a hard time just letting it roll off. Did you talk to him, too?"

"If I must. I'm appealing to you first. Makes you think about our own masks, doesn't it?"

"Our own masks?"

"Yes. Think about the leaves, that the green masks their true colors. Do our faces reflect who we really are? Or do they mask someone else?

I wonder what's behind Malcolm's mask? Maybe it's worth your while trying to get a peek."

Ron could see he had touched a nerve. Tracy was clearly thinking about the concept.

"Look, Tracy, help me help you be as great in this as you were as Falstaff last year. Make this childish behavior stop. Please."

"I'm sorry. I'll try harder."

But Tracy just could not let it go. At least not yet.

15

Mountain Misadventure

COUNTING THE ACTORS, ORCHESTRA, STAGE CREW, AND SET DESIGNERS, Ron's production required the participation of a significant percentage of the student body. While coordinating it all was a definite strain on the director, it was no accident that so many were involved. Throughout the school year there were many activities designed to include as many students as possible. Some were simply for fun, like the all-school ski outings to nearby Whiteface Mountain. Others were in keeping with the philosophy that students should share responsibility for keeping the place thriving. Those activities, like harvesting potatoes in the fields beyond the greenhouses, or humanely slaughtering and plucking chickens when it was time—which generated a high percentage of new, albeit temporary, vegetarians—may not have been the most popular, but they helped bond the community more profoundly than could any Friday night football game.

The Saturday following Ron's lake walk with Tracy dawned cool and clear, ideal for such a school-wide community activity. To fulfill their responsibility as stewards of a two-mile stretch of highway adjacent to school property, Glencoe students and faculty were to collect roadside trash.

Hamish's decree brought the usual undercurrent of groans. Although Glencoe students were accepting of the school's long-standing commitment to public service, as modern-day adolescents it was their duty to voice some displeasure at being recruited to perform manual labor; they fervently upheld their end of the bargain. Since the school's inception, all manner of chores and community service had been a staple of the program, as important as the academic curriculum. From the beginning, Glenn Stallings and Susan Coe made their expectations clear. There would be no maple sugaring in the spring unless everyone pitched in to split the wood the previous fall. There would be no skating on the duck pond if no one cleared the ice of snow. There would be no downhill skiing or jumping on the ski hill behind the school if students didn't sidestep their way up for the first run to tamp down fresh powder. No SnoCats at Glencoe. Work was simply a part of how an intertwined farm and school community functioned; no job was beyond the capabilities of its students who came to understand, if not always appreciate, what it took to make things work.

As everyone filtered out of the dining room to collect jackets, gloves and hiking boots from the large mudroom down the hall, Tracy stopped briefly at his cluttered cubby, overflowing with soccer garb, lacrosse sticks and assorted water bottles, bandannas, and baseball caps to grab his nylon day pack. Like salmon swimming upstream he bucked the traffic of students heading for the doors, making his way to the nearest stairwell. Assured that no one had seen him enter the Science Room, he quickly fulfilled his quest and only three minutes later was back at his locker, where Jake was waiting impatiently.

"Where'd you disappear to? Got better things to do than wait for your ass all morning."

"Sorry, Jake. Quick dump." He grinned, then swung his backpack over his shoulder, feeling a thump as the glass jar inside knocked against his shoulder blade. The two boys headed toward the door, passing close to Malcolm's locker, where the stocky boy sat wrestling new hiking boots onto his feet. Unable to restrain himself, Tracy reached into Malcolm's locker, slipping the boy's denim barn jacket off its hook and dropping it over his head.

The predictable stream of invectives belched out from beneath the jacket. "I should have smelled you coming, peckerhead," he growled, heaving the closest thing at hand, which happened to be someone else's math book from an adjoining cubby. Jake hooked Tracy's arm in an attempt to hustle him out of the building before things got out of hand, but Tracy slipped the grip.

"Come on, would ya?" Jake implored. "Leave this turkey be."

"Yeah, go with your boyfriend, Ganymede," Malcolm sneered.

"Hey, watch your mouth, bud," Jake warned, wagging a finger in his face. Then Pete Hedges stuck his head in the door and defused the situation with a simple "Last one out gets to unload the truck."

The boys hustled out of the locker area and caught up to Pete. Tracy walked beside him, matching his stride as if in military lockstep. Pete led most of the more challenging hikes. Tracy and Pete had spent considerable time together on those weekend challenges and shared an easy familiarity.

"Hey, Pete. Was that your T-shirt Christine was wearing the other day?" he teased. "Did you trade off or something?" Pete threw an elbow in Tracy's direction, cuffing him playfully in the ear.

"Ow!"

"You have a point to make, sport? Or are you just trying to add me to the growing list of people who'd like to see the sewers of Jakarta back up into your breakfast?"

"I'm supposed to understand why that's funny?" Tracy challenged, then turned his attention to the milling crowd that had gathered outside the gym to await instructions. He spotted Malcolm and steered him out of earshot of the others.

"I'll bet you your Saturday-night ice cream you can't keep up with me hiking up Balanced Rocks," Tracy sneered, pointing to the top of the nearby mountain Malcolm had struggled up to hear Pete Hedges's geology lecture his first week at school.

"I hate that place," Malcolm retorted. "But I'm happy to take your ice cream."

"After we're done with the highway cleanup. Just you and me."

Tracy could see the wheels turning in Malcolm's head. Was this a setup? Tracy was counting on two factors that would prevent Malcolm from turning his back on it. He wouldn't want to give Tracy any reason to call him a coward and might see an opportunity to prove his nemesis wrong. Tracy knew there was more risk in this caper than he should be taking, but it was so tempting to take care of the bully once and for all. If they got caught, however, he figured there was a good shot Hamish would kick them both out. For a fleeting second he thought back to the day his family had dropped him off back in September, when his parents had encouraged him to make the most of this year. Was teaching the sonovabitch who had ruined his boots a lesson he would not soon forget worth the risk? He knew the answer but that did not get in his way.

"Nobody'll notice," Tracy said, mind-reading Malcolm's hesitation. "We'll be back before dinner, unless you're even a worse hiker than I think you are. Jake and I do it all the time to keep in shape," he lied. "Let's see if those slick boots of yours actually work on rock, not just a stupid highway."

After sweeping both sides of the road for two hours, Hamish motioned for the crews to make one last deposit of garbage from the burlap gunny sacks they carried into the back of the trailing pick-up. When the last load had been dumped and the truck was on its way to the transfer station in Lake Placid, the headmaster announced they would all eat lunch together on a picturesque isthmus, a small strip of land that bifurcated the two Cascade Lakes. Tracy had mistakenly assumed he could persuade Malcolm to sneak off during lunch. He counted on having enough time to get up and down Balanced Rocks and back to school without running the risk of missing dinner, during which their absence would be noticed. As students and teachers strolled down to the nearby lunch spot Tracy calculated they could still make it, but now the margin of error was much smaller. Ironically, considering how mercilessly he had teased Malcolm about his hiking prowess, he had to hope the boy was not as slow as he feared or they would both be in trouble.

The students naturally divided up to eat their bag lunches with friends, largely left alone by the faculty content to settle down in their own groupings. The younger kids, too antsy to simply sit, eat, and converse, began skipping stones into Lower Cascade Lake. The ninth graders sought out a grassy spot facing the Upper Lake, as far as possible from their more boisterous schoolmates. The gorge formed by Cascade Mountain on one side and Pitchoff on the other created a natural wind tunnel, which explained why everyone kept their wool hats and parkas on despite the strong sun.

Sitting with Tina, Jake, and Libby, Tracy wondered if his anxiety was obvious. While his housemates chatted amiably, eating leisurely after the efforts of the morning work, Tracy wolfed down his sandwich and appeared disengaged.

"What's eating you, dude? We worked hard this morning. Enjoy the break," Jake said. "You got a date or something?"

"And who would that be with?" Tina teased.

"Some sixth grader would be about his speed," Libby smirked.

"Pre-boobs? I don't think so," said Tina.

Tracy threw them a withering stare. He was careful to shield his day pack away from the others, worrying what he would say if one of them happened to feel the jar that held the precious cargo he was carrying.

"Sure you're okay? You usually don't take crap from us without a fight," Jake said.

"I'm fine. Just tired, I guess."

After what seemed an interminable amount of time to Tracy, Hamish gave a signal that everyone should collect their things and start to hike back to school via a private trail that cut through the woods. Christine Mason stationed herself at the entrance to the trail, counting heads as they walked by. Tracy trailed Malcolm, walking by himself, as usual, and tapped the boy on his shoulder as they reached an indistinct fork in the trail. "This is it," he said, pointing to the faint path that led away from the route everyone else was following back to school. "Is you in or is you out?" Tracy challenged. Malcolm nodded in agreement. He did not look his usual belligerent self, Tracy thought.

Before long the boys were climbing a steep, rocky trail soon to be laced with the snows of an early winter. Given his weight and the new boots, it was tough for Malcolm to maintain Tracy's pace, but his pride pushed him on.

"Too many pancakes this morning? I doubt you've got enough energy to haul your fat ass up there." The hook was baited; now for the bite.

"Just because I don't waste my time hiking as much as you don't mean I can't keep up," Malcolm huffed. "I'm tasting your ice cream already."

Tracy grinned and picked up the pace. "Here's a chance to prove yourself."

"No . . . problem."

At the base of a steep section of rock, several hundred yards below the open summit where the two gigantic boulders known as the Balanced Rocks lay perched like proverbial bowling balls of the gods, an indistinct side trail cut away from the main track, following the base of the cliffs. Tracy led Malcolm around a bulge of rock. Above them was blue sky and scrub spruce growing determinedly out of the rock.

"Okay, Malcolm, now it gets interesting," Tracy said, scampering crablike directly up open slabs. He turned to see if Malcolm was following, then continued up a long, easy-angled, vertical crack. Here he could walk almost upright, using his hands to steady himself at the few precarious places. The smooth rock looked slick. Melt from morning frost ran from every interstice in the rock. Experience had taught Tracy the friction on the anorthosite slabs would easily hold him despite the exposure.

Malcolm followed tentatively.

Tracy calculated that his speed and experience would give him time to reach an unseen vantage point where he could unfold the next scene in his passion play. If everything worked according to plan, Malcolm would not bother him the rest of the year. Maybe he wouldn't bother anyone else either.

The rock steepened as Tracy worked his way up the crack. After a run of thirty feet or so the fissure ended in a blank wall. Above him and to his right he saw a small outcropping, large enough to sit down. With confidence he left the security of the crack and danced gingerly across the open expanse of pebbly rock, smearing his rubber soles on microscopic rock crystals that kept him from slipping. In ten quick steps he reached the ledge and sat down.

Below, he could hear Malcolm struggling to negotiate the crack. Hidden by the slight overhang, Tracy knew Malcolm would soon appear where the break in the rock came to an end. He unshouldered his backpack and lifted out the jar and its precious contents, taking care to rest it solidly on the ledge. Three garter snakes slithered actively within, reacting to the sudden exposure to light and the chill wind against the glass.

Just then, Malcolm's head poked up. He saw that Tracy had not gotten too far in front, but the expanse of blank rock ahead made him stop.

"How am I supposed to get over to that ledge?" he muttered.

"Say what? You're not whinin' are you, Malcolm? It shouldn't be hard for someone tough enough to put chicken shit in someone else's boots. Just go for it."

Tracy saw a look of recognition crossing Malcolm's face. *You think this is all about embarrassment?* Tracy thought. *That's just the start of it, buddy.*

Locked in a rigid position, Malcolm's legs began to shake involuntarily, a phenomenon known to rock climbers as "sewing machine legs." Tracy knew, watching from above, that a move was necessary before Malcolm lost control. This was not part of the plan. The first hint of doubt crept into Tracy's mind.

"You go on. I think it'll be faster if I go the other way," Malcolm said meekly.

"Don't think so," Tracy called out. "It's a lot tougher going down than it is getting up. Your best bet is to traverse over to me. Come on, you don't have a choice. You can do it."

Taking a deep breath Malcolm stepped tentatively away from the crack and onto the smooth rock, fingertips and toes searching for ridges, eyes glued to the next few inches ahead. His inexperience gave him no context for understanding that the way forward was completely within his capabilities. Adrenaline coursed through his body at the speed of light and fear of shame kept him moving upward.

"There's one thing I forgot to warn you about, Mal," Tracy called as he unscrewed the top from the jar in his lap. Malcolm had gingerly worked his way halfway to Tracy's ledge and was beginning to gain confidence. "This route is full of rattlesnakes and they're real nervous in the sun." He tipped the jar, sending the wriggling garters skidding across the slabs. At the word "snakes" Malcolm looked up and exhaled sharply as the serpents, equally panicked, slithered toward him. Forgetting his precarious position, Malcolm straightened up and took a blind step backward and shrieked. He took another step backward and began a head-over-heels tumble down the slabs, emitting a high-pitched scream that Tracy would never forget.

From his place on the ledge, Tracy watched in horror as Malcolm disappeared. Then came the crunch of breaking branches.

"Goddamn . . ." Tracy held his breath, waiting anxiously for an answer. He heard the wind whistling up from the Cascade Lakes far below. There was nothing else.

"Oh Jesus." He scrambled to his feet and traversed over the slabs to the vertical crack. He could feel his heart beating furiously as he realized the gravity of what he had just done. Leaning forward with one hand gripping the crack, he could see below Malcolm's body, arms and legs akimbo, spread across several stunted spruce at the base of the rock.

"Malcolm . . . Malcolm . . . Oh my God . . ." Tracy whimpered as he half-climbed, half-slid down the crack to Malcolm's resting place. The boy's face, contorted in a grimace, was wet with blood from a gash on the back of his head. Tracy began to sob, reaching out hesitantly, frightened, to touch the boy's jacket. He tugged gently, willing Malcolm to revive, to sit up and sneer at him again, anything to break this awful silence. There was no response.

"Shit. I'm so sorry," he moaned. "Hang on, I'll get help." Tracy left his unconscious companion and bushwhacked through the cripplebrush at the base of the rock until he reached the main trail. Petrified he would not get help in time, he bounded down the steep trail, grabbing at tree branches to maintain his balance until he reached the valley floor, then broke into a jog where the trail permitted. Tracy heard the faint gong of a bell and he knew from the sound that it was time for students in charge of setting tables to head to the dining room. For a split second his mind shifted away from the grisly scene he had just caused and marveled at how that resonant noise, a Pavlovian trigger that pealed fifteen minutes before every meal, could travel such a distance.

Tracy couldn't wipe away the sight of Malcolm's bloody face, vacant of expression. But as he approached Dewey Hall his resolve weakened. How could he describe what had just happened and what his role had been? Though he had never seen a dead body before he was sure Malcolm was close to checking out. Would it do anybody any good to tell the whole story now, before it was clear whether Mal would pull through?

Maybe better to just let things play out. But that's not how he'd been brought up. He had to try to save Malcolm. After all, it was an accident. His brain pulsated, a wave of nausea overwhelmed him, and he vomited.

16

A Life Hangs in the Balance

ANNOUNCING DINNER WAS ABOUT TO BE SERVED, A LITTLE BELL MADE the last of its thrice-a-day runs through the halls of Dewey, ringing in the hand of an earnest fifth grader proud of the responsibility. The Glencoe community filed quietly into the dining hall for the evening meal, fanning out to their assigned tables and standing in silence until Hamish made a move to sit down. One vacant chair remained at Ron Handy's table. He waited a good ten minutes, time enough for the quesadillas to cool before interrupting his own dinner to seek out Malcolm's houseparent for an explanation of the boy's absence. The students at Christine Mason's table ignored Ron's presence, continuing a debate about the prospects of whether more guacamole might be available.

"One of your brood under the weather this evening, Mademoiselle?" Ron asked, a twinkle in his eye.

"Pardonnez moi, monsieur?"

"Malcolm did not grace us with his presence this eventide, so I assumed he was at home recuperating . . . or plotting."

"News to me, Ron," Christine said seriously. She checked her watch as if it held the answer to the mystery. "He didn't come to dinner?"

"No. Did you see him when we did the head count after the road cleanup?"

Christine's cheeks flushed. It was her responsibility to be certain all of the students had left the lunch spot, crossed the road, and started on the trail back to school. She had taken a head count.

"I thought I had everyone. I'm sure I did. I'll run up to the house and check to see if he's there." She excused herself from the table and headed for the door. When she reappeared ten minutes later the dining room held a buzz of anticipation, energy that often preceded Saturday-night ice cream and evening activities. She walked directly to Hamish's table. Normally, she would have simply stated her business, but because of the student involved, she made it clear she preferred to speak with him in private. Hamish stood up and stepped away from the table.

"Malcolm seems to be missing. He didn't come to dinner and he's not up at the house. I was sure I counted everyone before we left the highway but now, I'm not certain. I'm sorry."

"Thank you, Christine. Considering the tight-rope we're all walking with this boy, that's discouraging."

At the next table, Payton Henderson overheard the conversation and caught Hamish's eye. Wordlessly, so as not to draw the attention of the students at his own table, he shifted his gaze toward an empty seat there, as well. *Who?* Hamish mouthed. *Tracy,* Payton responded in kind.

Hamish debated momentarily about the wisdom of getting the whole community involved. Whenever possible, he sought to keep student problems confidential but now it was more important that he learn whatever he could as quickly as possible. He rang the bell for quiet.

"I know you're all itching to get your ice cream and then to enjoy this evening's dance in Marcy Hall. By the way, you have my congratulations on a job well done this afternoon; the highway we have adopted has never looked so presentable. I have already received a thank-you call from the Essex County Department of Public Works. Your effort does not go unnoticed, and it is appreciated." A smattering of applause followed.

"One more thing before you begin clearing the tables for dessert. Was anyone with Malcolm before supper?" Silence. "Who saw him hiking back to school this afternoon?" More silence. "How about Tracy? Anyone with him this afternoon?"

Sitting in the back of the room at Pete's table, Jake looked in Libby's direction, then toward Tina. Neither girl returned his stare.

"Okay, did any of you pick up trash alongside Malcolm or Tracy?"

Three or four hands rose weakly in the air and the whispers began.

At that instant, Tracy walked into the dining hall, clearly out of breath. Hamish took his shoulder, turned him around, and walked him out into the foyer. He did not have to prompt Tracy, who fairly exploded.

"Hamish! There's been a terrible accident."

"Malcolm?"

"Yes," Tracy said, "You missed us?"

Hamish just frowned in response.

"Of course you did," Tracy sighed.

"Where?"

"Balanced Rocks. I know, I know," he said defensively. "We shouldn't have gone on our own but it was just a quick hike after the cleanup and . . . um . . . he fell . . . on the slabs . . . pretty bad."

Hamish was stunned. "You went up there? Just the two of you?" he gasped.

"Uh huh," Tracy answered, eyes to the floor.

"We'll deal with that one later, son. How did you leave him?"

Tracy sighed. "Unconscious. I think he cut his head. I couldn't help him on my own so I got here quick as I could. I'm really sorry."

Though they couldn't hear the conversation through the glass doors that led out to the foyer, it was obvious to anyone looking that Hamish was beside himself. From his body language it seemed like Tracy was trying to bore a hole in the floor to get away while the headmaster gesticulated wildly at him. Jane Henderson finally left her table and went out to see what the haranguing of one of her house members was all about. All eyes in the room followed her.

" . . . absolutely irresponsible, Tracy," Hamish cried as Jane approached. The headmaster turned to her, face crimson. "Malcolm's taken a fall on Balanced Rocks . . . Don't ask . . . I'm going up now. Ask Pete to catch me up as soon as he can pull gear together. Take this boy home before I do something I'll regret." Hamish spun away and headed out into the evening, forcing himself to put his fury aside and think through what he would need to grab from his house to carry up the mountain.

As he hurried to the farmhouse, Hamish scrolled quickly through the contact list on his cell phone. New York State Department of Environmental Conservation Dispatcher Liza Butler answered immediately and listened intently as Hamish breathlessly recounted the salient details of the accident.

"Are you with the individual?" Butler asked.

"No . . . I need to find him . . . I'm on my way."

"You don't know where he is?"

"Yes. Approximately." Hamish then described where he believed the victim lay.

"And you believe the victim may have life-threatening injuries?"

"I fear so," Hamish said, worrying that time was not their friend.

Dispatcher Butler calmly responded, "I am going to send six New York State forest rangers to your location. Forest Ranger Ecklestone will be in charge. I am also going to page out the Lake Placid Fire Department, the Keene Fire Department, as well as the Keene Valley Fire Department Wilderness Response Team. They will assemble at the Pitchoff Trailhead and a Hasty Rescue Team will head in your direction.

"When you reach the patient, please dial 911. Your location coordinates can then be pinpointed for the responding rescue teams. Expect a call from Forest Ranger Ecklestone for updates within the next twenty minutes. Everything is going to be okay, sir. Good luck and stay safe."

Ten minutes later, Hamish raced out of his house, swung his backpack over one shoulder and switched on the headlamp atop his wool hat. As he crossed the lawn behind Dewey Hall and set out on the trail that led to Balanced Rocks a familiar face emerged from the darkness.

"Holy Christ, Rambler, you scared the wits out of me," Hamish swore. The old dog gave him a *Well, what are we waiting for* sort of look. "You up for this?" Hamish asked. Rambler barked and trotted out ahead of the Scotsman. She knew the trail by heart without any need for the beam of a headlamp.

Forty minutes later the two companions reached the cliff area Tracy had described. Hamish's chest heaved from unfamiliar exertion and he sat for a moment to catch his breath. The afternoon had been warm, a perfect Indian summer day, but after sundown the temperature plummeted. Perspiration on his back began to chill as he zipped his parka all the way up. Rambler sat beside him just for a moment to survey the scene. Then she trotted off on a mission of her own.

It didn't seem so long ago, Hamish recalled, that he could jog up and down this small promontory and barely elevate his heart rate, let alone break a sweat. Flexing his sore knuckles, he remembered that they didn't always hurt so. Once, he could dangle by his fingertips on impossible overhangs while sorting out the next gymnastic move that required his left foot to be placed above his right ear or some other absurdity. To scale sheer rock faces he could jam his callused knuckles into sharp-angled cracks pitch after pitch. Now, the calluses were smooth, arthritis was creeping, and prescription painkillers were his only relief from a barking back and troubled memories. A quarter moon floated over the rumpled carpet of peaks spread out before him, insufficient light to easily locate an unconscious or dead body. He blew on a whistle. Far below his feet the lakes shimmered in the dim lunar glow. Cumulus clouds scuttled across the sky, dappling the mountains below in mirrored shadows. Rambler responded with a single bark. As Hamish rose to begin the painstaking search, the breeze died for a moment and he heard something unrelated to the movement of air through trees, a faint groan somewhere not too distant. Then, another bark.

"Malcolm?!" Hamish yelled. He blew the whistle once again and held his breath to focus his hearing. Another groan, not necessarily a response, just a groan. The Scotsman scrambled across a tricky precipice to a place where scrub spruce broke the expanse of open rock. Just below, Hamish's headlamp caught Malcolm's motionless body. Rambler stood beside him, licking the boy's face.

"God Almighty," he murmured, sliding down on his rear the last few yards to Malcolm's side. A check of his vital signs verified that the injured boy still had life. His core temperature had fallen desperately low and his skin felt clammy. Dried blood from a gash on his head looked like tar. Where was Pete? Ron Handy would have been his preferred companion, someone with a high degree of emotional intelligence as well as good sense. But Ron was well beyond being called out for search and rescue. Though Pete was young, he and Hamish understood the fellowship of the rope as reliance upon each other, a mantra among mountaineers. And Pete possessed sufficient training in basic wilderness first aid to provide physical, if not emotional, support to Hamish.

Hamish pulled out his cell and dialed 911 as instructed by the DEC dispatcher. While he was describing the scene, the location in reference to the nearest trail, and his best assessment of Malcolm's condition the emergency response system was pinpointing his location using cell tower triangulation.

Those coordinates, and the patient's current medical status, were then relayed via radio to the responding forest rangers, fire department EMTs, and Technical Rescue Personnel that were already very efficiently assembling one mile and a thousand vertical feet below, at the Pitchoff Trailhead.

Hamish stripped off his parka and laid it gently over the inert form, checking to make sure the boy was breathing and that his airway was sufficiently open. Out of his pack, he pulled a space blanket, metallized to reflect ambient heat back against the body, and tucked it carefully around the boy. There was no way to tell if internal bleeding was causing Malcolm to go into shock, draining away the boy's ability to sustain life. Other than the dried blood on his head there were no other signs of a wound. Hamish checked for a pulse and found it slow, but steady. Further investigation for fractures or worse would have to wait until emergency medical technicians arrived.

"Don't be leavin' us, Andy," he whispered, touching Malcolm's head tentatively, then realized he'd used the wrong name. Instead of the injured boy struggling to survive, Hamish could only see the young English medical student on a stormy Scottish cliff so many years prior. Murmuring a prayer that this accident would not end as had that long-ago episode, he turned away from Malcolm and busied himself with lighting a stove to brew tea as Rambler lay quietly, head on her paws, her nose touching Malcolm's inert form.

Ten minutes down the mountain, Pete Hedges swore as he lurched over boulders and roots, sprawling headlong more than once, dislodging his headlamp. Lungs bursting, dripping sweat despite the chill in the air, he reached the summit area and called out. Hamish whistled in response. Pete scrambled down to the accident scene and immediately pulled out a down sleeping bag, which he tucked around Malcolm, allowing Hamish to retrieve his own parka from the boy.

"He's in bad shape, Pete. Really bad shape. God help me if we lose him." The sober reality of seeing a child in such dire straits was a shock for which no amount of experience could prepare them.

"We'll get him through this," Pete whispered. Malcolm's still body frightened him. Malcolm was never still. "This is crazy," Pete said. "What the hell was he doing . . . ?"

"Doesn't matter now," Hamish said brusquely, "I doubt they'll send a helicopter in the dark."

"They better."

"I barely feel a pulse, Pete," Hamish choked.

"Head wounds bleed a lot," Pete said, feeling the sticky pool that had formed on the rocks under Malcolm's cheek. "Keeping him warm is what's important now, right?"

"Aye. The rescue team will be here soon. That's all we can do now."

The calls to the DEC and 911 mobilized rangers, medical technicians, and numerous volunteer climbers. Given the potential life-threatening injury to the victim, and the fact that darkness had already fallen, the reaction was swift. Some responders from the local towns were at the trailhead on State Route 73 in minutes; others answering their pagers or cell phones from locales an hour away grabbed their personal gear and headed out into the cool autumn evening knowing their involvement was uncertain. It would not be unusual for more than thirty people to participate in rescues of this nature. At least this evening would not also involve a search, for the location in this case was clearly known.

One volunteer, Carl Goblish, from the Town of Keene, hurried to the fire station. His role for the last twenty odd years on the search and rescue teams was to assure a truck was equipped for rescues and ready to roll. When Carl's pager crackled with a report of a person in need only a few miles from where he and a few neighbors were engaged in a Saturday-night poker game, the lean forty-five-year-old electrician, a former Olympic biathlete, tossed in his hand of cards, pushed his chips toward his host with a request to sort out the cash at next week's game. His companions were used to the all-too-frequent interruptions this volunteer position imposed on their friend. They knew this was an important, almost religious aspect of Carl's life and his way of giving back to the mountain community to which he was so dedicated.

Carl jogged down the street of their small village, picked up the key to the emergency vehicle at the fire station, and made the short, seven-mile drive up to the trailhead. He was not nervous, but the uncertainty of each rescue, and the inherent risks to the rescuers, put everyone on edge. The unknowns were scary.

At the trailhead there already were several state trooper squad cars directing traffic, ensuring the lane nearest the beginning of the trail up to Balanced Rocks was clear for emergency vehicles, gear, and the crew that would soon be gathering. Carl found Jeff Ecklestone, the ranger in charge, and began checking out the arriving teams for preparedness. Many faces were familiar, folks with whom he'd spent many hours backcountry skiing, climbing and drinking a brew or two. But everyone had to pass a rigorous check for fitness, friend or not. He checked clothing, footgear, and, especially as it was Saturday night, he paid attention to anyone showing signs of inebriation.

A Hasty Rescue Team of six, consisting of one forest ranger, two EMTs, plus three Technical Rescue Team members, quickly headed up the trail, headlamps illuminating their way, to find the victim and determine the severity of his injuries. Having heard that Malcolm was incapacitated "on a slab," they did not yet know the severity of the angle. The steeper the pitch, the more complex would be the rescue; and safety of the rescuers, not the victim, was always their primary concern. They carried enough equipment for any eventuality—rope to secure the rescuers and the litter carrying Malcolm, nylon webbing, Prusik loops used to slide someone up a rope, waist harnesses from which to connect the ropes, assorted carabiners, pulleys, anchor plates, and descent control devices. They also carried a light, two-piece, titanium litter, plus a backboard. A mile above, Hamish asked Pete to work his way back to the main trail to meet the ascending team and guide them to where Malcolm lay.

It was past eight when the Hasty Rescue Team reached Hamish. The forest ranger on the team radioed their status and then flagged the route as Hamish led the EMTs through the brush to Malcolm. Two Technical Rescuers followed and began cutting a trail to the patient while the third

Technical Rescuer began to assess and formulate an evacuation plan based on the terrain.

Meanwhile, a string of volunteers distributed themselves at points along the trail, to relieve each crew carrying the litter above them. At the base of the mountain, an ambulance sat, engine idling. There would be no helicopter involved, a complicated process at any time, but especially after dark.

Once the medical evaluation had determined that Malcolm could breathe on his own, that his head wound appeared to be superficial, and that the angle of the rock was not terribly steep, they carefully strapped him to the backboard, lifted him onto the litter, and set up a low-angle rope system to control his descent down the trail. Hamish and Pete said little. They watched, anxious but curious, as the rescue squad went about their practiced routines. Years before, Hamish had been one of these volunteers. He no longer felt up to the physical challenge, nor did his professional responsibilities allow for random disappearances from school, but he marveled how the years since his participation had brought about remarkable improvements in equipment, as well as team coordination.

Once back on the state trail, four litter carriers began the perilous hike down the mountain. An emergency technician walked nearby, trying to stay out of harm's way but needing to be close to repeatedly check that Malcolm's airway remained open. Yet another volunteer kept tension from above on a rope attached to the litter, to prevent it from careening down the trail if the litter carriers should stumble. At the steeper sections the entire operation came to a halt. They passed Malcolm to another group assembled on the trail who, standing close to one another, carefully "caterpillared" the litter from person to person until the trail resumed a less severe angle. There, another crew of litter carriers would take him on again, synchronizing their steps in descent to minimize jostling his body.

Mountain rescue is necessarily a slow process; it was nearly midnight when Malcolm reached the main highway. And that was precisely when he regained consciousness. Had he remained unresponsive, a helicopter was waiting in Lake Placid to transport him to the nearest head trauma unit in Burlington, Vermont. But thanks to a groan and the opening of his eyes, the medical team directed the ambulance to the hospital in

Saranac Lake, not to the helicopter pad in Lake Placid. Assuring Hamish and Pete there was nothing more they could do, Ranger Ecklestone urged them to go back to school and get some rest. Before Hamish could even think of asking for a lift, the assorted volunteer rescue crews had departed, leaving the Glencoe men and a weary border collie alone on the dark, chilly, highway.

"I'm no EMT," Pete said, "but I know it was huge that Malcolm opened his eyes there."

"Aye, but they'll be testing him for TBI, nonetheless," Hamish nodded, referring to the traumatic brain injury protocol they would certainly put him through as soon as he was secured in Saranac. "He's a ways from being out of the woods," Hamish added.

"No pun intended," Pete said wryly.

"No joking matter," Hamish said. "Lemme give Bonnie a call. I'm sure she's anxiously waiting to hear from me and would be happy to pick us up so we don't have to hike all the way back," he said, attaching a leash to Rambler's collar.

The two men found a boulder safely off the shoulder of the narrow mountain road and sat down to wait for their ride. Pete snapped off his headlamp; only one of them needed to light the way for Bonnie to spot them. Nearly half the night had passed since Hamish had first stood atop Balanced Rocks, searching for the lost boy while aware of the extraordinary beauty of the night. The moon was low in the sky now, yet still graced the lake before them with silver reflection.

"It's so weird to be witness to this amazing beauty that was just the scene of a horrible event," Pete said,

"I understand," Hamish said. "How can we distance ourselves from the fact that a child in our care nearly died? May still die, if God wills it. You know me well enough, Pete. I'm no religious zealot. But to let myself, even for a moment, set that accident aside and appreciate how blessed we are to live in a place like this . . . It's as spiritual as I get . . . I'm almost ashamed."

"I wonder if we'll ever know how this happened," Pete said. "Or if we're getting the whole story. I feel personally responsible yet I had nothing to do with it. It's a helpless feeling knowing I could not have prevented it. What should we do now?"

"You saw how that crew worked tonight. It's a complicated, awesome display of teamwork that's been honed over many years, but there's no getting used to the human aspect of it. We had some accidents when I worked at Outward Bound back in Scotland," Hamish said. "A girl swept overboard from a mast that broke in a storm, a falling rock, secure for hundreds of years, peeled a student off a cliff; it's not something you ever get over. You just try to get past it."

Hamish thought again about the other accident, of his own making, on a wintry night when he should have known . . . did know . . . better. Though the years mentoring his younger protégé had brought him as close to Pete as anyone, he could not share that painful memory. He forced that ghost back into the shadows. "Thanks for your help tonight, Pete."

"I'm not sure I added much value," Pete said, sensing Hamish had held back something important. "But I sure learned a lot from the S&R folks. I'm thinking I should volunteer. My wilderness first aid skills are solid, I think. And it's a way to give back. I owe so much to this wilderness preserve."

"It's a great idea, Pete. I'll introduce you to Carl Goblish—he was the one manning the emergency equipment truck—and he can tell you how to get involved. You'd be a wonderful addition."

Pete checked his watch. It was close to one a.m. "Are you heading in to town?"

"Aye. I'll drop you and Bonnie at school and then check in on the lad. I'll just pace the floor and keep Bonnie up if I don't."

17

Don't Judge a Book

FOR THE FIRST TIME SINCE HE'D COME TO GLENCOE, TRACY DID NOT enjoy a Saturday-evening dance. He hung outside the auditorium, wishing to be invisible, but there was no way he could avoid his best friend. Jake confronted him by the water fountain and interrogated him closely, searching for any flinching facial muscle. "What do you know about this deal?" he asked. Tracy gave him the story he'd decided he could share.

"I know what you're thinking, Jake. I just wanted to show him up, that he's too fat and slow to keep up with me. Stupid idea, I know. I'm in deep shit for it, that's for sure."

"You got that right, bro. It's been nice knowing you."

"I wouldn't wish this on anyone. Even that guy."

About halfway through the evening dance, Payton Henderson found the disconsolate boy tucked in a corner of the auditorium and suggested they walk up to Phelps House together. Tracy was only too happy to get away from the crowd but he dreaded the conversation.

"Want to share with me what happened?" Payton asked, gently.

"No excuses, Payton. We shouldn't have left the property. I know the rules. Between you and me, it's not the first time I've gone up Balanced Rocks on my own, and I just figured that me and Malcolm might work out some of our issues if we did something together, you know?"

"You mean breaking the rules together would bond you in some way?" Payton asked, skeptically. Tracy shrugged. The less he had to say, the better. It was bad enough that he had to admit breaking one rule. Giving Payton all the details was just too much. "There's good reasons for those rules," Payton said. "We just need to know where everyone is if we are responsible for you. Your parents expect . . . no, demand that. It's not because we want to clip your wings, Tracy. We just can't run a railroad that way. Insurance companies rule the planet. We just get to live on it."

"I get it. We screwed up. I just hope he's gonna be okay. What do you think Hamish will do to me?"

"I can't say for sure. He's all about getting Malcolm down safely tonight. That's where his focus is and where it should be. You're better off letting him sleep on this one. Snap decisions are generally not good decisions, and he's one man who likes to think things through. He's very fond of you, Tracy. He'll give you a fair shake."

Libby and Tina arrived at the house a few minutes later with the rest of their Phelps housemates. The girls were anxious to hear what Tracy had to say. Everyone assumed he knew something about Malcolm's whereabouts and the teachers seemed to know nothing. Or at least they weren't talking. Libby found him in the large communal bathroom brushing his teeth. She sensed immediately he was holding back; that was obvious from the look in his face. She blocked the doorway to keep him from leaving.

"So? Do we have to pull it out of you by force?" Libby challenged as Tina joined her in the hall. Normally, Tracy would have leapt at the question, offering any amount of money to have them make good on their offer. But he looked ready to cry and Tina saw that the ever-buoyant boy had changed and pulled her friend to one side to let Tracy by. They followed him down the hall to his room. When he did not attempt to close the door in their faces, they followed him in and sat down next to Jake on the bed facing Tracy's.

"Finally got the chicks in here voluntarily," Jake said, smiling.

"We all make mistakes," Libby said. "Won't happen again."

"So?" Tina asked. "We're all friends here. What the fuck happened up there?"

"I dug myself a pretty big hole," Tracy admitted. He shared with his stunned housemates the basic details but steered clear of the reason for Malcolm's fall. He felt the hole getting deeper.

"I don't get it," Libby said when Tracy had concluded his brief description of the afternoon's events. "You despise that kid. Why would you pick him to go hiking up there?"

"It was a spur-of-the-moment thing," he lied. "I wanted to show him he wasn't the big shot he thinks he is, and bet him an ice cream he couldn't keep up with me. And I was right."

"Doesn't look like it was worth it now," Libby said. "You may be hanging with your old Vermont buddies in a day or two."

"I just hope Malcolm makes it," Tracy said. "What happens to me now isn't that important."

Tina stood, crossed the space between them and sat next to Tracy. She put her arm around his shoulders and hugged him. Libby admired that her friend could comfort this irritating boy, but also was concerned that Tracy would take it the wrong way and embarrass Tina. Tracy pursed his lips, placed a hand on Tina's knee and said, "I really appreciate that, Tina. It means more to me than I can say." It was not the reaction Libby had expected from him. She felt a twinge of envy.

"Of course," Tina said, tousling his shaggy red hair. Her fingers lingered longer than one would have expected. "You're my house brother!"

Libby just realized that Tina seemed to have figured there was more to Tracy than just a hormone-driven adolescent boy.

Tracy did not fit the mold of an ambitious preppy. He gravitated to the school's maintenance garage rather than the library or the basketball court, preferring the company of the local maintenance crew who lived off-campus and motored in every morning to keep the facilities ticking. He did not seek out the crew to learn how to shingle a lean-to or replace a toilet. He dropped in for the off-color jokes and the occasional (not serious) offer of chewing tobacco. There was no pressure; he could be who he was with no apologies, a country boy from Vermont who didn't consider himself above these guys who swung hammers for a living.

Back in their room, Libby couldn't wait to ask a question that had been gnawing at her.

"I'm pretty good at picking up stuff between people, Tina. And I'm picking up stuff between you and our 'house brother,' as you called him. What's the story? Am I crazy?"

Libby thought Tina looked guilty. "You're not crazy. There is something I never told you. We had a bit of a thing last year."

Libby felt unsettled in her gut.

"*A Thing?* What sort of *A Thing?*"

"You know."

"I don't know," Libby retorted. "Tell me," though she was not sure she wanted to hear it.

"We kind of bonded after that episode with Hahnemann last year. We made out a couple of times. Goofed around. It didn't mean anything. We were both just having some fun."

"How far did it go?"

"Let's just say I'm still pure as the driven snow, though the snow has been messed with a little," Tina grinned. "Lighten up, Libby. He's not the only guy I've ever fooled around with. But he may be the only one who's cool with it and doesn't expect more."

"Jesus, girl. I can't believe you didn't tell me."

"Well, now you know. There's a lot of really good stuff in that kid. He just doesn't let most people see it. He lets me. What can I say?" Tina said, spreading her arms. "I've got a soft spot for him."

"Yeah, well, you don't make out with your *brother*. That's sick."

"Okay, my cousin, then," Tina said with a twinkle. "You have to admit, he's a damn good-looking kid now, isn't he? Those red curls sticking out of that cap? That faraway look like he knows what you're thinking? He'll be breaking hearts left and right if he ever figures out what makes us tick."

"He's tall now," Libby said, grudgingly.

"Oh, come on. You don't see what I see?"

"He's too obnoxious for me to see what you see. I don't know why he's not like that with you," Libby said.

"Last year we just somehow got past that. But I wasn't in a place to get serious, whatever being serious as a fourteen-year-old even means. He was a lot shorter, looked more like a little kid. Something happened to him over the summer, that's for damn sure."

"Well, we're living under the same roof all year so I guess I'll have plenty of opportunity to see if anything's changed other than his shoe size. Maybe rooming with Jake will mature him a little. Jake knows how to talk to us. Hopefully, some of it will rub off. But I'm skeptical," Libby said. "But if you two decide to have another *Thing* would you at least give me a heads-up?"

"Not happening. But I promise."

Over the next few days several more late-night conversations occurred among the four seniors in Phelps House, usually in Libby and Tina's room, which was the neater of the two. Libby came to understand that Tracy felt more at home hanging out with the blue-collar guys in the maintenance garage than he did with the bevy of rich kids, such as herself, or Malcolm, whose seemingly unlimited resources just made him feel inadequate. These moments of Tracy's self-reflection shook the stereotype she had formed of him, unsettling her. Somewhere, underneath all of his adolescent bluster, there lived a sensitive person longing to fit in.

18

Dealing with Fallout

THE NEXT MORNING RUMORS FLEW THROUGH THE HALLS ABOUT MAL-
colm's whereabouts. Students from Marshall House reported that
Malcolm had not been seen at home the previous evening and his bed
remained untouched. His roommate had nothing more to offer, either.
Following Hamish's wishes, all teachers had refrained from providing any
details. From the drawn and drained looks on all the grown-up faces, it
was obvious something bad had happened.

Hamish spent most of that Sunday in Saranac Lake waiting for any
news on Malcolm's prognosis. His efforts to locate Malcolm's guardian
aunt had been unsuccessful. According to her assistant, she was flying
back from New Zealand and would not be available by phone until
the next morning. When it became clear Malcolm was stable Hamish
returned to school late in the afternoon. As the school community filed
in to the auditorium after dinner that Sunday evening for the weekly
Silent Meeting, he could feel the tension.

Silent Meeting was held every Sunday and always began with music.
Sometimes Ron Handy graced them with an elegant Mozart sonata
on the baby grand piano. Other weeks, student ensembles performed.
Patterned after a Quaker ceremony, the Meeting was devoted to individual contemplation, not religion, but that didn't mean there was silence.
Anyone who wished could stand up and say whatever was on his or her
mind. Sometimes no one said anything. Often a teacher broke the ice by
sharing a poem or mentioning something that had happened at school or
elsewhere in the world, something they felt personally significant. There

was never a sermon, just a chance for quiet reflection on one's place in the universe. The oldest students generally distributed themselves along the last two or three rows of chairs, not to enable discreet whispering, for teachers intermingled to prevent such disruptions, but simply because it had always been that way. Younger children filled the front rows as if the view was better from there. In truth, there was nothing much to look at for the focus was meant to be inward.

On this particular Sunday, a group of sixth and seventh grade recorder players, seated on a small raised stage at the front, provided a rendition of "Greensleeves" as students and faculty found their chairs. Hamish stood at the rear of the room, waiting for the last straggler to settle down. He looked haggard.

After nearly ten minutes of silence Hamish rose from his seat and cleared his throat. All heads swiveled toward him. He had the community's undivided attention. "Before we complete another day at Glencoe, I must share some very difficult news with you." Jake turned to look at Tracy, seated beside him. He watched his friend's face as Hamish spoke.

"You are part of a challenging school. We wish it to be so," Hamish went on, choosing his words carefully. He was clearly shaken. "And we believe such challenges strengthen you and provide you with self-confidence to succeed in this difficult world. But it is never our intent to push you to your absolute limits, or to ask you to be something you are not.

"Some of you are brilliant students. Some are gifted artists. Some will find that your love of horses or mountains will burgeon into lifelong careers. Who knows? It is our role to expose you to new adventures and opportunities." He did not mean to ramble but it was his nature, and at this particular time he was finding it especially difficult to focus.

"I am deeply saddened to inform you all that a member of our community, Malcolm Dandridge, suffered severe injuries from a fall yesterday on Balanced Rocks. We don't know yet exactly how it happened or why he was there. As you know, Malcolm is a tough lad and it looks like he will pull through, but it's unclear if he will be well enough to come back to us this year. If you have a few minutes and would like to make a card for him in the art room, I know he'll appreciate it." The room let out a collective gasp and furious whispering began. "Please . . . a moment more," Hamish implored, waiting for the room to become quiet again. "We have all let this boy down. That's not to say I blame anyone here for what happened. It appears to have been a tragic accident.

"I know Malcolm could be a challenge, and some of you had your run-ins with him from time to time. Regardless of what you may think of him, he was and is one of us," the headmaster continued. "I am sure you will all remember that if the doctors decide he is well enough to rejoin us, we will be there to welcome him home."

Hamish took his seat. He looked for Tracy and tried to stare into his head. Jake was doing the same. Tracy kept his head down, eyes on his feet. Hamish decided the only way they might learn how it all happened was dependent upon hearing Malcolm's side of the story. Maybe Malcolm wouldn't make it. Maybe he'd never come back. Hamish had to move forward assuming what he now knew was all he would ever know.

After the midday meal on Monday, two visitors were seen observing the students filter out of the dining room on their way to afternoon classes. Hamish had expected them, though not so soon. Perfunctory handshakes were exchanged and he motioned them toward his office. Ron Handy passed the trio in the hall. It seemed to him that Hamish had aged ten years since the previous night.

"Mr. MacLean, as we discussed over the phone this morning," said the woman as she took a seat across from his desk, "whenever an accident of this nature occurs, the Department of Health must determine whether proper procedures were followed and whether supervision was adequate. I appreciate your cooperation as we investigate."

"We've never had a serious injury at Glencoe before," Hamish countered, defensively.

"According to our records, that appears to be true," the man agreed. "Are you in the habit of exposing these children to the dangers of rock climbing?" The insinuation rubbed Hamish the wrong way, but he restrained himself.

"Do we rock climb? Aye, under strictly controlled conditions, led by teachers with impeccable credentials. However, there was no rock climbing planned on our school-wide road cleanup yesterday. It was strictly community service. From what we can tell, Malcolm Dandridge split from the rest of us and chose to climb up Balanced Rocks with another student, who alerted us that the accident had occurred. Clearly, the two of them broke school rules and will be dealt with."

"Then the obvious question we have is why he was not being supervised during the walk back to school," the woman interjected. Hamish shot her a withering glare.

"We had nearly twenty staff members to cover seventy-seven children. That's a better ratio than you'll find anywhere. But you're not asking me why no one was holding his hand, are you?"

"No need to get antagonistic, Mr. MacLean," the woman said, glancing at her coworker with a look that said *I told you he'd be like this.*

"Well, what's the bottom line here?"

"Let's not get ahead of ourselves. I'm afraid it's premature to give you an answer on that," the man replied.

"What's it going to take to get an answer? We can't live under a cloud of suspicion."

"Let the process take its course, Mr. MacLean. There are protocols to handle such circumstances and we intend to play this by the book."

"Bureaucratic mumbo jumbo," Hamish muttered.

"If you don't mind," the man said, appearing to ignore the headmaster's goad, "we'd like to interview others who were involved in this activity. Also, we need some background on the procedures your staff follows for leading children. Then we'll make a recommendation as to the disposition of this matter."

"It will take a couple of weeks, I should think," the woman responded.

Hamish stood up. The meeting was over as far as he was concerned. "We'll cooperate any way we can," he said. "I would appreciate it if you would make your requests to my office directly. I will see that you have access to whomever you need. But if this becomes a witch hunt, make no mistake, I won't stand idly by," he said, wagging a finger.

"I assure you, we're not looking for scapegoats," the man said, collecting his coat. "Our only priority is the safety of the students under your care."

"As is ours. Good day to you." Fuming, Hamish ushered them to the door. Cathy Swenson stuck her head round the corner from her desk.

"What now?" He sounded defeated.

"It's Mrs. Graham. Her attorney's on the line, too."

"Isn't that called *piling on*?" he mumbled, slumping down into his chair. "Hello, Mrs. Graham," he said to Malcolm's guardian aunt. "Welcome back from Asia. Have you spoken with the hospital this morning?"

"Of course, Hamish. Please call me Mathilda. I've asked my lawyer, John Helderberg, to be part of this conversation, if you don't mind."

"Of course. Good morning Mr. Helderberg."

"How do you do, sir?" came a third voice.

"Mathilda, I don't know how to tell you how sorry we are. This was not a planned trip. He and another boy took it upon themselves to go for a hike unaccompanied. We're addressing that with the other person involved but what's most important, of course, is getting Malcolm through this critical period."

"Thank you for your sentiments. It seems Malcolm brought this on himself, as is his habit," she said sadly, catching the headmaster by surprise.

"Our only concern is his well-being right now, Mathilda."

"Mr. MacLean," Attorney Helderberg interrupted. "In the event the boy doesn't survive, my interest here is seeing that Malcolm's body and personal effects are handled properly. Mrs. Graham has asked me to come out there to oversee the matter, if you don't mind. I will leave it to the authorities to determine responsibility here. We know the type of child Malcolm was and how difficult he was to look after."

Hamish was stunned by the businesslike tone Helderberg used, as well as the lack of any compassion, especially as it seemed Malcolm was not in danger of dying.

"That's true, Hamish," Mathilda broke in. "We are grateful you took him in the first place. I only wish it had worked out this time."

"We're terribly upset that it has come to this. But I, for one, am not ready to write him off. He's been a handful, I admit, and now he's putting the doctors to the test. He's one tough kid, your Malcolm, and he may continue to surprise us. I certainly am hoping for the best."

"Thank you, Hamish. John will see you the day after tomorrow. I will follow him if the doctors feel I can be of service," Mathilda finished.

"I'll be in touch," Hamish responded.

During the next few days, the community went about its business in a state of collective shock. Students and faculty alike were stunned by the news of Malcolm's accident. Privately, many felt an absence of personal anguish. Rather than a good-riddance response, the prevailing sentiment was more accurately better-him-than-me.

At the weekly faculty meeting there was spirited debate about how Tracy should be dealt with. Leaving campus unsupervised was unquestionably a serious breach, worthy of expulsion. Others had taken excursions in the past to local convenience stores for candy and cigarettes and had been suspended. No one, to their knowledge, had chosen to go hiking for a few hours. Clearly, the accident underscored the importance of adult supervision and, from a cold-eyed business perspective, the insurance liability problem the school now faced. Tracy had so many fans that the consensus seemed to be to give him some consideration for being such a good citizen. In the end, it was decided he should be grounded from off-campus trips for a month and restricted to the library between the afternoon outdoor activities and dinner. Until it was known if Malcolm would return at all, the discussion about him was tabled, though all assumed the punishment would have to be the same.

Many teachers expressed a feeling of helplessness as to how best to console the younger students who might fear for their own safety. Hamish announced that Ms. Foxworthy, the school psychologist, would visit each class and meet privately with anyone, faculty included, in need of therapeutic counseling. At week's end, Hamish drafted a letter to parents describing the events and the school's response. He telephoned all members of the board of trustees to brief them personally. Predictably, the stress and strain found its way to the most vulnerable part of his body. By Sunday morning, Hamish was unable to rouse from his bed, so acute were the spasms in his back. He remained immobile through the morning but around two in the afternoon, while his wife, Bonnie, was visiting friends in Keene Valley, he struggled to his car, drove into Lake Placid, and refilled his Percocet prescription.

True to form, Malcolm surprised everyone, including the attending physicians. After three days he was sitting up, beginning to take food orally and threatening to wear out the batteries in his TV remote control, not to mention the patience of the nursing staff. He had legitimate reasons to be grouchy and in need of painkillers. His chart described several lacerations requiring stitches, a moderate concussion that left his head throbbing and dizzy as well as one cracked rib, which made it painful to breathe. Mathilda's lawyer, Helderberg, decided his presence had no purpose and left before Malcolm had even regained consciousness. Hamish visited each morning, once bringing a get-well card signed by those children who had not yet borne the brunt of Malcolm's wrath. He had come armed with *Robinson Crusoe*, planning to read aloud, but Malcolm waved him away, preferring the TV, even on mute.

Once Malcolm had regained his ability to converse, Hamish asked him to explain how he had come to be on that side of Balanced Rocks in the first place. That proved futile, for Malcolm had no memory of the event. The doctors were not surprised by the amnesia, but told Hamish they didn't rule out the possibility that Malcolm might regain a full understanding of the events at some point. Nevertheless, Hamish left the hospital each day wondering if this was all just a game and he was the one being played. But if so, why? If Malcolm had been led there, he'd be able to finger the culprit, and would relish the chance to do so. The pieces didn't fit.

On Halloween eve, Malcolm returned to Glencoe with a definite swagger, like a conquering hero. His powers of healing had proven remarkable and the stint in the hospital had left him ten pounds lighter. It was near six p.m. when the car bringing him from the hospital arrived back at Glencoe. From all corners of the campus, students and teachers alike slowly converged on Dewey Hall for dinner as the table-setters finished their tasks within. Tracy and Jake sat on the stairs outside the dining room door poring over a map of the Adirondack High Peaks and dreaming of extreme trips they might take in this, their final year at Glencoe. The boys yearned to bag as many mountains as possible, especially under the most trying winter conditions. It chagrined Tracy that he could not participate on trips going out during his suspension, but he looked forward to the dead of winter when the climbs required more technical skill. As the doors swung open and students and teachers fanned out to their assigned tables, somebody strode by, tapping the bill of Tracy's ball cap down over his eyes.

"What the hell . . ." Tracy said, glancing up to see who was responsible. When his eyes fell upon the bandaged head of Malcolm Dandridge, his eyes widened.

"Wow," Jake exclaimed. "Look who's back from the dead."

PART II

You must study the endgame before anything else; for whereas the endings can be studied and mastered by themselves, the middlegame and the opening must be studied in relation to the endgame.
— José Raúl Capablanca

19

Exit Strategy

SERGEANT HANK CASSIDY CHECKED HIS WATCH AND BLEW THREE short bursts on his nickel-plated whistle. Break time was over. As the shrill sound evaporated into the dense stand of spruce that lined the two-lane county road, a dozen men in Day-Glo orange jumpsuits stubbed out cigarettes, gathered their tools and shuffled off toward the woods to resume clearing brush. They grumbled that the guard's watch was fast, just like yesterday and the day before. Ignoring their practiced complaints, Cassidy eased his belly behind the steering wheel of the Adirondack Correctional Facility minibus and flipped through the girlie magazine in his lap, the waning light of an early November afternoon failing to leave any warmth on his neck. He had scarcely read a page before the argument erupted.

"Take back that shit, Butch," Vinnie Johnson warned, brandishing a shovel menacingly at Butch Carver, his much smaller adversary.

Cassidy tossed the magazine onto the floor and swore. "Jesus Christ, why can't they keep their traps shut and get the work done?" He grabbed his nightstick from beneath his seat, stepped out of the van, and strode angrily toward the inmates circling each other like bull moose in rutting season. Other inmates crowded around, eager for entertainment. Carver lunged at Johnson like a fullback bursting through the line of scrimmage. The whippet-thin Johnson crumpled beneath Carver's assault, responding with a desperate, wild swing of his shovel as he fell. It crunched his assailant's left shoulder, barely missing a tattooed spider on the back of Carver's shaved head. Clutching and grabbing, the two men rolled off into a drainage ditch between the road and the trees. The raucous crowd rushed to the edge of the ditch, yelling encouragement.

Cassidy shouldered his way through the mob that closed ranks behind him. He glanced around. He was severely outnumbered but still possessed the only weapon in the bunch. He focused again on the men grappling in the ditch below.

"Get off'm, Carver!" barked the guard, snapping his lead-filled nightstick into his free palm. He was so vulnerable because his partner had broken regulations by leaving Cassidy, picked up by his sister for some unexpected chore that would only take, she assured him, thirty minutes at most. *You're risking our fucking jobs*, Cassidy had pleaded. But he was the junior officer, and his concern fell on deaf ears.

Relax, Hank, I'll be back before you know it. My sis must be obeyed, his partner had chuckled.

The two inmates continued to fight, ignoring Cassidy's presence. Laughter at his feeble attempt to restore order rippled through the mass of inmates egging on the antagonists. Cassidy jumped down into the ditch and swung his nightstick solidly into Carver's lower back, catching the man flush in the kidney. The little bulldog howled in agony, then dove again onto Johnson. They rolled, snarling and spitting, farther away from the guard, who stomped after them.

At the edge of the huddle, Garth smiled. The swarthy lumberjack towered above the knot of inmates surrounding the skirmish, his dark eyes sparkling. As Cassidy clubbed the combatants indiscriminately, LeGrange grabbed the elbow of Ramon Ortiz standing beside him and whispered, "Surf's up, Jack. Let's boogie."

"Now?"

"Yeah, now! Those two won't fight all day." He pulled Ramon away from the clutch of men and they edged off into the woods. For a hundred yards, they darted through the trees on a course that paralleled the road. Ramon followed blindly, afraid to look back, lungs burning from the effort. They emerged at a roadside turnout where an empty van sat parked, a faded diaper service sign on its side panel. Garth bent down and ran his hand under the front bumper from which he extracted a key.

He and Ramon were several miles down the road before Cassidy managed to separate the brawlers and radio for support. Not until the corrections officer realized he was down two men did he understand that the bleeding, exhausted inmates, chained hand-to-foot but chatting amiably, had staged a neat diversion.

"We aren't going to outrun 'em in this, are we?" Ramon glanced back anxiously as though he expected to see squad cars already in hot pursuit. Garth sat calmly behind the wheel, a toothpick dangling nonchalantly from tobacco-stained lips.

"I thought you was streetwise," Garth sneered. "'Course I don't plan to outrun 'em. I'd like nothin' better than to dump your Puerto Rican ass first chance I get. But that won't be today, Jack. Thing of it is, we have to make them think we died or disappeared."

"My name's Ramon, not Jack."

"Everybody's Jack to me."

They were an unlikely duo, toiling together on the road gang that left the prison each morning to clear the sides of the nearby rural highway of all vegetation before the construction crew came in with heavy equipment to widen the right-of-way. Digging ditches, whacking weeds was easy work for Garth; he'd handled hundred-foot spruce, oak, and maple with a heavy chain saw since childhood. For Ramon, however, it was torture. His hands had blistered the first day after persuading the powers in charge that he needed fresh air, that he was suffering allergic reactions to the dusty books in the library. The blisters reopened every day, but Garth advised him to suck it up, his days of suffering would soon end.

Ramon looked down at his standard-issue prison garb. Alone he had no chance. Garth could melt into the wilderness without a trace, while Ramon's olive skin and prison uniform would stand out as a beacon in any rural New York bus station. Ramon realized Garth was right; the ruthless logger was his only ticket to safety. As misgivings began to incubate, he thought of the telephone call to his brother that had triggered his rash decision to join the escape.

"How'd you get Carver to pull that stunt?" Ramon asked.

"He owed me," the woodsman smirked. "That boy's got a weakness for meth, and I found a way that he didn't have to do without. It helps to be incarcerated in my own backyard. Maybe you haven't been up here long enough to know but there's guards here worse'n the inmates. I went to high school with more'n a couple and we got some history." Ramon recalled the warning he'd gotten from the corrections officer who had gone to school with Garth. *Stay away from that one, He's bad news.* Too late, now.

"Thing of it is, I kept Carver happy long enough where he knew there was a favor coming down the road and this was it, Jack. There was no way he could turn me down. A few weeks in the hole is worth all that crystal. Let's call it a good-bye present."

There are few paved roads in the heart of the Adirondacks and the one they were on led directly past the entrance to the correctional facility they had so recently called home. Ramon was stunned to see the gate come into view and slunk low in his seat. "Want to stop by the guard-house and say 'Good-bye?'" Garth smirked. Ramon was petrified. This was no game now. The target now on his back might as well have been tattooed on his skin.

On the outskirts of Lake Placid the laundry van turned off the main road onto a secondary route that threaded through a mix of countless evergreen and hardwood. Around a sharp bend, Garth pulled over to the side of the road behind an empty Ford pickup pockmarked with rust. He turned off the ignition and shifted the transmission into neutral.

"Okay, Jack, let's give Smokey Bear something else to think about," Garth said, referring to the state troopers who already would be mounting a search. Together, they pushed the van down a steep embankment into heavy underbrush. Repeating his earlier maneuver, Garth removed a key from underneath the bumper of the Ford and kicked the road-weary vehicle into life, wheeled it around and drove back to a fork in the road they had previously ignored. They braked and swerved around yawning potholes that threatened to snap the axles of the dilapidated truck, heading them ever deeper into the Adirondack wilderness. Garth knew these woods like the back of his hand. Hardened by years of backbreaking labor as a lumberjack and emotionally cauterized by a childhood of neglect in Tupper Lake, he felt lost everywhere but here.

Just as Ramon figured they'd come to the end of what a vehicle could navigate, Garth spun the wheel hard to the left, jouncing the truck onto an indistinct old tote road, evidence of logging activity from years past. A hundred yards farther on they came upon a small log cabin, tucked unobtrusively into the forest. This time a key was found beneath a flowerpot and a musty mix of pine, wool, and camphor greeted their entry.

"We've got maybe two hours before they'll be swarming. We'll take what we can carry and get the hell outta here," Garth said, gesturing toward a considerable supply of camping equipment stacked neatly in one corner. He set about loading two backpacks with food, a cookstove, some clothing, a rifle, knives, sleeping bags, insulated pads, plastic sheeting, and canisters of white gas for the stove. He strapped two pairs of short aluminum snowshoes to the packs with bungee cords. While Garth worked, Ramon examined the dank two-room cabin. Rustic Adirondack chairs surrounded an antique potbelly stove set into the fireplace. Against the far wall sat a simple sink, fed by a single cold-water tap. In the back room Ramon noted two double-decker bunks built into the walls. Kerosene lanterns hung from the rafters in each room. Over the hearth hung a crossed pair of ancient bearpaw snowshoes laced with shellac-stiffened rawhide. This certainly was alien territory to a boy raised on the streets of New York City.

"You sure we aren't better off in the truck?" Ramon asked worriedly.

"Thing of it is, there'll be roadblocks from Albany to Canada. We wouldn't stand a chance in that Ford. Our best bet is to cut overland and avoid the roads. After they've lost interest in us, we can hike out and go our own way. Don't sweat the details, Jack. I know a place where we can hang out."

"How long we got to stay out there?"

"Couple, three weeks, maybe. Nobody'll find us, and even if they do, we're just hunters. Do as you're told. I'll cut you loose as soon as I can, you can be damn sure of that. I ain't no kinda babysitter. Just do what I tell ya and we'll get outta this okay." Garth tossed some oversized wool pants, shirt, and a pair of insulated rubber boots in Ramon's direction and motioned for him to change out of his prison garb. After they dressed, Garth took down two camouflage hunting jackets from pegs behind the door and handed the smaller one to Ramon. They were lightweight but trapped body heat extremely well. Matching camouflage hunting caps, replete with fur-lined earflaps, completed their "uniform."

"What do we do with the jumpsuits?" Ramon asked, scanning the room for hiding places for his prison garb.

"Into the crapper."

"Huh?"

"The outhouse. That hole's one place they're not too interested in checking out. Come on, let's move." Garth grunted as he lifted a pro-digious pack onto his shoulders, a .22 gauge "hunting" rifle protruding from the top flap. Ramon grabbed a somewhat smaller pack and followed Garth to the outhouse where they paused to dispose of their old clothes and left the clearing as darkness fell.

The first few hours of freedom were critical. Garth explained to Ramon that he wanted to make the police widen their search and stretch their resources to the point where the bosses would calculate the costs and begin to question the feasibility of continuing.

The rear of the cabin sat perched above an energetic brook, perhaps twenty yards across. The sound of its flow suggested prodigious volumes of water were passing over the rocks—too swift and deep to ford safely in the dark. Following the top of the riverbank, the two men wove through aspen groves for half an hour. Finally, Garth stopped beside a large sugar maple whose trunk was far too stout to reach around. A ladder made of hemp hung from unseen branches above.

"Think they'll sic the dogs on us?"

"You can count on it," Garth said, unslinging his pack. "But dogs ain't smart enough to sniff where we're going. Just trying to buy us some time."

Ramon noticed a separate nylon rope hanging down next to the ladder. The end of the rope had been doubled back on itself, forming a loop to which a carabiner was attached, a metal clip used by rock climbers shaped like the letter D. Ramon watched as Garth hooked his pack to the carabiner and let it dangle. Then he started to climb the rope ladder. Ramon watched with growing unease as Garth passed the lower branches of the maple, his camouflage clothing gradually merging with the dark mesh of tree and night.

The sound of Garth's ascent was soon lost in the music of the brook. Then, as if from an unseen hand, the pack beside him began to lift. In a moment it, too, had disappeared into the crown of the tree. Ramon felt a strong urge to run back to the road. He peered into the darkness, trying to locate the direction from which they had come. But every way looked the same. He might wander all night without finding the right route.

"Look out. I'm dropping the rope," the disembodied voice of Garth LeGrange boomed from somewhere above. "Hook your pack like I did, eh?"

Ramon peered up into the tree. In a moment he saw the rope snaking down to him, the carabiner hopping at the end like a hooked trout. When it halted in front of his face, Ramon grappled with the mechanism until he figured out how to open the spring-hinged gate. He hung his pack as Garth had done. "Okay, it's on!" he called. Immediately, it began to rise in upward jerks.

"Your turn, Jack. C'mon the hell up, we ain't got all night!"

Gingerly, Ramon stepped onto the lowest rung of the hemp ladder and began to climb toward the dim light of Garth's headlamp. When he'd ascended about thirty feet, his eyes distinguished the dark outline of a rudimentary wooden platform. As he hauled himself up to the precarious perch, Ramon noticed a metal hook that had been screwed into the trunk above their heads. Two lines of taut nylon rope stretched from the hook into the darkness.

"This is where we lose those suckers," Garth announced, hauling the rope ladder up to the platform. Now and then a rung would snag on a branch, but eventually, he coaxed the entire length up to their perch.

"You're not planning for us to spend the night here, are you?" Ramon asked skeptically. "I can't believe they won't track us to this tree."

Garth began to laugh. "Man, I've got a goddamned moron with me, don't I? We're goin' over the brook, Jack. If you don't piss in your pants after this trick, I'll know you're not such a candy-ass after all, eh?" Ramon was dumbstruck. He watched uncomprehendingly as Garth unclipped the carabiner from the rope he'd used to lift the packs, coiled the rope neatly over his shoulder and laid it on the floor of the perch beside the ladder. From a pocket on his pack he produced three other carabiners as well as four pieces of one-inch-wide nylon webbing, the ends of which had been sewn together to form loops approximately eighteen inches in length. To each loop he clipped a carabiner.

"Watch carefully," Garth cautioned, "If you screw this up, the best that can happen is you'll get wet. The worst is, you'll break your back. I ain't haulin' no paraplegic around the woods, so get it right the first time." He took two of the nylon "slings" and tied each one to the top of each pack. A third he handed to Ramon. "After I get over to the other side, send a pack over. Clip the carabiner onto the zip line like this," he demonstrated. Garth lifted Ramon's pack, held it with one arm while he snapped the carabiner against the zip line that stretched away from the hook in the tree trunk. Had Garth let the pack go, gravity would have pulled it down the rope and across the brook to some unseen destination point. "When I give you a shout, send the next one. When I shout again, clip yourself in and come on over."

Ramon began to feel lightheaded and queasy. He watched Garth unclip the pack, set it back down on the platform and clip his own sling onto the zip line.

"Wrap your wrist around the sling a couple of times," Garth said, "but whatever you do, don't grab the rope. The fucking friction will take your skin off like nuthin'." Then, he stepped off the platform. Almost immediately, Ramon lost sight of him in the inky blackness. He heard the hum of steel carabiner against nylon rope as Garth hurtled across, but a second later the sound was absorbed by the moving water. Alone in the darkness on a tiny perch in the top of a tree in the middle of nowhere with police in hot pursuit, Ramon felt helpless and scared.

"Send the packs over!" Garth barked.

Seeing no alternative, Ramon responded as he had been instructed. Lift, clip, zip. The first pack shot out over the water. Silence. Then a shout. Lift, clip, zip. Pause, then another shout. Now it was his turn. Ramon clipped his own carabiner onto the rope, muttered a Hail Mary and stepped into thin air. He felt the sickening drop, then the glide as his body hurtled past the maple branches, the wind whistling across his face as he slid above the open water. In seconds, his feet slammed against the incline of the far bank and he crumpled upon root-strewn ground. Two strong arms hauled him up. "Hell of a ride, eh?"

Ramon smiled in relief. All business, Garth unclipped him from the zip line and walked back away from the water to a tree that held the other steel hook and against which their two packs rested. He untied a knot in the zip line and reeled in the rope, feeding it through the higher hook above their platform on the other side of the river. Before long, another knot reached his hand and he paused to untie it, then resumed pulling. When the last end went through the far hook, they heard it slap to the ground then hip-hop across the water like a flitting dragonfly.

Garth coiled the rope, stowed it in his pack, and motioned for Ramon to follow. Using his compass and occasionally consulting a map by the light of his headlamp, Garth led them through the forest, avoiding established trails, walking up ice-caked streambeds whenever possible to camouflage their presence.

It was just past seven in the evening when the German shepherds, straining at their leashes, halted their dash through the woods, muzzles sniffing around the base of a majestic maple tree. In the dim light of a quarter moon, the team of New York state troopers cautiously approached their frustrated dogs, guns drawn. The canine whines were nearly drowned out by the white noise of fast water tumbling over stones in the adjacent stream. The troopers shortened leashes and trained their powerful lights up into the empty crown of the maple. The scent inexplicably stopped here, and both men and dogs shared similar bewilderment.

As Garth and Ramon climbed, fewer instances of open woods appeared, where walking was easy and the route straightforward. With the valley soon far below, hardwoods became less prevalent, replaced by an ever-thickening latticework of evergreen. Young spruce grew up between the interstices of spiky blowdown, making travel slow and complicated. Ramon found it backbreaking work, stumbling toward God knows where. Sharp branches caught his clothes, scraped and punctured any exposed flesh, threatening to poke his eyes out. He cursed Garth, cursed the ice-covered fallen logs and streambeds, and above all, he cursed himself for being so foolish. Prison was a blessing compared to living here, like this. He might as well have escaped to the moon. As one more hidden branch snagged his legs, causing another headlong plunge, ponderous pack pinning him to the ground, Ramon thought longingly of the snug, tidy apartment on the Lower East Side and a family that surely worried what had become of him.

The walk was tortuously slow. Garth worked carefully to leave as few clues as possible. Rather than avoiding bogs and streams, they slogged straight through them, making it as difficult as possible for man and dog to follow their path. It was not until late in the afternoon on their third day of freedom when they reached Lost Pond, just south of a peak known as Mt. Street that had no maintained trail and saw infrequent visitors. Several inches of rotten snow already covered the ground.

"This is home, for now," Garth announced, unbuckling his pack.

"Here?" Ramon asked, slumping down on a fallen log.

"You'll see." Garth walked to one side of the open space and began to paw through the snow like a dog searching for a lost bone. Ramon watched as the lumberjack extracted half a dozen rough-hewn poles, each approximately three inches in diameter and of varying lengths. "Give me a hand while I lash these suckers."

While Ramon held them steady, Garth constructed a skeletal frame whose front poles extended higher in the air than the rear by a good twelve inches. With his Smith & Wesson carbon steel military knife, he hacked an armload of spruce boughs and laid them across the roof poles to effect a sloping ceiling. Then, he spread clear plastic sheeting over the boughs, letting the excess hang over the sides and rear of the frame as a windbreak. Through metal grommets spaced along the outer edge of the plastic, he threaded nylon rope, tying the sheeting to the four vertical corner poles using a marlinspike hitch and a small length of wood as a handle that made it trivially easy to control tension on the line. Then he stood back to admire the rough lean-to.

"How'd you know there'd be poles here?" Ramon asked, beginning to unload his gear into their shelter.

"How'd I know? I cut 'em, that's how I know."

"When?"

"Years ago. I got other spots all over these woods. I like spending time away. Figured it might come in handy someday."

Garth disappeared into the brush for a few minutes, returning with an armload of balsam that he spread over the snowy floor of their shelter. Ramon unrolled his insulated pad on the springy fir mattress, fluffed up his sleeping bag as he had seen Garth do, and stretched out. He was bone tired. Three days of splashing up icy brooks, branches thwacking him across the face, downed trees catching his clothes and snaring his backpack had taken their toll. He imagined scores of bloodhounds straining to find him and rip him apart. It was even more frightening than the thought of his stricken mother lying in an overcrowded New York City hospital ward. He glanced at Garth, who whistled softly as he pumped pressure into their cookstove. Their ordeal left the man looking fresh and relaxed. Ramon worried the fearless logger might choose never to leave this godforsaken place.

20

Community Response

TRAFFIC INCHED FORWARD ON THE NARROW MOUNTAIN ROAD, SNAKING ever closer to the roadblock. Lights pulsated blue-red, blue-red, atop the squad cars. Hamish saw there was no accident, no ambulance. A clutch of troopers huddled around each vehicle as it reached them. *If it's a sobriety check, I'm in big trouble,* he thought. How did two Guinness, just consumed at the Maple Leaf Inn, translate to a blood-alcohol level? Or was it three? He couldn't remember. There was no mistaking his light-headedness as alcohol mingled with the medication he'd taken for his chronic back spasms. They were smart to set up the roadblock here; the road was narrow and one squad car sat parked a hundred yards beyond the checkpoint on either side, cleverly positioned to intercept a motorist who tried to evade the confrontation. Hamish stroked his beard, flecked now with more salt than pepper, regretting that he'd stopped in at the Maple Leaf. It would certainly not end well if the headmaster of Glencoe School was found to be driving under the influence of all kinds of things. He could already anticipate how the conversation with the board chairman, Phil Connaughton, would go, resulting in his termination. At the age of sixty-three, finding another prep school head job was a dubious proposition, especially with a DUI on his record.

The cars ahead moved slowly forward. Nearing the flashing lights, he struggled to maintain focus as Guinness and oxycodone coalesced in his blood stream. It was an old foe, this predilection for medicating himself. Once upon a time, there had been an injury, a severe rending of muscle fibers in a valiant effort to save a mountain climber's life. Though the fibers had seemingly mended, the need for pain relief, physical as well as psychological, had never disappeared.

No one, except Bonnie, his wife of thirty-two years, had any inkling of this problem or the details of its origin. Certainly not his doctors, who unwittingly provided him with more opiates than he could safely use. Though Bonnie knew well the genesis of his addiction, she was frustrated in her inability to help her husband confront it. Their decision to leave Scotland for the United States was based, in part, upon Hamish's desperate hope that the demon would not cross the ocean with them, but of course it had.

Hamish MacLean was a studiously disciplined man, devoted to Bonnie, to mountaineering, and to educating youngsters. His inability to overcome his dependency on painkillers was a profound personal embarrassment, and he labored not to let it compromise his ability to lead. Several years after their move to Lake Placid, Bonnie sadly concluded that her husband would not find the key to his nemesis without drastic measures, so she laid down an ultimatum: *Quit once and for all or I leave for Edinburgh. I cannae stand by while you destroy us.* Petrified that she would make good on her threat, he tried mightily to comply, resisting the urge to refill his prescriptions, comforting himself only with the occasional Guinness down at the Maple Leaf. But the root cause remained just below the surface, ready to erupt at the next source of stress. His just-completed trip to New York City for the Glencoe board of trustees' meeting had provided just such a source. Bonnie did not, in the end, follow through on her threat, but the rift became a chasm in their marriage.

Hamish shifted from neutral to first as the car in front of him lurched ahead, and he began to rationalize his latest fall from grace. There was no harm making the long drive a bit more comfortable. The board of trustees meeting he had just endured was worth forgetting, if only for an evening. Several times a year, he was summoned by the board to review the health of the school and discuss his plan for the future. In the early years of his tenure these meetings had been almost pleasurable. Glencoe had been easier to fill, and the trustees let him captain their ship unfettered. Now the landscape was different; rising tuition meant it was harder to find eligible applicants, harder to balance the budget. Never mind that Glencoe was a nonprofit organization; the board could not allow it to run at a loss, at least not for long. The generosity of its wealthy benefactors was limited, as his nemesis, Connaughton, constantly reminded him.

As Hamish drove north following the weekend meeting, even the crooning of the Tannahill Weavers that filled his car with comforting Scottish ballads couldn't shake his anxiety about the school's future. *A financial disaster is in the offing unless you turn this ship around,* Connaughton had cautioned. *Don't change the program, just find more families who don't need scholarships . . . or hire better fundraisers . . . or we'll have to look for someone else who can.*

Hamish was close enough now to see what was going on within the circle of lights. Two state troopers, shotguns at the ready, ordered the motorist just ahead of him to unlock the trunk of his car. A third trooper, wielding a powerful torch, directed its beam into the trunk, following the aim of the shotguns. The beam illuminated only a spare tire, and the motorist was ordered to move on. This was clearly no sobriety check.

Hamish waited anxiously as the same operation was performed on a car coming in the opposite direction. Then it was his turn. He rolled down his window, the chilly night air causing his eyes to tear just a little, and waited for a trooper to approach. Two policemen flanked the car, one panning the back seat with his light, the other focusing his beam on Hamish. The trooper on the driver's side eyed him closely.

"Sorry for the delay, sir."

"No worries, officer," Hamish responded, looking forward rather than directly at the uniform to prevent his beery breath from being detected. "How can I help?"

"Lookin' for two escapees from the Corrections Facility in Ray Brook. Pretty sure they're armed. One's Caucasian, the other Hispanic. Have you seen anyone hitchhiking along this road?"

"Nae, not a one." He was not about to explain that he'd been at the Maple Leaf for an hour imbibing alcohol by himself, with no escapees as companions. The troopers checked his trunk, curtly thanked him for his patience, and instructed him to move on.

As he continued up the twisting two-lane road back to school, Hamish shifted his worries about the financial state of the school and his own problems to the back burner. He switched off the Scots Highland music and considered next steps. He would convene an emergency faculty meeting that night, for the school would surely be inundated with calls from concerned parents as soon as news trickled out. The faculty had to be informed, and they had to present a consistent message when dealing with the outside world. Hamish wondered whether several emails from board members might already be sitting on his computer, requesting a detailed policy statement on how he proposed to protect students from hostage-takings.

Following the graceful curves of the valley floor, the country road switchbacked steadily up through spruce and birch, breaking out briefly into the clear as it approached the narrow Cascade Lakes at the height of land between Cascade Mountain on one side and the jagged cliffs of Pitchoff Mountain on the other. Reflections from a quarter moon shimmered on the surface of the frosty waters, the last vestige of an ancient glacier that had carved this pass.

A police helicopter churned above him, searchlight trained on the ground below as Hamish wheeled the Jeep onto school property. There wasn't one chance in a thousand that a helicopter could spot anyone hiding in the woods at night but their presence underscored for him that law enforcement thought the men were in this vicinity. He drove by the barn, past the lower pasture flanked by dormant flower and vegetable gardens. Anyone could hide in the piney shadows that bracketed the garden plots, waiting to snatch an unsuspecting student out for an unauthorized moonlight walk.

School security at Glencoe had never been a pressing issue; the place was truly off the beaten path and enjoyed a low profile in the region. Few buildings had locks, and strangers entering the property would immediately be recognized as such and confronted. Through his years as headmaster, Hamish's chief security worry had been that a distraught noncustodial parent feuding with his or her spouse, might swoop in, collect their child, and leave. That was the kind of event that triggered AMBER Alerts, initiated in 1996 after nine-year-old Amber Hagerman was kidnapped and murdered by a stranger in Texas. The thought of convicts on the lam grabbing a Glencoe student as a human shield or negotiating chip gave Hamish the chills. This was no longer a hypothetical problem to be discussed at fall faculty orientation. This was real, and in his backyard. No time for a committee to promulgate a new policy; it had to be in place before the night was out. Whatever Guinness/oxycodone buzz that existed when Hamish left the Maple Leaf Inn had been thoroughly metabolized by the time his farmhouse came into view.

Measures Must Be Taken

HAMISH EASED HIS JEEP INTO THE SNUG GARAGE A FEW STEPS FROM the farmhouse he and Bonnie called home. Generations earlier it had been the only structure on what was once a hardscrabble farm owned by a multigenerational family too set in its ways to admit defeat against the unforgiving challenges of a short growing season and fields of stone. Over the decades since Glenn Stallings and Susan Coe had purchased the land to start the school, modern horticulture, greenhouses, and countless students picking rocks and spreading compost had done wondrous things for the land. It was now as productive a patch as could be found at an altitude of two thousand feet. Hamish wished the founders could see what their vision had wrought.

As he collected his suitcase from the trunk, Hamish's thoughts lingered on the roadblock he had encountered earlier at the bottom of Cascade Road. Fall was nearly half done and his outdoor program, which called for hiking trips into the Adirondack High Peaks every weekend, was in full swing. Winter came early in the North Country, but weather never slowed Glencoe activities. But the rules might just have changed, and his chief worry now was how to keep students safe from becoming human shields rather than frostbite.

A warm glow radiated from the MacLean kitchen as he approached the house. Waiting by the storm door, nose pressed to the glass, sat Rambler, tail wagging like a metronome. The wise old dog had cleared a spot on the foggy glass, and Hamish knew that meant his wife was baking. As he opened the door, humidity and wondrous aromas welcomed him into the kitchen. He reached down to scratch Rambler behind her ears and kissed Bonnie, elbow-deep in a batch of c'raisin bread dough. Sweet pungency of cinnamon and yeast permeated the bright kitchen. Bach's violin concerto in E Minor wafted in from the living room. A sense of calm and orderliness pervaded the house and Hamish felt the pounding in his temples subside. A calm, orderly, home was one of Bonnie's greatest gifts to him.

"How was your trip, dear?" she asked, lifting her head to meet his lips, recoiling slightly as the aroma of hops, barley, and malt passed between them.

"There've been better. The board wants me on the road, marketing the school like a dime-store huckster and beating the bushes for endowment gifts. I cannae fight these battles much longer, Bonnie. If they think I'm more valuable buying dinners for big shot consultants than I am teaching these bairns the value of a well-tilled field, an elegant rock-climbing route, or a properly conjugated French verb, then our time at this establishment may have run its course."

"I'm sure you'll see things in a better light after you've had a good night's sleep. I know how these trips drain you. By the way, did you see Pete and Christine down at the Maple Leaf?" she asked mischievously. Hamish looked up, surprised that she knew he had stopped off to have a drink. "Your breath's so strong you might as well hang a neon sign around your neck that says *Guinness on tap*." She studied his face and sighed. "Your eyes look funny, Hamish. You've started the Percocet again, haven't you?"

"Nae, Bonnie, I'm well shy of hammered. Ye know what long drives do to my back. It helps relax the muscles is all."

"Relax? You'll relax your way on the bru," she huffed, using the Scots vernacular for the unemployed. ". . . and out of a marriage." He shrugged as if it were something completely beyond his control. Though they both understood her words were hollow, they still stung. "Don't you see what's happening to you? It's harder and harder for me to watch and say nothing. But my words fall on deaf ears. When will you ever face it head-on?" she pleaded.

"I don't want a battle. It's under control. And, no, I did not see Pete and Christine. Were they meant to be there?" he said, eager to deflect the conversation away from his addictions.

"A little bird told me they shared a meal at the Maple Leaf this evening," she said, with resignation. "Haven't you noticed what's been going on with those two, Hamish?"

"Perhaps not."

"Forget how to recognize romance when you see it?" she asked, with a too familiar sadness.

"Romance? I recall it fondly," Hamish said, immediately regretting the comment. "But there are more important things in my head tonight," he said, reaching for the phone on the wall.

"Is there anything more important?" she said, placing a hand on the phone. "Are we done with this conversation?"

Hamish stepped back to look at the love of his life. Her face was as fair as the day he'd spied her across the room in a Scottish pub, but years of disappointment had taken its toll on the rest of her. Now a matronly partner to her husband, Bonnie was physically unrecognizable from the lithe cross-country runner who captivated him that rainy November afternoon following the Scottish University Championships in 1969.

. . .

A wisp of a thing, bundled in an overcoat the older man next to her had draped over the sweaty tunic she still wore, Bonnie animatedly described the grueling race to the two companions who shared her booth. Her face glowed recounting those stirring moments. The proud fisherman and his wife, who had ventured from their homestead on the Inner Hebrides to see their youngest daughter run, hung on her every word. Their other four girls were back home, left to mend nets while their parents stole a rare day to visit the child who wanted higher education, wanted to train to be a midwife, wanted a broader world than the land across the waters of the Minch could offer.

From his table across the room, Hamish watched with envy this loving family in jovial banter, such a contrast from the emotional wasteland that had characterized his own upbringing, of which he rarely spoke. The warmth she exuded in that drafty old pub was magnetic. He had to find a way to meet her, battling the shyness that normally stood in his way.

After finishing her story and her tea, Bonnie Berwick and the older pair got up to leave. Hamish watched wistfully, fearing his chance was lost. Through the front windows he could see a steady rain pelted the pavement, a rude change from the cold, dry conditions the racers had enjoyed earlier. With no taxis in sight, nor umbrellas in hand, the Berwicks stood forlornly under the awning, contemplating a ten-block walk to their hotel.

Take a bloody chance, Hamish muttered under his breath, and grabbed his coat. "Please, I couldn't help but witness your distress," he said, joining them outside the pub. "May I offer you a ride to wherever you may be staying?" Though Bonnie was about to politely decline such an offer from a total stranger, her father, accustomed to such courtesies in the Hebrides, quickly accepted. And so began a torrid romance, punctuated by marriage a year later, with all the promise two young lovers could anticipate.

He found a teaching job at the Albyn School in Aberdeen while she completed her midwifery training at Robert Gordon University. Bonnie's ability to help mothers bring babies into the world brought her immense satisfaction and she longed to experience it herself. But pregnancy eluded her. With each passing month, with each medical exam, her spirit deflated. Just when she had given up hope she could ever conceive, just when her dream of replicating the large, close-knit, family to which she was so devoted, it happened. And then a second time. And once more. But she was unable to keep any of them. Her final miscarriage was accompanied by hemorrhaging so severe her gynecologist counseled her never to try again. Hamish implored her to consider adoption, but Bonnie kept finding reasons why it wasn't a good fit until it became clear that a child of their own, from any source, was not to be.

Thus began the slow deterioration of their love affair into a workmanlike partnership in which the nurturing and education of other people's children became their life's passion. They remained devoted to each other, ever compatible, with a love weighted by dreams that remained impossibly out of reach.

Bonnie became Earth Mother. Hers were the shoulders the youngest students leaned on to cope with homesickness, a predictable occurrence each fall. She was the one the older students sought out for reassurance when high school application deadlines approached. For faculty with young children scheduling a rare night off to spend time together, Bonnie was the babysitter of choice. Glencoe was an intense place to work and play, a 24/7 commitment, and Bonnie provided a release valve for everyone. Mothering seventy-odd children at Glencoe did not erase the pain she carried from not having one she had birthed, named, and reared. To alleviate her own disappointments she constantly baked, eating much, sharing most, and only occasionally daring to confront the demons she and Hamish battled. Their periodic debates about his dependence on alcohol and painkillers, or her reliance on comfort food, were always difficult and readily postponed, though they continued to go through the motions, hoping something, one day, would change.

. . .

"I am truly sorry that I cannae make our problems disappear," Hamish said, enveloping her in a warm embrace. "I will never stop trying. But tonight, right at this moment, I must deal with keeping our children safe." The irony of his choice of the word *our* was not lost on either of them. "When I left the Maple Leaf I ran into some state troopers looking for two escapees from Ray Brook. It happened this afternoon. They think the two may be up in our woods and I'll not wait for the morn to talk to the faculty."

Bonnie sighed, extricating herself from his hug.

"I promise we can talk about my ghosts later, if we must. I do appreciate your pushing me, even if it doesn't show," he said. Conflict avoidance, especially for him, was a practiced dance. "Would you please find refreshments while I call the police?"

Heartbreak tucked away once again she resumed her domestic role. "Yes, of course. Does this old farmhouse even have a lock that works?" she asked. No one secured doors at Glencoe, apart from the walk-in refrigerator in the Dewey Hall kitchen and the maintenance garage, which contained power tools not meant to be freely available.

Bonnie wiped a stray strand of hair from her cheek, managing to daub the red bandanna holding her silvery hair with a healthy dollop of cinnamon dough. "Would you pass me the wax paper, love? I'm a bit sticky just now." Hamish's thoughts were elsewhere as he handed her the front section of the *Lake Placid News* while again lifting the phone. Rolling her eyes, she went to the sink to rinse her hands.

"Sergeant Parker?" Hamish asked, the burr in his brogue announcing immediately his identity to the officer on the other end of the line.

"Yes sir, I'm well, thank you . . . She's fine." Hamish patiently performed the necessary rituals of small talk with the local constabulary. "Tell me about this prison break." His bushy eyebrows arched upward as he listened, like twin caterpillars dancing a jig. His fingers impatiently drummed the countertop. "Not helpful, Sergeant. You know how I hate fencing these children in . . . but if it must be," he sighed. "Right . . . Good night to you, sir."

Hamish hung up, a look of resignation on his face. "Parker says it's nothing to fool with. One of these fellows is an accomplished woodsman and pretty dangerous. He asked if we could curtail our wilderness program for a bit. You know how important it is to get these puppies out of here now and again."

"The students' security comes first," she cautioned. "Do you really think it's wise to let them go roamin' in the woods under these circumstances?"

"Parker should do his job and catch those characters. Then I'll be able to do mine. What if they never turn up? Am I supposed to post armed guards and have the kids play dodgeball in the gym from now on?"

"Why don't we hear from the others?" Bonnie offered.

"That's my intention, honey."

While Hamish grumbled about how quarantining the entire student body would impact Glencoe, Bonnie poured crackers into a bowl and collected hummus, baby carrots, blocks of cheddar cheese, ginger ale, and beer from their second refrigerator in the basement. Hamish telephoned his most senior faculty at their various residences on campus, letting them know they were expected at his farmhouse after their students were settled in bed. Bonnie brewed him a cup of Earl Grey, which Hamish gratefully accepted. To collect his thoughts, he climbed the creaky stairs to his study, eased himself into a straight-backed rocker facing the window and gazed out onto the Adirondack wilderness that somewhere secreted two desperate men, no doubt uncomfortable and scared in a cold, remote hideout. He didn't envy those men, but worried about how to protect the Glencoe community. Locks were a problem.

While awaiting the arrival of his senior staff, Hamish diverted himself at the antique walnut desk he'd brought from the family homestead in Scotland. On his laptop he retrieved dramatic photos of towering minarets of rock and ice, scenes he had captured during a mountaineering expedition to the seldom-visited Chinese Himalayas. The American Alpine Club dinner was only a few weeks away, scarcely enough time to put together a decent presentation. He felt the weight of Rambler's aging body as she settled against his feet.

Without taking his eyes from the screen, he groped for his tea, a man equally comfortable corralling boisterous children, wrestling a fractious stallion, tinkering with a balky tractor, or holed up in a snow cave at twenty thousand feet. Being headmaster at Glencoe afforded him decreasing amounts of time to do the things he enjoyed most, which did not include those infernal quarterly trustee meetings. In the early days, board members focused on the progressive education principles espoused by the founders, Stallings and Coe. Since Phil Connaughton, the British barrister, had assumed the reins, however, new trustees were recruited from the corporate world, their emphasis morphed toward financial sustainability, and the pressure on Hamish to raise money increased exponentially.

Shortly after nine, Hamish heard the front door open. Bonnie's voice welcomed the first arrival. He saved his presentation, lowered the screen, and headed downstairs. The select staff filtering in to the MacLean living room were less than enthusiastic about extending their already long day, but as this was an unscheduled event, it was apparent that something unusual was in the offing.

"Mmmm, smells heavenly," Jane Henderson said, popping her head around the corner of the pantry where Bonnie was unloading several pans of cinnamon raisin bread onto metal racks to cool. "Are they for us?"

Bonnie beamed. "Depends on whether you're here long enough for these to cool, Jane. Where's Payton? Does he get the night off?"

"No, we came together. He's bringing in a few logs for Hamish."

"I haven't seen your peripatetic four-year-old in a while, Jane. What's he up to these days? Torturing amphibians?"

"I think the frog population is safe from him 'til spring, but if I have to play one more game of Go Fish I'm going to scream."

Bonnie's eyes sparkled. She often babysat for Nicky Henderson to give Jane and Payton a precious evening out once in a while. Hamish well understood those evenings were bittersweet for her, wishing she had been blessed with a child of her own. He knew she had come to believe, after three devastating miscarriages, that their destiny to guide generations of young people at Glencoe was, in some way, compensation for having been denied motherhood. At least they had Rambler.

Pete Hedges walked in next, chatting with Ron Handy, who came toting a book in one hand, a load of leather for a shoulder bag he was fashioning in the other. Ron was always well-fortified with busywork to distract himself while the others debated whatever it was they always debated. In truth, the music teacher generally contributed the most wisdom. He was the lone faculty member who had actually worked for the founders. He was the sole repository now for the institutional knowledge that threaded generations of students and faculty at Glencoe. In his idle time, when not concocting the next great Thanksgiving musical extravaganza, Ron had begun to write a memoir, for he understood it fell to him to document the institutional memory of Glencoe.

As the two men removed their boots inside the front door, Ron's beagle, Peppy, brushed ahead of his owner, for experience had taught him it was first-come first-served on the coveted hooked rug in front of the MacLean fireplace. If he didn't get there before Rambler, the old dog would occupy it for the duration of the meeting.

Steve Jacobs, tall, blond, and lanky, sauntered in without the usual sheaf of science papers to grade. Like most faculty at Glencoe, Steve was uber-athletic and responsible for some component of the school's afternoon sports programs. On a snowy February afternoon, you would likely find Steve tinkering with the rope tow on the ski hill behind Dewey Hall, or atop an all-terrain vehicle dragging a grooming rig around the ring road that circumnavigated the campus through the woods, preparing it for cross-country skiers.

"Evening, Ron. Has Hamish asked you to read us a bedtime story, tonight?" Steve asked with a smile, fingering the well-thumbed paperback Ron carried.

"You might enjoy it, Steve, but it's a bit dark for this crowd," Ron chuckled, as Steve read the blurbs on the back cover of Cormac McCarthy's *The Road*.

Pete Hedges joined their conversation, beer in hand. "Either of you know what's itching MacLean tonight?"

"I hope we're not going to discuss Malcolm Dandridge again," Ron said. "I advised Hamish that boy would be a tough project. Hamish thinks he's turned the corner, but I suspect we're in for more fun and games."

"I'm the one who's got to live with him," Pete reminded everyone. "Even after the sympathy he got after that bizarre accident on Balanced Rocks, he's not helping build chemistry in Marshall House. He's been here, what, five weeks now? And has mastered the art of turning off every other kid in the house. Christine and I are about ready to decapitate him."

Hamish descended the stairs from his study to join the small group of invited guests chatting idly in the living room below. *An energetic, creative bunch*, he marveled. *I'm awfully lucky to have them.* The core of the Glencoe faculty, this was a supremely independent-thinking group of educators. No mere rubber stamp, blessing his every suggestion, this unofficial executive committee had provided many vibrant, argumentative evenings for their chief. But that was what he wanted, what he needed to keep his outlook fresh and his leadership properly focused.

"Thanks, everyone, for joining us on such short notice. I know none of you is thrilled to add another meeting to your day, but your input is needed right now," Hamish began.

Pete chuckled. What choice did they have?

"Nowhere else we'd rather be," Ron teased.

"Okay. Let me get right to the point. Earlier this evening I drove through a checkpoint down by the Maple Leaf Inn," Hamish said. "It seems that two convicts have escaped from a work detail near Ray Brook, and the state police believe they may be nearby. I spoke with Sergeant Parker earlier this evening and he feels we ought to take precautions against a possible hostage-taking. You all know how I feel about restrictions on the movement of our children. Their parents didn't send them here to be fenced in. But I must take this seriously. I called this meeting to ask for your advice on how to proceed. How much information do you think the kids ought to hear? Should we curtail their activities, their trips? What do we do about the lack of security in our houses? Let this be a free-form discussion. I'm here to listen."

There was general silence while everyone absorbed the news. No one relished the thought of transforming the lifestyle of Glencoe to accommodate the needs of the police department, but the risk of a hostage situation could not be dismissed lightly. Ron Handy spoke first.

"We could suspend the trip program until Thanksgiving. Having all the students here on campus will make my life easier. It would be helpful for me to know everyone can be available for rehearsals."

"That's all well and good," Payton Henderson interjected. "But what happens if these characters are still at large after Thanksgiving? What if they've left the area and are never caught? How can we just pick a date when we feel it's now safe to go back into the woods? Some of our best hikers are going to be really disappointed if we have to cancel big trips."

"I'm much more concerned about safety in our own homes," said his wife, Jane. "We can't lock our houses at night, and our numerous canines," she added wryly, "are so used to strangers they would probably welcome these convicts with tails wagging. If I were a parent of one of these children—come to think of it I am—I would want some assurances that my son or daughter could go to sleep at night without worrying myself sick."

The discussion went back and forth. Hamish said little, preferring to listen to the animated give-and-take as he pulled slowly on his beard. At 10:30 he abruptly called a halt to the proceedings.

"The hour is late. I thank you all for your contributions. Please don't mention the subject of this meeting to the students in your houses. As much as I hate doing it, tomorrow I will instruct the maintenance crew to install combination locks on the doors in each of the houses. Just as soon as the police can round up these two neaps we can put the locks away. However, I do not see any point in advertising the reasons for our security measures. I'm thinking that copies of the *Lake Placid News* ought not be available in the library for a while. I wonder how many students will even notice," Hamish said. "If we're lucky, it will be settled in a day or so and no one will be the wiser."

"Hamish, someone's bound to hear about it on the radio," Pete said.

"Our kids don't listen to the radio," Ron countered. "But word may have already gotten out beyond our little bubble here. All it takes is one parent to see or hear this story somewhere, call his or her child, and we end up looking foolish."

"Ron's right," said Jane Henderson. "Maybe you should consider an email to the parents, explaining what we are doing to ensure the safety of their children. I think hiding this will only backfire in the end."

"I'm primarily concerned with protecting the younger ones, but I suppose there's no way to keep this cat in the bag. I'd like each set of houseparents to discuss the issue with their own students after dinner tomorrow night. Having done that, if you feel anyone seems particularly frightened, please let me know. Jane, your suggestion of a mailing to the parents makes sense. I'll get on that.

"As for the outdoors program, I think it might be a good idea to reschedule any mountain or riding trips that may be on tap during these next several weekends," he said, looking at Pete Hedges, who was responsible for coordinating hiking trips in addition to his duties as an English teacher for the upper grades. "Sergeant Parker sounded like a seagull screechin' on a wire. Wouldn't let me off 'til I'd agreed to all his safety measures. I hate like bejesus to take these steps. It goes against my very core, but I don't feel we have much choice.

"As usual, you've all been very helpful. It's late, and I don't deserve to take up any more of your time. See you in the morn." There was no lingering, save for cordial goodnights to Bonnie, who sent them packing with a healthy slice of the cinnamon raisin bread wrapped in tinfoil. Hamish had already disappeared back into his study at the top of the stairs.

22

Separation Anxiety

RAMON SOON CAME TO UNDERSTAND THAT LIFE ABOVE LOST POND WAS its own kind of prison. Although he no longer had to contend with concrete walls, steel bars, and Hector Mercado, Ramon's city smarts did not prepare him for a psycho lumberjack, infinite forest, and, after two weeks in the woods, a persistent chill he could never quite shake. He tried to convince himself there was still a way out, that he was not thoroughly trapped. Now that the adrenaline-fueled escape was behind them, he had time to think more clearly about his rash decision to follow Garth. Two months to possible parole; that's all he had needed until maybe they'd have let him go. But go where? In two months, his mom and brother might be dead. They needed him *now*, not in two months. As he lay in his sleeping bag, Ramon replayed the consequences of his choices. Could he really have been able to help anybody with cops combing his neighborhood, just waiting for him to surface? It was crazy. Ramon pinballed between anger and depression.

Rising from his sleeping bag each morning took enormous determination and a growing sense of frustration. Except to pee, there was little motivation for Ramon to move from the stink of his nylon womb. Staying alive was increasingly challenging with each colder dawn. There were only a few chores that had to be done. Their water supply came from a small brook that fed Lost Pond. Though it was ice-clogged each morning, it was still possible to break through to fill their pots. Soon, Garth warned, they might have to resort to melting snow, which would require more precious fuel to bring to a boil.

There was little chance anyone would just happen upon them, so remote was their location. With no maintained trail anywhere near the frozen pond that lay below their shelter, Garth felt they would be secure as long as they made no large fires and stayed under cover of the canopy. He permitted no fires at all during those first days when helicopter overflights could have spotted them. Depending upon how long Garth chose to remain in this spot, gas for the stove could run low, making fires essential. Each time Ramon broached the subject of their expected length of stay Garth cut him off. The man had a plan that he refused to share, or he was just playing by the seat of his pants. Either way, the uncertainty left Ramon terribly unsettled.

At first, Garth performed virtually all the chores in the early days of their residence at Lost Pond. He foraged for food, trapping or shooting small game when he could, built and tended their fires when he felt it was safe to do so, and handled all the cooking. Ramon worried out loud that using a rifle would attract attention, but Garth shrugged it off. As it was deer hunting season, he had little concern that someone within earshot of a rifle report would become suspicious; lots of folks were out there firing away, he argued.

The only chore Garth assigned to his inexperienced companion was the gathering of firewood. Eventually, Garth permitted Ramon to use a hatchet and prepare their campfire. He taught Ramon to break fallen branches in the crotch of a tree, to use birch bark as tinder, and how to find dry kindling when birch bark was unavailable by splitting open a branch and carving out splinters from its heart. The twigs and branches were then reduced to lengths that would easily fit their small fire ring, the only place the snow did not permanently cover.

As much as he despised the lumberjack, Ramon appreciated the chance to contribute something positive to their dreary lives. He came to revere the little orange flame that lived and died at his pleasure. The flickering light became a companion. Its crackle and dance was the only thing Ramon could control, the only comforting aspect of an increasingly demoralizing existence.

Eva Ortiz had raised her children to be meticulous about their grooming, no matter how desperate their living conditions. Even in prison, Ramon had not neglected his appearance, often rinsing his socks in the sink. If Garth had ever said that escaping from prison meant he'd have to wear the same set of soiled clothes for days on end, Ramon would have categorically refused to go. It revolted him to be near Garth, let alone sleep inches away from him, not only because the man was so brutish, but because his body odor was so foul. In truth, Ramon knew his own condition was just as bad. There was one piece that just didn't seem to fit. Not a meal would go by after which Garth would fish out a small toothbrush, its handle sawed short to conserve a few ounces, and scrub his teeth for an inordinate amount of time. When the toothpaste ran out Garth used salt, but he rarely failed to attend to that one part of his personal hygiene. The routine included meticulous flossing with what seemed like an endless supply of thin nylon string. The man's body reeked but his teeth always sparkled. Ramon thought it bizarre but never dared to speak of it. He worried his own teeth were beginning to rot away.

Then there was the issue of toilet paper. After ten days, the two rolls Garth had taken from the cabin were gone. When Ramon sheepishly asked what they should do about it, Garth just laughed and shrugged his shoulders.

"Maids didn't bring none this morning, eh?" he smirked.

"Come on, Garth. What are we supposed to do, stop shitting?"

"Quit eatin' the beans."

"I'm serious, man. What the hell are we supposed to do?"

"Rub your butt against a tree. Crissakes, I ain't your mama. Use leaves if you can dig 'em out, or the damn snow if you're worried about splinters on your ass. Eat with your right, wipe with your left, assuming you're right-handed," he smirked.

"Maybe it's time we got the hell outta here," Ramon fumed.

Garth stopped laughing. "I go when I'm ready. You can take off any time," he glared.

With his insides screaming with semi-reconstituted chili, Ramon decided he had no more time to debate the issue. He hurried off to the site of their rudimentary latrine, a designated area downhill from their camp, and struggled to put his new lesson into practice. It was clearly a practiced art, to squat in such a way that you did not soil your pants nor tip over backward into the latrine. As he balanced precariously over the hole, an eerie chorus of yowls echoed through the woods, a haunting sound that sent a jolt up his spine. He could not tell if it came from near or far; it seemed to saturate his tiny world from all directions. He hurried to finish his business and get back to the relative safety of their little camp.

The days passed, the supply of downed limbs nearby became scarce, and Ramon was forced to roam farther. He dreaded those forays, so intimidated was he by the remoteness of their camp. As soon as he lost visual contact with their shelter, he felt uneasy until he'd gathered a reasonable bundle and could retrace his steps to the campsite. He knew it was ridiculous to be afraid, that he would never fail to find the shelter, for it was effortless to follow his own tracks in the snow, at least in daylight. He worried, however, about what would happen if Garth ever sent him out to replenish their wood after dark. He imagined having to call for help and, hearing no response, would wander aimlessly, crashing into trees, shouting until he was hoarse. Even his flashlight wouldn't save him, for he'd never know which tracks would lead him back.

Occasionally, when Garth became particularly obnoxious or aggressive, Ramon forgot his fear and used wood gathering as a means to escape, at least for a while. He discovered a ledge a few hundred yards above their shelter from which he could see the rolling expanse of distant mountains. Lingering at the ledge, he was often tempted to simply walk off, assuming at some point he'd cross a trail or meet a hiker who could direct him to a trailhead and freedom. He had to try to get to the city. It might be the scariest thing he'd ever done, but to stay with Garth was insane. Maybe Garth would be relieved if he left or angry enough to follow and kill him.

One night, as they lay in their bags, waiting for sleep to overtake them, the ubiquitous yowls came again. There was something about the mysterious call that Ramon found especially disturbing. "I've been hearing that sound a lot," Ramon whispered. "What the hell makes that kind of sound?"

"Could be coyotes. Could be coy-wolves. Could be both. Coyotes and wolves from Canada are breeding and no one's thinning the packs. They're more active at night so that's why you're hearing them now."

"Anything we need to worry about?"

Garth chuckled, "Not unless you look like a rabbit or a deer or you're standing between them and food." It was clear the logger was not only unconcerned, but totally relaxed and at peace in their remote hideaway. For the first time since they had banded together, he offered details about his life before prison, warming to the story and tolerant of the occasional questions Ramon asked. At one point, Ramon felt safe in asking where the scar on his cheek had come from and whether or not it was acquired by choice. Garth hesitated and Ramon steeled himself for the inevitable insult. Instead, he got the whole story, including the deaths of two Mohawks responsible for his branding. Ramon was the only person he had ever told, Garth admitted. And if he ever breathed a word of it, well . . . the threat was clear.

Maybe he was misreading the lumberjack, but Ramon felt their relationship had just changed. Just a little, perhaps, but this was the first time Garth had ever offered a glimpse into his personal story. Ramon decided to risk a question.

"So, what's the deal with the flossing?"

Garth was quiet for a moment. It had been a habit for so long he'd nearly forgotten its genesis. "Been doing it since I was little," he said, wistfully. "It was real important to my dad, and he always took time to make sure I flossed, at least when he was sober. He'd hang over me until he was satisfied I'd done it right. Don't know why it was such a big deal to him, but it stuck with me—the only thing he taught me that didn't come with a slap or a kick. That's about all I inherited from the bastard."

"I gotta admit," Ramon joked, "you smell awful—maybe no worse than me—but those teeth are a shocker."

Garth laughed. "Maybe I got a career in the movies."

"Maybe not," Ramon said. "But you'll have a damn sweet mug shot."

"I ain't gettin' no more mug shots, Jack," Garth snapped, the joviality gone. "If I can get over the border and hook up with some lumber camp, nobody will see my ass in this country ever again."

Ramon finally stopped asking when they would leave. He knew it had to be soon but he also wanted to avoid the rage that question caused. Garth was like a stick of dynamite whose fuse was always smoldering. No matter how hard Ramon worked to avoid sparking the woodsman's temper, their exchanges became tenser as the inevitable day approached when they would leave the camp to finish their escape.

Besides wood duty, Ramon was also responsible for alerting Garth when the pot reached a boil and for keeping it refilled. Water that was not used to prepare their meals was used to wash their hands and their utensils and to fill their water bottles. Garth had told Ramon once that it was important to bring the water they heated to a full, rolling boil, especially that which came out of the brook feeding Lost Pond, but never told him why. Ramon usually followed instructions but sometimes his impatience prevailed. *It's hot enough now,* he thought. *Why waste fuel making it boil when we have to wait until it cools before we can use it?*

Garth imposed such strict rations of their dwindling supplies that it became impossible to ingest enough calories to maintain their strength. Breakfast consisted of one packet of instant oatmeal mixed with a few tablespoons of hot water. Every other day they treated themselves to a cup of cocoa. For lunch, a chunk of hard salami and crackers. For dinner, Garth alternated between beans and rice, pasta, and once in a while, a freeze-dried meal-in-a-bag, such as chili or shrimp Creole. To make their resources last longer, Garth laid some wire snares and built crude deadfalls at some distance from their camp to catch small game, mostly rabbit or squirrel. Every couple of days he would walk the trapline, bringing his rifle to finish off the unlucky creatures who had been lured by his bits of apple or popcorn.

Ramon worried that Garth had little use for him now. He had served his purpose as a pack mule, hauling gear into their backwoods hideout. But the beast of burden had to be fed every day. Ramon was certain Garth resented every time he had to share their meager rations.

"Don't you think they've given up on us yet?" Ramon asked one evening between spoonfuls of watery onion soup.

"Given up? No. But spending time on other business? Yeah, more every day," said Garth, wiping dribbled soup off his beard.

"I didn't risk my life breaking out of that joint just to sit in this hell-hole and eat your lousy cooking," Ramon muttered. "I'm getting damn tired of this. I want to go home."

"You can leave any time, Jack. Sooner the better. And if you don't like the food, get your own, eh? Now's as good a time as any. Get out of here." Garth set down his cup and approached Ramon menacingly. "I mean now! Leave!"

Ramon raised his hand to the advancing giant and tried to speak in a more conciliatory manner. "Whoa, take it slow. I didn't mean nothing."

Garth kicked the soup out of Ramon's hand and pulled him to his feet, his breath hot on Ramon's face. "If it wasn't so fuckin' hard to get rid of a body, I'd shoot your ass right now and be done with you. You got a problem with any of this, you just take your chances out there, got it?"

"Okay, okay," Ramon stammered. "Sorry. Didn't mean nothin' by it. Jesus."

Garth returned to his log, the flashpoint dissipated. "If I gotta stay out here a few extra days to avoid going back to prison, I'll deal with it. Figure another week, maybe," he said, rummaging through their food bag to take inventory. "I don't want to wait 'til we've got nothing left, just in case something comes up. Like I said, you're free to leave, anytime. There's the door," Garth smirked, gesturing toward a nearly impenetrable wall of spruce.

On those rare days when the November sun burned through the overcast, Ramon sought out that rocky ledge above their camp where he could take in the meager warmth on his face and reflect on the irony that while no cell still confined him, he was still every bit a prisoner. Was it possible to ever return to a normal life? Having learned of the casual murder of the two Mohawks, Ramon knew what Garth was capable of, and that he would not be going to Canada with the lumberjack. The fright of escaping on his own began to look more appealing than the chance of taking a bullet when Garth no longer had use for him. For his own survival, as well as his self-respect, he needed to control his own destiny.

Ramon listened to the soft snoring from his sleeping companion and the gentle pelting of sleety snow on the plastic sheet above their heads.

As best he could figure, tomorrow would be the two-week anniversary of their breakout. The folly of his decision to join in the escape ate at him. Only two months to a parole hearing and, with luck, freedom. Well, that was off the table now. He'd have to live the rest of his life on the run, or go back to prison for a longer stretch. *You're one stupid sonovabitch*, he thought. But sitting in this tiny clearing with a dangerous companion who might already have decided to kill him seemed the worst option.

Just past ten, with a full moon casting an otherworldly glow through the cloud cover, Ramon slipped quietly out of his sleeping bag, pulled on his parka and his foul-smelling socks and boots, and gathered a few essentials he thought he'd need. His precious headlamp, a water bottle, the last fresh batteries, and a few granola bars went into the top pocket of his backpack, Garth's prized Smith & Wesson hunting knife went into the main compartment, along with a hastily stuffed sleeping bag and a hundred dollars in twenties that he stole from Garth's pack.

True to his impetuous decision-making, Ramon thought little about the details of making his escape. He had no map and little idea of what direction would take him back to civilization the fastest. Garth had made passing remarks about where the closest trails lay and although Ramon had sought to file those comments away for future use, they were vague and not particularly useful. But it seemed sensible to try to reach a trail at night and get out to a parking lot before there was much activity. The fewer questions he had to answer, the better. Descending was the easy part, for he understood that trails to civilization lay below them on the valley floor. What direction to take once he hit such a trail, he did not know. He had barely given any thought to how challenging it would be to hitch a ride toward New York City. Now those concerns flooded his mind. Bus stations seemed too risky. He tried to visualize a successful outcome. He would find a trail sign; he would meet a sympathetic hiker going his way; a trucker heading south would pick him up. Anything was better than staying here and waiting for the inevitable moment when Garth would kill him or leave him to wander aimlessly in the woods until he succumbed to the cold or was captured.

Hiking without a compass or a map, Ramon only concerned himself with walking as directly downhill as possible. His headlamp cast a narrow beam, illuminating only the next few trees. He tried to keep a straight line but was often forced to weave around downed trees and dense underbrush. Each exhale was lit by the beam of his headlamp, a constant reminder of the frigid night air.

Within a quarter mile of their camp, a series of broken cliffs blocked his way. He nearly stepped off the first one, grabbing a tree trunk as one foot slid into thin air. Ramon backed away and took some breaths to settle his heart. He realized his strategy of beelining downhill was suicidal. He traversed the lip of the first cliff until he was able to locate a narrow chimney that allowed a safer descent. Dropping to a sitting position, he inched his way into the chute, grabbing flimsy branches to control his speed. Wet, cold snow found its way under his parka and shirt, melting on contact with his warm back. Progress was slow as he solved one steep section after another, but the wetness and cold increased, sapping his strength. There was no way to get warm. He had no matches or ready kindling to build a fire. His stumbles increased, and his resolve began to crumble. He felt panic creeping in as his breath quickened. There was no way to know how much farther he might have to travel to hit a trail. He had to keep moving to combat the growing chill but the way was so difficult. Moving fast was impossible, a slow road to hypothermia and death.

Ramon checked his watch. It was one a.m. For three hours he had been moving almost nonstop, pausing only to munch on an energy bar or to take a gulp of water. Each respite was brief, for the chill overwhelmed him almost immediately. He recalled it had taken them three days to get to their Lost Pond campsite the first time after the original escape. Then, they had been carrying huge loads and moving cautiously. If it took anywhere close to three days to get out now, he'd never make it.

The cliff section passed and he found it easier going by following a shallow depression that seemed to avoid the trees. It felt almost like there could have been a trail beneath the layers of snow and ice, and Ramon began to relax. With luck, this "trail" might take him all the way down to the valley floor. At that moment, to avoid a pair of large rocks, he stepped between them and plunged into icy water up to his knee. It took several seconds before the nerves in his leg reacted to the shock and, by then, his other leg had followed suit. With no discernible trail to descend, he had been tracking an ice-covered stream that finally gave way beneath his weight. Ramon immediately knew he was in serious trouble. The panic welling in his chest felt all too familiar and a frightful memory overwhelmed him.

. . .

It was August 1997. Ramon had just turned fifteen. New York City was sweltering, and its residents, at least those without the blessing of air-conditioning, were desperate for a break in the weather. Each night, Eva rinsed out sweat-stained T-shirts and hung them in colorful rows to dry in the shower, though damp was about all she could expect by the next morning, which brought another round of hot, fetid air, driving the family out of their sauna-like apartment and into the streets. The only relief Ramon and his siblings enjoyed was to dash in and out of the stream from a fire hydrant down the street that had been wrenched open by unknown benefactors. The fun lasted until the fire department came and recapped the hydrant.

Aunt Consuela showed up for dinner one Friday brimming with excitement. "We're going fishing!" she exclaimed, peeling open a big envelope. Eva chuckled at her sister's enthusiasm as she readied a cold salad. The energy and passion her sister brought to the family helped erase the gaping hole left by the loss of a father. It was a blessing for a single mother overwhelmed with three nearly uncontrollable boys and a baby girl physically spent from battling one infection after another. Pablo reached for the envelope and extracted a colorful card that described a fishing expedition on the Great South Bay, off Long Island.

"I won it at the raffle!" Consuela cried, taking the card back from her nephew.

"I never win anything. What raffle?" Eva asked.

"I told you I was going to a fundraiser at the Boys' Club last night, sister," Consuela smiled. "Your kids spent half their life there. Miguel is on the swim team there, right? We need to support that place or they'll shut their doors and these chickadees will be back on the streets," she said, poking Ramon in the ribs. "Anyways, I bought a few tickets to be a nice neighbor and next thing they are calling out my number for this trip. Anybody want to come with me?"

"When's this supposed to happen?" Pablo asked.

"Tomorrow!" Consuela exclaimed. "Early bedtime tonight little bebés. We catch a train to Long Island, and the boat will be waiting to take us out on the water. It's a day out of this stinking heat."

"I don't know how to fish," Miguel said.

"From what your mama tells me, you're half fish yourself! They'll teach us. That's what the brochure says," Consuela assured him. "They provide everything. We just show up and try to catch ourselves some dinner."

They boarded *Pollywog*, a twenty-eight-foot Boston Whaler in Bay Shore, after a couple of hours snoozing on the Long Island Railroad. Consuela and Eva had flogged them out of bed at six to catch the train, and it showed on everyone's faces. The captain, Charlie Crowell, met them on the dock. He looked to be in his early seventies from his weathered face and crooked posture, but he danced off the boat to greet them with the agility of a much younger man. Lean and tanned, he sported a scruffy white beard that looked to be of the permanent three-day-old variety. Atop his head was a grease-stained baseball cap that scarcely kept his beak nose in the shade. Ramon noticed a kid not much older than himself organizing fishing rods in the stern of the boat. Crowell welcomed them and introduced the kid as *Billy, my guy that makes the boat go.*

They eased away from the dock a little before ten, towing a small dinghy off the stern. Consuela was determined to enjoy the trip to the fullest and she maintained a nearly nonstop chatter with the captain. The rest of the Ortiz family remained almost mute, gazing at the disappearing shoreline and beginning to feel early onset of queasiness from the constant swell. Ramon took deep breaths to quell the nausea and noticed his siblings were looking a little green around the edges as well.

They had been steaming into the Great South Bay for about thirty minutes when Ramon saw the captain berating *his guy that made the boat go*. Embarrassed to be publicly chastised, Billy just stared at his sandals as Crowell laid into him. Suddenly remembering his guests, the captain turned away from Billy and clicked on a frozen smile. "Seems we've forgotten the lunches," he said. "I bet those coolers are sitting on the dock right where we left them."

"We going back?" Pablo asked, hopefully. He had already suffered enough deck rolling for one day.

"And ruin your trip? No sir. That's why we tow this dinghy, for emergencies like this. I'll shoot back there and get the food while Billy holds down the fort. He'll show you how to use the gear, and I'll be back before you know it. Surprise me with some bluefish." Crowell gave an apologetic shrug to Consuela and turned off the *Pollywog*'s engine. Billy hauled on the rope to the dinghy until it bobbed alongside. Crowell climbed in, Billy tossed the rope into the bow of the dinghy and Crowell roared off.

All eyes turned to Billy, who had yet to utter a word since they had left Bay Shore. Ramon felt sorry the shy boy had had to suffer such a verbal beating in public and was curious to see how the departure of Crowell would affect him. Billy removed his sunglasses and wiped off the salt spray with his T-shirt. He looked up, smiled wanly and said "Sorry. I screwed up."

Ramon suspected it was easier for Billy to admit a mistake to this group of strangers than to Crowell. He wondered if they were family or just boss and hired help. Eva walked across the deck and placed her hand reassuringly on Billy's elbow. "I'm afraid we don't know the first thing about fishing. Can you teach us?" she asked.

Billy smiled gratefully. "It's pretty easy, as long as you pay attention to the hooks." He patiently explained how to use the heavy rods, baited the hooks with bits of eel for everyone and kept a close eye on their casts. Pablo and Miguel took to it right away. Ramon became bored after a few casts of his own and started helping Marianna, who couldn't really handle the weight of the rod. Eva and Consuela chatted with each other, letting their rods sit unattended in the holders screwed into the side of the boat.

The wind freshened, and whitecaps curled over little blue-green waves across the bay. *Pollywog*'s roll became more pronounced in response to the breeze and with it came nausea again. Whether it was an impulse to escape the shifting deck or just an urge to cool off, Ramon could not have said. Without a word to anyone, he pulled off his shirt, scrambled away from where his siblings were casting, and dove overboard. The cool water immediately refreshed him, and his nausea disappeared. Ramon had taken swimming lessons at the Boys' Club when he was six or seven, but those days in the crowded pool did not really prepare him for open water like the Great South Bay. His brother, Miguel, on the other hand, was a natural, proficient enough to lead the Boys' Club teams to numerous medals in city competition and might one day earn him a college scholarship.

Ramon quickly found that the waves with their little foaming caps sloshed against his face as he swam away from *Pollywog*. No matter how he timed it, each stroke brought another dose of salt water into his mouth. *Maybe this ain't such a cool idea*, he thought, and began to tread water to keep his head higher. He looked back at *Pollywog* and saw no one watching him. There was shouting. Cheering. Someone must have caught a fish. He felt intensely alone and regretted not being on board to share the excitement. Keeping his head as high as possible, he began dog-paddling back to the boat, the wind now at his back. This was better. The waves no longer splashed into his mouth for they were moving in his direction but as he glanced up at the boat it seemed he was making no progress. He swam more vigorously but the distance continued to grow. *Pollywog*'s large surface area gave the wind a bigger target than his head poking above the waves, and so it drifted more quickly than he could swim. Ramon realized he was losing ground, and the anxiety caused him to breathe more rapidly.

On board *Pollywog*, no one heard Ramon's shout. All were cheering for Pablo as he wrestled a twenty-pound bluefish. The two women screamed with delight and Billy leaned over the railing to collect the fish as it broke the surface of the water, wriggling and glistening in the sun. It was then that Miguel realized his brother was not celebrating with them. A quick look about the boat confirmed for him that his older brother was not aboard. He scrambled to the bow and saw the waving figure in the water, now about a hundred yards away. "Ma!" Miguel shouted. "Ramon needs help! I'm going in." And he dove into the Great South Bay.

Billy dropped the bluefish into a bucket of salt water and rushed to the wheel. He could get *Pollywog* to Ramon a lot faster than Miguel could swim but when he reached down to the ignition he swore. The key was gone.

"Whatcha looking for?" Pablo asked.

"The key. It must have slipped out of the ignition with all the rocking, maybe," Billy said. The alarm in his voice was unmistakable. He sprawled on the floor, looking under the seats and in every nook and cranny he could see, but the key was nowhere to be found. Consuela was screaming at her nephews and Eva was standing in shock by the railing, her face cradled in her hands.

"The captain must have taken the key," Billy said to Pablo, who was watching him closely.

Consuela heard him and screamed, "He *better* have taken it. Where is he?!"

There were plenty of life preservers and foam noodles aboard to keep people afloat, for fun and for emergencies, but Miguel had leapt in before Billy had a chance to give him one. The boys in the water were on their own.

Ramon was now in full panic mode, hyperventilating and thrashing to stay afloat as the whitecaps repeatedly doused him, unaware his younger brother was closing in. He imagined slipping beneath the surface and watching the sun gradually dim as he sank. Miguel approached Ramon cautiously. He had never taken a lifesaving course at the Boys' Club, but he had observed classes from time to time while awaiting his chance to do laps, and one detail had stuck. He swam behind Ramon, reached around, and put him into a headlock, linking his fingers behind Ramon's neck. He worked desperately to keep Ramon's back arched out of the water and his flailing arms at a safe distance. Miguel scissored his legs madly under the water to keep them both afloat, and tried to calm his bigger, stronger brother, whose frantic motions would exhaust them both. Every few seconds another whitecap broke over them, but as Miguel had them facing the disappearing *Pollywog*, the waves hit them from behind, not directly into their faces, it became easier to breathe.

"Billy!! Where the hell are you?" Miguel shouted. "Bring the goddamn boat!!" But *Pollywog* drifted farther away.

The brothers could not know the chaos that was unfolding aboard *Pollywog*. The women were out of their minds with two boys in the sea and a nearly catatonic first mate. Billy slumped in the captain's chair, looking frightened and helpless. Pablo and Marianna clung to each other, their eyes glued to their brothers' bobbing heads that came in and out of view as a new set of waves rolled over them. The slowly unfolding tragedy continued for the next fifteen minutes, though everyone, in the water and on the boat, could have sworn the agony took so much longer. Miguel was beginning to tire and the fear Ramon was feeling became a shared experience.

"There he is!" crowed Consuela, pointing to the fast-approaching little dinghy. As Crowell steered his skiff to the drifting *Pollywog*, he could see no one happily angling for bluefish. It had been just over an hour from the time he had left them, nearly long enough for two of his clients to drown.

. . .

The panic Ramon felt deep in his core as the waters of the Great South Bay sucked him down was close to what he now experienced, clinging to a dwarf spruce tree, desperately rubbing warmth into his drenched legs. He was exhausted and slowly freezing to death. There was no Miguel to rescue him this time. Ramon tried running in place to get the blood moving out of his chest to his freezing legs but it was difficult to maintain his balance in the unconsolidated snow. There was no way to build a fire. He trained his headlamp on the tracks he had produced to get to this point and knew instinctively that, to stay alive, his only option was to abandon the escape and climb uphill to generate warmth, even if it meant returning to a murderer. Heart pounding, Ramon willed his legs to move, punching them at every stride.

It was near dawn when he reached their campsite, totally spent. Garth was still slumbering as Ramon carefully replaced the cash and the knife he had taken in the logger's backpack, keeping a single twenty-dollar bill for himself. He peeled off his wet clothes and laid them inside his sleeping bag, hoping his body warmth would eventually dry them. It seemed like hours before his shivering ceased, but at last his body relaxed and slipped into unconsciousness.

23

A Change in Plans

AFTER TWO WEEKS OF INTENSIVE SEARCHING BY STATE AND LOCAL police, scant evidence of the escaped prisoners had emerged. The stolen laundry van had been found, as had the truck Garth and Ramon had left at the cabin. Bloodhounds confirmed that the two men had, indeed, visited the cabin, but the dogs had lost the scent at the base of a towering maple tree within a quarter mile of the building. Blowing snow had obliterated all tracks and the dogs were their last and best hope. The *Lake Placid News* no longer updated the story on the front page. Down at Harry's Barber Shop, where Hamish MacLean visited like clockwork every two weeks, the talk in the chair turned to the weather and the hopeful crush of Christmas tourists arriving to partake of the winter sports that made Lake Placid a destination each year. The promise of early snows meant good news for downhillers at Whiteface and cross-country skiers at the Van Hoevenberg ski touring center, and good news for every restaurant and hotel owner in town. Consensus had it that the convicts had either perished in the wilds or managed to elude police roadblocks and were now the problem of some other community, maybe even some other country.

Initial news reports on the escapees had been sketchy. They were an unlikely pair to be traveling together—a Hispanic kid from Manhattan and a lumberjack from nearby Tupper Lake. As an experienced woodsman, Garth probably knew how to survive in the woods without provisions or equipment in winter conditions, the *News* pointed out. It was precisely that experience, the story continued, that would have convinced him to find warmer surroundings as soon as possible. The reporter opined that weeks in the wilds would have been especially difficult for the downstate fellow, who presumably did not have winter camping experience.

At Glencoe, students were still forbidden to walk on campus without an adult after dark, a practice they'd long cherished. But the outdoors program was reinstated, and gradually the school community returned its focus to matters closer to home.

Libby loved the calm of the evening reading period. Even the controlled chaos of baths, showers and group studying that followed comforted her. Each fall, students arrived at Glencoe hoping to have been assigned to Phelps House because of Payton and Jane Henderson. They ran a tight ship, but a supportive one. They were there to nudge, prod, cajole, hug, criticize, even reprimand when necessary. Most of all, for Libby, their guardianship was a safety net that never failed her. The warmth and camaraderie of Phelps House were so unlike the sterile rigidity she felt in her parents' vast New York City apartment. When the time came to create her own nest, she resolved to model it after Phelps. Though she loved spending idle afternoons in the art room with Christine Mason, who was much like an older sister, Jane Henderson felt more like what she imagined a loving, but firm mom should be. Her real mother, a source of perpetual mystery and disappointment, was like neither Glencoe woman. Feeling grounded and protected for the first time in memory, Libby was grateful to have been assigned to the Hendersons' house rather than the semi-controlled chaos that always seemed to rule other houses on campus, including Marshall, which Christine and Pete shared as houseparents, though not as an official "couple," for each had their own small apartment. The model worked well, but the fact remained, houseparents most sought-after by the kids tended to be those married to each other, like the Hendersons. That model just seemed closer to the nuclear family and less like a dorm with adult supervision.

A week remained before parents were to arrive to spend Thanksgiving Day with their children at Glencoe. A final week to perfect *The Truth about Zeus*, a final week to build sets and paint flats.

Following dinner in Dewey Hall, the Glencoe community fanned out to their respective houses on the hill, guided in the chilly darkness by a full moon highlighting the flanks of Cascade Mountain, visible above the trees. Libby and Tina reached the steps to Phelps House just as reading period was about to commence. As they discarded their barn boots and jackets in the mudroom cubbies, their high-spirited banter elicited a gentle reproach from Jane who was trying to subdue the other Phelps House students.

"Girls . . . please get your books and find a chair. It's past seven already."

"Sorry, Jane," Tina called. "We'll be right there."

"Too much sugar in the dessert tonight?" Payton cautioned. "I wish we could harness the energy in this house and sell it back to the power company."

At the dining room table Tracy and Jake were glued to an August issue of *Sports Illustrated* magazine, to which Tracy had a subscription.

"Reading period applies to you guys, too," Payton said.

"What you see here, Payton, is Tracy studying for his future career," Jake said, playfully cuffing Tracy across the back of his scruffy head. The magazine was opened to a story called "Super Man," describing Lance Armstrong's fourth consecutive Tour de France victory in July.

"And what career would that be, I wonder?" Payton asked. "Brilliant federal investigator going wherever the facts may lead? Or a lying sonovagun with strong legs and huge lungs who doped his way to the top?"

"The French looked into it. They didn't find anything," Tracy said, lamely. From his rather deflated look one could conclude he had his own private doubts about whether Lance competed cleanly.

"I recall having a conversation with you the day you arrived this fall, Tracy," Payton said. "I believe I expressed my doubts about the fellow's honesty and you didn't want to hear about it."

"This is the classic Hero's Journey that our whole semester's English class is about," Tracy said. "I've been following Lance since I was a little kid. Cancer in his groin, in his brain, triathlon career in the toilet. Worked his way to the very top through sheer hard work. He's blown away the competition four years in a row in the hardest athletic event there is. I mean . . . if that's not a Hero's Journey, what is?"

"He endured a lot. I agree. But I don't think he did it on his own. Time will tell. Look, Jane's going to kill me. You guys need to get in to reading period. But I will leave you with one lesson. Ever hear of Occam's Razor?"

Jake and Tracy shrugged. "Don't think so," Jake said.

"You've heard the phrase 'keep it simple, stupid,' or KISS for short?" Tracy nodded.

"William of Occam was an English philosopher, among other things," Payton continued. "He lived in the 14th century. This is a gross oversimplification, so apologies to the Occam family, wherever they may be, but he was the father of the Keep-It-Simple proposition. It's really hard to believe that one man could suddenly dominate the sport of cycling so completely, right? How could he do it? What are the chances that he inherited, or developed, the perfect mix of human attributes that enabled him to emerge from the pack the way he did and dominate so profoundly? Occam's Razor suggests that if there is a simple explanation for some set of circumstances, and a complex one, put your money on the simple solution being the likely one. Odds are, he's doping, and he's probably not alone. That's the simple answer. Occam would advise you to bet on it."

Tracy looked crestfallen, like he had lost his best friend. Not an uncommon reaction when one's previously accepted gospels are suddenly called into question with an argument not easy to refute and, in truth, jibes with your own deeply buried misgivings. This one was a bit more profound, perhaps, than discovering that fortune cookies are actually not a staple of Chinese cuisine.

Tracy picked up Alfred Lansing's *Endurance,* the book he was reading for English, and walked into the living room to find a chair. The class had not yet gotten very far into the classic adventure story of Captain Ernest Shackleton's heroic attempt to save his crew after his 1914 expedition to the South Pole went awry, but Tracy was already engrossed. The lecture from his houseparent, though, had left him wondering whether Shackleton would also end up with feet of clay like he feared for his modern-day counterpart, Armstrong. This hero business was perilous stuff.

"Tough losing an idol, huh," Jake snickered, following behind him.

"Who the hell is this Occam guy and what does a razor have anything to do with this?" Tracy muttered.

Jane or Payton usually bathed their son Nicky during reading period. Despite their best efforts, his squeaks and squeals would inevitably filter down to distract Libby and her housemates, curled up with their books in the Phelps House living room. One after the other would pick their heads up from their reading and scan the room to see who else might be giggling. Even Libby could not contain herself when Tracy, the bane of her existence, began to mimic Nicky's noises from the bathtub. Eventually, the room would dissolve into laughter until one houseparent or the other intervened to restore order.

This night, before escorting his irrepressible son up the stairs to another date with Mr. Bubble, Payton had filled the living room hearth with birch and maple logs, cut the previous year from the woods beyond the arc of student residences. As Libby scanned the room for a comfortable place to read, the fire was already crackling merrily. A Mozart piano concerto echoed softly in the background. Outside, an arborvitae swayed in the breeze, its lower branches gently rasping the cedar clapboards.

Jane sat at the table in the adjoining kitchen sewing down booties, a Christmas gift for her son, when the telephone rang in the foyer. Reluctantly, she set aside the booties and hurried to answer it. Half-listening from her chair, Libby sensed from the formal tone of Jane's voice that the caller was not a personal friend, but, clearly, an acquaintance. Jane was obviously struggling to remain civil.

"Oh . . . I see . . . can't be helped? That's really unfortunate. I'm sure she'll be disappointed," Jane said testily. There was a long pause as the caller tried to convince Jane of something. "After last year we were hoping to see you and Shelley for Thanksgiving this time. . . . Well, let me get her for you. Bye, bye." Jane poked her head around the corner of the living room doorway.

"Libby, it's your dad," she whispered, obviously irritated.

Partly due to a lack of cell phone coverage in the mountains and, more importantly, to eliminate the social distractions that modern-day cell phone ownership and usage had promoted, Glencoe required students to communicate with their families by traditional landlines. Cell phones were officially off-limits.

Libby closed her copy of *Endurance* and walked to the foyer to take the phone from Jane, who held it at arm's length as if it were contaminated. Jane squeezed Libby affectionately on the shoulder and returned to the kitchen. Though she tried to concentrate on her sewing, it was impossible for her to ignore half of the conversation.

"Hello?" Libby asked tentatively. Calls from her family were both infrequent and generally upsetting.

"Libby, it's Adam. How are you, darling?"

Adam. Not Dad, or Daddy, or Papa. Adam. She bristled at the "darling," as if he didn't have the right to use such a term of endearment.

"Oh, hi . . . Is everything okay?"

"We're fine, just fine. Shelley's in California for three weeks at a retreat. She told me to give you her love when I spoke with you."

Why didn't she tell me herself? Libby wondered. *She knows my number.*

"We need you to come to New York next weekend," her father continued, the first hint of discomfort in his voice.

"Next week? But that's when we do the Thanksgiving play. You and Mom are supposed to come see it. Remember? You must have gotten some mailing about it. Tina's folks can't make it—they're in Nepal—and I promised we'd take her out to dinner." Libby felt a battle coming on, a recurring script that began with a lump in her throat and ended with tears and frustration. She despaired of arguing with her parents; it was a painful pattern she seemed destined to repeat.

"That would have been nice, dear, but not this year. All the arrangements have been made. We want you to be with us. We're hosting a group from Kibbutz Harduf. It's in the north of Israel. Remember your mom and I spent a week there two winters ago? As you may recall, they run a wonderful Waldorf Steiner program in the Galilee and they will be here for a few days to see New York, learn about our school, and then visit Boston as well."

"Sorry, I don't remember the details about your trip. That was when you sent me to stay with Aunt Esther," Libby mumbled.

"Well, it's important that we be here as a family to celebrate their arrival. So, this takes precedence, I'm afraid."

"Who cares?" she grumbled.

"Excuse me?"

"I said why do you care whether I'm there? They don't know me." She already knew it was hopeless, but she couldn't just give in that easily. "You're being totally unfair. Everybody's parents come up for Thanksgiving. I've been working hard on this show and I want you to see it. *I* want to see it, for God's sake!" she said, her voice rising with an intensity that surprised them both.

"I'm sorry you're disappointed, Libby!"

"Disappointed? When did that ever matter to you and Mom?"

"I understand your feelings, Libby, but not your hostility," her father countered, trying not to rise to the bait. "The Kibbutz Harduf program is extraordinary, and we have so much to learn from each other. I wish you had more appreciation for what your parents have built here and wanted to be a part of it."

"Yeah, right," she mumbled under her breath. Adam barreled on, oblivious to her sarcasm.

"There is so much in common with how Glencoe was formed and, I hope, how it is run today. Progressive education on an organic farm? That's Harduf . . . and Glencoe. At least that's what we are led to believe," Adam said, a bit of skepticism in his voice. "It may not be a Steiner education precisely, but we hope it is the best place for you at the moment. Just not that weekend. You know we're always here for you, and . . ."

"No . . . you're never *here*, Dad. That's the problem. You're always *there*."

"We are your anchors, not necessarily your babysitters."

"I wonder what would happen if *Eyewitness News* received an anonymous tip about how the prestigious Austro-Lab founders treat their child?" she taunted.

"Elisheba Goldman! I'm ashamed of you," he said, using her Hebrew given name. "Our family has played a pivotal role in getting Austro-Lab off the ground. You don't realize how important your mother and I are in this endeavor. We're extremely proud of what we've accomplished and if we decide it's in your interest that you should be enriched by Steiner education in other parts of the world you must respect that, even if you don't agree with it. As far as Thanksgiving is concerned, you must be here. Period."

"Do they even speak English?"

"I beg your pardon, young lady," Adam sputtered. "Don't get snarky with me, I'm beginning to wonder what kind of an education you're getting up there."

"If you came up occasionally, you'd find out." Libby slumped down into one of the birch cubbies that cantilevered from the walls of the foyer and began to sob quietly onto her sleeve. In the adjacent living room, reading period had ceased to function. Her housemates exchanged concerned looks as the one-sided conversation became more heated. In the kitchen, Jane had abandoned her sewing and paced the floor.

"You criticize us for sending you to boarding school, but when we want to bring you home for a visit, you object," Adam Goldman continued. "I'm sorry if you're disappointed, Libby, but there will be other plays. I'll speak to Mr. MacLean tomorrow about arranging transportation. I've got some other calls to make before it gets too late, dear. See you Wednesday." Click.

Libby felt herself sinking into a sea of helplessness. Stuffed into the back of her cubby, eyes screwed shut, arms hugging her knees, she felt her chest constrict with anger. Yet again, the pattern was repeated. It always seemed to end like this with her parents. Just as Libby was about to storm out the door, reading period be damned, an arm slipped around her shoulder and Jane's gentle voice broke through.

"Libby, come up to the study. Nicky is tucked in. Maybe you'd like to talk to Payton and me about this, okay?" She opened her eyes and took a breath. She would not have to go it alone. Libby smiled gratefully and followed her housemother upstairs.

24

An Unexpected Visitor

IT SEEMED EVERY OTHER DAY ANOTHER STORM WAS BLOWING THROUGH the Adirondacks. A fresh eighteen inches of snow met Garth's eyes as he rolled to a sitting position in his sleeping bag. A wintry sun devoid of all warmth was just illuminating the frosty tips of the spruce above their heads as Garth grunted toward his companion, "Okay Jack, time we got serious about getting the hell outta here." Garth had mentioned to Ramon that he could carjack his way to the Canadian border, then cross it on foot well beyond any customs checkpoint. Border security was a myth as long as you knew how to travel in the bush. Ramon knew he was not part of that plan.

The gamy stench escaped from the sack as Garth stretched out an arm, reached for a stick and stirred the remains of the previous evening's fire, searching in vain for a living ember. Ramon poked his head out of his own nylon cocoon, ski hat pulled low to cover every possible inch of exposed flesh. Though he'd ached to hear those words again, Ramon felt anxious, not excited.

"Now? Today?"

"Soon as we can button this place up. We gotta tear everything down and make sure we don't leave much evidence."

"I still hear helicopters every day."

"Ahh, routine flights is all. The DEC's in love with those birds," Garth said, referring to the New York State Department of Environmental Conservation. "There's jokers getting lost every day. Those flights ain't got nothing to do with us, Jack. Wish I knew what day of the week it was. Should'a kept better track."

"Who cares what day it is?"

"I'd rather not head outta here on a weekend if I got a choice. Too many dudes wandering around."

Ramon looked about him. He realized he had become accustomed to their rough abode and scarcely noticed how grim it was. Every notch in those poles he knew as intimately as the lines in his own hand. The pattern of boughs across the roof was more familiar than the cracks in his bedroom ceiling at home. In a weird way this hovel provided a sense of security he was hesitant to abandon, especially now that he understood how risky it was to get away on his own. The devil you knew versus the devil you didn't.

As they ate their meager breakfast, the oatmeal cooling and congealing in their cups like bits of glue, Garth announced that they'd sleep only one more night above Lost Pond. Though he'd waited for weeks to leave their woebegone campsite, Ramon was still uncertain how he could manage on his own, unobtrusively leave the woods, get to a bus station, pay for a ticket, and travel safely back to New York City. Assuming Garth would just let him go, unharmed, he thought he could hitchhike away from Lake Placid, explaining that his car had broken down, but he had no idea where the bus stations were. More importantly, he had no money, save the twenty he'd taken from Garth the night of his abortive attempt to flee. Where was this ticket going to come from? And, most importantly, how could he safely resume life back in the city? What if his mom hadn't survived? Or his brother? Were they even still in New York City? Were the police watching the apartment, just waiting for him to surface? It seemed hopeless.

After breakfast, Garth left camp to collect their traps for the last time. "Fill the water bottles and cook some pasta. That's about all we got left. I want it hot when I get back." Since his own bottles were still full, Ramon retrieved Garth's and set them down beside the small camp stove to await the transformation of snow to potable water. He shook the stove to see how much fuel still remained, decided it would suffice without refueling, and pumped up the pressure. With a now-practiced hand, he cranked open the valve, sending a vapor of white gasoline up against the brass burner. At the touch of the butane lighter, a vigorous blue flame snapped to life, accompanied by the familiar low roar. He scooped up a potful of snow from behind their shelter, added the remains from his own water bottle, collected from a surprisingly open spring the day before, to speed the melt. As the snow began to liquefy, but well before it reached a rolling boil, Ramon poured the water into Garth's bottles, ignoring the odd pine needle and bit of bark that flowed in as well.

Chores done, Ramon left the shelter midmorning and headed upslope, away from the pond, to his favorite outlook. From this rocky perch Ramon could see ridges of mountains all the way to the horizon. Garth had taught him most of their names one day when his mood was expansive. Somewhere in between was a road that could take him south.

After maybe twenty minutes of enjoying the sunshine, he was about to depart this vantage point when a subtle, rhythmic noise caught his attention. The sound of ski poles crunching the snow reached him before he spotted a figure clad in purple passing just below his outlook. He held his breath and watched, afraid to make a move. The snowshoer appeared to be alone, expertly gliding through the dense undergrowth until intersecting Ramon's prints in the snow. Abruptly, the person halted and looked around.

"Shit!" Ramon whispered.

After a moment's hesitation, the figure turned to follow the line of prints up the slope. Ramon froze.

"Holy moly, you scared me!" the young woman exclaimed, shielding her eyes, from the sun. Before him stood a beautiful twentysomething blonde. Her hair was held in place beneath a purple headband that matched her parka and she wore form-fitting black tights and red gaiters that protected her calves. The sun glinted off her aluminum snowshoes. Despite the fullness of her pack and the surprise meeting she seemed at ease. As she leaned on her poles, her stance suggested the grace of an accomplished athlete.

When Ramon remained silent, the woman approached more cautiously. "I never expected to see someone else up here," she said, coming closer. "My name is Carly Perryman," she said, sticking out a mittened hand.

Still flustered, Ramon bent down and shook it. "Nice to meet ya." He wasn't about to tell her his real name, and he couldn't lie quickly enough to make it seem natural. Seconds ticked by. "Hunting," he said nervously.

"That's your name, or what you're doing up here?" she giggled.

Ramon smiled shyly. "What we're doing. Mostly rabbits," he said.

"Huh. It's a long way to come for rabbits."

"And squirrel," he added, thinking that might make the story more believable.

"I haven't seen a soul since yesterday morning," Carly said. " . . . and this is the last place I thought I'd run into anyone. You camping here?"

"Yeah," Ramon said, gesturing vaguely in the direction of the pond.

"Down by Lost Pond?"

"You know it?" Ramon asked. He thought no one but Garth knew about this area. He wondered if he should talk loudly to warn the lumberjack.

"From maps. Never been here before." She extracted a topographic map from a nylon pocket on her shoulder strap, unfolded it, and peered at it. "So you're not here alone," she said, looking up from the map. Ramon's guard went up even higher. He suspected he did not look like a typical hunter in the Adirondacks and worried about the conclusions she might be jumping to about who he really was.

"Uh . . . No. I got a buddy. He's checking our traps."

She started stamping her feet to keep warm. It was apparent to Ramon that she was not going to be satisfied until she'd received more information. He had a panicky thought that she might be an undercover cop. *Maybe she's already figured out who I am*, he thought.

"I'll stop and brew up some tea, if that's okay," she said, glancing at her watch.

Ramon jumped down from the rock and led the woman back to the clearing. Garth had returned and was sorting gear that he'd laid out on the space blankets that served as a floor of their shelter. He looked up as the two approached and Ramon saw a flash of alarm on his face, though he casually waved a hand in greeting.

"Hey, how ya doin'? I'm Carly," she said, not attempting to shake hands. "Mind if I get a hot drink here?"

Garth shrugged. "Name's Eric. I guess you've already met . . . Jack. What brings someone like yourself up here?" Ramon noticed the hatchet scar begin to twitch on Garth's cheek. He was certain Carly didn't miss it either.

"Oh, killing time while I wait for a guide job to open up. I'm not from around here so I figured I'd better do some homework. Get familiar with the territory, you know? It's tough to be a guide if you haven't been around the block so I figured I'd better do some hiking on my own first. They tell me Lost Pond Peak's one of the hundred highest in the Adirondacks so that's why I'm here," she said, waving vaguely toward a small hump that overlooked Lost Pond. "I climbed Street and Nye and bivouacked for the night," she said. "It sure was a wild day up here yesterday. Nice to see the sun again." She unsnapped the top of her sack and began searching through it. "Your friend tells me you're up here hunting rabbits."

"Uh . . . Yup."

"Been here a while from the looks of this place."

"We're in between jobs, too. I've always liked this spot. Real quiet," Garth said.

"Hard to figure this as a place to come for rabbits," she said, attaching a gas canister to her stove. She lit it and set a small pot of snow to boil, pouring in a bit of water to start the melt. Ramon watched with a growing sense of foreboding.

"How long you figure to be out here?" Garth asked.

"Another day or two, maybe. I moved out east a couple of months ago 'cause my boyfriend's working in Lake Placid. I used to be a mountain guide in the Tetons. In Wyoming?" She looked from one to the other, receiving blank stares. "The winter's kinda slow unless you're on ski patrol, which I wasn't. When my boyfriend got a job here at the Olympic Training Center, he told me to check out the guide services here. So far, nothing's opened up, but I figured the quickest way to learn the mountains here is to get out and climb 'em, so that's what I'm doing." The water in the pot began to bubble. She placed a tea bag in the pot and watched it bounce.

"Hiking alone, good looking woman like yourself. Not the smartest thing, eh?" Garth said. "Most folks don't hike in the woods by themselves this time of year. Shit happens."

Ramon felt Carly's attitude immediately change. He noticed the muscles tense around her eyes. "Oh, my boyfriend knows my route. If I didn't make it back on time he'd find me," she said quickly. She poured her tea and tea bag into a thermos, gulping some. Ramon thought she looked scared. "Well, I better push off if I want to reach Wallface Pond before dark," she said. Watching her with a laser-like focus, Ramon saw her bite her lip, as if she immediately regretted having mentioned her true destination. She shook out the last drops of tea into the snow, nested her stove inside the aluminum pot she'd used to boil the water, then placed both into a bright red nylon ditty bag and stowed it deep within her pack.

Ramon imagined Garth's brain was in overdrive. To let her go was to risk everything, especially considering how eager she was to leave. Garth glanced over at Ramon who shook his head slowly as if to say, *I'm not in this with you.*

"Happy hunting, guys," Carly said, tightening her shoulder straps. She took a compass bearing and hurried away from the clearing.

"Shouldn't have let that happen," Garth muttered as she disappeared from view.

"What choice did we have?"

"Got to take care of this." Garth said, his scar thrumming on his face. He rummaged through his pack, producing the Smith & Wesson carving knife he used to skin the animals that came their way, strapped on his snowshoes and strode after her.

Carly Perryman was an accomplished athlete and in extraordinary physical shape. Her experience living in the mountains out west had taught her how to live comfortably in the wilderness regardless of weather or season and that time had left her tough as nails with enormous stamina. But traveling solo was risky, breaking a cardinal wilderness safety rule. Even the fittest of climbers weren't immune to accidents and occasionally, as had been witnessed from time to time along the Appalachian Trail, women hiking alone became victims and headlines.

As she left the Lost Pond campsite, Carly set a furious pace. She jogged when the dense undergrowth permitted. Unseen roots caught her snowshoes and snow-laden evergreens showered her head and shoulders. When she finally descended to Wallface Pond, where she had told Ramon and Garth she intended to camp, she pushed on, never stopping until she had reached the parking lot at the Adirondak Loj, well after dark.

Garth descended rapidly following Carly's snowshoe tracks, which stood out as clear as a highway. Back at Lost Pond, Ramon worried what Garth would do with her once he caught her. Those tracks would lead others to the dirty deed as well. As far as Ramon knew, Garth had yet to take someone else's life in a premeditated fashion. There had been that incident Garth had told him about the Mohawks who had challenged him outside a Tupper Lake bar, the same ones, Garth was certain, who had given him the face brand. Ramon understood what Garth was capable of if pushed to the edge. He recalled the warning he had gotten from the corrections officer at ACF to stay away from the lumberjack. Lot of good that warning did, he swore to himself. Maybe chasing down this woman was a dry run for what Garth might do to get rid of him, too.

Ramon was no woodsman but he doubted it would be easy even for Garth to dispose of her body when he finally caught her. With a downed deer, if it was too difficult to haul it out, you could just leave it there and let nature take its course. Not so tidy getting rid of a human. He wondered if Garth would even tell him what he had done with her.

After an hour, the tracks were still easy to follow but Garth began to doubt he could catch her. The longer this business took, the longer the return would be, as well. As one hour turned into two, and two into three, Garth's resolve weakened. In his haste to hunt her down, he had neglected to bring a headlamp. It was a long climb back to their camp, and he could not do it in the dark.

The sun dipped below mountains to the west, leaving only the summits of the MacIntyre range aflame in rosy alpenglow. Ramon gazed at the rocky, windswept Algonquin soaring above wooded flanks already in the shadow of dusk. As those last rays of sunlight escaped their campsite

as if in a hurry to abandon the gathering chill for someplace more inviting, Garth appeared, looking angry and exhausted. Ramon hoped Garth
could see he had not been sitting on his ass, and had cleaned up the
campsite as instructed; he had packed his gear and deconstructed the
shelter. He had piled the poles in the woods around their campsite; the
plastic sheets that had served as their makeshift roof were neatly rolled
beside the small firepit, which would be eliminated the next morning. It
looked quite tidy after weeks of disarray, as if it had never been inhabited.
The next snowfall would complete the job. Without a cover over their
heads, this night would be a cold one, a last reminder of the harsh conditions they had endured.

Would Garth tell him what had become of their unexpected visitor?
Ramon was not sure he wanted to know.

"What a fucking waste of time," Garth muttered, slumping down
on a log adjacent to their firepit. Ramon waited for more details. He had
learned that he got less abuse when he asked fewer questions.

"I couldn't catch the bitch and forgot my damn light. From the looks
of her, I bet she's gonna report meeting us and that means we need to get
the hell outta here quick before this place is swarming with cops. Shit.
After all this careful planning she's gonna make us scramble. I'm damn
pissed I didn't take care of her when I had the chance here."

Ramon knew he had better not cause any further irritation, or he
might become a problem Garth could take care of that evening.

"Sorry, Garth. It did look like she wanted to get out of here fast.
Maybe we're making too big a deal out of it."

"It is a big fucking deal!" Garth seethed. "We've been out here for
more than two weeks for a reason. Not for our health, for sure. To make
them lose interest. Now they're gonna be interested again. And know
where to look. If she gets all the way out tonight, we're in a race for our
lives tomorrow." Garth glanced around the campsite. "You did a good job
breaking this place down," he said. "That's helpful."

"Why don't you eat something while it's still warm?" Ramon said,
allowing himself to feel a bit of pride at being recognized for anything.
He had already prepared the pasta and consumed his share, being careful to leave more than half. As Garth stirred the cooling pot of viscous

noodles, Ramon imagined he was trying to divine how much it had originally held, and if Ramon should be screamed at for taking too much. But
no accusations came forth on this night. Garth devoured the remainder,
washing it down with one of the bottles of water Ramon had prepared.
They shared a candy bar and settled into their sleeping bags shortly after
sunset.

"Soon as we can see, we go. That'll give us enough time to reach the
trailhead right around dark, so if we meet anyone, they won't get too good
a look at us," Garth declared. "Makes no matter now if we're quittin' this
place, but when you were chattin' up that bitch, I was getting zero return
on my trap line. The snares worked all right. We'd caught our fair share,
but when I got there all's left was bones and fur. We got competition."

Garth had said *we*. *"Soon as we can see, WE go."* That was one positive
Ramon could hang on to. Maybe he could get out alive after all.

. . .

Carly called ranger headquarters in Ray Brook early the next morning. Betty Lawrence, a temporary secretary on her first day in the office,
was trying to get the coffee maker to work and let the call go to voice
mail. It was not until the following day that Betty remembered to check
the recording. With no telephone message pad within reach, she tran-
scribed the message on the back of a used envelope and stuck it on her
boss' desk, wrong side up. When he arrived later that morning, assuming
the torn envelope was to be recycled, the Zone Supervisor tossed it in the
blue bin adjacent to his desk.

. . .

Ramon awoke later than usual. Since their escape Garth had always
shaken him at dawn, growling at him to get up and get the stove going.
Ramon sat up and looked over where the giant's huddled form still lay
entombed within his nylon sleeping bag. Above him a cloudless sky
already exhibited a deep cobalt hue.

"Garth?"

"Hmm," he grunted, moving nary a muscle.

"Shouldn't we get outta here?"

"Hmm."

"Sun's getting high."

"Can't do it today, Jack."

"You wanted to clear out first thing, remember?"

"Up half the night with the shits. I can't move."

Ramon lay back down, vaguely recalling Garth stumbling over him during the night.

"My insides are a mess. Just gotta hope that ho didn't turn us in. Lemme sleep."

Ramon lay restless for some time, finally extricated himself from the warm bag, dressed quickly to maintain bodily heat and lit the stove for cocoa. There was nothing else to do. No demand that he scrounge for wood or scrub pots. No insults, no slaps against his head. Throughout the day his tormentor left his sleeping bag only to stagger to their stinking latrine. He declined food, asking only that his water bottle be refilled. Late in the afternoon Garth ordered Ramon to rebuild the shelter, if only temporarily. Ramon thought Garth looked defeated. Scared even. The intestinal bug seemed to have sapped his strength to the point where running from anyone was impossible.

"We gotta take care of something. No . . . you gotta take care of something. Before the sun goes down, I need you to find those poles and put up our shelter again. I know it won't be as good as we had it, 'cause you ain't got a clue how to do it, but we don't want another night or more out in the open. Thing of it is, we come too far now to freeze our asses before we can get me healthy." Ramon understood that in the absence of medication Garth's gastrointestinal problem could take a while to overcome.

Ramon resigned himself to taking the abuse that would accompany his clumsy attempts to reconstruct their little lean-to but he had little choice. He set about reversing the actions he had just taken to deconstruct their shelter, while Garth orchestrated from the relative warmth of his sleeping bag.

After Ramon had finished the task Garth had another command. "Even though I ain't got an appetite now, I need you to check the traps again so we got something half decent to eat if we gotta stay here a few more days."

"I don't know where you set them, Garth."

"Yeah. I get that," he said. "Serves me right for not bringing you with me at least once. Okay, I'll get my ass in gear and show you the ones close by. But I'm only doing this the once. Memorize it." Groaning, he eased himself from his sleeping bag and pulled on his outerwear, shivering more from illness than the cold. The two men left the camp while the last vestiges of light remained. On unsteady feet, Garth led Ramon along his regular route that linked a half dozen carefully laid snares. Though he had initially been disgusted by the small rodents Garth would bring back to camp, Ramon came to accept, if not enjoy, the small pieces of roasted meat they relied upon to augment the dwindling rations from Garth's cabin. He had to stop thinking of squirrel as the dirty animals he threw peanuts at in the park and look at them, instead, as desperately needed protein. On this particular evening, their traps revealed similar results to Garth's last run. A few of the deadfalls and snares had caught prey, but once again, nothing edible remained, just discarded scraps. Garth appeared more irritated with each successive failure while Ramon concentrated on committing the route to memory.

Garth reported no improvement the next morning when they awoke to fresh snowfall. With growing snow cover, at least they had a roof over their heads once again. "Think you got the flu or something?" Ramon asked.

Garth grunted weakly. "My guess is, it's beaver fever."

"Beavers? From the pond?"

"Naw. Giardia. From water that's got bacteria in it; from animal shit, mostly. My stomach's turning itself inside out trying to get rid of something. You been boiling like I told ya?"

"Sure," Ramon said defensively. "If I hadn't, wouldn't I get sick, too?"

"Not necessarily. It's a crapshoot," Garth snickered at his unintended pun. "Just dumb luck who swallows the little buggers and who don't. It's not like you get a dose in every cup."

Ramon thought about his fear of running out of wood or gas. He knew he'd occasionally failed to bring the melting snow to a prolonged boil, as Garth had ordered. He recalled that when he'd melted water for Garth's water bottles the last time, he'd taken the pot off early and hadn't filled his own bottle. He realized what he was now feeling was a mix of regret and a hint of satisfaction.

"You're gonna have to do the chores around here until I beat this thing. Jesus, I feel weak."

"I can manage."

"If I got giardia, it's gonna be a few more days before I'll be feeling better, so you'll just have to sit tight. We just got to hope that bitch never turned us in."

25

Thanksgiving

THE DAY BEFORE THANKSGIVING, WHEN GLENCOE PARENTS HEADED TO Lake Placid to join their children for the weekend, Libby Goldman packed her suitcase, drove to the end of the road with Payton and flagged down a Trailways bus bound for New York City. As the bus pulled away, Libby began to cry. On her lap, *Endurance* remained unopened as she played out in her mind the battles she would face when she reached the city. She suspected her parents were using the Kibbutz Harduf party as a bogus excuse to ease her out of Glencoe.

She knew her parents had already received a letter Hamish had sent to each family describing Malcolm's tragic fall. She feared her parents would use this as evidence the school was not a safe place for her, that the leadership was incompetent. She imagined they would claim she'd grown too dependent upon Glencoe and tell her it was necessary to look for a better school. They would argue, they would cajole and, in the end, another set of roots would be ripped away. *This time I'm not going to give up without a fight*, she decided. *Maybe a tantrum in the middle of the party will make them take me more seriously.*

By the time the bus pulled into the Port Authority terminal, Libby had worked herself into a real stew. When she stepped onto the narrow concrete peninsula that led into the depths of the bus station, her senses were bombarded by the clamor of passengers and exhaust from a multitude of idling buses. A couple of months in the mountain air and calm of Glencoe had swept away her internal shield against city tumult. Lungs burning, eyes tearing, Libby struggled to gain her bearings and locate her belongings among the mountain of suitcases disgorged from the under-belly of the bus.

"Libby? Libby Goldman?" She looked up to see who was calling her name. A middle-aged Hispanic woman wriggled her way through the bustling crowd like a salmon swimming upstream. Libby held her ground until the stranger was beside her. "Are you Libby?" the woman asked in a thick Spanish accent.

"Yes. Who are you? Where is my father?"

The woman looked uncomfortable. "My name is Eva Ortiz. Your father asked me to meet you," she said, apologetically. She smiled and something softened in Libby's well-honed defense mechanism. "He is so busy right now. Getting ready for the party, yes?" She gestured to Libby's suitcase. "I'm sorry but I can't help you with that," she said, tapping her chest. "My heart's not so good."

Libby dismissed Eva's apology with a hand wave and hefted the bag herself. *What a shock. Dad failed me again,* she thought. *At least he's consistent. He fails me in all the little ways as well as the big ways.* "That's okay, I can handle it. Is there a stupid party every night for these people? I'm not sure I can get through it all."

"It will be a busy time for sure, but you can hide with me sometimes if it gets too much for you," Eva laughed. *What a delightful face,* Libby thought. *Wonder how she got the job.* "Normally, I just do housekeeping for your parents, but your father asked me to help since there's such a large group at your home. It's okay," she said, poorly hiding her ambivalence.

There was a dignity in Eva's manner that surprised and disarmed Libby. Her black hair, flecked with gray, was pulled neatly back into a bun and secured with a handsome leather pin. Together they braved the Port Authority terminal crowds, swollen with holiday travelers and opportunistic panhandlers, and made their way out to the street.

"Don't you get to be with your own family for Thanksgiving, Mrs. Ortiz?" Libby asked as they hailed a taxi for the three-mile ride uptown to her parents' condominium.

Eva shrugged as if to say some things couldn't be helped. She smiled shyly and looked down. "My kids know if I don't work, they don't eat. My sister, Consuela, will look after them."

"Sounds like you couldn't say no to my father."

"It's no problem for me. Don't worry." But Libby could see a glistening in Eva's eyes.

"Mrs. Ortiz, I'm sorry he made you come get me. He gets everyone to do his dirty work. I don't want to be here, to be honest. Maybe I sound like a selfish daughter, but if you've worked for my parents for a while maybe you know what I mean."

"Please call me Eva," she said, patting Libby gently on the arm. "They have been good to me. It's not for me to judge. Maybe we can get to know each other a little bit. That would be nice."

The Goldmans owned and occupied the top three floors of a pre–World War II apartment building on Manhattan's Upper West Side. With some last-minute rearrangements of furniture on the middle floor of the triplex and a lot of overtime work from Eva, Libby's parents had prepared sufficient accommodations for the eight-member delegation visiting from Kibbutz Harduf.

By the time the taxi pulled up outside her building, Libby was glad Eva would be staying the weekend. They took an elevator directly to the penthouse. There was no hall, no other doors leading to other apartments. The casual visitor could not have reached these floors without a special elevator key fob.

The doors opened onto a brightly lit foyer. The antiseptic feel of the Goldman home always struck Libby as a missed opportunity. There wasn't a single cozy spot, no place to curl up with a good book on a rainy afternoon. The common rooms were furnished in postmodern white leather. Track lights bisected the ceilings, trained down on expensive oil paintings of primary-colored rainbow stripes that relieved an otherwise unbroken expanse of white walls. Beyond a set of French doors on a wide, flagstone patio overlooking Riverside Park and the Hudson River, a ten-foot-high stainless steel George Rickey mobile danced in the wind, its trio of polished polygons bending and pivoting in carefully predetermined geometric perfection. The sounds of a string quartet wafted in from a distant room.

"Here, give me your coat, Eva. I know where the closets are hidden," said Libby sarcastically. A young man in a tuxedo approached them bearing a tray of stuffed mushrooms.

"May I help you?" he asked, pausing to shift the tray to his other hand while he held the closet door open for Libby.

"Are they kosher?" Libby cracked. The man looked confused.

Eva placed her hand gently on Libby's arm as if to say, *It's not his fault. Don't embarrass him.*

"Pardon me?" said the flustered young man.

"Sorry. I'm only thinking about our guests," said Libby sarcastically.

"Certainly," the waiter said, moving off quickly.

"I hate this," Libby said. "It makes no difference whether I'm here or not." Eva surveyed her with a quizzical look, a mix of shock and admiration.

"There is a Sabbath dinner planned for Friday," Eva said. "Tonight is a simple welcoming party."

"Simple? I bet it costs thousands."

"Oh, there you are," called a familiar voice. Shelley Goldman approached her daughter and hugged her.

"Hi, Mom."

"Eva, there must be something that needs doing in the kitchen," Shelley said abruptly, turning her back to the housekeeper to face Libby.

"Yes, ma'am," said Eva obediently and walked out of the room.

"That was rude," Libby said.

"Excuse me?"

"You spoke to Mrs. Ortiz like she wasn't a human being."

Shelley looked puzzled. "I don't know what you're talking about, dear. She's our housekeeper. She works for us."

"She still deserves respect, doesn't she?"

"Libby, you've been here five minutes and you're trying to pick a fight with me? Let's not go down that route, please. Come and say hello to our guests. We can talk about this some other time."

"Pencil me in for next Tuesday," Libby muttered under her breath, too softly for her mother to hear.

Despite being a small, private, institution, Austro-Lab was among the most well-endowed Rudolph Steiner schools in the world. Libby rarely talked about the prodigious wealth her family enjoyed, though she was proud of the dramatic tale of her great-grandparents' escape from Algeria during the German occupation in World War II.

. . .

Charles Goldman was one of the wealthiest Jews in France, amassing a small fortune in precious stones, mostly diamonds, which prompted frequent trips to the Congo. Often, he would stop over in Algiers to see an old friend, Henri Aboulker, a prominent Jewish physician and professor at the university. When word reached Charles that the German ambassador to France, in collaboration with the Nazi-friendly Vichy regime in Paris, had begun fingering rich Jews, expropriating their money, and shipping them off to Polish death camps, Charles realized that it was time for desperate measures. Letters from Henri confirmed that the Nazi iron fist was impacting the lives of Jews living in North Africa as well. Although death camps were not yet established, Jewish property was being confiscated, many were being sent to labor camps, both in Africa as well as in Europe. Henri suggested a plan to be discussed on Charles' next trip to Algiers. Time was of the essence, he cautioned.

Two weeks later, on a cool, fall evening, while sipping espresso at a neighborhood Algiers café, Henri advised Charles that the time was near for a bold attempt to change the course of history.

"My son, Jos, whom you've watched grow up, is quietly organizing his Jewish friends into a resistance force that will surely impact the war here in North Africa. Charles, I advise you in the strongest terms that *now* is the time to bring your family here," Henri pleaded. "Jos will be turning this place upside down and once that happens, I don't know if ferries from France will still run, or if we can spirit you out of here. But you've a better chance running from Algiers than you do from Paris."

It was November 6, 1942, when Charles secured passage for himself, his wife, and his daughter—Libby's grandmother—known to her now as Bubbe. The previous week he had transferred the bulk of his fortune out of France using a series of convoluted transactions. With fake documents procured through his friends at Credit Suisse, the three fleeing Goldmans took the daylong ferry ride from Marseilles, leaving their lavish Paris apartment with only two suitcases in hand. Two days later, 377 Algerian resistance fighters, 84 percent of whom were Jewish, under the command of Jos Aboulker, stormed the Algerian police headquarters and radio station in fake Vichy-style uniforms. During the chaotic next hours, as they broadcast news meant to confuse the Nazi-sympathizing government in Algeria, General Dwight Eisenhower landed two thousand American troops on their shores and threw out the ruling powers. As "Operation Torch" was unfolding, the Goldmans, with the help of Henri Aboulker, made their way out of Algeria. Two weeks later, they booked passage on a steamship out of Rabat, Morocco, bound for Canada, their wealth secure in Swiss banks.

. . .

Libby trailed her mother through the apartment. Shmuel Friedman, the senior member of the delegation from Kibbutz Harduf, was holding court in one corner of the living room. When he saw Shelley, a smile lit up his face. His skin was remarkably smooth for a man well into his seventies. It glowed red from a combination of high blood pressure, frequent saunas, massage, and liberal doses of anisette. A still-thick mane of white hair was pulled back severely into a pony tail that extended well below his shoulders. He wore sandals that revealed immaculately pedicured toes, beige linen slacks and a matching tunic, open at the throat. He looked like an aging yoga instructor from Southern California, not a rugged kibbutzim elder.

"Dr. Friedman, please meet my daughter, Elisheba," Shelley said. Libby reached out her hand but their guest ignored it and moved in for a warm hug, surprising her.

"I'm delighted to meet you, Elisheba. That's a beautiful name. I understand you came back from school just to meet us. We are very honored." Libby nodded dutifully. There was a charisma about the man that left her confused. "I've heard so much about you from your parents," he said, looking her straight in the eye. She squirmed beneath his gaze. "I understand there were school activities you would have preferred not to miss. Thank you for making this sacrifice to honor us."

"You're welcome," she mumbled with as much enthusiasm as she could muster.

"I'm hoping we can get to know you much better when you come to do high school with us at Kibbutz Harduf next year," he said warmly. "After your experience in upstate New York, perhaps there are a few things you can teach us about experiential learning," Shmuel said affectionately. "I look forward to that."

Libby was stunned. High school in Israel? When did this idea get cooked up? She decided not to confront her mother and embarrass Dr. Friedman. Instead, she nodded politely and said, abruptly, "Where should I put my things this trip, Mom?"

Shelley laughed uncomfortably and turned back to Shmuel.

"With all the comings and goings around here, we never know where our daughter will be sleeping. I think Eva made up the back bedroom upstairs, dear, next to my office." Shelley gave her daughter a quick squeeze on the shoulder, looked past her into the adjoining room and steered Dr. Friedman toward another group of well-wishers.

"Wait! Mom?" Libby demanded, catching her mother's sleeve. "Are you going to have time for me this weekend?"

"Of course, dear. We'll shop Saturday. I'm sure you could use a few things."

. . .

On Wednesday evening before Thanksgiving, Glencoe parents began to arrive at local hotels, motels, and weekend rentals. They were invited to a community luncheon the following day, after which *The Truth about Zeus* was to be presented. Attendance at Friday morning classes was also expected of parents before they were allowed to whisk their beloveds away for the weekend.

Wendell and Emily Barcomb were among the first to arrive, for they had personal and professional agendas of their own. Tracy met them in the parking area unobtrusively tucked to one side of Dewey Hall, surrounded by trees and invisible from Dewey.

"How's it going, son?" Wendell asked, changing from his casual shoes to calf-length Bean boots. His wife kissed Tracy through the open window, then slid over to get behind the wheel.

"Okay. What's up? You just got here and now it seems you are going somewhere else?" Tracy asked, puzzled.

Wendell laughed. "Very aware, Tracy. We purposely came early because I want to tour the barn and meet with the farm manager about the new composting unit that Glencoe installed. I called ahead to make an appointment. We have plenty of time later to catch up." Composting had been a habit since the founders first opened the school, but now they had equipment which produced impressive quantities of nutrient-rich material that enabled quantities of vegetables and flowers no other farm, especially an organic one, could match at an altitude where the growing season was so brief. "I expect I can learn a lot from the folks here which can help us back home. We'll see," Wendell said. "Want to join me?"

Emily waved to Tracy and backed out.

"Thanks, but I've seen that thingamabob a million times. Where's Mom going?"

"Mom's got stuff to do for her research. She scheduled interviews with several summit stewards at the Adirondak Loj," Wendell said, referring to those intrepid souls who routinely braved brutal conditions atop the highest Adirondack peaks to educate arriving hikers oblivious to proper etiquette in a delicate alpine region. These men and women worked tirelessly at ground zero, for meager compensation, in the effort to forestall the relentless onslaught of hikers who had discovered the wonders of the High Peaks and whose overuse of that natural resource was transforming a once-pristine trail system into eroded alleyways of mud, tangled tree roots, and bare rock sections devoid of topsoil. At the heart of Emily Barcomb's thesis was the question of whether a permit system for trail access was a successful way to save wilderness areas from overuse.

"Those conversations are important for her doctoral thesis," Wendell continued. "That's why we showed up early. We wanted to take advantage of the trip over here but not take time away from you. Is that okay?" Wendell smiled, slapping his son affectionately on the back.

Tracy did not answer. He was still trying to process this curious episode and whether or not to feel hurt.

"We'll take you out to dinner in Placid. Let's meet here around six. Does that work?"

"Okay, Dad. I'll go study my lines, I guess."

Moments before the luncheon for two hundred began on Thursday, a Chevrolet Suburban transporting Mathilda Graham and her companion, John Helderberg, pulled up at Dewey Hall. Ms. Graham, Malcolm's guardian aunt, emerged from the oversized black SUV in heels that were no match for the rough gravel covering every lane on the Glencoe campus. Wobbling uncertainly, she clutched the arm of her companion, eyes peeled for Malcolm.

To accommodate so many guests, the dining hall was transformed from its usual dozen or so well-spaced, tables of six into one long serpentine surface comprised of all the individual tables plus many other rented ones, following the perimeter of the hexagonal-shaped room.

Several tables laden with an awesome variety of vegetable and salad dishes produced from Glencoe's own fields and greenhouses were arranged in the middle of the room. Adjacent tables held twenty golden brown turkeys from a nearby farm. Hamish welcomed the families, some traveling thousands of miles, including more than a handful from overseas, to experience Glencoe at its best. After the meal and brief remarks, which varied little from year-to-year, the Scotsman led the community out of Dewey, to Marcy Hall for *The Truth about Zeus*.

Ron Handy skipped the meal entirely in order to meditate on the minutiae that would make or break the success of his opus. As the community finished their Thanksgiving repast, Ron paced Marcy Hall, waiting for the crowd to migrate over from the dining hall. His intestines were in turmoil, a final revolt to the stress he imposed upon his body every fall.

Standing behind the back row of the balcony, Pete Hedges and Christine Mason watched the guests file in, buzzing with excitement to be with their children and grandchildren. The small orchestra, comprised of both students and faculty, struck up the overture as the curtain rose, and Pete gasped at the spectacular set his girlfriend had helped construct.

"Jesus, that is awesome," he whispered to her, wrapping his arms around her. She beamed.

The performance was brilliant despite Ron's abject fears. Following the show, guests returned to the dining hall for light refreshments, which meant juice and homemade cookies. Hovering over the food, Mathilda Graham looked completely out of place, dressed for a Broadway opening, not a junior-level boarding school production.

"Introduce me to those people," she ordered her companion, Helderberg, elbowing him in the ribs and nodding in the direction of the couple pouring juice beside them. He sighed and complied. "I need to hear what others think before I volunteer anything," Mathilda said in a stage whisper.

"Good afternoon," he said, turning to the Barcombs. "I am John Helderberg, May I introduce you to Mathilda Graham? We have come from Ohio to visit her ward, Malcolm Dandridge," he said with discomfort.

"Perhaps you know him?" Mathilda asked, extending a gloved hand to Wendell and Emily.

"Yes, we have heard the name from our son, Tracy," Wendell said, giving his wife a quick glance. Tracy had reported on the new "bully" and had delivered the same edited version of the Balanced Rocks episode Tracy had offered Hamish. The Barcombs had wondered to each other if there might have been some details omitted. "This is your first year here, is it not?" Wendell continued. There was no sign of recognition on Mathilda's face when Tracy's name was mentioned.

"Most assuredly," Mathilda said. "And I wonder what you two thought of the production we just witnessed. I must say it was not at all what I expected. In fact, I was a bit shaken by what was happening on that stage. Do those children have any idea?"

Emily laughed knowingly. "This is our third Thanksgiving play, and we are no longer shocked by what we see here. The fellow that writes it all is a trip. I hope you get a chance to meet Ron Handy. He's been here forever, should probably be working as a musical director on Broadway, and amuses himself with productions that the kids love to put on and the parents think should be rated for mature audiences. I often can't believe the words coming out of those kids' mouths. His young actors have no clue."

"He's a very creative guy who doesn't get hung up on how old his performers are," Wendell added. "Out of the mouths of babes, and all that . . ."

"We don't see children's theater like this in Shaker Heights, where this girl is from," Mathilda said, smiling. "This is pretty mature stuff for children to see, let alone perform."

"The kids are so focused on remembering their lines and being in the right place at the right time, I don't think they give the subject matter much thought," Wendell said.

"Our son, Tracy, barely mentions the show when we speak on the phone. He's so intent on being appreciated and admired by everyone that I doubt he has time to think deeply about everything he is saying. He's just trying to get them spoken correctly . . . But maybe I'm wrong," Emily said.

"Anyway, very nice to meet you, Mathilda . . . John," Wendell said, extending a hand to each, in turn. "I hope your boy grows as much from this place as ours has."

"Where is that boy of ours?" Emily asked.

"Probably sharing a celebratory beer with his buddies," Wendell joked. "He deserves one for the job he did up there. I'm really proud of him."

As the Barcombs walked away from Mathilda and John, Emily asked her husband, "She's related to the boy who had that accident with Tracy, right?" Her husband nodded. "She didn't seem to register who we were," she continued.

"I had the same thought. Weird. Maybe her boy doesn't communicate as much as ours does, even if it's only part of the story."

At the Goldman residence in New York Thanksgiving dinner for eleven came off without a hitch, though Libby could not stop thinking about what she was missing at Glencoe. Not only did she resent having been denied the chance to see *The Truth about Zeus*, but also from being forced to exchange tedious pleasantries with the Israeli visitors. And she couldn't help wonder if these people were going to be her teachers in high school, and how was she going to extricate herself from this mess. She wondered if a call to her dad's mother, Sarah, her Bubbe, was her only hope of salvation. Bubbe actually listened to Libby and didn't always take her son's side. Maybe she could put an end to this Israeli school nonsense.

During the course of the weekend, Libby hung out in the kitchen, or wherever Eva happened to be working. She admired the quiet elegance with which the housekeeper performed her duties. Though Libby probed, Eva provided few details of her own life. Instead, Eva turned the questions back on Libby, who was eager to vent her frustrations to a willing listener.

The Sabbath dinner on Friday evening was mercifully brief. Dr. Friedman and her father gave short speeches extolling the virtues of a Waldorf education at Austro-Lab, and hopes for fruitful collaboration between the New Yorkers and Israelis in the future. Libby sought out Eva after the meal, locating the housekeeper on her knees in the kitchen, cleaning up someone else's mess.

"Come look at the sunset with me," Libby urged, leading Eva by the arm out onto the patio. Across the Hudson River, the last rays of the setting sun glanced off the crest of the New Jersey Palisades, leaving the face of the cliffs and the river itself in shadows. "How long have you been working for my parents?"

"About a year," Eva answered, hugging her thin sweater to her chest to ward off the biting wind.

"Don't you think this place is strange?" Libby asked. Eva shrugged her shoulders. "You know what I'm getting at, though."

"This is a beautiful place," Eva said, unwilling to offer criticism of her employers. "I do my job and that's all. Your parents treat me well."

"They are passionate about this stupid school movement. Sometimes it feels like a cult."

Eva was taken aback and answered carefully after a moment's pause. "I don't know very much about what they do. Perhaps it would be a good place for my children?"

"Tell me again. You have three?"

Eva smiled. "Four, actually. If I didn't have my sister, as I told you, I don't know how I could do this work and be a mother, too. Three boys and a little girl, Marianna. My baby," she said, fluttering her hands.

"I hope to meet your children one day," said Libby. She and Eva had now completed one circuit of the penthouse patio as dusk settled over the city.

"You are very smart," Eva said, walking back toward the doors that led into the breakfast room adjoining the kitchen. "But so unhappy," she said, taking both of Libby's hands in hers. Libby was surprised how easily Eva could get to the crux. "Why are you sad?"

"I don't hide it, do I?" Libby acknowledged. "Sometimes I feel like I can't breathe, like there's this heavy pressure on my chest. Usually, it happens after I've had a fight with my parents, or they're bringing me home, or not letting me come home. It almost doesn't matter what they say anymore, I don't agree with them, just because."

"When it's time for you to be a mama you may see it in a new way. Maybe it is good to not fight your parents every time. They give you everything you need, no?" Eva thought of her own tiny apartment, of her own frustrations with growing children fighting to be seen, to be heard, and to be independent.

"They give me clothes and stuff. Whatever I ask, I guess. Except time. Time is too expensive. I don't know if they love me. If they do, they sure have a funny way of showing it."

Eva turned to Libby and embraced her. "There are many ways to do that. Sometimes it is hard to see. I don't have money . . . " Eva smiled sadly, "and my kids fight with me sometimes. They think I am crazy with rules but they know it comes from love. Be patient, Libby. Be patient with them. They want you to be happy. And safe. There is nothing more important a parent can do than to keep their children safe. It's not as easy as it may seem."

There was no shopping spree on Saturday. By Sunday afternoon, Shelley Goldman's smartphone demanded that she be at La Guardia Airport, dropping off the Israeli contingent on their way to Boston, not at Bergdorf Goodman's with her daughter.

"You look wonderful, dear. That North Country air is doing great things for your skin," her mother said as she straightened her scarf in the mirror near the elevator door. "Thank you for coming in this weekend. It meant so much to your father and me."

"What happened to that shopping trip you promised, Mom?"

"I'm so sorry, dear, I'm hopelessly double-booked. Please understand."

"And when were you planning to tell me about this idea of high school in Israel? I have to hear about it from your Dr. Friedman? Did you think I might want something to say about my future?"

Her mother looked very uncomfortable. "Libby, I'm sorry we didn't bring it up sooner. Your father and I think it would be wonderful for you to spend a year or so at their kibbutz, furthering your Waldorf education and learning more about your Jewish heritage. It's a logical extension to your time at Glencoe. We're very excited about the idea, and part of bringing you here was to let you meet Dr. Friedman and the others, and maybe get excited about it yourself."

"If it was so important to you maybe you could have let me in on the plan ahead of time. This is kind of a shock."

"I'm sorry, sweetie," Shelley said, self-consciously. "I'll call you soon and we can talk about it further, I promise . . . Have a good trip back to school." She air-kissed Libby on both cheeks and hurried out.

"It was so nice to meet you," Eva said as she embraced Libby at the Port Authority gate. "This summer, maybe you can meet my family and come to our home."

"That would be great, Eva. And thanks for helping me get through this weekend."

"Do you have a long trip now? Where do you go?"

"Back to Glencoe. My school is about a five-hour ride to Lake Placid. Someone will pick me up there."

At the words *Lake Placid*, Eva's eyes widened. She'd had no idea that's where Libby went to school. The first time she had heard those words was November 2, the day after her son had fled the work detail. It was now burned into her memory.

. . .

Eva and Consuela were preparing dinner when the phone rang. Pablo answered it and called, "Mama? There's a policeman wants to talk to you. From Lake something. He wants to talk about Ramon, Mama."

"Your baby in trouble with gangs again?" Consuela said. Ramon had told them a little about Hector Mercado during those first weeks at Comstock, but the sisters had never learned how truly dangerous it had been.

"This is Eva Ortiz. Who is this?"

After a pause, her hand flew to her face. "I don't understand. He was coming home soon. Why would he do such a thing? He had no reason." She moaned. Another pause. "No, I have not heard from him."

She held the phone away from her ear so Consuela could hear.

"We hoped you could tell us where he is, ma'am," came the voice on the other end. "He's in big trouble, Mrs. Ortiz. If you want to help him, please get in touch with us if he contacts you."

. . .

As Libby hugged Eva and boarded the bus, it seemed to her that her parents' housekeeper had suddenly seen a ghost. The woman wiped her eyes on the sleeve of her coat, clutched a plastic bag with leftover turkey close to her chest, waved goodbye, and melted into the crowd.

26

Call of the Wild

THERE WAS NO TURKEY, GIBLETS, OR GRAVY AT THE CAMPSITE ABOVE Lost Pond. Thanksgiving came and went with no acknowledgment of its passing. And what was there to be thankful for? Freedom? They were too preoccupied staying alive. It was now about a week since Garth had announced they were leaving, but the virulent attack of giardia had weakened him to such an extent that movement was impossible. During his period of recuperation, the mountains had received an unseasonably large amount of snow. By the end of November, he was only just regaining enough strength to attempt what would be a nerve-racking, exhausting effort to gain full freedom. Ramon assumed the plan would somehow include getting rid of him, thus he was on edge.

Ramon managed to avoid the malady, a fact Garth continually brought up in the most unflattering ways. Ramon understood he was supposed to feel inferior in every way, including his immune system. The extended stay in the woods, however, had taken its toll. Though Garth was vastly more accustomed to prolonged periods of living hand-to-mouth in the wilderness than was Ramon—his youth had largely been spent preparing for such a trial—a weakened constitution and the stress of playing the most serious kind of foxes-and-hounds took its toll on both men. As their rationed reserves of food and fuel ran low, Ramon counted on Garth's experience and ingenuity to maintain their strength for the final break that had to come soon. Instead of encouraging words, however, what came out of Garth's mouth with increasing frequency was frustration, invectives, and a second-guessing of their plan.

With each passing day, their camp seemed to sink another inch or two beneath the ever-thickening blanket of winter. Their shelter displayed the ravages of the season, as well. The plastic sheeting above their heads was now rent in multiple places by rips and punctures from falling branches.

The night after Thanksgiving, a fresh storm buffeted them, blowing a layer of snow three inches deep on top of their sleeping bags. As they slept, heat from their bodies ventilated through the Fiberfil insulation and the outer shell, creating a thin veneer of ice to form where snow met nylon.

Garth sat up to greet the chilly winter sun peeking over the MacIntyre Range. He rubbed his arms vigorously to encourage circulation, causing the coating of ice on his sleeping bag to crackle and slide off like shards of crystallized sugar. He looked over at Ramon and muttered, "You still here, eh?"

Another slight. Ramon was tired of him, too. Tired of living under his thumb, at the mercy of his erratic, frightening companion. Every aspect of Garth's personality irritated him; the man's habit of beginning sentences with *The thing of it is* or ending them with *eh*? Most of all, he hated being called *Jack*. Weeks of waiting had given Ramon ample time to contemplate how he had gotten himself into this predicament, trading decent meals, a shower and a bed for a broken-down plastic-covered stick shed with no central heating or plumbing. He thought of the phone calls with Pablo that had provided him with the impetus to run, and wondered whether his mother and brother were now okay. It may have been idiotic to join Garth in the first place but the only way to make sense of it was to get out of these damn woods and find out what was happening at home. His failed first attempt at escape was never far from his thoughts. To try again would be just plain foolish. He had no desire to relive the abject fear that had accompanied his last dash to freedom. He would just have to trust that Garth would get him to a place where he had a fighting chance to get back to the real world. After all this time together, his companion would not just shoot him or leave him to fend for himself, would he?

"You ready to leave this dump?" Ramon asked.

CALL OF THE WILD

"I was ready days ago, but that was before you made me sick. Getting to Canada ain't no picnic. I need all the strength I can get."

"I don't see how you're gonna get stronger on the crumbs we're eating. We're pretty much out of supplies."

It was true. They were rationing everything they had and there wasn't much left. Whatever was stealing from their traps had all but removed rabbit and squirrel from their diet. The situation was getting dire. "I can't argue with you about the food stocks. I didn't figure to be out this long or you to eat as much as you do. Check on the traps one more time. Do you good to get some exercise anyways," Garth ordered.

"Maybe we can buy some real food when we get outta here. We got any cash?" Ramon asked, though he knew the answer.

Garth flashed a suspicious look. "Maybe. But don't expect me to buy you a bus ticket, if that's what you're thinking. Some trucker will get me near the border or I'll hotwire a car and once I hike into Quebec, I'll find a logging camp, make a few bucks and fatten up for a while. Then, I dunno, head for the Rockies. A man can become invisible in the Canadian Northwest. Best I can look forward to is a doublewide someplace the hell away from here," he grumbled.

Though he had fantasized of nothing else since those first days in the woods, Ramon felt anxious and unprepared for what lay ahead. As dismal as this existence had been, he had finally grown accustomed to the simple routines of staying alive. When it sank in that they would be living at this benighted spot for a prolonged amount of time, he had learned to cope, had broken each day into manageable chunks. First, he would focus on the preparation of each meager meal, then find a modest project, like whittling rudimentary figurines, that would fill time until it was time to eat again. The best he could say about his current life was that it was dreary and uncomfortable. The future looked intimidating and scary.

Garth rolled over, still in his sleeping bag, and checked the pot of water on the stove. The surface was still frozen from sitting out all night. There wasn't much gas left, either; he made sure the lid was securely on to capture every bit of heat the stove generated.

"I hate to leave this area. I know it better'n anywheres else, that's for damn sure. I don't know nuthin' else but logging. Logging is still pretty good in the Pacific Northwest and Alaska, I think. Sure is far from here, though."

For the first time, Ramon heard vulnerability in Garth's voice. Putting aside all the abuse he had taken, Ramon needed Garth to be strong for both of them. Maybe Garth felt just as cornered as he did.

"Hell, there are a million logging camps I can get lost in," Garth said, pepping himself up. "I'll be long dead before they zero in on me."

Ramon thought he didn't sound all that convinced. He shook out his sleeping bag and hung it on a branch to air. The day passed uneventfully. Garth took it easy, puttering around the camp, testing his energy levels, gauging whether he would soon be strong enough to make the final break. Ramon spent as much time as he could up on the ledge, away from his tormentor, mulling over his limited options for the future. When he returned to camp at dusk, Garth immediately found a way to torture him once again.

"You can bet they got your mama staked out just waiting for you to show. Unless you got friends to put you up and a way to make money, I can't see how you going home is gonna help nobody," Garth warned.

It was a depressing truth. Maybe the only way out was to turn himself in. He couldn't imagine living the rest of his life on the run. Whenever his thoughts ran to how helpless he was, anger rose toward the man who had persuaded him to jump ship in the first place.

"That's not what you said when we talked this over in your cell," Ramon grumbled.

Garth started to laugh. "We got different agendas, Jack. I needed a pack animal. You fit the bill. Whatever it took to get you outta there, that's what I told you. Not my problem it's not working out like you planned. What's your play? Gonna go back to dealing drugs?"

Ramon had often imagined a new life, a legitimate one with no shadows, but the details of this dream were always fuzzy. To stay clear of jail he needed a job, but his only qualifications for making a decent living involved illegal activities. It was a vicious cycle with no obvious exit.

"No. I won't deal drugs again. Maybe a bike messenger."

"A what?" laughed Garth. "You gonna make a living ridin' a bicycle? As an errand boy? You living in Fantasyland."

"Ahh, go to hell." Ramon stalked away from the shelter toward their latrine.

"Where you think you're going? Traps is that-away." Garth snapped.

Ramon hoped the logger had forgotten his earlier order but apparently that was not to be. "Just taking a dump. Then I'll go. Can I take the rifle?"

"Over my dead body," Garth muttered.

When Ramon returned from the latrine Garth was brandishing his Smith & Wesson long knife. Ramon was startled and considered this was the moment he had most feared.

"Relax, Jack. I'm letting you have this for your walk. In case you have to cut something loose, or finish them off. Can you handle that?"

"Guess so. Thanks."

"Bring that sack with you," Garth said, pointing to a burlap bag that hung from one of the poles. "In case you get lucky."

Ramon checked his headlamp, stuffed the sack into his coat and headed out of the camp, following a reasonably good set of tracks toward the first of the snares. The recent snow had not completely filled in the remnants of their last trip or he'd have been quite at a loss to find them. The path led down toward the edge of Lost Pond and around its perimeter. As he approached the first trap the sun had already dipped below the ridge, leaving the woods in a flat light that made him nervous. He had never noticed the transition from day to night when he lived in the city. Streetlights made the event irrelevant. Now, he was so aware of the passage of time and how he interacted with his surroundings at all times of the day. He flicked on his light and scanned the forest floor for the first trap, a clever deadfall that Garth had fashioned to crush an unsuspecting rodent with a heavy rock. The light found the rock, which had, indeed, fallen atop a rabbit's head. The snow was stained dark from blood oozing from beneath the rock but the body was still intact—the first successful catch since Garth had become ill.

Ramon rolled the rock off the rabbit and used the knife to separate the head from the body. He had no idea how to set the trap again. That would have to wait for Garth, but he felt good about bringing home something they could eat. Maybe Garth might not chew him out for a change. As he tossed the rabbit into his sack, his light locked onto a pair of eyes, staring at him from a thicket, perhaps fifteen yards distant. The reflective glow stunned him. When the yipping began, a slug of adrenaline shot up his spine and a sweat broke out. The yipping was answered, then became a chorus. As he swung his head, the light caught several other pairs of eyes. They were talking to each other, assessing the intruder who had stolen their rabbit.

Ramon slowly backed away, discarding any thought of proceeding to the next trap. He turned to run. Blocking his path stood an animal that had anticipated his flight. Reminiscent of a dog, this animal had a sharper snout. He estimated the wiry animal weighed about a hundred pounds, two-thirds his own weight. All muscle and sinew, its coat was shaggy, multihued, though in the dark it was tough to tell actual colors. There was no tail wagging, just a confident stare. Ramon held his breath. He felt trapped and sensed the others were now closing ranks behind him, though he dared not look. No doubt these were the coy-wolves Garth had described, a hybrid predator that was slowly invading the Adirondacks from the north. This was their territory and he was taking food from their mouths. They waited for the interloper to make the first move.

"Easy boy, easy," whispered Ramon, seeking to communicate a lack of fear. The eyes of the coy-wolf before him darted from the sack holding the rabbit, to Ramon's face, then to his hand, which still carried the knife. The yips turned to low growls and he sensed his time was limited. Finding his courage, Ramon screamed, meant to shock his adversaries and hopefully, alert Garth. The ears twitched and the coy-wolf bared his fangs. It seemed a signal to the others and then they were on him. Ramon felt the first bite on his legs from behind. He roared, kicking spasmodically, and whirled around to try to cast them off. They snarled, swarming over him. He felt a weight on his back, fur and hot breath around his neck. He slammed himself against a tree to shed the attacker and lashed out blindly with his knife. The sack was torn from his hand and his headlamp flew off into the snow. He was now blind and defenseless. The yowling grew in volume and he resigned himself to a gruesome end. Then, as suddenly as it had begun, the attack ceased. Their attention seemed elsewhere and he took the opportunity to slip away from the grisly scene. By pure luck, he saw, to his left, the glow of his headlamp, half buried in the snow, a cold fluorescent beacon of safety. He reached for it and pointed it in the direction of the snarling. In its light he saw four coy-wolves tearing into the burlap sack. They had what they'd come for. They had no quarrel with him now.

Alive and able to move, Ramon scanned the ground for a sign of his own tracks. He knew their camp was uphill from the pond. It didn't take long for him to locate the path he had taken. With heart pounding he sought to put as much distance as possible between himself and the animals, only stopping briefly to take stock of his condition when he had gone a few hundred yards. His boots had seemingly stopped the lowest attacks but his pants were ripped about the calves. The wet on his exposed skin was probably blood, he thought. Now that the adrenaline had subsided, he felt pain on his right ear. He reached up and felt some skin hanging loosely by his ear lobe. His fingers came away warm and sticky.

When Ramon staggered into camp, Garth was sitting up, still in his sleeping bag, holding his rifle across his lap. "I heard your shout," he said. "What the hell happened? Anything to do with those howls I heard about the same time?" Ramon slumped down by the firepit and held up his hand to show the blood.

"I think I need some first aid," he said. His voice was shaky; he was in shock.

"Let's get something warm into you. Get a pot going. I'll dig out the kit." Garth reached for his enormous pack and felt for the small box that held an assortment of bandages, alcohol swabs, painkillers, and the like. Ramon noted it was probably the first time he had ever seen Garth concerned for someone else's welfare. He fired up the stove and put a pot on to boil, then sat down and reviewed his injuries. "We can bandage you up okay," Garth assured him, "but there's not much I can do if those puppies gave you rabies. We'll just have to wait it out."

"They were after the rabbit," Ramon said, beginning to regain his composure. "The first trap had one and I had just put it in the sack when they attacked me. Once I dropped the sack they lost interest in me, thank God. Four of them jumped me. Man, I was scared."

Garth cleaned the gashes and puncture wounds with some snow and alcohol wipes, causing Ramon to grit his teeth in pain. He covered them with gauze and tape and pronounced Ramon good as new. "Don't hear about human attacks much," Garth mused as he poured out a cup of cocoa. "Just dumb luck, I guess. Explains all the trap problems we've been having. I'm going to keep the rifle handy tonight in case they decide to wander up here looking for you."

"How do I know if I got rabies?"

"I'm no expert, but I think it's not something you'll feel right away. It could take months. But if you do get symptoms, like a coma," Garth laughed, "you're shit outta luck. As long as you can get to a doctor pretty soon to check it out, or give you shots, you should be okay. But don't take my word for it. I've seen rabid dogs but no rabid people. We shoot the dogs. If you want, I could take care of you that way," he laughed again. Ramon flipped his middle finger at him, undressed and gingerly slid into his sleeping bag, physically and emotionally shattered.

"It's a bitch we lost the rabbit," Garth said, clicking off his headlamp.

27

Vision of the Future

"Do you know what you want?" Emily Barcomb asked, looking up from her menu to the two boys sitting across from her. It was nearly five, early for dinner, but four hours of driving remained before she could drop the roommates off at Glencoe, followed by another two to get home to Burlington. This early stop in Bow, New Hampshire, was more to give her a break than to satiate the hunger of her passengers. There would be fewer restaurants, especially those of the non-fast-food variety, the farther they drove through Vermont and into the Adirondacks.

Jake thumbed through the multipage laminated tome of the Greek diner's menu. "I don't know the first thing about running a restaurant," he said, shaking his head in wonder. "But it's got to be a nightmare having to stock the ingredients for so many different things."

"You got your breakfast foods twenty-four seven," Tracy chuckled. "Sandwiches as thick as your fist, and your traditional Greek dishes. Did you see those cakes when we walked in? They must be six inches high. Does anyone actually eat that stuff?"

"I'd much rather support a family business like this than take you to a Mickey-D or some other chain," Emily said, waving over a waitress. "Make up your minds. I've got a long night ahead of me."

The companions were on their way back from visiting Philips Exeter Academy, one of the nation's premier prep schools. This was but one of several fall trips that Glencoe ninth graders endured as they prepared for the next phase of their educational careers; at least those who were not intending to enroll in a local public high school. As an academic whose schedule was more flexible than her husband's, it made sense for Emily to chaperone this trip. Wendell had already taken Tracy to see Putney, the other leading candidate on his list, and much closer to their Burlington home.

"Thank you for bringing me along, Mrs. Barcomb," Jake said, after they had ordered.

"Of course. And for the umpteenth time, please call me Emily," she said.

Jake nodded. "I don't know how I'd have gotten there without you. My mom doesn't drive. She was a city kid like me, and never needed a license. Plus, we don't have a car."

"Happy to do it. So? What did you guys think of the tour guide?"

"She sounded like she was reading a script," Jake said.

"She was cute," Tracy added. "I was impressed by how she could walk backwards all over the campus so she could face us while she talked. Imagine doing that at Glencoe, with all the rocks and roots and stuff. She wouldn't last ten yards."

"Can either of you see yourself going there next year?" Emily asked.

Tracy folded up the paper sleeve from his plastic straw into an accordion puck and idly pushed it back and forth with his fork like a stick-handling hockey player. He had agreed to this trip mostly to satisfy his dad. "I don't know, Mom. Feeling comfortable there would be the best acting job of my life. Putney's got a farm like Glencoe, and cabins to live in, and work jobs like we have. It felt like a larger version of Glencoe. Plus, they have a great outdoors program. I'm really pumped to get to know the White Mountains and Putney takes trips there."

"I would like to climb in the Whites, too," Jake said. "Exeter is like an hour closer than Putney is, just so you know."

"Sounds like you've already made up your mind," Tracy said. "Exeter, man, that's pretty buttoned up. It felt so formal. Like calling teachers mister or missus. Everything seemed so, I don't know, orderly. Careful. I think I'm too loosey-goosey to fit in there. Not to mention having to wear a jacket and tie every day. I don't think I even own a jacket that fits. Jake and I were the only kids on the tour who didn't show up with jackets. I felt out of place from the get-go. I bet they'd kick me out for some dumb thing. Anyway, I doubt they'd take two of us from the same school. If you apply, it's probably a waste of time for me."

"Why? Because I'm smarter than you?" Jake teased. "Or because I'm Black?"

Tracy punched him lightly in the arm. "Probably both," he said. "Though I hadn't thought of that."

"Of course, you haven't," Jake said. "It's true, Exeter is a lot different from what we're used to," he continued, addressing Emily. "During the math class I sat in on the teacher stopped lecturing because there was a guy leaf blowing outside. They have an army of maintenance guys keeping the place looking perfect. At Glencoe we'd be the ones out there. But with rakes."

"When did you ever rake leaves at Glencoe?" Tracy joked. "Leaves are natural. Hamish would probably say they have as much right to be on the ground as we do."

"You take everything I say literally, Tracy. I was just agreeing with you that Exeter would be a serious wake-up call."

"The place gave me a stomachache. I couldn't sleep. I don't think it's for me," Tracy said. "I know Dad will be disappointed."

He knew his mother's preferences and expected to see her smile, or show some sign of approval. But her face remained passive. *If Jake wasn't here, I bet she'd be high fiving me*, he thought. She and Wendell had argued throughout the fall about which school would be best for their son. Tracy knew she saw much of herself in him—his love of wilderness, wild imagination, boundless energy. He worried a place like Exeter would fit him like a straitjacket. His dad was torn. Go to the local high school, he would say, prepare to take over the farm, and save us a boatload of money, or aim for the stars and go to the most prestigious place you can. Putney was a fine school, Wendell would agree. An extension of Glencoe, but wasn't it time for Tracy to grow up and find his place in the real world? That argument didn't cut it with his mom. She wanted the "real world" to be more like Glencoe. Or Putney. Reasonable people might debate whether a place like Exeter was behind the curve on where the real world needed to be—where young adults learned to be accountable to each other and to the planet on which they were stewards. Maybe Exeter did that for some students, but not in so obvious a way as did Putney, the Vermont boarding school, inspired by the same Dewey principles as Glencoe. Even the states in which the two schools sat demonstrated stark differences; Vermont reflecting a liberal bent, New Hampshire, perennially run by Republicans.

Jake eased out of the booth and stood. "Just be a moment. Gotta get some relief," he said, and headed for the restrooms. Once he was out of earshot, Emily dropped her even-handedness. "How did the evening go for you? I was up all night worrying about how you were feeling."

"Honestly, Mom, I would dissolve at a place like Exeter. I couldn't wait for the visit to be over. I felt like it was a world I had nothing in common with. The kids they put you with must be trained to market the school so who knows if what they tell you is the truth. I didn't ask much. I bet the admissions people grill them after we leave about whether we were loony-tunes. I just want to climb mountains or ride a bike for a living, maybe get some endorsements from companies so I can live out of my van, be a dirtbag, and just travel around—sorry, Mom," he said, catching his mother's arched eyebrow. "It is a beautiful place, though. I'll give it that."

The waitress brought their food just as Jake returned. He slumped into the booth with a very sour look on his face.

"Do you think you'll apply, Jake?" Emily asked.

He took a long sip of water and stared at his hands. "It's complicated," he said.

"How so?" she asked pleasantly, not picking up on the change in Jake's mood. "I know you grew up in a different kind of place than Tracy. The whole rural-urban thing. But you love Glencoe every bit as much as Tracy. Could you see yourself thriving in a more conservative atmosphere?"

Ding went an alarm in Tracy's head. *Conservative.* He was pleased that his mother was showing her cards a bit and was curious to hear Jake's response.

"This has been a tough twenty-four hours for me," Jake said. "I don't like talking about what I'm going to talk about because you probably won't understand and I'll get frustrated and . . ."

"Whoa," Tracy exclaimed. "What's up with that? I've been with you nearly every minute since we got to Exeter and I didn't see anything that upset you. You seemed pretty cool with the place."

Tracy could see Jake was nearly trembling. Emily sat quietly, letting the boys sort it out. All of them ignored the steaming plates of food before them.

"No, Tracy. You didn't see anything. You *don't* see anything. That's why I love you and also why you're part of the problem."

"What problem?" said Tracy perplexed.

"Go pee."

"What?"

"Go pee."

"I don't have to pee."

"Go anyway."

"You want me to go to the restroom?"

"Yup."

Puzzled, Tracy got up from the booth and walked to the back of the diner.

"Sorry, Mrs. . . . um . . . Emily. I'm not trying to be difficult. And thanks again for bringing me on the trip, and for dinner, and for that knucklehead son of yours. I love him to death."

"You're welcome, Jake. I think he's pretty special, too. And I'm thrilled the two of you could do a visit together. Exeter is not my cup of tea. Tracy knows that. But I am not going to try to persuade him that it isn't a good fit. It's got to be his decision."

"He may be too much of a free spirit to be happy there," Jake agreed. "I've spent enough hours with him in the classroom and in the woods to appreciate how unique he is. He may not be the best student academically—though he is whip-smart—but he's taught me so much about being at one with the wilderness."

"Say more," Emily said, her heart filling.

"Let me give you an example," Jake said. "One trip stands out. I'll never forget it. We were bushwhacking from one mountain to another. You don't normally climb them that way and it meant travelling through some of the thickest, most miserable terrain. As we descended the first peak to the low point between the two, everyone was getting whipped in the face by branches, tripped by roots we can't see, regretting we'd ever signed up for the trip. I can't remember who the trip leaders were, which teachers, but they were as unhappy as we were. It was slow going, getting late, and it looked like we'd have to bivouac without tents in the middle of that crap if something didn't change.

"We break out of the woods for a second and there's this stream, going our way. Tracy sings out 'let's rock-hop down. It'll be a gas.' Without asking, he takes the lead and dances down like it's a ballet. At first, everyone's cautious, picking their way down carefully so as not to get wet, and he's rocking and rolling like it's nothing. He's in seventh heaven and it became contagious. We realize we're not in the awful brush anymore, we're making great time, probably won't run out of daylight. Everybody starts bouncing down, shouting, laughing. It was such a relief and he was magnificent. That's where he's happiest, and it rubs off. He's like a pied piper. I don't know that he could feed that part of himself at a place like Exeter."

Emily had tears in her eyes but said nothing.

"I'm looking for different things in a school, Emily. Exeter would be a big change, but my mom is pushing me because she thinks it's a way in to a world that's usually closed to folks like me. She's already decided I can be anything I want . . . as long as it's a lawyer or a doctor. Maybe that's not who I am, but she's done so much for me, I can't say no; at least not now. Sending me to Glencoe was the first step in that journey. A place like Exeter is Step Number Two. I owe it to her to try."

After a few moments Tracy returned and slid in next to Jake. "Did you send me away to tell my mom some deep, dark secret?"

"What did you see in the restroom?" Jake asked.

"What did I see? Some sinks and urinals and stalls I wouldn't be caught dead going in. What else would I see?"

"How about the message scrawled on the door as you were leaving the restroom?"

"I don't pay attention to graffiti," Tracy said.

"It obviously upset you, Jake," Emily said. "What did it say?"

Jake pushed his plate away from him, appetite gone. "Something like all people that look like me should get our dirty asses outta here. Sorry, Emily."

Emily blanched.

"I'm choosing not to give you the exact words. And this is New Hampshire, not Mississippi," Jake muttered, shaking his head.

"Didn't pay attention to it," Tracy said, missing the fact his friend was seething.

"Here's the thing, Tracy. You didn't see it and I knew you wouldn't. I saw it immediately. I live it all the time. I just don't talk about it."

The waitress approached their booth, noticed most of the food had gone untouched, and asked, "Is everything all right? Did I mess up the order?" She looked at the plate Jake had pushed into the middle of the table and said to Tracy, who was closest to her, sitting on the aisle, "Did the cook burn your friend's hamburger?"

"I'm not his friend," Jake said. Emily and Tracy looked at him, wide-eyed. The waitress shifted uncomfortably. "I'm his brother," Jake continued. "And the burger is fine, thanks."

The waitress looked at each of them and fingered the collar of her blouse nervously.

"Brother from another mother," Emily said, trying to cut the tension. "The food is great, miss. We just have a lot to say to each other, that's all."

"Okay, whatever," she said, leaving abruptly.

"What was that about?" a bewildered Tracy asked. This was a side of his roommate he had never seen.

"I wanted to make a point. What went through that waitress' head—what I have to go through all the time—is that you're white and I'm Black. The two of us can't be brothers because I'm different. Every minute I'm different. Color is what she saw."

"That is a horrible thing someone wrote in the restroom," Emily said. "You have a right to be upset."

"It's more that it comes on top of all the things I was thinking about while we were at Exeter. You're right, Emily. I am happy at Glencoe and yet Exeter may be my best move, if they take me. Like I said, when Tracy was in the restroom, not seeing the world I live in, I need something different from high school than he does."

Tracy was upset, finally. He could now see the turmoil Jake was in. He felt badly that he had not seen the graffiti or, if he had, subliminally, it had not registered even after his friend had ordered him to go to the restroom. That was even worse. Tracy didn't think he saw race, rarely gave it a thought, and until now, never discussed it with his roommate.

"Here's the thing," Jake continued. "Glencoe isn't real life. Not for someone from Bed Stuy. I don't feel like people look at me at Glencoe and see a Black kid, but the fact is, there are only a handful of us there, and I feel responsible for making sure they're all okay. I'm always checking in on them, and it's exhausting. They don't know I'm doing it but it's how I am. At Exeter it will be different, not necessarily better. At least there will be more of us, people of color. And I'll be one of the younger ones and won't feel like I have to take care of everyone else. But we're all tokens. We let the school feel good about itself, that it's saving another few Black kids. As long as I play my part and don't make trouble, they'll let me in their club. I get a ticket to the best colleges, and access to their elite world. Changes my life. Do I feel good about the part I have to play? No. But will I do it? Probably. And it makes me sick to even think about it that way."

"That's an awful weight to carry," Emily said.

"I never realized you worry about how people look at you, Jake," said Tracy.

"Are you kidding? When you go into a convenience store, does the guy behind the counter call out to ask you if you can find everything you're looking for? He does that to let me know he's got his eye on me. Do people cross the street rather than walk past you? Do you ever worry about walking around with a bunch of guys because other folk will think you're a gang? It's constant, and not something I will ever get used to. So, I build walls for self-protection. It's not me, I tell myself. It's them. I was taught early on by my uncle to be aware of stuff like that. He called it the 'odious red badge of opprobrium.' I didn't know what those big words meant exactly but I knew where he was coming from. He repeated it so often it stuck with me."

"You have a wise uncle," Emily said.

"The red badge?" Tracy asked, looking from Jake to Emily.

"Odious red badge . . ." Jake said, smiling. " . . . Of opprobrium."

"Sorry, I feel like an idiot," Tracy muttered. "Help me out. I really want to understand."

"I think what Jake's uncle meant," said Emily, "was that simply having a different skin color is like being branded. The world—the white world—will shun you, avoid you, watch you. Opprobrium means public disgrace. It's a heavy burden, sweetie," she said, looking at Jake. He nodded appreciatively.

"You're my best friend, T-Man," Jake added. "But you don't have a clue about the race thing. And it's not about money. You can't tell who's on scholarship at Glencoe and who's not, but you sure can tell who's got a different skin color. I don't think about it every day at Glencoe but I sure as hell do everywhere else. I'm sure I will at Exeter and that makes me sad. I am not looking forward to graduation because it means I have to leave la-la land and face the real world, a harsher kind of world than you'll ever see, Tracy. And it just gets harder the older you get. I don't need anyone to teach me that. I live it and I know it's true."

"Does this happen when we're hiking, too?" Tracy asked, looking bewildered.

"It's more subtle," Jake said. "Folks aren't used to seeing a Black kid on the trail for some reason. I guess they think we aren't supposed to leave the city. It's a subtle reaction to me. Forced conversation. I'm a curiosity. They don't leave the trail to get away from me. But I can see discomfort in their eyes. I'll get some small talk, to show me they're at ease. But they're not. So, I keep it short and move on."

"I had no idea," Tracy sighed. "I guess I'm in my own world."

"You think?" Jake teased, punching his friend lightly on the shoulder.

28

Preparing for Adventure

THE DINING HALL AT GLENCOE WAS THE MOST HEAVILY USED SPACE IN the school, a place for wholesome, family-style meals that utilized as much produce as the farm program could harvest, as well as quiet games, study hall, and the occasional rock climber enticed by its floor-to-ceiling fieldstone hearth. Beyond the glassed double doors that separated the dining room from a generous foyer, Pete Hedges had stapled a trip announcement. The bulletin board was littered with all manner of notices: chore designations for the week, newspaper clippings heralding the success of the soccer team, a five-foot-high cardboard rendering of a maple leaf, the ever-climbing colored portion indicating the number of cords of wood split by students to boil sap during the spring sugaring season.

Everyone participated in the outdoors program to some degree, but only an elite cadre, in dogged pursuit of the forty-six Adirondack peaks over four thousand feet, was fit enough, or crazy enough, to willingly volunteer for the kind of challenge Pete had advertised on the bulletin board. The notice displayed an artful rendition of the MacIntyre Range in pretty pastels, lovingly produced by Christine Mason, offering to the first eight hardy souls the opportunity to join Pete and Christine on a strenuous two-day traverse of three mountains in the range: Algonquin, Iroquois, and Wright Peak. It was scheduled for the upcoming weekend and, considering the depth of late-fall snow already on the ground in the higher elevations, promised to be a challenging alpine experience.

The MacIntyres cut a wide swath through the heart of the Adirondack High Peaks. They are named for Archibald McIntyre, without an "a," founder of the famed Adirondack Iron Works, source of the nation's finest steel-producing iron ore for a thirty-year period just before the Civil War. The roller-coaster ridge of peaks and saddles in the Mac Range runs northeast to southwest with formidable, rocky-topped Algonquin at its apex, the second-highest peak in New York State, topped only by Mount Marcy, a nearby neighbor. Deciduous stands of maple, beech and birch carpet the lower flanks, giving vent to explosions of vibrant color each fall. The higher elevations are laced with rings of stunted coniferous balsam and spruce, hardy denizens struggling to prosper in a harsh environment. Winter lingers through April, allowing tender buds only a few precious weeks to grow and prosper. Although numerous Adirondack peaks have open, rocky tops, Algonquin is one whose summit cone is naturally bare. Most owe their treeless crowns to fire and erosion.

At the northern end of the range stands Wright Peak, named for an early governor of New York, Silas Wright. A half-mile south of Wright, as the crow flies, stands Algonquin, linked via a broad alpine ridge to Boundary Peak, not a recognized 46er because it sits too close to its higher neighbor to qualify as a distinctly separate entity, some say representing the border between the land of the Algonquin and Iroquois tribes, whose namesake peak rises farther to the southwest on this wide whaleback ridge. Beyond Iroquois Peak, a forbidding string of cliffs and a promontory known as Shepherd's Tooth block the way to the smallest peak in the range, Mt. Marshall.

Enthusiasm for climbing the High Peaks took years to germinate. Those seeds can be traced back to Bob and George Marshall, two brothers who, under the tutelage of a local guide, Herb Clark, explored the region as teens during summers at Saranac Lake. Bob wrote about their adventures in a 1922 booklet and grew up to become the nation's leading advocate for forestry conservation, indelibly affected by those hiking weekends in an upstate New York wilderness struggling to recover from widespread fire and clear-cut logging. For his efforts, Marshall was honored by Congress, which named a Montana wilderness area after him.

Bob Marshall's pamphlet, plus a history of the region published five years later, sparked the interest of a church group from Troy, New York, a couple of hours south. Thus began a concerted effort to reach the summits of all forty-six peaks that had been correctly (and incorrectly) surveyed to be at least 4,000 feet in height. In 1948, a nonprofit organization, the Adirondack 46ers, was formed, which kept records of everyone who self-attested to have reached all of the summits. Tracy read each issue of the club's biannual magazine, *Adirondack PEEKS*, to which the Glencoe library subscribed, and looked forward to seeing his own name in the roster they published each spring with the list of finishers for the previous year.

The term "peak bagging" was a sensitive one at Glencoe. It connoted a systematic conquering of summits with little regard for the journey. As a headmaster who lived by the precepts of wilderness preservation, Hamish made clear to his staff how he wanted the tripping program to be run.

We have an opportunity to train these children for a lifetime of enjoying the precious wilderness in our backyard, he lectured. *Checking off summits is fine, but it's just a statistic. Make sure they experience all the miracles along the way. If they don't see a burl growing out of a tree and wonder why, they've missed a golden opportunity. If they don't marvel at the intricacies of a moss field, they've wasted their time. If they don't marvel at the fragility and resiliency of lichen clinging to ancient rocks, their world is too small.*

We have multiple senses to experience the world we live in. None of them involve counting summits. Walking in the Adirondacks is a privilege. Let's make our students appreciate the means, not just the end.

Those lessons Hamish hammered home certainly found fertile ground in Tracy Barcomb. As ill-equipped as he was at picking up cues from other human beings, Tracy missed nothing when walking through the wilderness. For that, among other attributes, he had become one of Hamish's favorites. And the feeling was mutual; Hamish was not an intimidating, remote, authoritarian to Tracy. He was a mentor, a grandfatherly figure, whose stories and wisdom Tracy sponged wherever they spilled.

As Libby walked out of the dining hall following a typically hearty breakfast of grapefruit sections, a hot cornmeal cereal everyone called sawdust, and pecan-topped sticky buns, she came upon a boisterous debate, with Tracy holding court, as usual.

"I can't believe you put your name on this list," Tracy said, as he poked Jake Thompson in the ribs.

"I figured you'd need a babysitter," retorted his buddy, faking a left jab at Tracy's chin.

"You might want to think this through, Jake. I hear you Black folk don't do well in cold weather," Tracy teased. "Better use that eraser while you still have time. Pete's going to be taking the sign down tonight and if your name's still on it, you're toast."

Jake raised an eyebrow. "The red badge?"

"Sorry," Tracy groaned, recognizing the signal and immediately regretting his jibe. "I didn't mean it."

Jake pulled him away from the clutch of kids hovering by the bulletin board. "Given what we talked about in the diner the other day, I should be really pissed off."

"You should be. No excuses. The color of your skin doesn't mean shit to me," Tracy said. "You know that, right?"

"That may be what's in your head, but nobody knows what's in your head. Or your heart. Did my speech that night mean anything to you?"

"Jake, the last thing I want is to offend you."

"I cut you more slack on this than I should, Tracy. The other brothers and sisters here at Glencoe don't know you like I know you. And I don't like having to explain or defend some of the comments you make to me that they can hear."

"I didn't mean any disrespect."

"I know that. But it's a habit you need to break."

"I'm sorry. Sometimes I just say stuff before I think about it."

"That's an understatement. If you try that at your next school, with someone who isn't as understanding as I am, you may end up with a punch in the nose. Or worse. And you'll deserve it."

Tracy nodded, embarrassed. He extended a palm and Jake slapped it hard. They had an understanding and a bond too strong to be shaken by

Tracy's ignorance, but he could see how disappointed Jake was and that stung.

In truth, there was nothing the two boys liked more than to spend time together working their way through all of the Adirondack peaks. The same uncle who had schooled Jake on the *odious red badge of opprobrium* had also taken the time to introduce him to mountains. Many a weekend Terrence Thompson would collect Jake at home, shepherd him up to the Catskills for climbs, and regale him with stories of his own alpine adventures as a member of the army's 10th Mountain Division, based out of Fort Drum near the Canadian border. Once Terrence saw how his nephew enjoyed scaling the heights, he introduced him to rock climbing on the renowned Shawangunk cliffs in New Paltz. Soon thereafter, Terrence advised his sister that Jake would be a natural for a boarding school not far from where he had spent his army days.

As his uncle predicted, Jake fell in love with the Adirondacks and climbed as many of them as he possibly could. It was a passion he shared with his redheaded friend from Vermont. By the start of his ninth-grade year, Jake had thirty-five of the Adirondack High Peaks under his belt, many climbed during the winter months. None of the students, including Tracy, had much to teach him in that department.

"I hope this is the last time I have to point out how brain-dead you can be," Jake said, shoving his friend affectionately in the chest. He turned to leave and plowed right into Libby.

"Whoops, sorry," Jake apologized, catching her before she fell.

"I'm okay," she replied, linking her arm through his, as they strolled down the hall toward their next class. Tracy brushed past, feeling disgusted with himself and envious at the easy way Jake and Libby were with each other.

"I heard what Tracy said to you. How can you take such garbage from such a twerp?" Libby asked.

"You've got him all wrong," Jake said. "He's got a good heart, even if he doesn't know how to show it. I'd feel different if Malcolm came on to me like that. That guy must have a death wish the way he acts. He's like a one-car accident waiting to happen."

"As far as I'm concerned, those two deserve each other," Libby continued, as she and Jake stood outside Pete Hedges' English class. "If Tracy's such a good friend of yours, maybe you can convince him to stop making a fool of himself around the girls, and to keep his hands off us. He bugs Tina and me every chance he gets and we certainly don't provoke him. He's so full of hot air, Jake, I bet even *I* could go on that Mac Range trip and keep up with him."

"He can be charming in a half-assed way. I do my best to point it out to him when he's gone over the line," Jake said. "I guess it's hard for you to understand why he's my best friend."

"He's got a lot of growing up to do."

"Not like the rest of us, huh?" Jake said with a twinkle. "We've got the world all figured out, haven't we?" Libby punched him lightly on the arm.

"It's love, Libby, that's all. Tracy's dying to get your attention. If you'd give him the time of day, I bet he'd behave himself."

"If I give him anything, Jake, it'll be a well-aimed kick in the balls. The last thing I want to give him is encouragement."

"Okay, so he acts like a jerk sometimes. But don't put him in the same category as Malcolm. Tracy's a good kid when you get to know him—especially in the mountains. I've been on more than one idiotic death march where everybody's past their limit, ready to quit, and there's Tracy, cracking jokes, singing songs, keeping us going. He's terrific.

"Why don't you sign up for this Mac Range trip, Libby? Ask Tina to come along, too. We'll have a great time, and maybe it'll chill Tracy out a bit to see a couple of senior girls on a trip with Pete's rat pack."

"I'd rather get root canal than spend the weekend in a confined space with Tracy. But thanks for the invitation."

Pete Hedges opened the door to his classroom. "You guys coming to English or am I going to be lecturing to myself this afternoon?"

Dutifully, the two ninth-grade friends followed him in.

"I'm thrilled you all could make it," Pete said sarcastically after his class of eight had finally settled into their seats and pulled out their dog-eared copies of *Endurance*. "We're at an interesting point in the semester and I want you to show me I'm getting my point across. Okay, tell me what the Journey of the Hero means to you, as described in Lansing's book, after reading Homer's *Odyssey*," he said, pointing at Jake.

The Odyssey and *Endurance* were the first two books Pete assigned to his ninth-grade English class. The former was familiar, at least by name, to every student. The latter, a grueling 1914 expedition, led by the English explorer, Ernest Shackleton, to sail to Antarctica and traverse it via the South Pole for the first time, was generally unknown to his students. Taken together, they illustrated how strikingly similar one could chart heroic journeys in literature, recognizing that one was fiction, the other not.

"From what we've read so far, I'm guessing you assigned both of these because of the challenges both heroes, Shackleton and Odysseus, faced trying to get home safely," Jake said. "The Hero is responsible for not only himself but so many that rely on him to lead them wisely. They have a plan but inevitably events make those plans impossible so they have to adjust, maybe go to Plan B or C. I am curious to find out what Shackleton's Plan B looks like," he continued.

So far, the class had learned that, upon sailing within sight of their first goal, Antarctica, the ship had become trapped in ice floes. For months they waited for conditions to ease but, with the onset of winter months, the pack ice became thicker, and eventually the hull of the *Endurance* was crushed. Shackleton ordered the crew to set up camp on the ice and there they remained for half a year, eating through their supplies, until spring thaw broke up the floes and forced them to make another fateful choice. Using three small lifeboats, the entire crew managed to sail to a deserted place called Elephant Island, where they set up a miserable campsite. The brilliance of their captain was his ability to keep the crew from psychologically deteriorating while he focused on how to get them all home.

The class would soon read that, understanding no rescue could happen if their whereabouts were unknown, Shackleton set out with five other crewmen in a single lifeboat, leaving twenty-two behind, aiming for the nearest whaling station on South Georgia Island. Seventeen days and eight hundred miles later, thanks to extraordinary navigation across the Southern Atlantic Ocean, the wildest stretch of open water on the planet, they reached the island, but on the opposite side from a manned whaling station where help could be found. Their final challenge was to traverse snow and ice-covered peaks with inadequate clothing and equipment to reach the far coast, shocking the whalers who assumed all had perished months earlier. Shackleton immediately set about organizing a rescue ship to retrieve whomever was still alive on Elephant Island. In the end, all twenty-two men were rescued and returned home, a heroic end to an unbelievable three-year journey.

"The Hero's task, as he moves from the known to the unknown portion of his journey, is to recognize how to learn on the fly, to adjust to new realities, and model behavior his or her charges can follow to survive their predicament," Pete said. "Shackleton had a resilient crew and he instituted regimentation in their daily lives to maintain their sanity and give them something to hang on to. Importantly, he also knew how to leverage the skills of his crew. An intelligent Hero knows it takes collective will to survive.

"Who can give me a current example of the Hero's Journey from your experience?"

After thirty seconds of silence Tracy raised his hand. "Umm . . . I think Neil Armstrong might be a good example. I might have said another Armstrong—Lance—but I'm having my doubts about that guy these days. I know Neil didn't go it alone; he had a crew in the Apollo 13 capsule and help back in Houston, right? But he's like Shackleton. He faced huge challenges on the way to the moon; they didn't know if the lander would ever lift off the surface. That qualifies as an ordeal to me. But they figured it out and made it home. I don't know what happens to Shackleton yet, but sounds like a Hero's Journey to me."

Libby and Tina exchanged glances. Tina's look conveyed: *See, he's not the simple ignoramus you think he is.* Libby's was: *I didn't think he had a thought in his head that didn't involve mountains or sex.* Each of them pretty much understood what the other was thinking. Libby then had another thought; one she did not try to telepathically share. For the first time she allowed herself to see Tracy as earnest, even thoughtful. And, *God strike me for even thinking this, sort of cute,* especially with that unruly red hair trying to escape that ball cap he always wore.

"Great example, Tracy. These stories are not identical but there are clearly similar patterns in how the Hero deals with hurdles thrown his or her way. Whether it's Shackleton, or Odysseus, or Armstrong, the hero chooses a profound endeavor and cannot manage it alone. They rely on others who can teach and help. There is the inevitable, unspeakable challenge that threatens the survival of the Hero and his team. The Hero must respond, begin to grow, and transform. They don't wait for events to happen; they force the issue. It is how they confront the Unexpected in the Unknown that enables growth and wisdom to emerge. Failure can still be heroic. Success is never guaranteed. Only in fairy tales. The concept of the Hero's Journey was well articulated by a professor named Joseph Campbell back in the 1940s. He recognized these patterns in stories from the early Greeks and Romans to adventures of the present, as Tracy suggested. At the end of the day, it is a universal story of triumph over adversity through the eyes of a heroic character who becomes profoundly transformed by the experience. So . . . I can't guarantee what happens to our friend Ernest Shackleton and his band of brothers, but please have it finished when we resume classes after winter break."

Later that afternoon, while adding the final brush strokes to a water-color pastiche of a mountain scene, Libby felt Christine Mason's gentle hand on her shoulder.

"Beautiful work, Libby," Christine marveled. "You've really found a style that works for you."

"Thanks, Christine. I have to admit it's an improvement over that backdrop I painted of Mt. Olympus for the Thanksgiving show. God, that was awful. Looked more like an ice cream cone than the home of the Gods."

"That's ridiculous," Christine giggled. "I'd say it was more like a massive pimple than an ice cream cone." Libby laughed, dipping her brush in water to clean it. "We sure missed you at the performance," Christine said. "You worked hard and I wish you had had the chance to enjoy the fruits of your labor. I got a lot of compliments from parents about the sets."

Libby shook her head slowly, remembering the long hours on the bus to New York and back, the disappointment with her parents and that one bright spot, her time with Eva. "I missed it too," she said quietly. "But there wasn't a thing I could do about it."

"That picture of yours reminds me," Christine said, brightening, eager to move the conversation away from Libby's sadness. "I've got a great trip coming up in the MacIntyre Range. Want to join us?"

"What is this, a conspiracy?" Libby smiled. "Jake just asked me the same thing. I don't get it. Why would anyone want to freeze their buns off when they don't have to?"

"I used to think the same way until Pete convinced me to give it a try last winter. I was hooked. Well, that may be a little strong. But it opened up new ways of looking at the world and experiencing your senses that actually helped me in the classroom. I'm now better able to help students get in touch with their ability to see things and convey it to canvas than before. I know it sounds crazy."

"So, you didn't like hiking until you came to Glencoe?" Libby asked.

"I never experienced winter hiking before I came here. I guess the last time I spent so much time around mountains I was probably still a teenager. The summer after my senior year in high school I did an Outward Bound course in Colorado. I think it was the three-day solo more than my artistic abilities that interested Hamish when I came up for my interview," Christine joked. "Why don't you come along, Libby? I think there are still one or two places left."

"I dunno. Cascade is the only mountain I've ever climbed."

"You're fit, Libby. Probably a lot stronger than you think. Anyway, I'd love to have you along. We need some gender balance. Too many male hormones on this trip."

"Will you promise to keep Tracy off my back?"

"I'm no miracle worker, but I'll do my best. Why don't you put your name on the list now before you change your mind?"

"Oh, what the hell," Libby said with resignation. She rinsed out her paintbrush, and headed for the stairs, taking them two at a time, relishing the moment when she could rub the news in Tracy Barcomb's freckled face and wondering why she cared at all. Past the empty classrooms she hurried, down the main hall of Dewey, to the atrium where the sign-up was posted. Passing a practice room, she heard Ron Handy at the piano, urging on a student clearly new to the instrument. Now that *The Truth about Zeus* was over, it seemed Handy had been reborn, his energy back to normal. For such a consummate artist, Ron was at his best teaching the beginners. His patience was legendary. After all these years working with hundreds of eager amateurs Ron could still be enthusiastic with students for whom a piano chord sounded like a kitten traipsing randomly across the keys. Past the door to the library Libby saw the more diligent students getting a leg up on the evening's assignments, past the indoor rock-climbing wall . . . A red blur swooshed past her left ear and landed with a thud at her feet. Involuntarily she let out a scream, jumping to avoid what had already hit the ground beside her.

"Hello, princess."

"Jesus Christ, Tracy, you could have killed me," she sputtered, thinking immediately of Tigger's infernal bouncing in the Winnie-the-Pooh story. "You're not supposed to be up on the climbing wall without a spotter."

"Okay, okay. No need for a hissy fit."

"Just grow up a little. I can't believe I'm signing up for that stupid Algonquin trip you're on. I should have my head examined," she muttered, turning to walk down the hall. Tracy watched her go, delighted.

As she approached the sign-up sheet, Malcolm was writing his name in on one of the two remaining empty lines. He was about the last person in school she would have imagined wanting to join this trip, aside from herself, that is.

"Are you seriously thinking about going on this trip?" Libby asked.

Malcolm turned and smiled. "Why, you think I have some irrational fear of heights now?"

"No," she stammered. "I just didn't think you'd want to start hiking again so soon after . . ." her voice trailed off.

"I'm fine," he said. "And maybe I've got something to prove. Anyway, I know I'm stronger than half of the wusses on this list. What about you?"

"Actually, I had just decided to try it, yes."

"Well, all right," Malcolm smiled. "That sure makes the whole thing a lot more interesting."

Libby grimaced, elbowed past him to the board and wrote her name on the last empty line. Unfortunately, there was now no more room for Tina.

Later that evening Libby blew off steam to her roommate in the privacy of their room. As Tina watched bemusedly from her bed, Libby paced furiously, rehashing all the reasons why she detested Tracy Barcomb and why this trip was probably the worst mistake of her life.

"What's the big deal?" Tina said when Libby flopped back down on her own bed, physically spent. "Tracy's harmless, immature, oversexed, your typical fifteen-year-old boy. He'll grow up someday and we probably will never know how he turned out. What is it about him that bugs you so?"

"I don't really know," Libby admitted. "He just knows how to push my buttons. I don't like how I get when he teases me."

"Flirts," Tina said.

"Whatever. I get mean and that's not who I want to be. Even with him. But the last place I want to be for two days is trapped in a group with Tracy and Malcolm. Watching them go at each other is painful."

"Malcolm? You can't be serious."

"Dead serious. He wants to prove something to everyone. I don't think he has any idea what he's getting himself into. I may not be experienced in this stuff, but at least I know I'm in good shape."

"Sounds like Pete and Christine will have their hands full. Just stay out of their way." Tina raised an eyebrow and grinned mischievously. "You know, Libby, I think you kind of like his wildness. In fact, I think you wish you could be more like him."

"Who?"

"You know who. Not Malcolm."

"That's the most ridiculous thing I've ever heard," Libby protested.

"You're wrapped pretty tight, girl. Tracy lets everything just hang out. He doesn't care what anybody thinks, he just does and says whatever crosses his brain. I bet you'd kind of enjoy acting like that once in a while. Yeah, the more I think about it, the more it makes sense to me. You've got a thing for Tracy Barcomb."

"I hate you, Tina."

. . .

Eight students and two leaders met in the gymnasium after dinner that Wednesday to assemble gear for the MacIntyre trip. While Libby struggled with her conflicting desire to bring everything she owned but also to carry as little weight as possible, Tracy and Jake pawed over group equipment, selecting the heaviest items—stoves, pots, and tents—their adolescent machismo driving them to produce the heaviest possible load. To the top and sides of their packs they lashed steel crampons and snowshoes.

After twenty minutes, Libby had made virtually no progress. Clothes and sleeping gear still lay about her in disparate piles; the still-empty pack at her feet.

"Looking for directions?" Tracy teased.

Libby threw up her hands. "There's no way I can fit all this stuff in."

"You don't need three pairs of everything," Jake said patiently. "No offense, but I think that terrycloth bathrobe's got to go."

"No way, Jake! I'd pay to see her wandering around in the snow in that thing," joked Tracy. "Where's the nightie?"

"You're an idiot," Libby snapped.

Pete looked up from helping someone else. "You guys done yet?" he said pointedly to the two boys. They nodded. "Then head up the hill, you're not helping here."

"Just offering some friendly advice, Pete."

"Thanks for your concern, Tracy, but I'll take over if that's okay."

"Go right ahead, but she'll need a llama to carry all that stuff."

Apart from the others, Malcolm meticulously sorted through a small mountain of the latest accessories he had just received from his Aunt Mathilda, who must have selected something from every page of the REI catalog. There was a sleek Black Diamond headlamp, a self-inflating air mattress, and gleaming Grivel crampons with easy step-in bindings, perfectly paired with Asolo mountaineering boots. He was stuffing a wine-colored Marmot sleeping bag, good to forty below zero, into the lower compartment of a Dana pack when Pete and Tracy walked over.

"Gee, Malcolm, you got a GPS gizmo there in case we get lost and an avalanche flotation device perhaps?" Pete Hedges asked, with a twinkle. Tracy was speechless looking at all the goodies at Malcolm's feet. If he could have written out a wish list for Christmas, all this gear would have been on it, though everything was way out of his family's price range.

"It's crazy, I know," Malcolm answered, ruefully. "I have no idea how all this stuff works. Blame my aunt. She wants to make sure I don't get myself into trouble. Probably had one of the clerks walk up and down each aisle tossing the most expensive things into a cart. Do I really need to carry all this crap?"

"Truth be told, she got you some great stuff. You're a lucky boy. I wish I had equipment half as good as this." Pete grinned at Tracy, who could only shake his head in awe. Apart from whatever his dad could afford from Army Surplus, Tracy made do with the flotsam and jetsam Glencoe had accumulated over the years. Pete glanced at the pile of clothes Malcolm had lugged down from Marshall House. "Mal, you should be prepared to hike with three layers from the waist down and four from the waist up—plus an extra layer for emergency in the pack. You good to go?"

"I guess. Maybe I'll pay some cretin to haul this stuff for me," he muttered. "Want to make a few bucks?" he asked Tracy, sarcastically.

"By the way, I'm really pleased you signed on," Pete said, ignoring the comment. "We're going to make this a lot more fun than the last time you took a hike." He had witnessed more than one cathartic transformation of a kid whose entire outlook about school had changed after a single challenging hike.

29

The Best-Laid Plans

FOLLOWING FRIDAY MORNING'S BREAKFAST ON DECEMBER 9TH, MEM-
bers of the Mac Range trip assembled outside the kitchen, lording it over
their fellow students who were obliged to attend class as usual. Libby
swore there wasn't a cubic inch of room available in her pack for anything,
but Christine somehow managed to wedge in some cheese and Triscuits.
Pete drove up with one of the school vans. One by one, the students
hoisted their packs to be stacked neatly behind the rear seat.

"I feel kind of queasy," Libby said as she boarded the van and sat
down next to Christine, snuggling against her for security as much as
warmth.

"Nerves. It's totally normal. Just go with the flow," Christine said,
tousling Libby's hair.

Hamish emerged from his office to watch the proceedings and wish
them good luck. He rarely participated in the outdoors program these
days, so preoccupied was he with administrative duties, but his heart went
along with every group. "Good to see you getting an early start," he said,
as Pete secured the rear liftgate of the van. "You should get some views
before the front comes through."

"Does it look like we'll be socked in the whole weekend?" Pete asked.

"Whatever comes, you're prepared, right?" Hamish grinned, clapping
Pete on the back. "Knock the bastards off!"

Twenty minutes later, Pete parked the van at Heart Lake, the jumping-off point for many trails into the High Peaks. Everyone anxiously
fussed over their gear one last time, tightening bootlaces, adjusting

shoulder straps, and using the restrooms in the visitors' center. Libby wandered over to the side of the van where Tracy had left his pack. She grasped the pack with one hand and tried to heft it. Failing to lift it even an inch, she tried with both hands, barely succeeding.

"Jeez," she exclaimed. "You're supposed to enjoy carrying this?"

Tracy grinned, shrugging his shoulders.

The group set out briskly on a well-traveled trail. Though countless hikers had packed the snow into a concrete-like state, regulations required everyone to bring snowshoes or cross-country skis when the snow depth exceeded eight inches. They didn't need them on this stretch of trail, but that would soon change. Once they began to gain altitude, the need for snowshoes became evident. For many of the students the use of snowshoes took some adjustment, resulting in a fair amount of stumbling. Not surprisingly, Malcolm found the wide appendages frustrating, generating a stream of curses each time he kicked himself in a calf muscle.

Nearly two and a half miles from Heart Lake, the trail passed a waterfall, its flow temporarily stilled until spring released its ice. When Pete called a halt, the kids unshouldered their packs and began pulling out sweaters, parkas, woolen hats, and mittens. Libby slumped down on the end of a snow-covered log with her pack still slung over her shoulders, resting it against a birch tree to relieve the complaining muscles in her neck and back.

"Anyone want some good ol' raisins and peanuts?" Christine asked. She circled the group with a bag of gorp in her hand and a few words of encouragement. "Libby, you ought to put on something warm," she advised. "Once you chill off, it's pretty tough to get warm again."

"I can't believe people do this on purpose. Maybe this wasn't such a smart idea." The cold began to penetrate, and she saw everyone else was donning an extra layer. Jake and Tracy tossed snowballs at each other, oblivious to the ordeal. They seemed completely at home on their snowshoes, prancing about as if the things didn't exist. Libby looked for Malcolm but couldn't spot him. She slipped out of her pack, unclipped the buckles securing the main flap and began searching for the down jacket that seemed to have burrowed its way to the bottom. "I think I'm strong enough to make it, but I'm not sure I can maintain this pace," she said to Christine. "Are we almost there?"

"Almost halfway to the first one," Christine chuckled. "You'll be okay. Just keep aware of your body's signals. Don't let yourself get too hot or too cold. Keep that jacket handy, put it on when we stop and take it off when we get going again. It's a simple rule, but people get lazy when they're tired and that's when accidents happen. And . . ." Christine smiled, "don't forget to enjoy yourself."

Libby instinctively went for her hairbrush as soon as she had donned the parka, grimacing as she stroked through the tangles and icicles.

"Where's Malcolm?" she asked no one in particular.

Christine scanned the group munching on gorp, passing chunks of cheddar around, and drinking from chilled water bottles. No Malcolm. At that moment, he emerged from the woods, making a big show of zipping his fly. He grinned at Christine.

"Had to drain the wick."

Observing this interaction, Pete shook his head in mock disgust, relieved Malcolm had not wandered off and, in fact, looked comfortable so far.

Fortified by Christine's encouragement and snacks, Libby shouldered her pack and waited for the others to fall in line. Tracy stepped past her and said, "We start really climbing now. Better lose that down jacket or you'll be sweating like a pig in ten minutes. Then we'll just have to wait for you while you get undressed again." Before retorting, she noted that the other kids were, in fact, removing their outer jackets even though they shivered as they did so. Following suit, she stuffed her jacket back in the pack, cinched down the waist strap and began windmilling her arms to regain warmth. Tracy and Jake seemed immune to the cold and the steepening trail, never complaining, never revealing fatigue, chatting happily to each other.

As the troupe wound its way ever upward through thinning spruce and birch, the snow deepened. Libby's second wind kicked in and her steps came easier. She was able to reach down for extra effort and feel her body respond. Despite the elements, she felt warm, more in control.

At the junction marking a spur trail to Wright Peak, Pete huddled the group together so they could readjust their clothing to suit the worsening conditions they could expect as they approached tree line. One of the kids asked if Wright was their first objective, which was what they had discussed during their first trip meeting back at school.

"That was the plan," Pete said. "But with this front coming through I want to make sure we get up and over Algonquin today. If the weather holds, we'll shoot over to Iroquois before bailing out to our campsite down by Lake Colden. I'm afraid we'll have to bypass Wright today. Always pay attention to the weather in the mountains. Ignore it at your peril." While they pulled out warmer jackets, hats and mittens, Pete began another story.

"You may be interested to know that back in January of 1962, a B-47 Air Force jet disintegrated just below the summit of Wright Peak, off to our left. For five days searchers combed the High Peaks by air before finally locating the site of the crash. Rescuers then were forced to wait several more days for a break in the weather before they could begin the grisly task of recovering the bodies of four unfortunate airmen."

"Did kids from school get to see any of the wreckage?" Jake asked.

"Yep. Sometimes we climb up Wright from a slide on the backside where the crash occurred. I'm told back in the day, some kids brought back small pieces of the plane, including dials from the dashboard. There's not much left now.

"Anybody know what that pile of rocks signifies?" Pete asked, pointing to a pyramid-shaped jumble of stones that jutted out of the snow a few yards farther up the trail.

Libby remembered having seen similar pyramids at periodic intervals along the trail. "It's a trail marker?" she volunteered.

"Duhhh," Tracy snickered.

"Okay, Tracy," Pete challenged. "If you're such an expert, tell us how cairns came to represent trail markers."

Tracy looked embarrassed and shrugged his shoulders. "I can't remember. Ask Malcolm. He knows everything."

"Hey, knock it off," warned Jake, giving Tracy a right jab to the shoulder.

"It's from Europe, I think. Maybe Irish?" Malcolm interjected.

Pete looked impressed. "Pretty close, Mal. Before we get too cold here, I'm going to give you a short course in mythology."

"Can't let a teachable moment go to waste," Christine teased. Even in that innocent jibe, Libby could sense the easy intimacy Pete and Christine shared. She felt a bit wistful about what that would be like for her one day.

"Ignoring that remark," Pete chuckled, "I shall continue. Cairn is a Scottish word, meaning monument. The word is relatively modern, but the myth it represents is quite old. The habit of leaving piles of rocks to mark a trail is thought to have originated with the ancient Greeks." Pete proceeded to recount the story of Hermes, son of Zeus, and of the trial this God of travelers, shepherds, and thieves had undergone.

"One of Zeus' wives, Hera, lost patience with the mischievous Hermes, who had caused the death of her favorite hundred-eyed watchman, Argus," said Pete.

"Arr-gus, ye'll swing from the yardarms," Malcolm crowed.

"Shut up, Malcolm," Tracy snapped. "He said Greeks, not pirates, you dimwit."

"Right," chuckled Malcolm. "We're so lucky to have Zeus and his play toy, Ganymede, on the trip with us today," he teased, nodding at Jake and Tracy.

Uh oh, here they go, worried Libby.

Ignoring the distraction, Pete continued, directing his words to the other kids who were listening intently. "After laying the facts of the case before the assembled jury of gods, Hera urged them to cast their vote by throwing pebbles in her direction if they felt Hermes was guilty, or in his direction for an acquittal. Hermes's arguments were so compelling that the pile of pebbles tossed by the gods covered him from head to toe, freeing him from punishment and, by the way, creating a shape that looks like the ones we use to mark the trail. To this day," Pete concluded, "the spirit of Hermes is believed to reside within each cairn to help travelers on their way. So, that's it. Test on Monday. Now let's get on our way before we turn into icy monuments ourselves."

"Nice to know Hermes wasn't just God of Purses," Jake laughed, looking at Tracy who had played that role in the just-completed Thanksgiving production.

With trees devoid of leaves, the hikers had a clear view behind them into the valley from which they'd come, but overhead storm clouds were brewing. Hamish had been right about the incoming front. Libby cocked her head, listening to the ominous roar of the wind somewhere above them. Pete ordered them to don their wind parkas and swap snowshoes for crampons, lacing them to the bottom of their boots. Although she had practiced this maneuver in the school gym when they were packing their gear, Libby discovered that with bare fingers in freezing conditions it was a challenging task. To her left, Malcolm stepped easily into his top-of-the-line crampons, snapping them into place with a few quick movements. Libby blew into her hands to make them work, then resumed her struggle with the neoprene straps that refused to cooperate.

Malcolm crouched down and said, "You do the left. I'll take care of this one. I hope these things work better than those dumb-ass shoes. I sure don't want to kick myself in the leg with these. They're lethal weapons," he said, rubbing his fingers along the sharp crampon points but smiling up at her. Libby thought maybe there was actually more to this guy than he generally let on. He seemed to show her a totally different side. Gratefully, she followed his orders and soon was standing ready to walk, hands numb but encased again in heavy woolen mittens.

As they emerged from the relative shelter of the trees and broke out onto the final summit cone of Algonquin, a blast of wind caught her flush, rocking her back on her heels. Invisible icy needles pummeled her cheeks. Struggling to maintain her balance, she leaned onto her ski poles. Glancing up, she hoped the open rocks above her represented the summit. She glanced east in the direction of Vermont and gasped. The vista was breathtaking. A white carpet of forest and frozen lake lay beneath her feet. Nearby, seemingly close enough to touch, loomed Wright Peak, laced with rime ice, its summit already enshrouded in a sea of clouds that came rolling in from the north, close to enveloping Algonquin as well.

Pete looked earnestly from face to face. "Ready?" he shouted. "The visibility is going to drop to nothing in a few minutes. Stay together.

Make sure you can see the person in front and behind you! We're not going to stay on top for very long. Let's go!" Anxiety again began to well up within Libby's chest as the group moved out from behind the protection of the boulder. She felt her heart pounding through five layers of nylon, fleece, and wool, as the buffeting wind and biting cold scraped away at the confidence she had worked so hard to build in the preceding hours and miles.

"I hope this guy knows what he's doing," she muttered to herself, lowered her head like a bull and stumbled into the gathering gale.

Ten minutes later, two hundred yards from the now-invisible summit, they entered the cloud. It teased them at first with thin gossamer strands, finally coalescing into an all-enveloping whiteout. In the lead, Pete slowed his pace, alert to the occasional cairns that marked the trail. There was little chance of losing the way, for as long as they continued upward, they could not miss the top. It would be a different story locating the correct route of descent.

Libby passed Malcolm, who had stopped to retie a bootlace, mittens gripped between his teeth. He glanced up and smiled warmly at her, a gesture that at once startled and relieved her.

"No problems?" she asked.

"Not yet," he grinned. "Pretty cool. The crampons are great, huh?"

Libby had noticed how positively the steel teeth bit into the ice underfoot.

"Yeah. I can't imagine taking two steps without them. Have you ever done this before?" she shouted.

"No. But it seems easy enough."

The tight line of hikers snaked upward between glazed boulders deposited by the last retreating glacier, following a trough worn down between knee-high, ice-encased cripplebrush. From her place in line just ahead of Christine, visibility was so poor that Libby could see only two other people ahead of her. All at once, the grade lessened and she came upon the rest of the group stomping their feet on a small plateau. Pete greeted her with a hearty clap on the shoulder, a twinkle in his eyes. Tiny icicles hung from his mustache.

"Is this it?" she shouted, surveying the barren moonscape. The wind at the summit rocketed at them with the power of a freight train.

"Yes, ma'am. Congratulations!" he grinned, then stumbled toward Christine, who had just joined them at the summit. It was urgent that they not linger for long.

Tracy sidled up to Libby. "Nice goin,' kid," he shouted at her above the roar of the wind. "You look like a ghost."

Libby stared, too tired to say anything.

"Bet you didn't figure Algonquin would be like this when you were sitting in the art room, huh?"

"I made it, didn't I?" she retorted. "God, it's cold up here." Her bloodstream seemed to be shutting down communications to her extremities and she felt attending to them was more important than battling Tracy.

"Did you bring a scarf?"

"I think so."

"Put it on. If your neck's warm it'll make your fingers warmer, too."

"You mean I have to take the pack off and look through everything?" she said with exasperation.

"I'll get it for you. Turn around. Which pocket is it in?"

"The one on the lower left. Or maybe the upper right. I don't remember."

Tracy unzipped and zipped until he had located the woolen scarf.

"Thanks," she said gratefully. She wrapped it around her neck and tucked the ends into her parka, then realized the rest of the group had already started down the other side of Algonquin toward their next objective, Boundary Peak. She could barely make out three or four colorful nylon packs humping down the slope. "Come on, they're leaving without us." She hurried off to join them when she heard a cry behind her. She turned to see Tracy sprawled on the rocks by the summit cairn.

"Shit, it's my ankle," he grimaced, clutching his lower leg as he struggled to a sitting position, fighting the heavy pack that had him pinned to the ground. *Don't fall for another Barcomb prank*, she cautioned herself.

"Give me a break," she snapped, turned away and scanned the slope for the others. She could now spot only one disembodied pack bobbing away from her like a cork in the mist.

"Hey!" she yelled. No response. "Help!" she yelled louder. The pack turned. It was Malcolm. Seeing Libby wave, he hesitated, looked back down the slope toward the others, and then began walking back up to the summit.

"I'm not kidding," Tracy moaned. "Gimme a hand, will ya?" Libby took one last glance in the direction the others had gone and reluctantly staggered back against the wind to him.

"If this is some kind of joke, it's a lousy time . . ."

"Help me off with this damn pack!" She knelt beside him, wrestling with the stubborn belt buckle. Once free, he rolled out of his shoulder straps and began unlacing his boot.

"What's up with you two?" Malcolm shouted as he regained the summit. "We gotta get the hell outta here." There was little doubt the wind was gathering steam.

"Christ, I caught my crampon between a couple of rocks. I sprained my ankle or something. Shit, that hurts," Tracy whimpered, realizing the implications.

Libby couldn't think straight. She was in a place as alien as the moon. Trying to make sense of how to help immobilized her. She just stared down at Tracy as he rubbed his ankle.

"I don't think you should take your boot off here," Malcolm cautioned.

"Oh yeah? What the hell do you know?" Tracy whined.

"Enough to know that thing will swell like a balloon if you don't keep pressure on it," Malcolm advised. Libby looked from one to the other, helpless.

"If it's not broken, you better try to walk on it," Libby urged. She wanted to get off the summit as quickly as possible.

"She's right," Malcolm agreed. "Put your weight on your ski poles."

"I'll give it a try." He hopped to his feet, testing the leg gingerly as Malcolm helped him on with the pack. "Maybe I can walk it off," he said hopefully. Once on his feet, though it hurt to put pressure on the foot, the ski poles acted as crutches and allowed him to move. Libby could sense he was struggling to decide which way they should go to catch up to the group. Libby had no idea; the whiteout was disorienting. There was no one to follow, no discernible footprints in the ice.

Libby felt herself losing control. "I don't know where they went. It all looks the same," she cried.

"Okay, lemme think," Tracy shouted. "We've got two options: try to retrace our steps down to tree line where the soft snow is. We'll find our footprints there. Or . . . somehow we find the route toward Boundary, where the others must be waiting.

The first alternative was a huge risk. Hamish had often spoken of the dangers of descending Algonquin under conditions such as these, how the topography of the summit cone seems to pull climbers into precipitous gullies between Algonquin and Wright. *The mountain will try to suck you to the right, if you let it,* Hamish had warned one night as Tracy and other aspiring Glencoe mountaineers sat around their headmaster's fireplace, listening to riveting tales from the headmaster's days in other mountains from other times. *If that happens, you may never be seen again.*

"You don't know which way they went, do you?" Libby cried. Tracy shook his head sadly. All directions looked the same to the three. Though a compass hung from Tracy's neck, since he carried no map, it was challenging to know the correct direction toward that next bump on the ridge where the others were headed.

"I've looked at the damn map a million times," Tracy moaned. "I should have it memorized!" Was Boundary due west? Southwest? South? Under pressure, it was a huge risk to make the wrong guess.

"We gotta get out of here!" Malcolm shouted, tugging his parka. "I'm freezing to death!"

"Actually, we shouldn't," Tracy shouted. It was a rule that had been drummed into him from his first trip into the mountains. If you are lost, stay put. But it was blowing near hurricane strength; the risk of hypothermia rising with every passing minute. Malcolm was right, Libby thought. They could freeze to death if they didn't get out of that relentless wind.

Libby had a macabre vision. If Tracy could somehow choose the right route, he would prove to everyone that he was every bit as adept a mountaineer as Jake. In her mind's eye she saw him coolly leading his helpless schoolmates safely out of the woods, into the waiting arms of the entire school. Hobbling in front of the cameras, he would casually recount their harrowing journey. Maybe he was actually enjoying this predicament.

A heavy gust slammed into them, knocking them to their knees and suddenly they all felt there was no choice. They must descend, as quickly as possible, no matter what the direction.

"The wind usually comes from the west!" Tracy shouted, bracing his body against the buffeting. "If we keep it to our right, we'll be heading south, which is where Boundary should be . . ."

"That way?" she pointed, at random.

"Let's go," Tracy yelled.

Sacrificing their right cheeks to the gusting knife-blades, they stumbled uncertainly off the summit. Usually, the wind was westerly. But the warm front that had passed just to the south of the High Peak region was followed by a blast of cold Canadian air that dove into the Adirondacks from the north. By keeping the wind to their right, Tracy was ensuring that they would never find Pete, for their course would take them due west, into a rugged trailless region. With each step, they moved farther from help.

Several hundred yards below, Pete and Christine gathered everyone in the lee of the summit cone for a clothing break. Something was wrong. A quick head count confirmed three were missing. Pete looked back up the slope, straining to pierce the cloud. He realized Christine should not be here if there were other students ahead of her in the line. In his haste to get everyone down off the top, he had neglected to remind Christine to bring up the rear. But he should not have had to do that. It was a basic rule of travel in the mountains—an adult should be at or near the front and definitely at the rear. In her haste to find shelter from the wind and blinding snow, Christine had simply headed down right behind Pete and had no idea one of their group had twisted an ankle with two others stopping to help him.

"Don't move! I'll be back in a minute," Pete shouted to Christine, who did not have to be told what had happened. As he hurried back up the mountain, he felt the first ripples of panic.

Scarcely a few minutes after the three hikers had stumbled off the summit, Pete negotiated the last few yards to the top of Algonquin. His hopes were dashed as he found the familiar plateau empty. He had counted on Tracy, not only to stay put, as he had been taught, but to save

Pete from the consequences of his own poor judgment. Again and again, he shouted their names, but as soon as the sound left his lips it disintegrated in the wind.

As Pete screamed on the summit of Algonquin, a mere hundred yards below, oblivious to the calls, Tracy delicately picked his way down, sharp pains shooting up his injured leg. Libby followed close behind, cupping the right side of her face with her mittened hand to ward off the wind that punished every inch of exposed flesh. Malcolm picked up the rear, nearly blinded by the driving, frozen mist. Scarcely twenty minutes elapsed before they reached the tree line. Tracy paused to adjust the drawstring on his hood. The snow was deep and soft here, layer upon layer blanketing a nearly impenetrable mesh of chest-high conifers in thick vanilla frosting. Tracy began to search for footprints, limping across the slope from left to right, descending, then traversing back again. Libby watched his dogged exploration, then looked back up the slope. Already, windblown snow had dusted away their tracks. No one would be able to see where they had gone.

Pete saw immediately that he was wasting valuable time standing at the top of Algonquin in a blizzard. Despite his familiarity with the terrain, he still found it difficult retracing his line of descent to rejoin the group, stopping often to consult the compass that hung from his neck. Finally, he emerged from the mist, alone. Christine's heart sank. His face told her everything she needed to know.

"They're gone! God knows where!" Pete shouted.

"We've got two hours before dark," Christine shouted back, searching for her watch beneath the layers of clothing.

"We have to trust that Tracy's experience will get them through the night. They've got good clothing and sleeping bags." But no tent and little food, he remembered. The five other children in the party looked anxiously at their two leaders. "We're doing no one any good standing here. We've got to get moving before we all freeze," Pete ordered. The beleaguered crew was beginning to feel the chill as their sweat stole precious heat from their cores. Either they had to establish a camp immediately, bundle up and begin the arduous task of cooking dinner under difficult, exposed conditions, or abandon their plans and beat a swift retreat back to the parking lot. The flat light of dusk was already making it difficult to read the terrain. Although in shock over the sudden turn of events, Pete knew he needed to think clearly to get the rest of them home safely, as quickly as possible.

"If we stay the night here," Pete barked, "it'll be that many more hours before we can get the word out and begin an organized search. We've really got no choice. Saddle up everyone, we're going home!"

Keeping close together now, Pete at the front and Christine at the rear, the shell-shocked band battled their way once again over the summit of Algonquin, pausing briefly at the top to make one, last, desperate search. Pete held his compass firmly in his mitten as they descended the northwest slope. He checked it frequently, praying that Tracy, Malcolm and Libby were just ahead.

Darkness settled over the mountains and the wind subsided as the group reached the frozen waterfall for the second time that day. In silence they hauled out headlamps and water bottles. Christine distributed the remaining granola bars, cheddar cheese and Triscuits. Until then, none of the children had dared to speak of the incident. Philip Carter, the only twelve-year-old on the trip, sidled up to Jake. "Think he planned it?" he asked, a sly grin barely visible in the gloaming.

"What are you talking about?" Jake demanded.

"Tracy finally gets to spend a night with Libby."

"What kind of an idiotic remark is that?" Jake sputtered, slamming a forearm into the surprised boy's chest. Pete jumped between them before Jake had time to tackle Philip again. "Hey! Knock it off!" he bellowed. "We got enough problems as it is without garbage from either of you, okay?"

30

Survival Instincts

TRACY PLUNGED RANDOMLY IN THE DEEP SNOW FOR FIFTEEN MINUTES, searching for tracks. His ankle held up, but when he sank into the snow, snagged for the umpteenth time in a hidden spruce trap, it was apparent he had no idea where they were. He sprawled out, frustrated and dispirited.

"Tracy, for God's sake, you don't have a clue, do you?" Libby accused. Malcolm's face showed fear but he said nothing.

Tracy looked from one to the other of his classmates. Their faces were easy to read. They counted on him to hold the answer. Libby's eyes were brimming with tears. Tracy felt at once embarrassed, sad, disconsolate.

"I'm really sorry, Libby. I don't understand. We kept the wind to our right, yet we don't seem to be anywhere near Boundary. Maybe we're headed toward Wright. I just don't know. It's so easy to get turned around up here." He lay back in snow up to his chest and closed his eyes. He seemed ready to give up.

"Come on, Tracy! Pull yourself together," Malcolm yelled. "You can't quit here! We'll die! We've got to get out of this wind. Come on! Get up!"

Tracy opened his eyes. "I'm just real tired right now," and he closed them a second time. Libby side-slipped down to where he was imprisoned, knelt down, and shook him violently. Then she stood up, unbuckled her waist strap and removed her pack. The wind stung her back, damp from exertion.

"Tracy! Please! We gotta move! Malcolm, help me," she implored.

Tracy stirred, opened his eyes and looked up at his worried companions. He saw fright, but no look of helplessness or resignation in their faces.

"Okay, okay." He scooped snow away from his chest until he could find the waist strap from his pack. He unbuckled it, slid his arms free and wriggled his way to the surface, gripping a spruce tree to avoid slipping into the hole again. "Pete must be tearing his hair out. I can't imagine what he and Christine were thinking when they started down without us."

"Maybe they were thinking of each other," Libby snapped. "I've got to eat something. I've been running on adrenaline and I just crashed. Do either of you have any gorp or something?" she pleaded. Malcolm searched his pockets for remnants of the nuts and raisins he had stored so casually that afternoon.

"Hang on, I think I've got something," Tracy offered. He dug into his pack for cheese and crackers that had been earmarked for lunch the next day. "Damn, I wish I had taken more food instead of these stupid pots and pans." He recalled the competition with Jake as they tried to outdo each other by loading their packs with heavy, bulky communal gear that no one else would ever volunteer to take. That machismo had now come back to haunt him. "Aha!" Triumphantly, he held up a box of Triscuits and passed it to Libby.

"Who ended up with the tent?" Libby asked.

"Jake," Tracy said sadly, thinking how much more comfortable the upcoming night could have been.

"Something to drink. We gotta keep drinking," Malcolm said.

"How come you suddenly know so much about survival?" Tracy challenged.

"Would you chill out?" Libby said testily. "Sounds like he knows what he's talking about. And at least he didn't get us lost."

That seared him to the bone. "Sorry," Tracy apologized. He presented a water bottle, semi-frozen, and generously offered it around. "Either of you got any?"

Libby had drunk half of one liter bottle, and Malcolm produced two nearly full ones. Unfortunately, they had been housed in external pockets and were nearly solid ice. Libby sipped from Tracy's bottle tentatively, savoring each drop.

"Wish I was sitting in Phelps House in front of the fireplace," Libby said wistfully. "Did you ever get invited by Jane and Payton for a cup of cocoa after all you guys had gone to bed?" she asked Tracy. "I don't think I was supposed to let anybody know about that," she muttered.

"No," Tracy said. "Bet you never got special treatment from Christine and Pete, huh, Mal?"

Malcolm shook his head. "Guess we're not cute enough, Tracy."

"Sorry. I'm just kinda feeling sorry for myself right now," Libby said. "Tracy, I want to sleep between my own sheets again. Get us home!"

"I'm trying. I guess the best thing to do is head straight down," Tracy suggested after they had packed the food and water away. Having eaten, he felt somewhat rejuvenated. "It's close to four," he said, consulting his watch. "We need to find a sheltered place while there's still some daylight. Let's put on the snowshoes here. I'm afraid we may not find a packed trail for a while." His mind was beginning to function again and the excitement of adventure almost crowded out his fear. He buckled his insulated black rubber boots, known as Mickey Mouse boots for their visual similarity to those worn by the cartoon character, into his snowshoes. He lashed neoprene straps behind each heel and over each instep. They might be lost, but at least their feet would not give them trouble. Pete had told them Mouse boots first became popular among American soldiers during the Korean War in the early 1950s. After the war, thousands of pairs made their way to army surplus stores in the States. Most collected dust on backroom shelves as winter camping was an avocation of the very few. With customary foresight, Hamish had stockpiled the school's hike house with Mouse boots of every size so that no student at Glencoe ever had to worry about cold feet as an excuse for begging off winter trips.

Tracy watched with envy as Malcolm effortlessly slipped out of his state-of-the-art crampons and stepped into brand new, lightweight, MSR snowshoes. Libby also had been given basic snowshoes, constructed from kits by students in an afternoon activity some years prior. Again, she was frustrated with the straps. Unable to fit the ends through the buckles, she discarded her mittens and almost immediately her fingers became useless in the cold. Tracy moved over to help, but Malcolm was there first.

"You don't have any thin gloves under those mittens?" Malcolm asked, pulling off one of his own to display a silk liner. "Or waterproof overmitts? Guess I gotta thank Aunt Mathilda whenever we get outta here. She did me a solid sending me the best of everything. Better put these back on, Libby," he said, handing her the mittens. "I'll do the straps."

"I'm not up on the latest mountaineering fashion," she said, slipping her hands into the still-warm mittens. "Seems like you're my strap guy today," she said, managing a weak smile. She hugged her hands to her armpits to will warmth back into her fingers as Malcolm bent to the task. Tracy muttered to himself and turned back to fastening his own shoes.

Properly shod, with headlamps affixed, the exhausted companions resumed their descent of the western flanks of Algonquin in silence, all attention devoted to the constant search for space in the dense forest. They used their ski poles to probe the snow before them for unseen spruce traps as the frigid winter night crept up from the valley below to meet them.

By six p.m. they had reached open woods and travel became somewhat easier, though their vision was limited by the strength of their headlamps. Traveling now between well-spaced birch and maple, they no longer felt trapped by the infernal spruce whose tentacle branches scratched and tore at their faces, depositing clumps of snow down their necks as they struggled past.

As darkness swallowed them, they lost all perception of distance, for their lights illuminated only the next tree, the next boulder. There was no way to judge how far they'd come, nor how far they had yet to travel. They walked without speaking, each lost in private thought, having plodded almost constantly since nine-thirty that morning with very little nourishment or rest. Just to be moving seemed a positive decision. They stayed warm while they moved, but with each pause to catch their breath or consider which direction to follow, an insidious chill crept into their exhausted bodies. Each time they resumed their task it took longer to rewarm. A lack of calories and hydration was starting to take its toll on their ability to move safely or think clearly. Conversation was sporadic as they retreated inward, struggling to keep panic at bay.

At eight-thirty they reached the valley floor, stumbling unknowingly across the Indian Pass trail, a route that would have led them back to the parking lot at Heart Lake, where they had started that morning. Unfortunately, exhausted and guided only by meager light, they crossed the thin path in the snow without noticing it. Just beyond the path they encountered an open area punctuated by large boulders. The faint sound of gurgling could be heard from beneath their feet. Despite his fatigue, Tracy recognized that if any of them broke through the surface of ice, frostbite would be nearly instantaneous. Using great caution and urging Libby to place her feet only where he placed his, Tracy delicately traversed the brook, feeling ahead gingerly with his ski poles to test the strength of the ice. On the far side, the terrain sloped upwards and they followed it several hundred yards before Libby stopped to rub her aching legs. After so many hours of descent, the "ascent muscles" in her thighs were unhappy to be called back to action.

"My legs are cramping, Tracy. I don't think I can climb much farther." She pushed up the sleeve of her parka, exposing her wrist, and focused the headlamp on her watch. "It's nine o'clock. I've got to stop."

"Just a few minutes more," Tracy urged.

"If she's done, she's done," Malcolm retorted.

"Ten minutes. I can do about ten more," Libby said. "But that's it. I don't think I've ever gone this long without having to pee."

"That's not surprising. You're dehydrated. Your body's got nothing to get rid of," Malcolm said. Tracy looked at him, saying nothing, but again surprised that Malcolm had any idea about such things.

"I've been eating snow all the way down, but it doesn't seem to help."

"Forget it. You're just wasting valuable calories melting the snow which could be used to keep yourself warm."

"What are you, a walking encyclopedia?" Tracy asked.

"If you're so smart," Malcolm shot back, "why are we climbing again? We can't possibly be on Algonquin anymore."

Tracy thought for a moment. "Probably not. Maybe when we get to the top of this little ridge, we'll see Heart Lake and the lights of Adirondak Loj."

"Fat chance," Malcolm said disdainfully. "You have no idea, do you? We're too low down to see anything but more trees, especially in the dark."

"I'm done," Libby sighed. "And I really need a drink. My throat is parched."

Tracy felt the same. Hours of gasping for frigid air had rasped their throats like sandpaper.

"This better be the last little bump," Malcolm said.

Ten minutes stretched to thirty, thirty to forty-five. Tracy stifled the urge to call a halt, desperately hoping they were just a hump away from the parking lot and a telephone. Yet they kept going relentlessly upwards. It was close to ten when they staggered to a halt beside an enormous boulder. Even he had lost the will to continue. Adjacent to the boulder stood a small grove of balsam fir, a sheltered flat spot where they could rest. No words had to be spoken; they all knew this was it for the night.

Discarding her pack, Libby wearily leaned it against the rock and watched Tracy immediately begin to prepare the space. Ignoring the dull ache in his ankle, he withdrew a Swiss army knife from the innards of his pack and began hacking branches off a nearby balsam tree. Malcolm pulled from his own pack a folding survival tool that offered a combination shovel and saw, another gift from his obsessive aunt. Tracy interrupted his hacking to marvel at the instrument, wondering what other goodies still remained in that mystery pack Malcolm toted.

The boys collected an armload of narrow-stemmed boughs, each thick with the distinctive flat needles that make balsam comfortable to lie upon. Libby stood by, windmilling her arms to keep warm, watching the boys work together to make their overnight stay as comfortable as possible.

With their backpacks propped against the boulder behind them as rude bolster pillows, the three lost travelers tamped down an area in the snow with their snowshoes, then scattered the balsam boughs Tracy and Malcolm had collected. They spread their wind parkas over the boughs as protection from the snow and any sharp needles. Tracy stared as Malcolm unfurled his self-inflating mattress pad. Next to his and Libby's thin, foam pads, Malcolm's looked like the fluffiest accommodation in the world. "My stupid aunt," Malcolm said sheepishly. "Only the best for her little baby."

The front had blown through, leaving the Adirondacks in clear, arctic air. Through the leafless canopy above their heads, billions of stars winked down at the exhausted hikers. Libby unlaced her Mouse boots, pulled off the top layer of sock from each foot, stuffed them into her boots and crawled, shivering, into her sleek nylon sleeping bag.

"How's your ankle do . . . doing?" she shivered.

"Not too bad," Tracy lied, fingering the puffiness. "It may stiffen up overnight but I should be okay to get us out of here tomorrow."

Malcolm gave a harrumph from within his sleeping bag.

"What's that supposed to mean, wise ass?" Tracy said, offended.

"Tracy!" Libby interjected. "If you two start in on each other, I'm going to scream. I'm hungry, I'm thirsty, I'm scared to death and now I've got you two idiots to deal with."

Tracy accepted the criticism and chose to move on. "Can I give you some friendly advice without getting my head bit off?"

"What about?" she asked guardedly.

"Your boots. If you leave them out like that, you'll never get your socks out in the morning. They'll freeze like rocks in there. Trust me, I've done this a few times and I'm just trying to help."

"He's right," came a voice from within Malcolm's bag. He had burrowed fully within it to warm himself.

"Okay, okay. You want me to sleep with my boots on?"

"No. But I would throw those socks inside the bag with you where your body heat will keep them dry. I sometimes sleep with the boots inside, too, but if that's too hard-core for you, at least put them under your head. It's not the most comfortable pillow in the world, but it beats stuffing your feet into frozen boots in the morning."

"You sure we're going to make it 'til morning?"

"No question. But I still can't understand where we went wrong."

"We shouldn't have moved off the top," Malcolm reproved. "Pete would have found us there."

"How do you know so much?"

"Am I wrong?"

"No . . . but, if you remember, it was pretty ugly up there and you were both yelling at me to make a decision and get the hell off the summit."

"Seems like eons ago," Libby sighed. "Do you have any idea where we are?"

"You know the answer to that," Malcolm said.

"Shut up, Malcolm," Tracy retorted. "Look, as long as my ankle holds up, we'll get out."

"With nothing to eat? How long can you keep going with no food?" Libby asked.

"Days, no problem. There've been miners stuck for weeks underground with no food or water, drinking their own piss to stay alive, but they made it," Tracy said.

"I'll die before I do that," Libby muttered. She lay back and stared at the twinkling sky. "Don't you think they're looking for us?" she asked.

"You can be damn sure Hamish is flipping out," Tracy said. "But my goal is to walk out of here without an escort. I don't want to be found. I want to get out on our own."

"I can't believe it," Libby said with exasperation. "You care more about your stupid ego than you do about our safety."

"I know what he means," Malcolm said softly from within his nylon chrysalis. "It's embarrassing getting lost like this. I want to get out on our own, too."

"Well, get over yourselves, guys. This is serious and whatever mistakes we made earlier, let's not make more now. Should we just stay here?" Libby asked.

"Where's *here*?" Malcolm asked. "I'm not sure we can hold out with no food and not much water until they figure out which direction our guide has led us."

"Drop the sarcasm for crissakes," Tracy snapped. "I'm doing the best I can, and we're all in this together, like it or not."

"Just get me home, Tracy, whether it takes a rescue party or not," Libby pleaded. "You know, if you quit trying to impress everyone all the time, you'd be better off. I'll never understand how guys think. You're a completely different species as far as I'm concerned."

The boys did not respond. Tracy recognized what she was saying was true. What was most important to him was approval. He thought about those weekend horseback rides with his dad on their Vermont farm. No matter how precise his canter or how he held his horse through a vault, the most he would receive was a nod of approval. Once he had purposely fallen, allowing himself to be dragged with one foot in the stirrup, just to gauge his dad's reaction. It was a ridiculously stupid thing to do and he was fortunate not to have hit a rock or been kicked by his surprised mare who came to a quick stop. Wendell rode up, noted that Tracy wasn't bleeding, and suggested his son would enjoy his ride more thoroughly from the back of his horse rather than under her belly.

"You respect Jake's opinion, don't you?" Tracy said, revealing her comments hurt. "He thinks I'm not such a bad guy."

"Maybe I'd think of you differently if you treated me like you treat Jake—like a human being, not a sex object."

"I guess I never figured out how to pierce that tough exterior you wear," Tracy sighed. "I've embarrassed myself trying."

"Should I take that as a compliment?" she asked, softening.

"Coming down Algonquin was about the worst bushwhack I've ever done and you stayed right with me without complaining. That was a shock. When I say you're tough, I mean not just physically. It's like you've got this brick wall around you. You're tough all the time, whether you need to be or not."

"Ouch, Tracy. I think you just found my hot button."

"What button is that?"

"My parents would smile if they had heard your take. For most of my life they've moved me around, prevented me from getting close to people . . . why am I sharing this?" she said, mostly to herself.

"Seems like they've succeeded," Tracy said.

"I hate them for it. And if we ever get out of here alive, there's no way my folks will let me stay at a school that got me lost. They'll sue the pants off Glencoe."

"I think I'm going to miss Glencoe," Malcolm said from the innards of his warm sleeping bag. "If they shut it down because of us."

Tracy thought with horror what a loss it would be to him if his missteps resulted in the closure of Glencoe.

"You think I'm tough?" Libby asked. "I don't think of myself as tough. Maybe you bring it out in me."

"See, I'm not the only one who sees himself differently than the rest of the world does," Tracy retorted. "You're cold, Libby, and you can dish it out pretty good."

"I'm not trying to be. Cold. Aloof, maybe," she said, staring up through the trees. Billions of pinpricks of starlight stared back. "But I hear you, Tracy. I'm just protecting myself."

"That may be the first time that you heard me."

"You said something worth listening to."

"Sure is nice to have somebody else getting dumped on," Malcolm said.

"I'll get to you later," Libby said, giving him a poke through the sleeping bags. "I can't believe I'm stuck here for the night with the two of you," she said. "I'm not quite finished with you, Tracy. If you quit acting out all the time and just were yourself, maybe I'd want to listen to what you have to say more often," she said.

"It's a tough habit to break."

"Amen," came a muffled comment from Malcolm's bag.

"Stuff it, Malcolm," Tracy snapped. "Wait 'til I get to you."

"I'd say you already have. Big-time," Malcolm said. A chill ran down Tracy's spine at that comment. He chose not to pursue it.

As Tracy stared up at the swaying canopy of branches, silver skeletons in the pale moonlight it occurred to him that, in all the rugged trips he had taken at Glencoe, he could not recall letting himself appreciate the wondrous beauty of the woods on a winter evening. If only this overnight was part of the plan.

"How long before they call our parents?" Libby asked.

"That depends on whether Pete and Christine bailed on the trip and went home," Malcolm opined.

"Definitely," Tracy said. "They ought to be home by now. Hamish must be going crazy."

"I wish I could be a fly on the wall listening to the phone call to my folks," Libby said. "Maybe this might actually get them to visit me."

"Assuming they've got us alive to visit," Malcolm said. "I don't want this turning into a body recovery thing."

"Don't say that," Libby said. "I'll never get to sleep if I'm scared shitless. Do these bags ever get you warm? Aren't you guys frigid?" she asked.

Malcolm chortled from the depths of his bag.

"Jesus Christ, you can't say anything without a boy thinking about sex," she snapped. Libby wrapped her sleeping bag more tightly around her.

"Be patient, you'll warm up," Tracy assured.

For ten or fifteen minutes they lay quietly, lost in private thoughts, dimly aware of how the bonds of shared misery were bringing them closer. The breeze picked up in the tops of the trees and the winter chill deepened. Moon shadows mottled the forest around them.

Libby sat up and looked first at Malcolm's idle form. She could hear his breathing, slow and even. She was bone tired from the climb, the shock of being lost, and the lack of food and water. She was almost too tired to feel scared. She turned to look at Tracy. Through dumb misfortune he had nearly broken an ankle and through simple circumstance she had been there with him instead of trundling down the backside of Algonquin with Pete and the others. But they weren't dead yet.

"How do you do it?" she asked.

"Huh?" he asked, half asleep.

"How come you aren't totally panicked?"

"Well, I admit it's not what I signed up for," he answered, grateful that he and Libby could, maybe for once, have an open conversation. She was right. He did hide behind his incessant teasing. Maybe he needed to trust who he was and drop the artifice. "But I've been in worse weather lots of times," Tracy said. "Last year Hamish took us up on the Dix Range and had us camp on the ridge to get a feel for real alpine conditions. It was wild, the wind whipping the tent all night long. I kept thinking what I would do if the nylon ripped and we had to dig a snow cave to survive. I slept with my boots on that night. This ain't so bad. Listen, if you want to get warm, roll over here next to me."

"Which am I, naive or stupid?"

"Suit yourself," he sighed, turning his back toward her.

"What else am I supposed to think?"

"That I deserve a little credit for knowing what I'm doing. If we can conserve body heat, we may survive just a little longer. Could make the difference between being found alive or as a couple of ice cubes."

"You're serious?" she asked,

"The best way to keep warm is to zip the sleeping bags together, but I don't think that's gonna happen."

She rolled over a few inches, cutting the distance between them in half. He rolled over in her direction and they were now face to face.

"Trust me, Libby. I've already done enough stupid things for one day."

"All right. Let's hope this is the last time we have to do this." She smiled, though he could not see it. "You have no idea where we are, do you?" she asked. "Are you scared they'll never find us?"

"Oh, they'll find us. When, is the question. I'm trying to think about how to get us the hell out of here before it becomes a retrieval, not a rescue," he added. It had been hours since he had been the old Tracy. That boy seemed to have disappeared atop Algonquin. Since then, he had been all business. He hoped Libby was grateful he hadn't crumbled.

"My gut tells me to be petrified," Libby said. "But I still feel hopeful. If you're calm, I'll try to be, too." She rolled the remaining inches toward his sleeping bag. "I haven't been much help to you," Libby apologized.

It was impossible to see her eyes in the dark. Tracy thought somehow that made it easier for her to speak. "I mean, maybe if I wasn't so inexperienced, I wouldn't have screamed at you to get us off the summit."

"Yeah, we wouldn't be in this fix right now if we'd stayed put."

"My face was freezing off and it was scary up there. What else could we have done?" she asked plaintively.

"It doesn't matter now, Libby," he comforted. "At the moment it seemed like the only option."

"How can you be so calm? You're either a great actor or the dumbest guy in the world. None of this seems to bother you," Libby said.

"Maybe I'm both. You may think I'm a schmuck some of the time, but I really believe we can handle this. When you get right down to it, all it takes is one foot in front of the other until we hit a trail or find someone. This ain't Alaska, and this ain't the Shackleton expedition. Reading that stuff in Pete's class actually makes me feel much better about our situation. We won't die as long as we stay warm and keep drinking. And, to quote some country song I heard somewhere, we're not a thousand miles from nowhere." Though he was parroting what he had been taught about survival, their predicament was not all that simple. They had a stove but somebody else was carrying the fuel. With no way to melt snow, drinking was going to be a serious problem. And if they couldn't drink, staying warm would soon become challenging as well.

Calmly he explained what he hoped to do the next morning to help them find a trail. The longer he talked, the more relaxed she became and never interrupted to criticize or complain. At the same time, Tracy found, as he sought to comfort Libby, that he was curiously happy. He was in his element, having spent enough hours on enough trips in the winter to feel confident about his experience, his ability to think rationally, and to assure others that he was someone to trust and follow. The lessons his dad had instilled about how to function comfortably under trying conditions, which were then enhanced by his experience climbing in all kinds of weather with Pete and Hamish during his time at Glencoe, stood him in great stead to think clearly and to step outside of whatever self-doubts he had to comfort his classmates.

The imprint of his mom on his spiritual connection with the backcountry was just as impactful, just as important to his feeling at home at this moment. The conservation philosophies of Aldo Leopold as well as the wilderness ethics from Guy and Laura Waterman that his mother had poured into him from as early an age as he could comprehend, contributed to his inner calm. Where he should rightly have been frightened, anxious, second-guessing his every decision, Tracy felt at ease and emboldened. And, he felt for the first time, that Libby and Malcolm respected him. Maybe even liked him a little.

Tracy could not have told you what irony meant, but what he was feeling at that moment was ironic. Here they were, somewhere deep in the Adirondack wilderness, with dwindling ability to keep themselves fed and warm, and yet Tracy could not have felt more at home. He had a fleeting thought that it would be a damn shame for this all to end and for all of them to just go back to whatever the old normal was.

"However," Tracy finished, "if we're not back at school by this time tomorrow night I may be crying on *your* shoulder." With that, Libby moved closer to him, bumped him affectionately and then, seemingly embarrassed by their sudden intimacy, twisted in her sleeping bag so that her back was toward him. He felt the weight of her against him. They were so close his breath warmed the back of her neck. He whispered, "Good night. Try not to worry."

"I'm counting on you."

"You can. Promise."

31

Dominoes Begin to Fall

LEAVING THE WATERFALL, PETE LED THE REMAINING MEMBERS OF THE shell-shocked group down the Algonquin trail to the Adirondak Loj, a rustic log hostel at the edge of Heart Lake. Herding the exhausted students into the warm, spacious living room, where a handful of guests eyed them curiously, Pete asked to use the Loj phone and dialed the school's number, followed by the MacLean extension.

"Bonnie, this is Pete."

"Pete? Where are you? Aren't you supposed to be . . . ?"

"Yes. I'm at the Loj . . . We have a problem . . . Is Hamish there?" Pete could hear muffled talking as Bonnie partially covered the receiver with her hand.

"Why the devil are you at the Loj?" Hamish barked.

All the way down the mountain, Pete had dreaded this moment. "Three of the kids got separated from us on top of Algonquin. I looked everywhere, Hamish, but they just disappeared. It was really ferocious up there. I couldn't find their tracks."

"Holy Christ . . ." There was a pause as Hamish relayed the news to Bonnie. "Where's everybody else?"

"Warming up here with Christine. They're pretty shaken. Can we get a pickup?"

"I'm on my way."

Twenty minutes later they were loading the van for the short ride back to school. Hamish asked no questions during the ride. It was clear he didn't want a discussion in front of the children. He knew, by surveying the group, who was missing. When he pulled the van up outside the Glencoe dining hall door, Hamish turned in his seat to face the quiet group. "You've been through a pretty tough day, haven't ye?" he said gently. Wearied nods acknowledged. "We've set up a couple of tables. Before I send you home to bed, I'd like to get some food in your bellies. I know your thoughts are with your schoolmates. We'll do whatever is necessary to have them back with us as soon as possible."

Subdued, they filed in to the darkened building, exhausted from the forced march, the unanticipated extra miles with full packs and the jolt of losing companions. Jake pulled Pete aside as they headed into the building. "Pete, if there's anything I can do to help, just ask. I'll go back out there right after dinner if you need me."

Pete's eyes welled up as he gripped the boy's shoulder. Jake was nearly as tall as Pete, and almost as strong. "Thanks for the offer, Jake, but right now you can help most by keeping everyone else settled down. Those three are in a tough spot tonight, but I'm confident Tracy's experience will keep them safe 'til we find them." Jake nodded agreement and headed in to eat.

The regular kitchen crew had long since departed for their homes in the surrounding communities, so Hamish ferried leftover lasagna and salad from the walk-in refrigerator. Pete put a double boiler on the stove to steam the lasagna while Christine started slicing the last freshly baked loaves of bread. In a state of shock, they murmured to each other while Hamish found some raw carrots and celery sticks and arrayed them on a couple of serving dishes while the students helped set two tables in the empty, partially lit, dining room. The mood was funereal.

Hamish approached Pete at the stove and placed a hand on the young man's shoulder. He felt Pete cringe beneath the light pressure.

"How did it happen?"

Without taking his eyes off the steaming pot Pete grimly summarized the day's adventures, sugarcoating none of his own shortcomings. Hamish asked a few questions but offered no criticism. Christine shuttled platters of hot lasagna while Pete and Hamish talked together in the kitchen. There was no banter at the tables. The food was devoured almost as fast as it could be delivered.

"Make sure they all get up to their houses without delay," Hamish advised to his dispirited teachers after the meal was concluded and the dishes deposited into the dishwasher for the morning crew. Pete nodded. Christine ushered the students to their lockers to get their hats and coats and headed out into the chilly night for the brief walk up the hill to their respective residences. Hamish turned off the lights in the dining hall and walked down to his office at the west end, his stomach churning. His desk lamp would burn long into the night.

After seeing the last of the students to their homes, Pete and Christine stood together under a tree. In the moon shadow Christine put her arms around him and squeezed. Pete choked back tears and laid his head upon Christine's shoulder. He was devastated, powerless to change the course of three lives whose future was now very much in question.

"Let's talk inside. I'm freezing," Christine said.

"At least we have an inside to go to," Pete mumbled, following her in to her apartment on the first floor. His place was directly above hers and they shared as many nights together as possible in one place or the other while discreetly keeping up the charade for the students in Marshall House that their relationship was platonic. "I can't believe what happened. I just want to go back and change what we did." He turned to Christine and cupped her face with his gloved hands in a warm caress. "Under no circumstance can you blame yourself, Christine," he said. "This is all on me."

"I lost my head up there," she whimpered. "I didn't want to lose sight of you, and I guess I panicked."

"I'm supposed to not let that happen. To the kids. To you. I know better," Pete sighed. "And now those kids are going to pay for my lapse in judgment. We've just got to find them . . . soon."

"How long do we have?"

"That depends on so many things," Pete said. "Are they hurt? Do they have enough food or water? I can't remember what each one was carrying. It's just a shit show. I can't fucking believe it. I'm so embarrassed and frustrated and angry," he sputtered. "I just want to get right out there, but that's not how rescues happen. I described the Balanced Rocks search and rescue to you, remember?" Christine nodded, rubbing his back tenderly.

"It's a very organized, disciplined process and the last thing they need is for someone like me to scramble out there and make myself part of the problem. I'd love to be a regular volunteer on the S&R crew," he said. "I told Hamish I'd like to be and he was going to introduce me to the right folks. Now that's probably never going to happen. Dammit, I'm going to show up tomorrow and offer to help in some way. I can't just sit here."

Christine kissed him and said, "Thank you for trying to make me feel better. As guilty as I feel, I know I can't do what you do and that makes me feel even more responsible. How can I show my face at school tomorrow? I should resign."

"That's not going to help matters," Pete said. "I know exactly how you feel. But the last thing Hamish needs right now is to have both of us walk out the door leaving him with big holes to fill. We just have to suck it up and do our jobs."

"I sure am glad I have you, sweetie."

"You're the reason I'm still here after five years. Don't even think of leaving," Pete said, moving in to envelop her in a bear hug.

32

The Crown Lies Heavy

NEARLY FORTY YEARS OF LIFE EXPERIENCE SEPARATED THE LOVESTRUCK couple from their boss and it showed in the respective complexity of their worries. Like checker players, Pete and Christine focused on how to salvage the pieces they had lost due to their momentary lapse in judgment atop a stormy peak. In contrast, with his chess clock ticking toward expiration, Hamish fretted about an endgame that could bring down his entire institution, not just spell disaster for three of his students. He had to finesse this endgame against an opponent he could not see, whose moves he could not predict.

It would be a long night, perhaps the first of many, for the man ultimately responsible for everything. Dreading the next few hours, Hamish fished in the back of his desk drawer for a vial of Percocet. He gulped down a couple of pills with a swig of scotch and dialed the number for Jeff Ecklestone. It was becoming an unpleasant habit, he thought, as he listened to three rings of the ranger's private line. Jeff's sleepy voice interrupted the answering machine that had already begun to play its message.

"Jeff, this is Hamish MacLean calling from Glencoe. I'm terribly sorry to disturb you; I seem to be a regular alarm clock for you these days. I need your help."

"Forget it. What's up, buddy?"

"Three of our youngsters are somewhere on the flanks of Algonquin tonight. Don't ask me how this could have happened. Can you give us a hand?"

"Did you already call DEC dispatch to report it?"

"A few minutes ago, yes. But I wanted to let you know directly. I need a lot of help on this, and fast."

"We won't have anyone ready to go in until first light, Hamish."

"I know, I know."

"If those kids have the proper gear, they should be able to hang on until we locate 'em."

"If they're not injured."

"I prefer to assume that," the ranger said. "You in the office?"

"Aye."

"I'll call you later."

Hamish paged through the student directory for the other numbers. He chose Tracy's household first. To his consternation, he got their answering machine. He left a short message summarizing what had happened and asked to be called back, no matter the time.

So loath was Hamish to speak to the Goldman family that he chose to re-fill his tumbler with another inch of scotch. His fumbling fingers caused two incorrect connections before a familiar voice answered. "Good evening. This is Adam. May I help you?"

"Good evening to you, sir. This is Hamish MacLean at Glencoe."

Hamish thought he heard an almost inaudible shift of gears through the wires.

"Ahh, yes. A bit late to be hearing from you, Hamish," Adam responded. "Do you normally make capital campaign solicitations at this time of night?"

"I'm not trying to raise money, Mr. Goldman." Hamish rarely let an opportunity pass to remind a potential heavy hitter that the school did not run on love alone, although this parent was probably one of the least likely to cough up extra dough. "I'm calling because there's been a problem with a mountain trip that went out today. Libby and two other students became separated from their group and have not yet been located. However, there is no reason . . ."

"Excuse me?" Adam interrupted. "Would you repeat that?"

"Let me finish, sir. Your daughter signed up for an overnight mountain trip that left this morn. They were not scheduled to return until late tomorrow. According to the trip leaders who aborted the trip and returned a couple of hours ago, the three apparently lost contact with the group on the summit of the first peak . . ."

"You sons of bitches," Adam rasped, almost in a whisper.

". . . conditions were rather severe, and it was impossible to see which way they went, I'm told," Hamish continued, ignoring the remark. "The trip leaders made an attempt to find them but it was too dangerous to keep the group up there on the summit. We are organizing a search and rescue party right now in conjunction with the park rangers . . ."

"Wait a minute . . . Shelley?" Adam called to his wife, not bothering to muffle the receiver with his hand. "I've got Hamish MacLean on the phone. He tells me they've lost Libby on some goddamned mountain."

"What!?" Shelley Goldman's startled voice intoned from across the room. "Hamish, how could you let this happen?" she said, obviously now on speakerphone.

"We'll be heading out to find them at first light," Hamish said with discomfort. "And I'm confident we'll have them back, safe and sound, within a few hours."

"You're waiting until tomorrow?" Shelley shrieked.

"The hell you are," bellowed Adam.

"Just a minute. We don't want them to spend a minute longer in the woods than necessary, I assure you," Hamish said. "But we'd only be putting others at risk if we started now. We need daylight to follow their route."

"You're telling me you've got three children roaming about in the snow by themselves in the middle of a December night . . . and this on the heels of that other accident you wrote us about? You people should be put out of business."

"I'd be happy to debate that with you at another time, Mr. Goldman. Your daughter is well-equipped to spend the night out. We'll find her as quickly as possible; I can assure you of that."

"You'd better." The phone clicked. Hamish shook his head sadly. He suspected he'd just heard the greatest display of concern they'd ever expressed toward their daughter. What a shame they couldn't show it in ways she could appreciate.

Despite all the perks and privileges that went with the job of head-master, despite the comfortable home and reasonable compensation, these were the times that made him wonder if it was all worth it. The weight of responsibility for the entire school community rested on his weary shoulders. Hamish wondered if the pain in his back would suddenly disappear were he to walk away. No one would blame him. He had left an indelible mark on the place despite the current stresses in admissions. If you took the long view, his tenure would be remembered as a time of growth and stability, a tenure during which Glencoe became known as a beacon of enlightened, progressive, education. Or so he hoped.

Next on the list: Mathilda Graham; yet again a call with rough news about her nephew.

Hamish dialed the Ohio number. After five rings, he was about to hang up when her voice came through. She sounded as if she'd just been running.

"Hell . . . Hello?"

"Hello . . . Mrs. Graham?"

"Yes. Excuse me while I catch my breath. I just got in. Who is this please?"

"Hamish MacLean, ma'am."

"Hamish, hello. How are you? Is everything alright?"

"We're workin' on it, Mrs. Graham."

"Mathilda," she cut in. "Didn't we establish that the last time?"

"Ahh, yes . . . Mathilda. I am sorry to report that we have a bit of a problem with Malcolm's whereabouts . . ."

"His what?"

"Where he is. He was part of a weekend mountain trip, Mathilda, and I'm afraid several of the children have gone missing. We are, of course, mounting an immediate effort to locate them and, I assure you, the children are capable of safely spending the night out until we reach them."

"Oh dear," she said quietly. "Oh dear. What can I do?"

"There is certainly nothing for you to do at this moment. We have contacted the rangers and are mobilizing a team to find them at daybreak."

"What is it with my Malcolm and mountains?" she asked softly.

"Mathilda, trust me there is no cause for panic. I believe everyone will be home safe and sound in short order." Confident though he was, Hamish was careful not to tie himself to any specific timetables for recovering the lost students. There were certainly many unknowns at this point.

"I fear it's too late to find a flight this evening, Hamish."

"Let's not be hasty. I suggest you give us a day or two before making travel arrangements. We may well have Malcolm on the phone to you before you can even get here."

She sighed. "Hamish, whatever you recommend. I'll say a prayer for the children and expect to hear from you tomorrow. Oh dear, that boy is a trial."

"Very well, Mathilda. Good night."

Another swig of scotch. There was one more call to be made. If he waited any longer, he knew it wouldn't be made. Perhaps he should talk to Bonnie first but better to act while he still had the resolve.

"Mr. Connaughton's office," intoned the woman's voice.

"Hamish MacLean, here, Victoria. Is Philip free?" It might be dawn in England but Hamish knew the chairman of the board would already be at his desk, his trusted administrative assistant there as well.

"Nice to hear from you, Hamish. Must be nearly midnight in Lake Placid," she said.

"Indeed. Glencoe never sleeps."

"Of course. I'll let Mr. Connaughton know you're ringing."

Philip Connaughton's upper-crust British accent identified him as one of the privileged set whose résumé included Eton as his finishing school and Oxford as his university. His father was a member of the House of Lords, and his physician mother the founder of the most renowned cancer clinic in London. Connaughton was a revered name in the United Kingdom, and their son, Philip, had leveraged the lineage adroitly. Still functioning as a managing partner of a boutique hedge fund, Philip had been the chairman of the Glencoe board of trustees for a decade.

"Good morning, Hamish. It is morning there now, isn't it?"

"Yes, Philip. I would rather be comfortably tucked in bed but events intervened and I felt the need to keep you informed."

"I'm listening."

"We've had an issue on one of our mountain trips this weekend, Philip. Three students have gone missing in a snowstorm. They are reasonably experienced and properly equipped, but obviously the next day or two will be critical to getting them home safely. I wanted to make sure you were fully apprised."

"Hmmm. You know I am a direct fellow, Hamish. My style is not to suffer fools gladly. Not to suggest you are a fool." Hamish squirmed in his chair. During the tough board meeting in the fall, where the pressure on him to increase enrollment had driven him back to pain meds, his chief adversary had been Connaughton. Although the other directors had challenged him, the chair's arguments felt more personal. He couldn't shake the sense that, at the heart of it, the relationship could never get beyond the fact that Connaughton was a blue-blooded Brit while Hamish was a Scotsman. It could be as deep-seated and simple as that. "I assume you've got the authorities organizing a search."

"Of course. At first light we will be combing the area."

"In brief, Hamish, how did it happen?" Hamish recounted the events as Pete had explained them, leaving out the fact that two of the three students were the same ones involved in the earlier accident on Balanced Rocks, an episode that had also brought ringing criticism upon his head by Connaughton.

"You've spoken to the parents?"

"Those of whom I could reach, yes."

"And sacked the teacher who led the trip?"

"I beg your pardon?" Hamish's heart sank. This was not an outcome he had anticipated.

"Hamish, we are vulnerable enough as an institution right now. Glencoe is a wonderful school, but the board needs to anticipate events beyond the horizon. There could be lawsuits emanating from this event that causes us financial ruin. Part of our protection strategy must be keeping everyone accountable. From what you describe, your teacher demonstrated malpractice. I'm not asking for your resignation . . . just yet . . . but he needs to go. Assure me that will be done."

Pete Hedges was jolted awake by the ring. Disoriented, his brain struggled to push the fitful sleep aside. It was just past five. He sat up, reached for the phone on his night stand, swung his legs out of bed and sat at the edge. Who and why someone would be calling before dawn? Then he remembered why he felt so foggy and what had transpired the day before. *They were found*, he concluded. *The nightmare is over.*

"Pete, it's Hamish. Sorry to wake you."

"Of course." Was this a call to announce what his brain had decided was spectacular news? Or to advise him of the plans for the search and rescue?

"I know this has been a rough time for you and Christine."

"Rough? Watching my dad sink into dementia was rough. This is devastating, even though it's not family. I feel so much responsibility just because it's *not* family. I don't know what to say, it happened so fast."

Hamish took a deep breath. He wanted to get this out before he had any more time to think about it. "I feel it too, Pete. I am ultimately called to account whether I caused the problem myself or not. And I have a solemn obligation to the Trustees as well as the parents. Bottom line, it should never have happened, Pete. We are responsible for the welfare of these kids. In loco parentis. There's nothing we do that's as important as keeping them safe. As much as I hate doing this, I have no choice but to let you go . . . "

"What?!" Pete said, stunned.

"I regret it's come to this, Pete," Hamish continued, staring at his desk. "But the fact is, I have no choice." *Sure you do*, he imagined Pete thinking, stunned at the harshness of this message. *You need a fall guy and I'm it!*

"God willing there will be no casualties but the school will be dealing with major public relations problems and possible lawsuits," Hamish paused to drain his glass, the scotch no longer a smooth comfort as it coursed down his throat. "My responsibility goes way beyond my loyalty and appreciation for the effort you devote to this job, Pete. I'll do whatever I can to help you find something else just as soon as this business blows over." It was torture, speaking of such things to someone he'd mentored almost as a son, but Hamish knew if he didn't say it out straight, with no emotion, he would lose his nerve. He silently cursed Connaughton.

Pete didn't respond. He slid off the bed and sat on the floor. He held the phone at arm's length as if it held poison. To Hamish, the silence was excruciating. *If I was in his shoes,* Hamish thought, *I would yell "How can you do this to me . . . over the phone?"*

"I wish there was some other way, Pete." Hamish said, breaking the stalemate. His stomach was in knots. This went against every fiber in his body. How could Connaughton make him destroy the career, the self-respect, of such a fine young man? What did that say about himself that he could not fight to keep his own faculty member? He spat out the next words robotically. "Please be out by breakfast and give me a call when you get settled."

"Can't we sleep on this for a night, Hamish?" Pete whispered. Hamish knew Pete was struggling to choke back tears.

Yes, that's what we should do, Hamish thought. *And then forget we ever had this conversation.* Pete was his protégé; this was not how you treat someone that precious. But he could not walk it back.

"Sadly, this is not up for debate, Pete. I will have Cathy put together termination papers. You can come in to get them within the fortnight. I'd rather you not be here when the children hear the news. Good night, Pete. I'm truly sorry. You've done wonderful things here." Hamish hung up, anguished that he had allowed a terrible injustice to occur.

For some time, Pete sat, numb, on the floor, his back to the bed. Finally, he struggled to his feet, tossed on some clothes, and went downstairs and out the front door. He knocked softly on Christine's door; her small quarters, consisting of a single bedroom, small sitting area and kitchenette, had its own entrance on the first floor. After hearing no response, Pete walked around the corner of the house to the window that faced her bedroom and rapped on the glass. After a moment she parted the curtain, her face filled with sleep and mystification. Pete motioned with his hand that he needed to speak to her and returned to the front. She opened it, dressed in sweatpants and a T-shirt. He embraced her, and all the emotions he had so carefully bottled up since that moment in the mist atop the summit of Algonquin bubbled up.

"Pete, what happened? Why are you here so early? You're crying!" she exclaimed, lovingly wiping her fingers across his cheeks.

"Hamish fired me. I'm supposed to be off the property before breakfast." She felt his weight slump against her.

"Come in. Sit down," she said, stunned.

Pete clung to her, sobbing uncontrollably. "I wanted to scream at him. How can he do this to me? After everything I've given to this place! And get this. He still expects me to do my job, rouse the kids for barn chores in ninety minutes, without letting them see how upset I am. Just go about my business, then get the hell out of here."

Christine gripped his arm as he stumbled to a chair.

"This is my fucking home, Chris. What happens to *us* now?"

She knelt beside his chair and hugged his legs as he cried, her head on his knees.

"Shouldn't it have been me? I'm the one who screwed up, not you." She was the one charged with keeping the students in sight, in front of her. But she had failed to pay attention on the chaotic stormy summit.

"What are you going to do?" she asked softly.

"What choice do I have? I can't very well punch him in the nose. I'll have to get out of here with my tail between my legs. It's humiliating."

"This doesn't seem at all like the Hamish I know," Christine said. "He's all about finding ways to keep people here, not get rid of them."

"It wasn't up for discussion. It was a quick call and I could tell he wanted to get done with it and off the phone. Look, he may have ordered me off the property but he can't stop me from helping find those kids. I'm not walking away from that, no matter what he says."

"It's all my fault. This whole thing should never have happened. I will give Hamish my resignation after breakfast," Christine said. "It's not right that you take the blame for me. You are a star here."

"I thought we covered that last night, Christine. Your leaving doesn't make things any better. If he wants you here, and you want to *be* here, then accept it. This is my battle. But I don't want to lose you, sweetie."

"You're not losing me. Call me when you know where you're staying and we will figure this out together. I'm so sorry, Pete. I love you."

"I love you, too. And thanks for letting me in," he smiled sheepishly.

She led him to the door, kissed him, and watched him disappear back upstairs to pack.

33

Day Two

AT FIRST LIGHT, TRACY SAT UP AND SURVEYED THEIR WORLD. NO MATter which way he looked, the forest was of a sameness that revealed no clue as to where they were or what direction would lead them home. There were no distant views by which he might orient himself and certainly no marked trails. Like snowflakes, every direction offered a similar, but not identical, landscape. *Shit, we could be anywhere*, he thought.

Tracy reached behind him for his pack and rummaged through it for the Triscuit box, then groped inside the bag for the water bottle he had kept close to his body. He nudged the sleeping form beside him.

"Libby. Breakfast is ready."

She opened her eyes, disoriented by seeing Tracy's face above her. Her practiced responses toward him returned. "Is this some terrible nightmare? What are *you* doing in my bedroom?"

"Hoping to get some liquid into you," Tracy retorted.

She rubbed her eyes and instinctively felt her hair for tangles. "Sorry, I was confused for a second. God, it's cold." She felt for remains of the crackers at the bottom of the box and extracted what she assumed was a fair share, washing them down with carefully rationed sips of water from the bottle Tracy offered. Mindful to keep the sleeping bag tightly wrapped under her chin, she twisted to look in Malcolm's direction. He was stirring.

"Hey," she said, nudging him with a foot, "don't oversleep."

"Did you have to do that? It was so nice and quiet around here," Tracy said.

"Don't you think he deserves some food, too?" Libby demanded.

"I dunno. He could still stand to lose a pound or two," Tracy muttered.

Malcolm sat up, blinking from the shock of the cold, still air. Without speaking, he accepted the Triscuits box and shook the remaining crumbs into his mouth. Then he reached into his pack of a thousand pockets and extracted a plastic bag with small packets of energy gel, yet another thoughtful gift from Aunt Mathilda. The gel was solid as a rock.

"Crap," he muttered, tossing a couple to Tracy.

Tracy grinned. "Could use these as door stops. Got any bagels in there?" He wriggled out of his bag, wrestled on his boots that were still warm from their residence within his sleeping bag and stood carefully on his snowshoes as a platform in the snow. Shivering violently, he packed away his clothes, stuffed his bag into its sack and started windmilling his arms to get some feeling back into his numb fingers. He knew the others would look to him for reassurance and that he should not look panicky, though that's exactly how he felt.

Resigned to the fact she could delay the inevitable no longer, Libby finally unfolded herself from the warm bag, fished out her socks and found them warm and dry. Mimicking Tracy, she sat upon her snowshoes so as not to sink into the snow as she laced up her boots. Then, she stood precariously and attempted to tighten the neoprene straps. Caked with ice, they refused to cooperate.

"Let me get that," Tracy volunteered. He bent toward her, broke off the offending balls of ice and cinched the straps tight. "What would you do without me?" he smiled.

"I wouldn't be here in the first place," she said.

Malcolm had also readied himself. "How's the ankle, Tracy?" he asked.

"Okay, I guess," Tracy answered, flexing it. "Can't afford to rest it now. You guys ready to split?"

"Gotta go to the bathroom first," Libby said.

"Why is it that girls always have to go to the bathroom whenever it's time to go someplace?" Tracy asked.

"I won't be long. About the last thing I *want* to do is drop my pants and freeze my ass off."

"Take as long as you want. Don't pee in your pants or flop backwards into the snow," Tracy joked. "We'll wait," he said, stomping his feet to get the blood circulating.

"Thanks for the helpful advice," she said, trudging off in the direction of an evergreen thicket that provided some privacy, still in the process of getting used to walking with flippers on her feet.

"Do you want to check out the compass?" Malcolm asked Tracy after Libby had gone.

"I'm afraid without a topo map to go with it and a view to help me orient myself, I can't make much use of it," he said ruefully. "But if I can just get a glimpse of some mountains, I should be able to at least figure out a general direction."

"So, what do we do now?"

Tracy was uncertain. He felt comfortable negotiating life in cold, snowy conditions but for how long? Without supplies they couldn't keep their strength up. They could stay put and conserve energy or make a stab at finding a trail. His restless constitution and mortification of being found like a lost dog refused to allow him to make the conservative choice. "Let's keep going up this slope. That's the only way I can get a view," Tracy said, with as much conviction as he could muster.

Libby rejoined them. "Feeling better?" Tracy asked.

"Don't you ever have to go?"

"Once a day, whether I need to or not."

"You're nuts, you know that?"

"I prefer to think of myself as . . . bubbly," he grinned.

"Remind me to thank Christine for persuading me to come on this trip," Libby said grimly. "Okay, get us home."

34

An Uneasy Alliance

AT DAWN ON SATURDAY, A HASTILY ERECTED COMMAND CENTER ADJA-
cent to the visitors' center at the Adirondak Loj became the jumping-off
point for the search and rescue effort. Pete Hedges watched volunteers
gather into small search parties under the coordination of park rangers.
He recognized a few organizers: Carl Goblish, who was handing out gear
from the back of his truck, and Ranger Jeff Ecklestone, clearly in charge.
Still reeling from being fired, Pete wrestled with shame and embarrassment. Part of him longed to put as much distance as possible between
himself and Glencoe, but this feeling was overwhelmed by his desire to
find the kids, preferably before anyone else could. One by one, parties
filtered out of the building to comb their designated tract of wilderness,
a painstaking, and tedious process requiring long hours and disciplined
execution. Pete stood on the porch of the visitor's center and watched
them, aching to participate but unable to step forward.

At eight a.m. Hamish drove into the parking area, accompanied
by a last-minute companion. He unloaded his pack and strode toward
the command center, trailed by Rambler. True to her uncanny ability to
sense crisis, the border collie had blocked the way as Hamish attempted
to back out of his parking space at school. Knowing Rambler was so
comfortable in the woods, even in winter, and feeling his own anxiety
about the impending search, Hamish relented and let his old friend into
the van. He called Bonnie to let her know he was taking their dog. Rambler would offer welcome companionship during what was likely to be a

difficult day or two. He didn't let himself even imagine what would happen if they failed to locate the students within the next forty-eight hours.

Passing Pete in the parking lot, Hamish nodded uncomfortably and walked over to talk to Ecklestone. Pete was stunned by the callous indifference showed by his friend and mentor. The ranger sat on a folding chair, his attention divided between topographic maps, a cellular phone and a shortwave radio.

"Morning, Jeff. Where's my team?"

"They're gone, Hamish. Where you been?"

"Fighting fires of my own back at the school," Hamish said ruefully. "It's amazing how fast bad news travels."

"I held the last group as long as I could but they took off twenty minutes ago. Want to catch up?"

"Too old for that. Got anyone else who needs a partner?"

"I do." Jeff and Hamish turned to see who had spoken.

"I don't think so, Pete," Hamish said uncomfortably.

"Why not?" Pete challenged. "I can't just sit here. I need to help." He turned to address the ranger. "I'll go out alone, Jeff, if my *former* boss finds it too uncomfortable being with me," he said bluntly.

"Let's not involve Jeff in our dirty laundry," Hamish muttered.

"The kids are more important than our *laundry*. The point is, Hamish, we both need a partner and we both need to be out there. But if it's too difficult for you . . ."

Hamish held up his hands in defeat. "Okay, okay, my needs are not what's important now. Where do you want us, Jeff?"

The ranger looked relieved. "I wish we had more volunteers show up today. Head up to Avalanche Lake. I think you have time to get to Lake Colden before it's time to come back out tonight."

"I'm not interested in coming back out if we don't find them today," Hamish responded.

"That's not how we do it, Hamish. You know that. I need to make sure all the rescuers are safe and sound and out of the woods come nightfall."

"Jesus, Jeff. I know the protocol, but every minute counts. We'll go rogue if that's what it takes. I brought what I need to stay out until we find them, goddammit."

"You're a pain in the ass, Hamish. You're my responsibility while you're on this mission."

"Aye. But these are my kids. I'm not sleeping at home tonight if they're still out there."

Jeff sighed. He couldn't force Hamish to adhere to his orders, so he might as well try to get the most he could out of him. "If that's the way it has to be, then camp near Lake Colden and come over the Indian Pass cutoff tomorrow. I don't really think they came down over there, but we gotta circle this damn mountain. Goblish will give you a radio. Stop at the Lake Colden DEC Interior Outpost Cabin and make sure you check in with me before evening so I know that you are safe, as well as where you are."

Hamish nodded. "Come on, Hedges," he called over his shoulder to Pete, who had been quietly waiting to see how this drama would play out. "Looks like it's you and me."

In addition to a radio, each search party carried emergency clothing, food, and first aid. If the lost trio could be located on or near an established trail, snowmobiles could be brought in to shuttle them out quickly. The fear was, of course, that they were off trail, perhaps injured or unable to respond to calls and whistles from the rescue parties. If that were the case, chances for a successful rescue would diminish.

Pete and Hamish spent the day in uneasy companionship, the younger man intentionally trailing the Scotsman by twenty to thirty yards. This distance kept their conversations brief, restrained, and limited to the mechanics of the search itself. Both found it too painful to vent their innermost feelings, for neither trusted the path such a conversation might take. Hamish understood Pete had to feel absolutely shattered, both for the act of losing the kids and for the sacking. Forced to spend this time together, even at a remove of many yards physically, rubbed salt in the wounds of both men. It was almost too much to bear and certainly too much to discuss. Constantly second-guessing himself, Hamish was heartbroken over Pete's distress yet unable to broach the subject as they tramped past Marcy Dam.

He had his own worries beyond what would happen to his protégé. If any child was found seriously injured, deceased, or, God forbid, never found at all—all outcomes that had happened in those mountains—it might prove impossible to keep the school alive. Was this concern selfish or self-serving? It was a convenient distraction to ponder as the angle of the trail increased and his breathing came faster. It had been a long time since he had shouldered so much weight. The old rucksack that felt as familiar as a trusted friend didn't sit as comfortably on his aching hips as it once had. Hamish was certain the strain would play havoc on his back and had tossed a new bottle of Percocet in the top pocket before leaving Glencoe. Sure enough, before they had gone much past Marcy Dam, the shooting pains returned, coursing down his legs like an electric current. Yet he kept a pace that had Pete gasping as he tried to keep from falling behind. Was this Hamish's way of putting *distance* between himself and Pete, of expressing his anger? Or was it a fear they both shared, that only speed and good fortune could avoid what looked to be, with each passing hour, impending tragedy? Rambler trotted along uncertainly between the two, seemingly aware of the tension in the air and appreciating every opportunity to stop and rest.

They snowshoed five miles up to Avalanche Lake, a spectacular pond nestled between the cliffs of Mt. Colden and Algonquin. This was one of Hamish's fondest places in the Adirondacks, reminiscent of the Scottish lochs he had frequented in his youth. After lunching in virtual silence on the rocks by the edge of the lake, frozen solid and blanketed with several inches of soft snow, they marched straight across the lake, eschewing the "Hitch-up-Matildas," an ingenious cantilevered platform of wooden slats bolted into the stone just above the water's edge, that served as the trail during the warmer months. So precipitous were the cliffs above them no one could have safely reached the bottom of the valley by that route.

"This feels like a waste of time," Pete said, as they stopped at the outlet of Avalanche Lake for a drink. "We both know the chances are slim they could descend this way." Communicating on this level, about routes and logistics was about all the two could manage given their current relationship. It was the only common bond they now shared.

"Aye. But we go where we're asked so all directions are covered. The sooner we can get around to the other side of the MacIntyres the better," Hamish agreed. "For today, we'll have to be satisfied with eliminating this side as a possible exit. We're nearly to Lake Colden. Maybe they came down the other side and are warming safely at the caretaker's hut by the lake. If not, it's a second night out for those poor souls without much in the way of food or drink. I am worried, Pete. Terribly . . . worried."

35

Race against Time

The morning hours passed slowly as Libby, Tracy, and Malcolm labored up a frozen creek bed, hoping against hope that an established trail was just over the next rise. Weakened by lack of food and water, they made slow progress, stopping frequently to listen for the calls of would-be rescuers.

"They must have started out after us, don't you think?" Libby asked, leaning against a tree. It was now early afternoon. Malcolm removed his pack and bent over, hands on knees as he tried to catch his breath. He had been unusually quiet during the morning hours as the physical strain took every ounce of strength. He was too tired to be angry.

"Sure. They'll be all over the place," Tracy answered. "Hamish must have blown a gasket when Pete and Christine got back. I'd much rather walk out myself than be found. I'll never get over the embarrassment."

"My ego isn't wrapped up in this like yours, Tracy. I'm not supposed to know what I'm doing. But I don't think I can spend another night out without food or water," Libby said. She glanced at Malcolm. "How're you doing?"

"Been better. I'm with you, Libby. I couldn't care less whether they all think I'm a sissy. I just don't want to die out here. You can have all this damn equipment. I ain't ever using it again anyway."

"Don't quit on me, guys," Tracy pleaded. "If we find a trail soon, we can get ourselves out before dark, get a shower and a hot meal, and sleep for twenty-four hours."

"Okay, boss," Malcolm growled. "But this climbing shit makes no sense to me. Why we got to go up to get out?" Tracy had no answer, only doubts.

Dehydration crept up on the lost hikers. Their mouths felt like sandpaper, their weary legs cramped with lactic acid. But they stumbled on, following the depression of a streambed, unknowingly moving farther away from their rescuers and toward increasingly dense stands of evergreen that ringed a small, mountain lake designated on topographic maps as Lost Pond.

"If this is the end of us," Libby said, "I'd just as soon drop my damn pack right here in the snow. What's the point?"

"We don't give up. Reach down, find that extra something," Tracy encouraged, though his own confidence was flagging.

Staggering behind Libby, strength gone and hooded head lost in cravings for a Coke, a chocolate chip cookie, anything with a calorie, Malcolm remained silent, matching each of her snowshoe steps with his own. Dense woods thwarted their aimless progress and clumps of snow pelted them from disturbed branches as they passed beneath. It was the freckle-faced boy in the lead who first sniffed the sweet scent of wood smoke. Tracy halted for a moment's respite to calm his aching ankle and strained to locate the direction of the aroma. Night would soon be upon them again, and the icy breeze carrying the smell of burning wood tantalized the Glencoe trio. The safety of a warm fire might be close, and with it, the end of their ordeal.

"Smell that?" Tracy asked.

Libby sniffed. "Yeah. Does that mean we're, like, close to the parking lot?"

Tracy did not see how that was possible. "I dunno," he said. The Adirondack Park spanned some six million acres and contained precious few trailheads or parking lots.

"We better find it quick. I'm beat," Malcolm pleaded.

Tracy eyed a nearby fir towering fifty feet into the Adirondack dusk. Most of the lower branches were free of snow, but the crown sported a newly fallen, fluffy frosting. He needed to figure out what direction the wind was blowing so he could tell where the campfire might lie. Bending his shoulder to the trunk, Tracy nudged the massive tree, causing only a slight shiver in the upper reaches, but enough to send some of the fairy-dust flakes wafting in the faint breeze that also carried the aroma of burning wood.

"See? There's a slight breeze from over there," Tracy called, pointing to his left. "The smoke's gotta be coming the same way."

Five minutes of struggling through heavy spruce seemingly brought them no closer. After ten minutes more, daylight had almost disappeared and the smell was no more distinct. Fighting off exhaustion, adrenaline took over, fueled by the seductive aroma of burning wood. With Tracy breaking trail in the deep snow, as he had done since their initial descent from Algonquin the day before, the three trekked on, each following in the leader's footprints to conserve energy, lost in private thoughts, the only sound their heavy breathing as they hurried to locate the source of warmth and safety. The breeze picked up as it often does at sunset when the temperature drops. It played with the woodsmoke as a feline with a catnip mouse. Now the aroma was strong, then it disappeared, only to return a few seconds later. *Where the devil was it?* Tracy wondered. Oddly, none of them thought to call out. Suddenly, Libby saw a glint of orange. She stopped, grabbed the sleeve of Malcolm's parka and pointed, wordlessly. Tracy saw it, too. "Let's go!" he said eagerly. Libby hesitated. "Come on," he chided. "What's the matter?"

"We're in the middle of nowhere. Why would anyone camp here?"

"Probably looking for us, Libby," he guessed, forgetting his earlier reticence about being found. "We're gonna be okay!"

36

A Ghost Revisited

WHILE HAMISH AND PETE TRAVELED THE LOWER ROUTE, OTHER teams climbed the normal trail to the summit of Algonquin. They methodically descended the peak, treating the slope as a grid to be traversed, hoping to intersect the route taken the day before by Tracy, Malcolm, and Libby. What began as a straightforward process on the open summit slabs became an arduous task as the search party reached thick walls of cripplebrush and scrub fir. A few minutes before darkness, however, their efforts were rewarded. One of the spruce traps that had almost swallowed Tracy had not yet completely filled in. Nearby, and a little lower, a second trap revealed itself. Three sets of tracks led down from there. The team excitedly called in the finding to Jeff Ecklestone at the Adirondak Loj who radioed all parties.

"Please be advised that the Algonquin summit crew has encountered what appears to be the route taken by the three. They estimate the route of descent to be two hundred seventy degrees magnetic north. Over." The ranger then directed all searchers to make their way to Rocky Falls lean-to on the west side of Algonquin at first light on Sunday, to begin an orderly line sweep of the vast woods on that side of the mountain.

It was technically still fall. Nearly two weeks remained before the winter solstice, but the gathering darkness came depressingly early. By the shore of frozen Lake Colden, Hamish searched his pack first for the headlamp, and then for the food bag while Pete unfolded fiberglass wands that became the framework of Hamish's alpine dome tent. "At last, they're on to something," he said. "It sure feels like those kids have been gone an eternity." They went about their practiced routines with no wasted movements and little discussion. The relief of being mostly apart during the day's hike could not continue into the evening. There was one tent and hours until morning. The time for two men uncomfortable with their feelings to avoid each other had passed. Had the circumstances been different, Hamish and Pete would have considered this a rare treat to be enjoying a night out together in the mountains beside a pristine mountain lake. Instead, it was sheer torture.

Hamish unrolled his sleeping bag and fluffed it up atop his sleeping pad on the floor of their cramped shelter. As he stood, pain radiated across his back, and he gasped.

"You okay?" Pete asked, seeing Hamish grab himself as if he had been knifed.

"Aye. Just my back. It'll pass. Lord, I hope we've trained these kids well enough that they'll find a way to survive this. I don't know how I'll live with myself if they don't."

"I was the one who screwed up," Pete sighed.

"What happened up there was unforgivable, Pete. My God, you're the last one I'd expect to let this happen. If this goes bad it will haunt you forever."

"You know how sorry I am. I'd do anything to change it. It was crazy up there. I know it's no excuse but all I could think of was to get the group off that summit." Hamish noted Pete had not looked to share any blame with Christine. *He's a damn fine fellow and I'm going to kick myself for a long time for letting that blowhard Connaughton twist my arm to fire him*, he thought. As miserable as it made him feel, Hamish could not bring himself to cross the chairman.

"We're in a bottom-line business, Pete. I know you didn't mean it to happen. The result is all that matters." Hamish bit his lip. He wanted to say this was not his call. He wanted to say it was out of his hands. But he didn't.

Sitting on a log outside the vestibule of their tent, they melted snow over a compact gas stove and privately contemplated the onset of night over Lake Colden. When the water had boiled, Pete poured off enough to fill two thermos bottles, one for tea, the other for soup, while Hamish readied macaroni to go into the remaining water. He crumbled a granola bar and laid it on a plastic bag for Rambler, silently apologizing for the meager rations. He poured water into a spare cook pot and set it down for the dog, who gratefully lapped it up. The men sipped the warming split pea soup in silence, the beams of their headlamps filtering through steam clouds that rose from the bubbling pasta.

After supper, while scrubbing bits of starchy noodles from the pot, Hamish's thoughts became more introspective. *Before you blame another for everything that's wrong, look in the mirror, you old goat, and deal with your own mess.* He knew how Pete was suffering because he had felt it himself. He was still feeling it so keenly that forty odd years later the memory of Zero Gully still seared. Deep in his gut, Hamish carried an unspeakable guilt, born of a calamity he could neither discuss nor erase. Maybe, he thought, it was time to share his ghost of Glencoe. It might help Pete understand why he could grant a boy like Malcolm so many chances yet extend a cherished friend and colleague no rope at all. He owed Pete an explanation, even at the expense of reopening his own wound.

Pete had moved into the tent and hung a small LED lantern from a loop in the roof. Millions of frost crystals clinging to the canted nylon panels of the dome magnified the humble glow. The young man peeled off his outer layer of clothes, spread them between his sleeping bag and air mattress, and slid into the chilly bag. Hamish felt Pete's anguish, knew how hard it must have been, must still be, for Pete to tolerate his company. Sleep, if it came for either of them, would be only a momentary respite.

Hamish waited outside, gazing up at the twinkling starlight while Pete finished organizing his side of the tent. A steady breeze blew across the lake. Frozen trees cracked like muffled gunshots as the wind tested their flexibility. Tufts of fair weather clouds scudded above the ramparts of Mt. Colden, briefly hiding the starlight as they raced parallel shadows on the rock, forest, and lake below.

"Ready," Pete announced. "Come on in."

"I imagine you think I acted a bit hastily," said Hamish in his gravelly brogue as he bent down to enter the tent. He grimaced as another spasm raked the muscles in his back. Rambler brushed by him and snuggled between the two sleeping bags, a familiar routine she thoroughly enjoyed.

"You have a school to run, and I screwed up. I wish you had taken more time to think about my fate, but right now it's not me I'm worried about. I don't know what I'll do if they don't come home in one piece," Pete said.

"You're taking this better than I would," Hamish said. "I know how hard it is for me, knowing I have so many friends, acquaintances, even complete strangers, out here somewhere trying to help. I appreciate how tough it is for you, as well. There's only one way for us to get this gorilla off our backs, you and me. We have to find these kids."

"Before anyone else," said Pete.

"That may be best for us, personally," agreed Hamish. "But what's best for the kids is to be found, safe and sound, no matter who does the finding. If the worst happens, and they are not found, or don't return in one piece, you will never put this behind you." He swallowed hard. "Something like that has eaten me like maggots in my gut for more than forty years."

"What's that?"

"My personal demon." Hamish lay back in his sleeping bag and stared at his breath as it lifted toward the ceiling, where it morphed into minute frozen stalactites.

"Sorry?"

"You think you've heard every one of my stories, but nobody . . . nobody 'cept Bonnie, has heard this one. Maybe it will do us both good for me to air it out."

Hamish rolled on his side and felt for the small nylon ditty bag he had deposited in one of the tent's cargo pockets. He pulled out a pill box and a small leather-covered flask, fished two tablets from the pill box, placed them on his tongue, unscrewed the top of the flask, took a long swig of the Scottish single malt and offered it to Pete. "Laphroaig? A bit peaty."

"No thanks."

"Ahh," Hamish groaned as he twisted to return the flask to the ditty bag. "This damn back . . . Well . . . Pete . . . it's like this . . . when I was in my early twenties, I spent nearly every weekend knocking about the crags near Glencoe in the Scottish Highlands."

"Glencoe?"

"Crazy coincidence. Probably has a lot to do with my being at this school. Glencoe is a small mountain village that has drawn generations of climbers. Wonderful granite in that part of the British Isles and no shortage of lads tossing off one audacious climb after another. In my day, the competition was fierce and, like most fellows that age, each of us, the good ones anyway, felt indomitable. Indestructible. I suppose it's a disease of youth in general, to ignore risks and think you'll survive anything. Looking back, it's a wonder any of us lived. Though the passage of time has blurred most of my foolishness, one still torments me. After you've heard the details, perhaps you'll understand."

Pete reached an arm out of his sleeping bag and scratched Rambler, lying between them, behind an ear. She licked his hand and settled back down. There was quiet in the tent while Hamish waited for the pills and alcohol to alleviate his pain before beginning his story.

"I lived in Edinburgh during college," Hamish began. "I was a diligent student Monday through Friday but come the weekend, when the fellas repaired to the local pubs, I often found a way to get up to the Ben Nevis area."

"That's the highest peak in the United Kingdom, isn't it?"

"Aye. Not as high as Algonquin, but it offers some of the best technical rock and ice climbing anywhere. The tourists can enjoy a hike to the summit without much stress. But that's not what drew me there. By the time I'd driven up from the city and hiked into the climbers' hut it was often the middle of the night. There was always a motley crew staying at the hut, including some of the leading climbers in the country. Legends like Chris Bonington, Dougal Haston, Hamish MacInnes."

Pete listened intently, his steamy breath coalescing in a cloud around the golden glow of the lantern.

"We fell over ourselves trying to impress them," Hamish continued, "hoping they'd invite us to join them on a climb. If that had happened our reputations would have been secured! I was spellbound listening to their stories in the evenings. Some of their early routes in the Himalaya have never been repeated. It was as if Michael Jordan showed up at a playground and chose you for a game of three-on-three. I was intoxicated hanging out with these folks.

"Maybe as a result of such heady company, my buddies and I challenged ourselves to go beyond our limits, trying to impress them and, I guess, prove we were worthy of their attention. We survived a few close calls, but I have never been called to account for the price an innocent lad paid because of my lack of judgment. I have never gotten over it to this day."

"Jesus, Hamish, you didn't kill anyone, did you?" Pete rolled onto his elbow to get a better look at Hamish, lying on his back in the down bag.

"All in due course. I had my sights on a climb called Zero Gully. It was on the north side of Ben Nevis and had only been climbed once before in the winter, two years before the weekend I am describing to you. I was to meet a friend from Glasgow who was every bit as talented and bold as I was. I stopped for supper at the Clachaig Inn in Glencoe on my way to Ben Nevis; we had agreed to meet there, my friend and I. He was to meet me at the hut—the CIC hut—which is the base camp for many of the hardest climbs on the Ben, as we call it. But he didn't show.

"That year was particularly stressful for me. I had to juggle my studies with a job at a local cycle shop, and I was forever trying to catch up on my rest. I was so knackered when I got to the hut, hiking in the dark after a long drive and a heavy meal with a pint or two, that I overslept. By the time I opened my eyes it was near noon and everyone had left to go climbing. Still no sign of my buddy, Robbie. I was pissed, having come a long way and planned to do this serious climb. I was a pretty decent climber then, but not so good that I trusted myself to climb Zero Gully alone."

As Hamish warmed to the story, his Scottish accent became stronger and even the choice of words seemed to transport him back to a different time and place.

"I remember cooking up some oatmeal and grumbling about being left behind when a young lad walked into the hut. As soon as he opened his mouth, I knew from his accent that he did not belong to the Weegee climbing club. They were a pains-in-the-ass lot, but that's another story."

"Weegee?" Pete asked.

"Someone from Glasgow. Slang for Glaswegian. This one spoke the King's English and for a Scotsman like me, just the accent and the perfectly trimmed blond hair was enough to put me off. I'm not proud of that. But at that time prejudices toward us Scots affected me much as it did many of my fellow countrymen. Anyway, the poor fellow was studying medicine in London and desperate for a break in the mountains. That was the only day I laid eyes on Andy Boarder, but he's haunted me nearly every day since."

Hamish paused, located the flask, and took a healthy swallow. The Percocet was beginning to take effect, easing the throbbing in his back and the tension in his brain. He seemed entranced, as if there was no one else in the tent.

"Andy was more than a novice climber," Hamish finally continued. "But the demands of being a medical student left him very little time for recreation. A nice chap, really. I knew it was not fair to dismiss him just because of his accent and social class. We were just really different, but rather than waste the weekend, I convinced myself that Andy could second me on Zero Gully despite his lack of expertise on steep ice. Our late start ought to have eliminated Zero Gully, but I was stubborn. He was game and the first few pitches went pretty well. I was in great form and Andy followed pretty easily. As the route got harder, and I took more time to sort it out, Andy had to belay me for long periods. I noticed him stamping around and he shouted his feet were going numb, could I speed up. This was tough stuff. There was no speeding up, and his suffering increased the longer it took me to solve the next climbing problem.

"After we had completed the hardest pitch, more than halfway up, I felt it was safer to press on to the summit and descend the tourist route. Down-climbing Zero Gully with him was out of the question. Or so I thought. As his condition worsened, I felt ever more desperate to get to the top and safety. On one particularly narrow ledge in the long chimney we were in, I'll never forget the fear I saw in his eyes. He refused to continue. I had to get him warm, but I wanted to get to the top, too. I needed to climb that bastard. It made me blind.

"The most prized book in my library is one by the famed French mountaineer, Lionel Terray, one of the most prominent climbers back in the '50s and '60s. It is entitled *Conquistadors of the Useless,* which is the perfect description of the fool I was. There shouldn't have been any question about which priority was more important. I am constantly reminded about a quote from the fellow who started the National Outdoor Leadership School back in the 1960s—Paul Petzoldt. Ever heard of him?"

"The name sounds vaguely familiar. Of course, I know NOLS," Pete said. "You sent me there after my first year teaching."

"Look him up when we get through with this. He was a legend, a fine climber in his own right and committed to the kind of education I revere. As you know, NOLS is a great companion institution to the Outward Bound School, where I cut my eyeteeth back in Wales. Paul once said, 'There are old mountaineers, and bold mountaineers. But there are no old, bold mountaineers.' That pretty much sums up Hamish MacLean. If I had remained the bold climber I was in 1959, reckless would be a better description, I would probably not be alive today."

"So, what happened to you and Andy?"

"Right. I digress. The point is, my pride got the better of me. I checked my altimeter and judged there were about three more runs of the rope before we topped out, maybe two-hundred-fifty vertical feet. I had several problems: a late start, an incoming storm, and a partner who refused to move. We had no business being out there. Yet, all I could think of was to complete the route, I'm ashamed to say. But Andy refused to budge. He knew he was totally puggled.

"There we were, stuck on this ledge with a winter storm about to hit. I had never climbed this hard a route, let alone at night, but at that moment, the difficulties didn't intimidate me. Frankly, I was more rattled by those eyes of his. I just wanted to get out of his sight. It was beyond ridiculous, but all I could think to do was keep moving up.

"Andy couldn't speak at that point. Just shivered, piercing me with those damn haunted eyes. I secured him to that ledge, left him a thermos of tea, and turned my back on him. In doing so, I broke a cardinal rule of mountaineering." Hamish paused. Pete watched him reach again for the flask in the side pocket of the tent for another numbing swallow of scotch.

"The fellowship of the rope," Pete whispered.

"Aye. The fellowship of the rope. One must never leave his companion behind, especially for some self-centered reason. The folly of my decision began to sink in soon after I left that ledge but I forced all thoughts of him out of my head. I concentrated only on the ice and rock above me. In my haste, I was placing my ice tools very poorly. By all rights they should have picked up my pieces at the foot of the climb, but still and on, I dinnae slip.

"I followed that chimney to the top, traversed over to the main gully, the true crux of the climb, and then managed a steep snow field to the summit plateau. By that time, it was about midnight. Then the storm hit full force. I learned later that the lads back at the hut, having read of our intentions in the logbook, had begun to talk about a rescue, certain that we'd never make it. And they were almost right. I realized that Andy would never survive alone up there if I went all the way back to the hut and tried to put a search party together. No way anybody would go out that night to rescue him, so what was the point? By spending precious time climbing to the summit, I'd practically sealed Andy's fate. There was nothing to do but descend the way I'd come and see if I could keep him alive.

"You can't imagine how dangerous it was to reverse my route back to him. I had nothing to eat or drink, nor the time to do that if I had anything. Though I found some old fixed gear in the wall now and again I didn't trust it would hold me on a rappel, and I didn't have enough of my own to just leave on the route, so I had to do a lot of downclimbing without any protection. It took so long . . . hours . . . to reach a point where my light finally lit up the ledge where I'd left him. His body was partially covered with snow and ice chips. I was sort of surprised to see him. I'm ashamed to say there was a part of me that wished he had blown off.

"The next hours were the worst of my life, trying to get him down. His legs were completely useless and he kept up this insane havering."

"Havering?" Pete asked.

"Uh . . . muttering," Hamish said, momentarily brought back to the present by Pete's interruption. "When I get a bit of the malt in me, I tend to reach for my old slang, I guess." It had been so long since he had permitted himself to relive those moments on Zero Gully.

"How did you get him down?" Pete asked.

"I won't bore you with the details, though nearly every move is burned into my brain. It took all the ingenuity I had to get the both of us down safely." Hamish paused for a deep breath, a shudder that was almost a cry. "Somewhere in that nightmare my back tore up. I've lived with that pain ever since.

"When we reached the bottom, I left him on the scree slope, wrapped in my parka, and stumbled to the hut. The storm had only recently passed over us so I was not surprised that no one had come looking for us. When I crashed through the door the lads thought they'd seen a ghost. My face was gashed, I was bent double from the pain in my back, and I had just enough strength to tell them where to find Andy before I collapsed.

"It was late the next day when I woke up. The caretaker of the hut told me they'd managed to get Andy down to the hospital in Fort William, and it had been a tough twenty-four hours for him. The doctors tried to save his legs, but deep frostbite, combined with the banging they'd taken during the descent, destroyed too much tissue. He would survive, but as a double amputee."

"Whew," Pete whistled softly.

"To my horror, I was treated like a hero who had practically lost his life saving the poor chap. No one knew of my decision to leave Andy in the first place. No one knew I'd gone to the summit. Aside from you and Bonnie, no one knows that Hamish MacLean completed the second winter ascent of Zero Gully. I was so ashamed of the whole business I couldn't even bring myself to visit Andy in the hospital."

From the downy recesses of his sleeping bag Pete asked, "Did you ever try to contact him?"

"Nae. Never had the nerve. The following week I read in the newspaper how grateful he was that I had saved his life. It made me physically ill to read that. He could remember nothing of being left for hours on that ledge, while I pursued my ridiculous dream. Every time my back acts up, it's a grim reminder of what I did to him. I can't put it to rest."

"Did he ever reach out to you?"

"Once. When I was at Outward Bound. I have no idea how he found me and I did not return the letter."

Hamish was silent. Pete stared at the lantern hanging from the tent ceiling. Rambler snored, tucked neatly between the two men. She spasmodically kicked a leg out in her sleep.

"She's chasing a chipmunk, poor dear," Hamish said, stroking her back. "I share this with you, Pete, in the hopes you can now understand how painful the loss of these kids is for me. How personal it is. These things just don't go away, as you will discover."

The headmaster had one more confession left.

"To ease my guilt, I started drinking a bit more than I could handle. To ease the pain in my back I started taking Percocet and refused surgery that might have left me unable to climb again. Before too long I couldn't function without it—the pills or the alcohol—or thought I couldn't." He reached again for the flask, shook it, and drained the last drops.

"Maybe this is something you can't handle on your own."

"That's what Bonnie says. I'm a stubborn man, Peter, and it's taken me too long to come to the same conclusion. If this search and rescue goes bad, I'm going to have a lot more serious things to worry about than addiction. What I've told you tonight stays between us."

"I understand. I may start drinking myself."

How could Pete accept that the man who had mentored him so thoughtfully, Hamish wondered, who had just shared a most intimate detail in his life, could be the same man who could summarily end his career at Glencoe? It was torture lying next to Pete, who was both friend and protégé and now, thanks to him, an outcast. It felt totally wrong. Could he empathize with the guilt Pete must be feeling? Could he summon the necessary generosity of spirit? Or was he wallowing in his own self-pity? This search could not go badly or it would haunt the both of them forever. These were feelings two proud men knew not how to discuss, and sleep did not come easily.

37

Campfire Confessions

THE SOUND OF CRUNCHING SNOW NEARLY CAUSED GARTH HEART FAIL-
ure. He looked at Ramon, raised a finger to his lips and pointed in the
direction of the sound. Ramon immediately thought of Carly. She must
have reported them and knew the coordinates of where they could be
found. Garth reached for his rifle. That's crazy, Ramon thought. If he
blew these folks away there would be others right behind them. Perhaps
the lumberjack was thinking the same thing, for he returned the rifle to
its sleeve. They would have to talk their way out.

"We've gone over this before. Don't open your mouth. I'll handle it,"
Garth whispered. Ramon nodded, his heart pounding.

"Thank God! We're gonna be okay!" Libby exclaimed to her companions when she saw the tiny fire and the two men squatting beside.
Plodding into the clearing behind her, Malcolm managed an exhausted
smile. He saw a log by the fire where he could collapse and rest his
cramping legs.

In the dim light it was hard to take stock of their visitors. Ramon
scrutinized each in turn. The heavyset one seemed too tired to notice his
hosts. The girl was just happy to be there; she raised no alarms. But the
other one, the other boy who had hung back a little when his companions
burst into their campsite, he was the one to watch, Ramon decided. He
seemed to be taking it all in. Ramon imagined what the kid was process-
ing: he and Garth didn't look like your average winter hikers; they didn't
look like rescuers. Seedy. Disheveled. Smelly. What the hell would they
do with these kids? He knew Garth's brain was working in overdrive but

they couldn't talk to each other openly now. *God help me if this turns into a massacre*, Ramon worried.

"Well, what have we here?" Garth exclaimed. Their tiny campsite suddenly seemed alive, and quite overcrowded. Ramon assumed Garth was thinking the same thing as he—better three teenagers appearing out of nowhere than a swarm of state troopers. Instead of an emergency crisis they had more of a slow-developing one. These kids should not be out here alone.

Tracy's eyes swept the scene and Ramon was absolutely certain this was the one to worry about. He could almost see the wheels turning in the kid's brain, trying to make sense of it all. The snow was unusually packed down around the firepit, and looked as if it had seen many fires. Dozens of questions should be coursing through this kid's head. Ramon wondered if he would reveal those thoughts.

"Boy, are we glad to see you!" Libby said, letting her pack slide to the snow and slumping down on a log before the fire. "We're the missing ones," she exclaimed hopefully. "Have you been looking for us?"

"Slow down, girl," Garth responded. "Where you been?"

"Can you guys spare some water?" Malcolm asked timidly.

Garth shot a glance toward Tracy. "Where you from, boy?" he asked, ignoring Malcolm's request.

"Uhhh . . . Glencoe School," said Tracy, hesitantly. From Garth's tone of voice Ramon could tell the lumberjack had reached the same conclusion as had he.

"I've heard of it," Garth nodded. "Do the teachers let you guys go off on your own like this?"

"We were up Algonquin yesterday but got separated from the rest of the group."

"You guys got any water you can spare?" Malcolm asked again.

Garth motioned to Ramon to toss over a water bottle. They each had two and never shared. Ramon grudgingly offered one of his to Malcolm who gratefully chugged from it, ignoring the odd pine needle, then passed it to Libby.

"We could use some help," Tracy said, almost in a whisper.

"Algonquin, eh? You kids have come a long way. The wrong way," Garth grinned. "Name's Eric. This here is Jack. Jackie, boy, see if we got any cocoa left," he said to Ramon.

"Maybe we could borrow something to eat?" Libby asked meekly. "We've had nothing but crackers." Garth rummaged through a stuff sack and came up with a couple of strips of dried beef jerky, grudgingly handing one to each kid. Libby thanked him, warily fingering the cardboard-like strips as though they carried disease. She didn't eat meat, more for political reasons than diet, but she bit into it hungrily.

Ramon scooped snow into the blackened pot, added a little water from his second water bottle to facilitate the melting process, and balanced the pot carefully on the glowing coals. They had suffered these many weeks waiting out the police only to become attached to a new set of search targets. The woods were no doubt swarming with rescue parties. To Ramon, the possibility of capture seemed almost welcome. He assumed Garth did not share that view and would fight to the death to avoid it.

Eyes on the fire, Libby began to describe how their trip had gone awry while Tracy sat, hugging his slow-warming body. He leaned over to Malcolm and, turning his head to conceal what he was whispering, said, "These guys don't seem like buddies out hunting, do they?" Malcolm shook his head almost imperceptibly. "They sure seem suspicious of us. Libby has no clue." He turned back to Libby, who had been chatting away to her new friends, explaining their predicament, and in a barely audible tone, mumbled, "These guys are bad news."

Libby's eyes widened. Malcolm looked up alertly.

"What'd you say, boy?" Garth asked sharply.

"Umm . . . Can you get us to Heart Lake?" Tracy asked.

"Could be. What was that junk that just came out of your mouth?" Garth snapped, then caught himself. "Anyways, after you've had a good night's sleep, we'll get you taken care of," he grinned. In the dim light Ramon saw the smile and shuddered.

"Jack, let's you and me go find some more kindling so these kids will be warm tonight, eh?" Garth reached behind him for a long leather casing, slung it under one arm and waited for Ramon to stand. Tracy watched closely as they stepped away from the clearing.

"Why are you so suspicious?" Libby asked when the men had moved off into the darkness.

Tracy put a finger to his mouth to signal quiet, and listened for the receding footfalls.

"That sure irritated the big guy," Malcolm said.

Tracy nodded at Malcolm. "Damn right."

"And the other one hasn't said a word. Something is off," Malcolm added.

"Right. These guys don't look like they go together. They took a rifle with them to collect firewood. What's up with that? What the hell did we just walk into?" Tracy said.

"They sure could use a bath," Libby sighed.

"My gut tells me we may have been a lot better off never finding these guys," Malcolm said. "Being lost feels a whole lot safer than being found by these guys. Did you see that cheek scar? Looked like a freakin' axe. Who gets one of those on his face? Gotta be one crazy dude."

"Yeah, I saw it," Tracy said. "Looked like a branding."

An anxious quiet fell over the group as they huddled by the small fire, lost in their own fears.

"Maybe I got off on the wrong foot with y'all at the beginning of the year," Malcolm said, breaking the silence.

"Maybe you did," Tracy agreed.

"Yeah, but maybe that's because you don't know nuthin' about me."

"You showed more'n enough for me to make up my mind," Tracy muttered.

"Maybe we need to cut everyone a break," Libby said. "You don't make that great an impression either, Tracy."

"Well, I seriously doubt there's anything new to be learned. I think I've got enough to know what makes him tick and he sure knows what I'm about. He's done nothing all year to make anyone want to be his buddy but, okay, we've got a long night ahead of us. I'm listening."

"Look, guys," Malcolm stammered, "if this is where it's going to end for all of us, I'd like to clear some things up. It's probably more important to me than you, Tracy, but let's put an end to this bullshit. I know I've acted like an idiot sometimes."

"Like the damn loom, Mal? Like Hamish's stained-glass window?" Tracy accused. "Like the chicken shit in my boots? An idiot? Sometimes?"

"Will you just give him a chance?" Libby retorted. "Just shut up for a minute."

"When I get angry something snaps. It's as if someone else takes over," Malcolm continued, grateful for Libby's interjection.

"Mal, you usually get angry over nothing," Libby said. "Those stupid girls on the looms were just teasing. They didn't deserve to have their work destroyed."

"You're right. I'm trying to figure it out. Why I snap."

"Everybody's got a story. We've got time. What's yours?" Libby asked.

"Born in Georgia. Dad was in the service but when I was three, I lost both my parents in a car accident," Malcolm said, matter-of-factly. "Honestly, I don't remember anything about my folks. They sent me to live with my mother's sister. We lived in an old broken-down shack in the boonies. It was like you see in the movies. Real rednecks-ville. I've never shared this with anyone. I don't talk a lot about myself." Malcolm's voice strengthened as he stared into the embers. Then he picked up his head, scanning the woods for signs of their hosts. "I'm pretty scared right now."

"Me, too," Libby said.

"Go on," urged Tracy. He was scared, too, and glad to hear he wasn't alone.

"She had lots of kids, my aunt. One more didn't make much difference. Her husband was a mean son of a bitch when he drank. Us kids figured out it was safer to disappear when he drank. It was a bad scene, a lot of 'domestic violence' they call it, right? He left one day and never came back. Things started settling down, I was just getting comfortable for the first time in my life, and my aunt sends me away. Boom, one day I'm there, thinking that with the old man gone I'm gonna have some peace for a change, next day it's me who's gone."

"You can't just kick a little kid out of the house," Tracy said, thankful for the distraction. He was dreading the return of the guy with the scar.

"Maybe she figured the welfare money would go farther with fewer mouths to feed. Last in first out? I don't know. I spent a few weeks in a foster home until this guy Wayne Dandridge shows up. He was my dad's younger brother. Until then, I never knew I had an uncle. He was a damn good sax player with a little apartment above a strip club in the French Quarter of New Orleans. He lived with this Hopi Indian lady."

"I was in New Orleans once," Libby interjected.

"At a strip club?" Tracy teased.

"Shut up, Tracy," Libby said. "Go on, Malcolm."

"I lived with them for a couple of years. They didn't have any kids of their own and he was always off on some gig, sometimes for weeks, over to Europe and Japan. Whenever he'd split, she'd take me back to her family on the reservation in New Mexico. Those Indian kids and me didn't get along so good," he chuckled.

"You sure have a knack for getting people pissed at you," Tracy said.

"True statement," Malcolm sighed. "Anyway, when my uncle got back, the two of them yelled a lot and I could tell it was going to be her or me. When he told me he was sending me to boarding school in Ohio, I threw his sax out the window."

"That's a lot of rejections for a little kid," Libby said.

"I guess. I didn't know what to call it then. They shipped me off to a military academy," Malcolm went on, "and he figured out how to stop being my legal guardian. Now I've got this foster lady, Mathilda Graham. She's not really my aunt but that's what she tells everyone. Even Hamish thinks we're related. She's just a rich bitch who wants to do some good, I guess," Malcolm smirked. "I do appreciate it, though. She gives money to groups that sponsor kids from tough homes and I guess she figured she should sponsor a kid herself. I know she cares about me'n stuff, but I don't think she'd ever really want me living with her, full-time anyways. That's why, when the military school didn't work out, she found Glencoe."

"How'd you screw up military school?" Tracy asked, anticipating more interesting details.

"It's pretty embarrassing," Malcolm said, rubbing has face to get the blood circulating back into his frozen nose, "but since I've gone this far,

370

I might as well get it all out there. You see, military schools have this tradition where the older kids pick on the younger kids."

"Hazing," Libby said knowingly.

"Yeah. I didn't care what they did to everyone else. They weren't going to give me any crap. Well, some of the upperclassmen were afraid if they let me avoid it, the tradition would be in trouble."

"You're talking eighth grade, man, not the army," Tracy said.

"We learn to be bastards at an early age," Malcolm said.

"Speak for yourself," Libby said.

"They make you do tons of pushups and hang from doorways by your fingers 'til you think your arms'll drop off. You know, stuff like you hear about."

"Sorry, I don't hear about stuff like that," Libby said.

"When you get to be an eighth grader yourself, then you can stick it to everyone else," Malcolm responded. "That's the way it's always been."

Tracy thought Malcolm had already mastered how to *stick it* to everyone else. "But you couldn't hang in there long enough to become the torturer, huh?"

"No, but I made an impression before I got my ass shipped out of there. One Friday night there was a dance at a girl's school nearby but I decided to skip it. About nine o'clock these four guys wearing ski masks burst into my room. They told me I wasn't showing enough respect and they were going to teach me a lesson. They grabbed me, stuffed some handkerchiefs in my mouth to keep me quiet, and dragged me over to the gym. They shoved me into one of those full-length lockers and threw a lock on it. Then they shut the lights and left."

"Holy shit," Tracy exclaimed.

"The locker had slits in it, so at least I could breathe. I spat out the handkerchiefs and screamed for a couple of hours, but no one showed 'til the janitor came to clean sometime Saturday morning."

"Did you know who did it?" Tracy asked.

"Yup."

"Were they expelled?" Libby asked.

"Are you kidding? I don't squeal. You of all people should know that," he said, staring at Tracy, who dropped his head to stare at his feet.

"Telling the commander is the last thing I'd ever do," Malcolm continued, content to let the barb remain. "I settle things my own way. The next weekend when everybody was out at a football game, I poured bleach over all the stuff in their closets." Malcolm smirked, recalling the event with pride. "I knew I'd get canned, but it felt great."

Tracy thought of how he had chosen to get even with Malcolm for the manured boots. Malcolm's seeming reference to that event sent a shock wave through him. Was the so-called amnesia all part of Malcolm's twisted code of honor? The kid seemed a helluva lot more dangerous now that Tracy knew what he had endured at his previous school and what he might do in retaliation.

"Glencoe's different," Libby said softly. "I've never been in a place where I felt so supported, especially by adults."

"Whatever," Malcolm muttered.

"Not *whatever*," she said sharply. "A lot of us have had a not-so-normal family situation or we wouldn't be at a boarding school at our age. I can't match the crap you had to deal with growing up, but I struggle all the time to understand how to make things better with my folks. They don't visit me, they only call when they need something, and they have no clue what *I* need from *them*. I can't tell you how much the Hendersons have helped me this year. And Christine. Other from persuading me to come on this trip, which I totally regret, she's been a huge help to me. But none of them could have made a dent if I hadn't given them permission. From what I can tell, Malcolm, you've never given anybody permission."

"From what he's gone through," Tracy said softly, "maybe I would have kept everyone at arm's length, too. That doesn't mean I think how you act is okay, Mal, but it does make me understand a little bit where this stuff comes from. It's like you expect to be kicked around so you kick first."

. . .

"We're in trouble, huh?" Ramon said when he and Garth had walked fifty yards away from camp.

"You got that right, Jack," Garth said. "The thing of it is they'll put more men in the woods to find three missing kids than two escaped cons.

That chick we met the other day may have reported us or she may not have, but this is the real deal. We stay with the kids, we're dead meat. You go find some sticks and head back to camp. I'm gonna get a head start on breaking trail outta here so it don't take us so long tomorrow. At least the search teams ain't thinking about *us* right now."

As he worked his way back to the campsite, picking up the odd piece of kindling that lay above the snowpack, Ramon knew he had a choice to make. He recalled the story of the Mohawks Garth had wasted and the close call with Carly. Garth had clearly made a decision. He figured the kids were doomed. It wasn't much of a stretch to figure he was part of the same plan.

Ramon found them in their sleeping bags, sitting close together with their backs against their packs, their sleeping pads protecting them from the snow. "We got to talk," he said, dropping his bundle of wood by the fire and settling down across from them on a log. The meager light tossed by the flickering embers made the surrounding woods totally black behind him. It would be impossible to spot anyone approaching until they pierced the circle of light, but Ramon figured he had some time before Garth returned.

"First of all, my name is Ramon Ortiz, not Jack. His is Garth. Maybe you heard of us."

"Garth?" Tracy asked. "Thought he said Eric."

"You may think everything's cool since you found us. Truth is—I wish you hadn't. You were better off lost. I don't know how much time we have, but there's a lot to tell you."

"What do you mean?" Libby asked.

Ramon banged a few snow-laden sticks against a log to clean them and threw them onto the dying coals. The wet wood steamed, leaving bubbling damp spots. "Did you know there were a couple of guys who escaped from a prison around here back in October?"

"Oh, Jesus," groaned Tracy.

Ramon nodded. "Bingo. I'm not your problem, guys. I was doing time at Ray Brook for selling drugs. I didn't hurt nobody. Only reason I broke out was to get home and help my family. Really dumb decision." Ramon slowly stirred the fire with a stick. Four pairs of eyes watched the embers jump back to life. Four minds lost in separate, but similar, nightmare scenarios.

"I'm telling you this because we're in this together now. There's lots of people trying to find you, but if they find us when they find you, me and Garth are going back to prison for a long time. Garth ain't gonna let that happen, you can be damn sure. I think he plans to get rid of you as soon as possible and he may want to get rid of me, too."

"What do you mean *get rid of us?*" Libby stammered.

"I'm not sure. He'll tell you we're leading you out to some trailhead. But that may not be true. I just don't know. He's out there breaking trail to someplace, but he didn't say where or why except that it will speed things up tomorrow. I don't think he trusts me so he didn't give me much."

Tracy buried his head into the collar of his sleeping bag, overwhelmed by the enormity of the challenge ahead.

"Why should we believe you?" Malcolm demanded.

"Why should I make it up?" Ramon retorted. "It would be easier to lie to you and just go along with whatever he wants to do. But I don't want no part of it and we're going to need each other."

"You'll let him . . . do . . . whatever?" Libby pleaded.

"I don't know what that is, or how to stop it. Not alone, anyway."

"Let's get outta here," Tracy said, shaking. "Do you know which direction Heart Lake is?"

Ramon chuckled. "I don't even know what Heart Lake is. Before they sent me upstate, I'd never been out of Manhattan." *Except for juvie,* he thought. "I tried to run a while ago and that didn't work out so good. Anyway, we'd never outrun him. He grew up in these woods. He'd follow our tracks and shoot us. I'm sure of that."

"There's four of us and only one of him," Malcolm offered bravely. "Let's jump the sucker when he gets back."

"Oh, yeah. Brilliant idea," Tracy snorted. "Did you see the size of that guy?"

"Actually, I had been thinking something like that, too," Ramon said. "But you have no idea what a crazy son of a bitch he is. You see that scar on his face?"

"Hard to miss," Tracy said.

"Well, a couple of Indians burned that into him."

"Jeez," Malcolm said. "And got away with it?"

"Not exactly. I can't tell you if it's true or not, but he says he killed the guys who did it and now he thinks of it as a badge of honor. Be careful if it starts to twitch; that seems to be some kind of trigger."

"Great," Libby said. "We walked in on an insane asylum."

"Why doesn't he just split on his own?" Tracy asked. "Maybe he's already on his way."

"All his stuff is here," Ramon said, pointing to Garth's large pack. "He's not going to Canada without it."

Ramon stood, walked the perimeter of the campsite and peered into the darkness. They had strength in numbers but Garth knew the plan and controlled the weapons. All they had right now on their side was time to get to know each other and concoct an alternate ending. But how much time? Ramon had no idea.

"Where you from . . . before?" Libby asked.

"The city," Ramon said, taking a seat again on the log and feeding the fire.

"Whereabouts?"

Tracy began to fume. They had just been handed a potential death sentence and Libby was chitchatting. He glanced at Malcolm, trying to read the other's reaction to the line of questioning. Malcolm gave Tracy an imperceptible shrug, as if to say, *That's a girl for you.*

"Ever heard of Alphabet City?" Ramon asked. He wondered the same thing as did Tracy. What difference did it make what was in their pasts. The future was all that mattered. "Avenue A? Avenue B? The Lower East Side?"

"I know someone from there. She works for my parents," Libby said. "I'm from the city, too, uptown."

"Can we talk about how we're going to stay alive?" Tracy snapped. "I mean it's great you two are practically neighbors but if we don't figure something out before he gets back, nobody's going home again."

"He's right," Ramon admitted, rubbing his unshaven face that sported only wisps of a beard he'd never been able to grow to any reasonable degree. "If this was my turf, I'd know how to handle him. But here?" He shook his head.

Libby reached an arm out of her sleeping bag and reached for a thin branch and tossed it atop the modest blaze. "I wondered what happened to you guys," she said, softly. "After a while, everyone figured you'd escaped."

"Or died," Malcolm added.

"I wish we had," Ramon muttered. "Escaped. This is no picnic. Life here is a different kind of prison." He peered into the blackness. Though the fire was small, it still destroyed his night vision. They'd never see or hear Garth until he was on top of them. "I guess that's where I'm headed. Back to prison. For a long stretch this time. And I only had a couple of months left," Ramon sighed, burying his head in his hands. "This was the stupidest thing I've ever done, and I'm going to pay for it."

"What made you run?" Malcolm asked.

"I called home one day and learned that my brother got knifed and my mother had a shock that nearly killed her. That's the only reason I took off with that bastard, to see them before maybe they died." Frustrated, he flung the fire poker he'd been using into the darkness where it fell mutely in the snow.

"When we get out of here and you want me to call her for you, I will," Libby offered.

"You gonna memorize my number?" Ramon challenged, doubting any of them would ever see a telephone again. She seemed awfully sweet and totally ignorant of the trouble she was in.

"You guys have no idea what you got yourselves into," Ramon said, rubbing his chin.

"I think maybe I do," Tracy muttered. "Nobody's hunting for us until dawn. We either get rescued here in the morning, if they found our tracks, or we split now and hope to outrun him. Am I missing something?"

"Or we kill the guy," Malcolm added.

"Not sure any of those make any sense," Ramon countered. "I've been living with Garth for weeks now and he scares the shit out of me. This ain't no video game, guys. You're crazy if you think you can handle him. Or just disappear."

Libby looked puzzled. "Just curious. What's her name?" she asked Ramon.

"Who?" Ramon asked.

"Your mom. I know only one Hispanic person in the world and her name's Ortiz, too. How common is that?"

"Come on, Libby," Tracy exclaimed. "I thought we were trying to figure out how to survive here. What difference does this make?"

"I want to know," she said firmly.

"Ortiz is like Smith," Ramon said. "There are a lot of us. But, to answer your question, it's Eva. She was cooking and cleaning for some folks uptown. She didn't talk much about it, but they paid well and it really helped keep food on the table. Some strange name like outer space. Astronauts, or something."

Libby sat bolt upright. "I knew it!"

Malcolm, who had been quietly listening, trying to find a way to contribute, suddenly heard the crack of a tree limb, somewhere beyond their small community circle. "Shhh," he rasped, putting a finger to his lips.

Libby ignored him. "It's Austro-lab, right? Where your mom works?"

"You a witch or something?" Ramon asked, clearly shaken.

Tracy glanced from one to the other, totally confused. "What the hell's going on here?" he asked. "You both freakin' me out." But his attention was mostly on Malcolm, who had risen and crept out of the circle of light thrown by the meager fire. Tracy stepped past Libby, who was completely focused on the seemingly impossible connection she had just made. He caught Malcolm by the shoulder and held him from moving further.

"I swear I heard someone out there," Malcolm whispered.

"My heart's beating so fast I can't hear anything," Tracy muttered. The two crept away from the campsite in order to filter out the conversation between Ramon and Libby. But they could hear nothing but the occasional snap of trees cracking in the cold air.

Back at the fire, Ramon stared at Libby as if she held some precious secret that could only be revealed if he stayed perfectly still. "This is crazy," Libby whispered. "I met your mother a couple of weeks ago when I went home for Thanksgiving. My folks sent her to pick me up at Port

Authority. She told me her name was Eva and when she found out I was going to school near Lake Placid, it was like I shot her."

Astonished, Ramon reached out to Libby and grasped her arms. "She's okay? What about her heart?"

"She mentioned she had been sick, but I guess it wasn't that bad. She sure worked her tail off for my folks and she still had time to help me get through that weekend."

Having allayed their fears that no one was lurking beyond their camp, Tracy and Malcolm returned to the fire. "What's the deal?" blurted Tracy. "Have you guys forgotten what we're doing here? We don't have a lot of time to figure this out."

"Unbelievable . . ." Ramon muttered, his mind whipsawing between what Libby had just revealed and the crisis at hand. He stood and reached into their near-empty food bag. Out came a dog-eared Hershey bar that he broke into pieces and offered to the three. Tracy sniffed it, then gratefully wolfed his portion as if it might be his last. "I tried to get away from that man once already," he lamented. "He knew I couldn't find my way outta here and he knew I wouldn't fight him or I'd be as good as dead myself. I've seen what he can do when he's angry and he's never even been arrested for the worst shit. Don't expect me to handle him on my own . . ." His voice trailed off.

They sat in silence. Having listened to Ramon despair over the impossibility of escape or ambush, all four found the last vestiges of bravery slipping away. There seemed no way out. "I guess it's my time to confess," Tracy said. "I gotta say something while I can." Ramon sat half-listening, since the story involved people he did not know. He waited impatiently for Tracy to get to the point, for he wanted to interrogate Libby further. Talking to this girl was the closest he could get to family and each word was like a life preserver.

Tracy had rehearsed this moment countless times. Even as he stumbled down the trail from Balanced Rocks to Glencoe that afternoon in October, he had tried to construct the words that would explain his awful prank. But when it appeared Malcolm had no memory of the event Tracy had stopped rehearsing. Now that he understood that Malcolm remembered everything, and had chosen to let it fester, Tracy could no longer keep that apology locked up. He talked about snakes slithering over rocks. He spoke of his horror in watching Malcolm cartwheel off the slabs to the scrub below and how helpless he felt, how frightened he was that Malcolm would die, or was already dead.

Ramon noticed Libby's shock, her look of disbelief, as she listened to the stuttered words, and watched Tracy's face dissolve into tears. Finally done, he tucked his head into the collar of his sleeping bag and wept. Through all of this, Ramon noticed, Malcolm never flinched, never took his eyes off the fire before them.

"Just couldn't keep it to yourself, could you?" Malcolm finally said in a nearly imperceptible voice. "You're an asshole." Waiting a beat to see if someone responded, Malcolm continued. "I figured we'd just let that one go, mostly because I couldn't decide how to get even without killing you. It seemed to me the less said the better. I don't come off all that cool in this story and you sure come out like a criminal. No offense," he said, glancing at Ramon. "I know I could have run you out of Glencoe if I had just spoken up, but that's not how I roll. That's sort of what I was trying to tell you with my own sorry-ass story. Maybe if I hadn't spilled my guts, you would have kept this to yourself, too. I'd just as soon you kept suffering, if you want the truth."

"Malcolm, you almost died!" Libby exclaimed. "How can you not despise Tracy?"

"He's not my favorite human being. But it's complicated."

"Complicated? That's the last word I ever thought I'd hear coming out of a boy's mouth," Libby exclaimed.

"Man, I hope you know it was an accident," Tracy pleaded. "I just meant to scare you. You have no idea what it's been like living with this. I really thought you were dead and that there was nothing I could do to change it. Then, when I found out you were going to make it, it was too late to say anything. I'm sorry, man, I really am. When I heard you'd come out of the coma I knew I had to face you. Then when you didn't remember anything . . . I was too chicken to do anything else."

"I was counting on that. If you knew I knew, then I'd have had to do something back. And I couldn't come up with anything. I have no idea how you knew I'm petrified of snakes," Malcolm muttered, almost cracking a smile. "That bit of detective work impressed me."

Tracy remained quiet.

"I bet I could press charges," Malcolm said.

"I have no idea," Tracy whispered.

"You bet your ass I could. But as long as we both know it, that's enough for me. What happened should have just been between you and me. I know I almost bought the farm, but the fact is, I didn't. I didn't even suffer all that much. Not that I recommend it or anything. Point is, it worked better for me that no one else knew what really happened. It kind of gave me a do-over at school when I got back from the hospital. But now you went and screwed it up so if we ever get out of this damn place you and I have to deal with this all over again. Unless Libby agrees to never mention it to anyone either."

"Wait a minute," she said. "Don't get me in the middle of this conspiracy. I think you're both crazy. The truth needs to come out and it's up to you guys to face it. Hamish needs to know."

"How about I sue Tracy, sue the school, make a fortune and never have to work a day in my life? Sound like a plan?"

Tracy shook his head in disbelief.

"Forget it, Tracy. Just move on. I have," Malcolm said. "I know your family is broke anyways. We got bigger shit to figure out."

Libby shook her head in wonder. "The Ninth Grade War is over. Too bad we may not live to tell anyone about it."

"Four against one," Ramon said with encouragement. "Only way we live is to work together." The others glanced at him, almost having forgotten he was there. No suspicion remained; their mutual survival would be driven by their degree of collaboration. It was clear the next few hours were critical.

Tracy wiped his eyes, a huge weight lifted. "I don't know how we're going to get out of this, but I won't quit on you guys," he said firmly.

"Me, too," Malcolm said. "I'm all in."

Ramon lifted his finger to his lips at the crunch of approaching snowshoes.

38

Struggle to Survive

RAMON LIFTED HIS HEAD FROM THE WARMTH OF HIS SLEEPING BAG TO see Garth stirring the dying coals with a striped maple sapling, as he had done, hours earlier. He checked his watch; it was just past five. The sky was beginning to lighten. Ten yards beyond the campsite their three visitors lay curled up together in their bags.

"You're up early," whispered Ramon.

"Never went to sleep," Garth said. "I can't afford to sleep until we get rid of our problem. We're too close to freedom now to let some stupid shit screw up everything. The woods will be swarming with people looking for our friends here. I want you to get up quietly and help me get ready to split. It's game time."

"How did the trail-breaking work out last night?"

"Not so great. I'm probably gonna pay for the energy I put out. I'm still pretty weak. But we can't stay another day. Not now."

Ramon was convinced Garth's top priority was shedding the kids somehow. But what about the lumberjack's next priority? Shedding *him*. He needs me to be part of his solution, at least for part of the day, Ramon surmised.

"They seemed awfully quiet when I got back last night. What did you tell them?" Garth said, waving in the kids' direction.

"Nothing about us," Ramon lied. "They were just happy to find us. I didn't do much talking. They asked me how to get outta here but I really didn't have anything I could tell them, since I don't know."

Garth considered that for a moment. "If you're shittin' me, Jack, it's going to be a hard day for you, too." He stood and rubbed his legs to get the blood flowing. Ramon could see Garth's breath in the frigid morning air and felt the giant's anxiety. "We're not going to wait for the sun to get above the MacIntyre ridge," Garth said, waving in the general direction of sunrise. "The sun brings rescuers. We need as big a head start as we can get. The trail's good 'til about halfway, but we still got work to do. Get packed."

"We gonna eat first?" Ramon asked warily.

"And waste what little we got? No. We eat when we don't have so many mouths to feed."

Ramon nodded. Garth stuffed his sleeping bag into his pack and strapped on his foam pad as Ramon did the same. All Ramon knew was that they would somehow separate from the kids and then boldly walk out to the nearest trailhead, trusting that most traffic would be looking for children, not convicts. In plain sight they would be invisible; security through obscurity.

Ramon gently shook the kids when the packing was mostly done.

"Wake up, guys. It's time to leave."

Libby rolled to a sitting position, sleeping bag wrapped to her chin. She poked Tracy, curled up on one side of her. Then she poked Malcolm, completely tucked inside his bag on her other side.

"Gotta get moving," Ramon urged. "We'll get you out of this." He felt Libby staring at him, as if demanding he provide some assurance he could deliver on his promise. But he doubted he could, and avoided her gaze.

Tracy opened his eyes to the still-gray light. It took him a moment to orient himself.

"I almost forgot to be scared," he mumbled to Libby.

"Welcome to the club," she said. "I'm petrified." Malcolm was the last to stir. He watched his companions extricate themselves from the warm bags and shove steaming feet into chilled Mouse boots, working the laces before their fingers ceased to cooperate.

"Damn," he said to his companions. "I wish I was at Glencoe. Boy, do I wish for that. Never thought I'd say that."

Tracy smiled. "I feel you, bro."

"Tell you what," Malcolm said, crawling out of the sleeping bag. "I'm not going down without a fight."

"Boys," Libby muttered, stuffing her sleeping bag into its sack. She began to sniffle and turned her back so Garth would not see her distress.

"Let's go, let's go!" urged Garth, keeping a careful eye on the kids as they finished their packing. "Happy to be going home, right? Everybody happy?"

An arm encircled Libby's shoulder, warm breath at her ear. "We'll find a way," Tracy whispered. Ramon was close enough to hear. In Tracy's eyes Ramon saw a determination that made him feel he might have help; whatever it was they could do when the time came.

"We are outta here!" Garth cried. His rifle was stashed behind a shoulder strap, not easy to detect unless you looked closely. "You'll feel better as soon as we get you back on the trail."

. . .

Daylight was still an hour away when Hamish unzipped the top of his sleeping bag and sat up, his breath steaming in the frigid tent. Pete lay patiently until Hamish had dressed, stowed his personal belongings and crawled out the door of the tent. While Hamish fired up the stove, Pete packed his own gear, shook off the frozen shards from their tent and stuffed it into its sack. They breakfasted on oatmeal and tea, eager to circumnavigate the southern end of the MacIntyre Range and enter the valley where the kids' tracks should have led. It was slow going for they were now in less-traveled areas where the trail was no longer maintained, the snow deep and unconsolidated. The two men traded the lead every fifteen minutes to conserve strength; there was little talk between them; recent events had torn them apart, too raw to ignore. Around noon they reached the Indian Pass trail junction and stopped to rest.

. . .

A high-pressure air mass out of Canada had taken a firm grip on the Adirondack High Peaks; cold, dry air, a cloudless sky, all the ingredients of a perfect mountain day. In single file, the Glencoe students trailed

Ramon out of the camp, following the path Garth had broken the night before. Garth picked up the rear in order to keep tabs on all of them and prevent Ramon from veering off route. Despite the tracks he had set the previous night, travel was slow. The snow was still so unconsolidated a brisk pace was impossible.

"Yo, Jack, pick up the pace. We want to get these little buggers back today, not next week," Garth called out. Ramon noted how upbeat Garth seemed. The happier the lumberjack appeared, the more worried it made Ramon.

Tracy locked into Ramon's easy pace, stepping where the man stepped. His ankle was still tender but at least it functioned. The cold had kept the swelling to a minimum. Libby followed close behind. As long as they were headed downhill, Malcolm managed to keep up, which saved him from Garth's wrath and occasional swats on his back to increase his speed.

The path Garth had broken led them gradually into a valley that intersected a lightly traveled trail near Scott Pond that was now hidden underneath unbroken snow. This was the most dangerous spot, crossing a maintained trail, which increased the odds of running into people. The group of five crossed the valley floor without encountering anyone and began to climb the backside of a peak known as Wallface.

At first, the fact they were hiking uphill did not concern Tracy. The Adirondacks are a series of ridges, sometimes they rise to tree line, sometimes just hogbacks between drainages. But as the ascent remained steady, Tracy began to fume. There was no logical reason they ought to be climbing so relentlessly. "How come we keep going up? We should be hitting the main trail by now," he said, turning to direct the question to Garth at the back of the line. "You sure you know where we're going?"

"Relax, kid," Garth said. "We got to get over this shoulder, okay? Then it's smooth sailing all the way down."

"Pretty big shoulder," Tracy muttered.

"What's that?" Garth asked sharply.

"Nothing."

They had long since reached the end of the snowshoe tracks Garth had laid down the previous night. Tracing new ground, their pace of travel slowed. Soft, virgin snow hindered their progress. The woods, so open near the valley floor, closed in again. As they climbed higher hardwood trees became fewer, evergreen more prevalent, growing closer together, hindering straight-line travel. *What is that man planning?* Ramon wondered. *The numbers aren't in his favor. Too many kids and me, a partner he don't trust.* The only thing he could come up with, especially with Garth at the rear, was that they were all going to be shot and left in the middle of nowhere. But then things got more complex.

Calling a halt, Garth fished a climbing rope from his pack and knotted an end around a carabiner that hung from his belt. He motioned to Malcolm to come over to him. Garth made two loops and fashioned a bowline. He passed the large loops over Malcolm's head and backpack and tightened it around his waist.

"What the hell is that for?" Tracy demanded. Malcolm looked bewildered.

"Just taking precautions so nobody does nothing stupid," Garth snapped. He pointed to Libby, "You next."

"So we don't run away. Is that what you mean?" Tracy snapped. Ramon threw him a warning look as if to say, *Don't press your luck.*

Garth took two steps in Tracy's direction and slapped him brutally across the face. The force knocked Tracy to the snow, where he lay stunned, eyes tearing. Garth ran about ten feet of rope through his hands and made two more loops, affixing another bowline around Libby's waist. Then he did the same with the now-compliant Tracy. Finally, he completed the maneuver by tying Ramon in at the end.

"Now we stay together and nobody gets lost again," he grunted, taking the lead.

"Guess Ramon was right," Tracy said to Malcolm. "This guy has no intention of helping us out." If there had been any doubts about Ramon's warning, those doubts were now erased.

"Wish we had a plan," Malcolm whispered.

"Read and react," Tracy said. "We outnumber him. That's all we have."

They now traveled through deep, untracked snow, which hid downed logs, roots, and rocks. The rope constantly caught in the branches of intertwined evergreen trees. Around noon, the grade eased, the trees

385

became shorter and denser, and views of surrounding peaks emerged as they approached a plateau. They had been walking since dawn in a heightened state of anxiety with no stops for food or drink and everyone was exhausted. They stumbled to keep up with Garth, the rope pulling painfully whenever they slowed. They emerged from the thick forest to a curiously unnatural open space. It had been cleared in haste a few years prior, allowing an emergency helicopter landing to rescue climbers trapped on the slabs of Wallface.

"Didn't expect this," Garth exclaimed, stopping at the far end of this clearing. "Enjoy the view, folks. While you can." Just beyond a large boulder, the mountain dropped a sheer eight hundred feet to an enormous jumble of glacial erratics in a col known as Indian Pass. The cliff was the source of the peak's name—Wallface. Scaling it attracted only a handful of expert climbers each year due to its remote location and extreme challenge. The Indian Pass canyon created its own wind and it welled up and over the summit lip.

As soon as Tracy saw the MacIntyre Range glistening in the noonday sun across the deep valley from where they now stood, he knew exactly where they were. He recognized the ridgeline and understood how far they were from any trailhead or rescue party. "This is bullshit!" he blurted. "Why are you doing this to us? We just want to go home!" His voice rose to a scream.

Garth ignored the outburst, slung his pack into the snow and motioned for Ramon to untie himself from the rope that connected him to Libby. As Tracy began to do the same, Garth stepped over to him and slapped him hard. "Not you, Jack. We can do this the easy way, or not." He dug into the top flap of his pack and pulled out his steel knife. After long weeks of waiting, Ramon could see the nearness of the final act exhilarated Garth. Malcolm and Libby stood transfixed. The lumberjack circled around them so that the kids stood between him and the cliff's edge. When they were found, as surely they would be, either this day or the next, tied together at the bottom of Wallface, no evidence would tie their bodies to a couple of escaped cons. The presence of a rope would be a puzzle to those who knew what the kids had taken into the woods but it would forever be just a minor unexplained detail in what would be a larger tragedy.

"Ramon, you gonna just let this happen? Help us, for Crissakes!" Tracy pleaded, using the man's real name.

Garth glared at Ramon and sprang at Tracy. He slammed his forearm across the boy's mouth, sending him sprawling to the snow with a spatter of blood. "Shut up, kid. I didn't ask you to get into our business." With a flick of his Smith & Wesson, Garth sliced the rope that linked himself to Malcolm. It took a few swipes to cut all the way through, while the others watched, dumbstruck. Then he spun toward Libby and grabbed her in a bear hug.

She screamed as Garth pinned her arms to her sides. She flailed helplessly as he dragged her to the precipice of the cliff.

"Ramon!" Garth spat as he struggled to control the desperate girl. "Get the fat one!"

Ramon stood immobilized, unable to help or hinder. Libby flailed and screamed, squirming in a fruitless attempt to break free. She was now close enough to the edge to feel a strong draft of air welling up from below. Twisting her head, her mouth grazed Garth's ear and she bit. Hard. Garth roared as blood spurted from his torn ear. He wrestled Libby closer to the edge, as she hung on to his ear, grinding it between her teeth. Then she vomited on him.

"Malcolm," Tracy screamed. "Grab something! If she goes, you go!" Events were moving at lightning speed but Garth's plan did not need to be explained. Once he got Libby over the edge, gravity would take Malcolm and then Tracy. Ramon recognized it as well, and in one nanosecond a small segment of his brain thanked Garth for disconnecting him from the kids. Maybe the lumberjack would let him live after all.

Tracy's scream drove Malcolm into action, just as the rope to Libby began to grow taut. He leaped for a nearby dwarf spruce and clung to it desperately. Tracy spat blood, scrambled back to his feet, and leapt toward Garth's legs. Arching his back, he lifted the ski poles he still held as high as possible and drove them deep into the man's thigh, snarling like a wounded bear.

Garth's strength was immense, but his recent bout with giardia, as well as the searing pain on the side of his head where only part of an ear remained, sapped him enough that he struggled to get Libby to the edge. Fighting to maintain his balance with Tracy hanging on to his legs the embattled giant screamed at Ramon. "Rip that kid off the tree. Now!!"

Playing the moves out in his head at millisecond speed, Ramon saw the battle was nearly lost. The strength of the deranged man was overwhelming. Ramon saw how vulnerable Tracy was clinging to Garth as the giant moved closer to the edge. The only thing preventing Garth from plunging the steel blade into the boy was Libby's struggle. As Garth bellowed in pain, he nearly dropped Libby while twisting away from Tracy. The knife fell from his hand as he tried to rip the ski pole from his leg while maintaining his grip on Libby.

Perhaps it was the sense his own life was in peril that made Ramon finally act. Perhaps his paralysis disappeared upon realizing this girl who had brought him such good news of his family was about to be thrown to her death. Perhaps watching Tracy act brought out his bravery. Whatever the reason, Ramon sprang toward Garth, raised his own ski pole and buried the shaft into Garth's back. The carbide tip pierced the lumberjack's coat and plowed into muscle already distended from exertion. Garth screamed as he hurled Libby over the edge.

They heard Libby's anguished cry as her body dropped over the precipice. Unable to counterbalance Libby's falling weight, Malcolm was ripped from the tree. With the edge of the cliff drawing close, he saw the sun glinting off Garth's blade and grabbed it as he shot by. A moment later he experienced the sickening sense of weightlessness. As the rope connected to Malcolm's falling body rapidly paid out, Tracy rolled to one side, wedged his body behind a small boulder, closed his eyes, and waited for the inevitable jerk.

With two ski poles still embedded, Garth turned to confront Ramon, who leapt sideways to avoid Garth's furious lunge. Ramon grasped his own backpack, the only movable object within reach, and swung it like a baseball bat. He caught Garth flush on the side of his face. Garth staggered, his nose exploding blood from the blow. Ramon stepped forward and swung again. Instinctively, Garth grasped for the only thing within reach, a coil of rope that still was linked to Tracy and now lay in the snow. Emitting an animal snarl, Ramon hurled himself feet first into the lumberjack, sending his body into the void. Garth uttered no sound as he flew into space, clinging to the end of his nylon lifeline. He grazed Malcolm, who was hanging upside down about ten feet below the top, and then just missed colliding with Libby's body, which lay in a gnarled clump of sturdy cripplebrush growing out of a small ledge five feet below Malcolm. He jolted to a halt as the rope became taut and his shoulder dislocated from the force of the drop. Garth gasped in pain but his grip held firm. Tracy felt an intense pull at the same instant; he now had two bodies hanging off one end of his rope, the lumberjack hanging off the other. His waist and chest were constricted near to the breaking point.

In the only good bit of fortune, the rope was slack between Libby and Malcolm, which meant Tracy did not have the weight of both kids to support. Braced behind the boulder, Tracy battled to maintain his position with Malcolm's weight pulling him one way and Garth's heft pulling the opposite way.

"Uhhhh," Tracy moaned, struggling to breathe. "Help me, Ramon. Please . . ."

Ramon grabbed the rope that led to Garth to relieve some pressure on the boy. Tracy caught his breath. "Goddammit!" Tracy cried, still in extremis, trapped by the ropes and at the total mercy of the remaining convict. "I'm stuck." When he could brace no longer, gravity would send four of them to their deaths. Ramon realized it, too. He could release his grip, turn his back, walk away from all this, and for the rest of his life try to forget this awful episode.

As they hung near the top of the wall, Malcolm and Garth could not know what was going on above them on the summit or how tenuous their safety really was. They wore no climbing harness that would have enabled them to hang comfortably, nor did they possess jumars or prussiks, devices that would have held their weight and enabled them to ascend the rope back to the summit. Malcolm had managed to get his head above his feet and was clinging to the rope to take some of the pressure off his waist. He stared at Garth, a few feet below, too shocked to be scared. Garth stared back, in agony, on his own rope. His exit strategy required that he climb, hand over hand, before the pain in his shoulder overcame him or his fingers cramped from exertion. He reached for a higher point on the rope with his good arm, momentarily relieving the pressure on his dislocated arm. There was no way to make progress without using both arms. He began to claw his way up.

Malcolm watched the giant ascend, his rope swaying only inches from Garth's. As the determined logger reached for a higher grip with his damaged arm, Malcolm reached over with his left hand, which still held the lumberjack's knife, and raked Garth's top hand. Garth screamed, releasing the rope. His body dropped three feet, then held, his good arm still gripping tight. He glanced at blood dripping from the injured fingers and swore. Malcolm did not wait for the next move. He attacked the giant's rope again and again, fraying the nylon strand by strand. Garth was running out of time to haul himself up and overcome the boy. The hatchet scar on his cheek twitched wildly.

Oblivious to the drama below, Tracy and Ramon struggled to hold onto the ropes on the summit. "Do you feel those pulls?" Ramon said, grimacing under the strain. Each time Malcolm slashed at the rope, it jerked in Ramon's hands. He feared Garth might be the only survivor left.

"We gotta find out who's still there," Tracy gasped, and called out the names of his friends.

Malcolm heard nothing. He chopped as fast as he could while Garth began to ascend again, unable to use the torn tendons in his bloodied hand and the disintegrating fibers in his shoulder. Garth reached for Malcolm's boot. The rope still held. Malcolm desperately kicked with his other boot, catching Garth flush in the face. The lumberjack absorbed the blow and surged upward, grabbing Malcolm's calf. With one last explosion of strength, Garth grabbed as high on the rope as he could. His face came up to Malcolm's waist as Malcolm slashed again at the giant's hand. It hit home, severing the tense muscles and the remaining nylon cords that held the man to the mountain. Spurting more blood, the logger dropped like a stone. Five seconds later, Garth hit the rocks at the bottom of Indian Pass.

On the summit, Ramon and Tracy felt one side of the rope go slack. A few seconds passed before they heard snapping branches and a distant thud on the valley floor.

"Holy shit!!" Malcolm screamed. "I got him!! I got him! Crissakes, don't let me go!!"

"Hijole!" Ramon gasped. Tracy began to shake.

"Malcolm! Y'okay?" shouted Tracy.

"Son of a bitch took a header. Feel it?" he yelled.

"Sure did," Tracy called.

"Get me the hell out of here! This fucking thing is squeezing me to death."

"Where's Libby?" Tracy held his breath for the answer.

"Below me," he called. "On a ledge. She's not moving."

"Ramon, step in and hold the rope," Tracy pleaded. Relieved of Garth's weight, Ramon wedged himself between Tracy and the boulder and took the still-taut rope that held Libby and Malcolm against his back, bracing his feet. Tracy wriggled out of the loops that held him, reeled in the end of the rope that had held Garth and tied it off expertly to the sturdiest tree within reach. "Okay, you're good," Tracy said, signaling to Ramon it was safe to step away. The strain of Malcolm's body now shifted to the tree. Ramon and Tracy scrambled to the edge.

There was no preparation for the shock of seeing Malcolm dangling, with Libby's inert body slumped on a tiny ledge just below. One shift of Libby's weight could send her hurtling off the ledge. Tracy needed help but that was hours away at best. His only hope was the young man beside him.

"Would you two stop staring at me and do something?" Malcolm pleaded. "I don't like heights, if you remember, Tracy."

Ramon turned to Tracy. "How can I help?"

"I have no idea," Tracy said. "If Malcolm wasn't dangling in midair and could walk his way back up while we pulled, yeah, maybe. But then we also have Libby's weight to worry about and she shouldn't be moved if we don't know what's wrong with her."

"Hang on, Mal, I'm trying to figure this out," Tracy called.

Because the top of the cliff jutted out into space a few feet, Malcolm was dangling, unable to place his feet against the cliff wall. Had there been no overhang, Malcolm might have managed to climb back up the cliff wall, relieving some of the weight from his waist and arms. But that was not the case, and he was not strong enough to haul his entire body weight up the ten feet or so that separated him from the summit plateau.

"Libby will get hypothermic pretty quick unless we can warm her," Tracy said quietly to Ramon. "And Mal can't hang there forever with no harness." His mind was going a million miles a minute, trying to shake off the shock of it all, and trying to sort out what was possible and what was critical. Ramon had no frame of reference to even offer a suggestion. He just waited to be told what to do.

Tracy leaned out over the edge, searching for solutions. Libby lay sprawled on a ledge below him about ten feet and to his right. Malcolm dangled immediately below him. Off to his left, about six feet away, but at the same level, was another small ledge, about two feet wide. A plan began to form in Tracy's head.

"Okay, here's the thing," Tracy said to Ramon after what seemed an eternity. "I can't send *you* down there," he said, pointing to the ledge where Libby lay. "I need *you* to get help. I realize what that means about your plans to get home, but I hope you see that's the only way to keep that girl alive. I've got to figure out how to rappel down to her. I don't know how the hell to get Malcolm back up without pulling her off that ledge. But, maybe, if I can get Mal over to that other ledge," he said, pointing to the one he had just spotted to his left, "we can make them both secure until help arrives. Let's see if your buddy had some stuff in his pack I could use."

"He wasn't my buddy. But we'll look," Ramon said. He had spent two months trying to avoid everyone and now his job was to find . . . anyone.

Tracy looked around as if reinforcements might magically appear. Assistance was miles away but with the MacIntyre Range clearly recognizable across the valley, Tracy finally had his bearings. "Now that I know where we are, I think I can get you back to a trail. I just can't figure out how the hell we ended up here," Tracy shook his head in disgust. He realized that he could not get either Malcolm or Libby on solid ground by himself, or even with Ramon hauling as well. There was just too much dead weight and Libby should not be moved until it was clear whether she had internal injuries. Libby needed immediate attention, but he also worried how long Malcolm could safely hang on. Those were a boatload of *Ifs*. He had to steady himself, breathe, and think these options through.

If Malcolm was right that she was just unconscious, then the biggest threat to her was hypothermia. She needed to be kept warm. It had been almost two days since they had had much to eat or drink. *If* Ramon could not bring help, there was only one way in which any of them could live—Tracy would have to leave the other two on the mountain. *If* he could figure out how to rappel down to Libby, that would be a one-way trip, and he would be sealing his own fate as well if Ramon did not come through. And could he somehow get Malcolm over to that small ledge? Lastly, he worried that the taste of freedom might overwhelm Ramon, or that he would get lost. Was it even realistic to think Ramon could make his way down Wallface by himself before nightfall? The odds of success were diminishing with every passing moment.

"Did you guys have a map?"

Ramon shrugged.

The prospect of picking through Garth's belongings repulsed Tracy. But there might be items that would keep them alive so he tipped the pack on end and dumped its contents on the snow. Out tumbled smelly clothes, cooking gear, a thermos bottle, a few granola bars and cans of sardines, another knife, revolver, some ammunition, a couple of wrinkled instant heat packets and another rope. Ramon poked at the heap with the toe of his boot as if it were contaminated.

"Maybe the side pockets," Tracy said. Next to a near-empty tin of chewing tobacco and half a dozen plastic dispensers of nylon floss he finally extracted a small folded map. He fingered it as if a priceless amulet. "This sure would have come in handy a couple of days ago." He removed the compass from around his neck and held it tight against his chest. He pointed it toward the glistening summit of Algonquin to get a bearing, then twisted the compass dial so that the freewheeling needle that always points toward magnetic north sat within a corresponding painted arrow on the compass housing.

"You need that to tell you which way is down?" Ramon asked.

"If that's all it took, you could have gotten out of here yourself weeks ago, right?" Tracy challenged.

"I already tried that once," Ramon said, nodding weakly. "It didn't turn out so good."

"I know where we are," Tracy continued. "But I need to teach you how to use it." He handed the compass to Ramon, saying, "To be sure you're heading the right way, every now and then hold the compass to your chest like I did. Twist your body until the red magnetic needle is lined up inside this other arrow on the dial . . . some call it a housing arrow. The red's in the shed. Remember it that way. Then walk straight ahead. Obviously, if you get to a cliff you need to skirt around it, but once you do, walk back about the same number of steps. That'll get you back on your original line. If you do it like I say, you'll be sure to cross the trail at the bottom. Here, let me show you on the map. He spread it on the snow and turned it slowly until Algonquin lay in the proper direction from where they now stood. With his finger, he showed Ramon where they were and traced the general route Ramon would follow. The actual distance was only about a mile from the top of Wallface to the intersection with the Indian Pass trail, but no one could easily walk that terrain in a straight line.

Ramon looked anxious. "How long you figure it'll take?"

"I have no idea. Depends how fast you go. And how cliffy it is." Tracy looked at his watch. It was a little past one. Three hours of daylight left. They would not easily weather another night out. "There'll be lots of people looking for us but if you don't find somebody before dark, we may not survive. You're all we've got, man. You gotta move."

"Hey . . . Where are you guys?" Malcolm called. "This rope is killing me. I gotta do something different here."

Tracy walked back to the edge and tried to act calm. "Just hanging out?"

"Still the clown," Malcolm muttered. "Is that all you got? I just killed somebody, man. And I don't want to end up where he went."

"Tryin'," Tracy called. "I got to get Ramon out of here. I'm coming down to help."

"Get on with it."

Tracy turned back to Ramon, and went over the process again, explaining how he needed to follow the compass in a northeasterly direction, skirting the cliffs, then descending until he finally met the Indian Pass Trail. "When you reach the bottom of the valley which runs north-south, hang a left on the trail, which I hope to God you will see. It'll run you into Heart Lake and you're bound to meet somebody." The two hugged awkwardly and Ramon turned to go. After several steps, he stopped to look back. "Take care of that girl," Ramon pleaded.

The wind whistled gently on the summit of Wallface. Except for the disturbed, bloodstained snow, and the drama on the cliff below him, it was hard to believe there had just been such turmoil. Worrying that with every passing minute Libby was losing her battle, Tracy turned his attention to the extra rope, which he secured to a tree. He unstrapped his sleeping bag from the bottom of his pack and slung the drawstring around his neck. He stuck Garth's granola bars and heat packets into a parka pocket, and a water bottle and the thermos into the sleeping bag stuff sack. He saw his hands were shaking and tried to settle down. He took several deep breaths, wrapped the rope around his back and over one shoulder and backed his way off the summit. The exposure of dangling eight hundred feet above the ground barely registered as he descended to a point level with Malcolm, who spun slowly in the breeze.

"Ramon's gone?" Malcolm asked.

"Yup. We gotta trust he'll do the right thing. I've got an idea how to get you over to that ledge," he said, pointing to the thin outcropping on the cliff wall. But take this first," Tracy advised. He retrieved the water bottle and a granola bar and handed them over. "I'm going to give you a push. You will swing out a bit, then come back at me. We push against each other again. Maybe a third time. The pendulum action should swing you over to the wall. Try to grab that ledge. Hopefully, the swing will push me over to Libby at the same time. I've got to get her warm," he said. "You'll be okay, Mal. That rope's not going to break."

"Okay. I ain't got any better ideas. But if you push me, I'm probably going to knock Libby right off that ledge."

"Jeez, you're right," Tracy said, realizing his two companions remained tethered to each other. "Good call. Slice the rope," he said, noting Malcolm still held Garth's knife, "and I'll tie her to me."

Malcolm waited until Tracy had grasped the rope and began sawing away at it. When it came free, Tracy quickly threaded it through his own rope and began the pendulum process Pete had taught him on the crags behind Glencoe. As both boys were suspended with no solid purchase, the initial push did not move them much. But as Tracy had predicted, with each successive collision, the boys moved farther apart, until Malcolm was able to grab the ledge, crawl onto it, and loosen the rope. Simultaneously, Tracy slowly swung the rest of the way to Libby's ledge. As he carefully steadied himself next to her, he looked across to Malcolm. "You did awesome, man," he said. "I wish I could have seen how you made that monster fly." Malcolm smiled, saluting Tracy with the granola bar.

Tracy secured himself to a scraggly spruce growing out of a thin crack on the narrow ledge he now shared with Libby. It was flimsy and probably wouldn't have held if he slipped but it was all that protected them from a free fall to the rocks below. So intent had he been on getting Malcolm to his perch and reaching Libby, he had allowed himself no thought to their precarious position. It was more than precarious; it was grave. Odds were low, Tracy understood, that they would ever be found; at least not until some intrepid rock climber managed to reach this height, months from now at the earliest. He doubted this forsaken place was on the list of spots the rescuers were now searching; it was so far removed from normal routes off Algonquin they might as well have been on Mars. All their hopes were pinned on a stranger they'd just met, someone who would have to sacrifice his own freedom to report where they could be found. He felt overwhelmingly sad.

Libby stirred, which brought Tracy back to reality for the moment. He removed the sleeping bag from its stuff sack, being careful to not drop the water bottle and thermos from the stuff sack, and fluffed it up. So as not to dislodge her, he tucked it beneath her head and over her body. It occurred to him that he had often dreamed of touching her face, her body. But this was not how he had imagined it. It was clinical now, urgent. Her face was caked with blood from the small gash in her cheek. She still wore her wool hat.

"Libby . . . can you hear me?" he asked gently. "It's Tracy. I'm going to take care of you." Libby opened her eyes and tried to lift her head.

"Do you know who I am?"

"Yes," she whispered. "My head hurts. Am I going to die?"

"No way," he encouraged. If she believed it, she stood a better chance. Shock was a huge concern. "Can you wiggle your toes?"

"I'm not sure. They're numb."

"Fingers?" He watched her mittened hands move slightly.

"I'm so cold."

Tracy decided to take a chance. If her neck was broken, she should not have been able to move her extremities. If he followed what he had been taught, he should not move her until help arrived and she could be properly stabilized. But if he didn't warm her now, she might not last long enough to be helped. Her trembling meant her body had not yet given up and was still trying to warm itself.

"They hurt . . . my toes . . . I'm so cold . . ."

He dug two chemical heat packets from his pocket, twisted them to blend the segregated liquids and slipped them underneath her parka near her belly. He felt his own body stirring as he did so, and fought with himself not to let his fingers linger. He wondered what she was feeling, if his almost caress meant anything to her.

"I'm going to give you something hot to drink," he said gently. "But don't try to move, okay?" Tracy pulled the thermos from the stuff sack and poured out a half cup of steaming cocoa, the one thing Garth had given them time to prepare that morning. He longed to sip it but resisted. The lumberjack's unwitting last gift of hospitality, he thought grimly. Tracy gently supported Libby's head in his lap so she could take a sip, while taking care not to cause a sudden jerk that might cause both of them to slide off the ledge. She drank feverishly, spilling half the contents.

"Oh! I'm sorry. I'm such a klutz! To think my parents actually paid for me to do this," Libby whispered. Tracy felt the cocoa dampness on his pants and knew it would soon freeze. He drank the remaining drops and poured her a second cup, which she gratefully accepted. Returning the thermos to his parka, he shyly wrapped his arms around her to steady her. As the heat packs warmed her, Libby began to cry. Tracy removed a glove and wiped the tears from her cheeks with his bare hand. She grasped it and held it against her chest.

"Don't let me fall," she pleaded.

Tracy could hardly breathe and did not move a muscle. "You're safe with me," he whispered, desperately hoping that was the truth.

39

Closing In

AT THE BASE OF WALLFACE, A GROUP OF SEVEN STUDENTS AND TWO outdoor education leaders on a wilderness leadership outing from Paul Smith's College had stopped for lunch. One of the students with a keen interest in ornithology scanned the towering wall with binoculars, searching for eagles. It was not a bird that caused him to gasp, but rather something distinctly larger that crossed his field of vision. Then they all heard the snapping of branches.

"Was that gunshot?" a student asked.

"Something just fell off the cliff," shouted the young man with the binoculars. "It flashed right by my eyes." Leaving their lunch, the group scrambled up through a steep boulder and scree field to the base of the cliffs. The going became tougher as the snow deepened and the angle increased. They fanned out to cover more territory.

One of the instructors was the first to come upon the site where Garth had landed. Though well versed in CPR and first aid, one look at the battered body made him gag. Averting his eyes from the mutilated face and the bloodied hands, Brooks checked the man's pulse and peered up at the rock face. No evidence of a climbing partner, nor any shouts for help.

"Makes no sense," the instructor remarked as his co-leader joined him. "No rope. No harness. No pack. No scream. Half an ear. Bizarre. This man is not equipped for ice climbing. I've never heard of anyone trying to solo Wallface in winter, especially in army camouflage. It's like he fell out of the sky."

"What a mess," his colleague agreed. "Cover him with a tarp and note the spot so the rangers can collect him later." The Paul Smith's group retreated from the accident site and continued north on the Indian Pass trail. Before long, they encountered two men sitting on boulders by the side of the trail, drinking tea.

"Afternoon," the older man said with a distinct Scottish accent. "Are you one of the DEC rescue teams?"

"'Fraid not. And it's too late for a rescue," said one of the instructors. "Time for a recovery."

Pete's heart sank. "You found them?"

The instructor looked confused. "Them? We found one guy who peeled off Wallface while we were having lunch. There's not much to rescue."

"On Wallface?" Pete asked, puzzled. "How old would you say?" He dug into his pack and extracted a radio, handing it to Hamish.

"Late twenties maybe," Brooks said. "Rough looking. Huge. Scraggly beard. Missing most of one ear. Didn't look like a rock climber. No equipment, no rope around his waist, no harness. Weird."

The radio crackled and Ranger Ecklestone's voice came through.

"Jeff, this is Hamish."

"What have you got?"

"Pete and I are at the old Lake Colden-Indian Pass trail junction and we've met up with some folks from . . ." He looked at the newcomer for help.

"Paul Smith's Outing Club," the instructor supplied.

" . . . from Paul Smith's, Jeff," Hamish continued. "They're not one of yours, I take it. They just came down from the Pass where they found a climber who had just fallen off Wallface."

"Jesus. What in heaven's name is going on out there?" Ecklestone exclaimed.

Hamish handed the radio to the instructor.

"Hello, sir. This is Ken Brooks. I'm an outdoor ed coordinator."

"Bottom line it for me, Ken," the ranger said impatiently. With one difficult rescue attempt and now a seemingly unrelated climbing death, resources were becoming painfully thin.

"One of my students caught the fall in his binoculars. Whoever he is, there's not much left of him. Really odd, sir. He had no climbing gear, no harness. He lost most of his face in the fall. Hands pretty sliced up as well. As far as we could tell, he was alone. If you follow the tracks we made in the snow from Summit Rock at Indian Pass you'll find him. We put a blue tarp over him."

There was a frustrated sigh. "I'll scare up a snowmobile and a sled to litter him out. Let me have Hamish, please." Brooks handed the radio back.

"You're earning your money today, Jeff," said Hamish. "I guess you've heard nothing from any of the other teams."

"Not yet. I figure you and Pete should keep walking down the Indian Pass trail toward Rocky Falls. We've got some search lines coming down Algonquin on your side. Here's hoping we get this done today."

"Aye. Better be so."

The college group headed off while Hamish waited for Pete to pack the stove they had used to brew tea. The two men set out together, but before long Hamish began to lag behind. Pete glanced back from time to time. His mind was in turmoil. Now and again, he would forget that he had just been fired, that he should hate the man he had revered for five years. To be thrown together like this, with a common goal, was excruciating. Pete felt increasingly certain that Hamish's heart wasn't in this decision to can him. He would never have shared the story of Zero Gully if he wanted to distance himself. It just didn't make sense. Pete wasn't sure if Hamish's inability to keep up with him on the trail was guilt, passive aggressiveness, or just plain fatigue.

After hearing the epic of Andy Boarder and Zero Gully lots of things about the Scotsman began to add up. Pete had often wondered what caused Hamish's Jekyll-and-Hyde behavior, sometimes rigid to a fault, sometimes patient beyond reason. The painkillers explained some of it. Mostly, it seemed that Hamish MacLean had never reconciled his decision to leave his climbing partner on that icy ledge. Pete felt simultaneously sorry for his old friend and furious with him. For her part, Rambler seemed to pick up on the tension, trotting back and forth between the two men as they traveled along the snow-packed trail from Indian Pass.

The dog suddenly ran ahead, stopped after thirty yards, sniffed, and barked at her two companions. As Pete reached her, he saw the distinct line of tracks perpendicular to their trail. Hamish joined him a minute later.

"Someone bushwhacked right across the trail. More than one, I'd say," Hamish exclaimed. "Nice work, Rambler," he said, scratching her behind one ear.

"Yeah. Multiple snowshoes. But why cross the brook? If it's them, this trail is what they should have been shooting for," Pete said. Multiple depressions in the snow led over a jumble of ice and rock in the now-frozen brook to dense woods on the opposite side.

"Most likely they came through here in the dark, Pete. They had no map, right? The trail is pretty obscure. At night they could easily have missed it."

"Look at how many basket holes there are," Pete remarked, recalling they had all brought ski poles to help with balance. "One person didn't make all those holes. What do you think, Rambler?" The dog barked and made a move to cross the brook, hesitating to see if the men agreed with her judgment.

Hamish gazed across the frozen brook at the tracks that led farther from any help. Time was running out. "I can't sit here and stare at these tracks. If we want to find those children alive, we've got to take a chance. Let's follow these tracks as far as we can while there's light. The kids will need to be warmed and fed if we can find them and we'll need it ourselves if we dead-end on this. Let's radio Jeff and tell him what our plans are."

40

Lost and Found

RAMON FOUND IT EASY FOLLOWING THE SNOWSHOE TRACKS THAT HAD led them to the top of Wallface, but before long the compass bearing led away from that route and into deep, untrammeled snow. He hesitated, looking at the tracks as if they were old friends. Panic welled up and he debated turning around. Better to be captured with the kids up there, than wander around, lost in the woods, until he collapsed. He recalled vividly his ill-fated first attempt to flee that ended in near-frozen legs. He crouched down, took a deep breath and tried to sort it out. He'd come too far now and, dammit, he'd saved lives up there. If he hadn't acted, they'd all be dead, and Garth would be on his way to Canada. That was a fact, and it gave him courage, even if it turned out he would be the only one who knew the truth. Ramon checked the compass again, picked out a line in the woods to match the arrow jiggling in its housing and plunged into virgin snow.

· · ·

Hamish and Pete snowshoed steadily through open birch woods, pausing every few minutes to blow on a whistle and listen for a response. Rambler's age had caught up to her. She had not been on such a strenuous hike in a number of years and, though the muscle memory was there, her stamina was lagging. Normally she would gallop ahead of the group, choosing the route, exploring the territory, looking for critters, then checking back with everyone. Back and forth, hour after hour, in her own slice of heaven. But that was then. She seemed to understand that was no longer possible.

Rambler was not the only one feeling her age. Thanks to the lack of wind and new snowfall, the Scotsman was able to follow the meandering tracks but struggled to maintain a decent pace. Father Time and the demands of a desk job were betraying the once-indomitable engine he'd always taken for granted. Once, he glided up rock and snow, leaving climbers half his age shaking their heads in wonder at a man who displayed that enviable combination of power and stamina. When he wasn't participating in an Alaskan or Patagonian expedition, he was training for one. It kept him at an exquisite level of physical fitness where his strength felt limitless and gravity barely contained him. As the stresses of guiding a school had stolen the hours he had systematically reserved for training, the almost superhuman fitness he had always taken for granted began to erode. They were quite a pair, he and Rambler. Neither one had any business being here, but events had intervened. Now both needed to reach down for that last bit of energy. In the flat light of late afternoon, Hamish stopped for a drink and to massage his cramping legs.

"Maybe you should go on ahead. I'm sure you could make better time."

"That's okay, Hamish. I'd just as soon we stay together."

Hamish figured Pete was hanging back to make sure he could be of help in case the old fart who fired him ran into trouble himself, but he was silently grateful.

Rambler looked up and barked. Hamish followed the dog's gaze but there was nothing to see. Suddenly, the fleeting movement of color against the snow-white background caught his attention. A lone hiker approached and Hamish's heart sank . . . it was not a familiar face. Rambler growled; a sound that rarely left her throat. She trotted up to the man, circled him warily while sniffing the complex mix of odors. Most of the smells were alien, distasteful, but interesting. She had never met coy-wolves but their dried saliva had left a mark that intoxicated her. And she also took note of a familiar aroma. She may not have known every student's name, but she knew their smell.

"Good day. I'm surprised to see someone out this way. Have you run into any lost youngsters?" Hamish asked directly.

"Yes, sir," Ramon stammered. Rambler circled him warily, prompting nervous looks from the young man.

"You have!" Hamish's eyes widened. "Where?"

"Up there," Ramon said, pointing vaguely. "A boy sent me to get help."

"For God's sake, man, what happened?" Pete demanded.

Ramon hesitated. "There was an accident. The girl . . . she's on a ledge and her friend, Tracy, I hope, is with her. The other one . . ."

"Malcolm?" Hamish asked impatiently, fearful there was bad news to come.

"Yes, that's his name, I think. He's hanging on a rope near the girl."

Hamish was bewildered. There were thousands of details he needed to know, but daylight was waning. They needed to get to them as quickly as possible. There had been no radio communication since their connection with Ecklestone at Indian Pass. Other S&R teams on the ground were in other areas.

"Were you up Wallface?" Pete asked.

"I guess so. Tracy called it that."

The story was thin and made little sense to Hamish. The young man looked nervous, and not just because Rambler was sizing him up. He smelled as if he'd been out in the woods for a long time. Nevertheless, the kids were alive. That news crowded out all else.

"Follow our tracks down to the Indian Pass trail," Hamish instructed. "I'm sure you'll run into a rescue party somewhere along the way. Let 'em know we're trying to get to the kids 'afore night. Tell 'em you met Hamish and Pete."

"Yes, sir."

"What did you say your name was?"

Pause. Not a hard question, Hamish thought. Why did he appear to be mulling over how to answer?

"Ramon . . . Ortiz." The name did not register at all with Hamish.

"Okay, Ramon. Thanks so much for the information. Great to hear they are alive. Stay safe getting out," Hamish said. The three men shook hands and parted.

"Name ring any bells?" Pete asked when they were again alone.

"Not really. You?"

"A little. Can't place it, though," Pete said. He excitedly relayed the information by radio to Ecklestone at the Loj, failing, however, to refer to Ramon by name. Ecklestone advised them he hoped a refueled helicopter could be at the Wallface landing zone within the hour. Perhaps they'd all arrive at the same time.

The news Ramon conveyed overshadowed Pete and Hamish's mutual discomfort with each other. At least for a time, the two were able to set aside their rift and focus on following Ramon's tracks up to Wallface as quickly as possible.

Ramon pocketed the compass, no longer needed, and followed the well-defined path into the valley. As soon as Hamish and Pete dropped from sight Ramon stopped and took in the silence. For the first time since he had been arrested, he was now truly alone, in control of his own destiny. Though he had resolved to do as Tracy asked, he took a moment to think it through one more time. If he followed the advice he's just been given, the full story would emerge and he would be back in prison that night. If he avoided talking to anyone he met along the way there was still a chance he could be free. After two months of doing everything in his power to avoid being seen, he could probably walk past every search party as if invisible. As scary as the scene on top had been for him, they didn't need his help now. Those two men he'd just left seemed to know what to do. He was off the hook.

There are not many forks in the road one encounters that can truly define a life's path, but Ramon realized he was now at one of them. What path to take? He had given someone his name and he had to assume it had been transmitted to the authorities. He believed the kids to whom he felt such a bond would be okay now. There was a chance he could still evade capture, but that window was closing fast, and his unfamiliarity with the trails made that option unlikely. Maybe the answer was to get to the regular trail the older man had mentioned, but stay off it until dark. Then he could walk out safely. He made his choice, and walked on.

. . .

Hamish emptied one water bottle, hoping the rehydration would reduce the cramping in his legs, and hiked faster. He tried to push Zero Gully out of his mind. If this didn't work out, his tenure at Glencoe was finished. Even worse, he would have three more souls on his conscience for the rest of his life. He didn't think he could handle the quantity of drugs it would take to keep those ghosts at bay. Following Ramon's meandering path, he and Pete continued upward through the dwindling light, stopping only to affix their headlamps and swallow energy bars. Rambler was struggling to keep up. She was game and trusted her companions unconditionally but the route was taking its toll.

Just past six they reached the summit. Silver moonlight bathed the open area where chaos had reigned a few hours earlier. Hamish noted two ropes leading to the edge, several upturned packs, a jumble of gear in the snow. He knew the kids had carried no ropes. Cautiously, he and Pete strode to the edge, peered over, scanning the cliffside beneath them. Hamish whistled.

Twenty feet below Tracy heard the noise and saw the LED light amid the stars. "Ho. Anyone down there?" the Scotsman's familiar brogue rang out.

"Hamish!! God, it's good to hear your voice," Tracy called. "Libby's with me but she's hurt. Mal is on another ledge right under you somewhere."

"Hey, Hamish. Can you get us outta here?" Malcolm called out weakly.

The scene was all too familiar—a ledge, an injured climber clinging to life on a frigid winter's night. Hamish shuddered. *This one will not slip away,* he promised himself. "Copter should be here 'afore long," he called. "We'll get you off 'a there soon as we can. Pete's here as well."

"Sorry, Pete. Sorry we screwed up," Tracy called. "How did you find us?"

"Ran into a fellow on his way down who said he'd been with you," Pete said. "He didn't say much but enough to confirm we were on your tail."

"I could use a warm drink," Malcolm moaned, a disembodied voice in the dark.

"You'll get all ye need, lad. Keep those limbs moving," Hamish called.

While he did not feel they should try to get the students off the cliff before the professionals arrived, Hamish knew they could provide psychological sustenance while they awaited help. A quick radio call delivered the news that a helicopter would be there in minutes to attempt a rare night landing. It seemed Libby was stable and, as Malcolm responded lucidly to questions, it appeared he was dealing with shock in a reasonable way. They just had to hang in there, Hamish kept reminding them. The ledges were secure, the ropes strong. By keeping them talking and reassuring them, he was trying to defuse their panic. Rambler crawled on her belly to the edge, curious to see what all the fuss was about. When she heard Malcolm and Tracy's familiar voices she woofed.

"Is that Rambler?" Tracy asked. Just hearing her, a symbol of life as normal, lifted his spirits.

"Yes. She insisted," Hamish chuckled. "So, tell me, why in heaven's name did the three of you decide dropping off Wallface was the best way home? Was this your idea, Tracy?" Hamish asked, trying to lighten the moment and reduce the likelihood of shock.

"Not our plan, Hamish. Remember back in October when you wouldn't let us go night-walking because of that prison break?"

The dots quickly connected for the Scotsman. "You cannae mean . . ."

"Yup. Same guys," Tracy said.

"That explains a lot," Pete exclaimed, recalling Ramon's camouflage clothing earlier that afternoon, on the heels of the Paul Smith's report of a dead body similarly clad.

"The guy you ran into on your way up here—Ramon—he saved our lives," Tracy said. "I wouldn't be here talking to you if not for him. None of us would."

"That may be true. But I've got to call it in," Pete said.

"They need to know what they're dealing with here," Hamish said in a low voice to Pete who was digging the radio out of his pack.

During the next ninety minutes Hamish and Pete were again witness to the professional artistry of a DEC-organized rescue. After some intricate logistics of rappelling and winching, the three Glencoe students were soon returned to the summit. Libby was placed on a Stokes litter and lifted up into the belly of the chopper. Aside from bruised stomach muscles from prolonged hanging on the rope, and dehydration, Malcolm was in remarkably good shape. As the helicopter lifted off in the darkness, Hamish fired up a stove and set a pot of water to boil. He, Pete, and Tracy would have to wait for the next shuttle, for the copter's weight limit had been reached.

"Tracy, maybe this should wait until we get back and get a chance to debrief, but this has been killing me ever since I went back to the summit and you weren't there. For goodness sake, why didn't you stay on the summit of Algonquin?" Pete implored. "This whole thing didn't have to happen."

Hamish had been thinking the same thing, now that Libby and Malcolm were on their way, and in good hands. Tracy hung his head, struggling to summon a response.

"I know. Stay put if you're in trouble. We had the exact conversation right after I hurt my ankle. I'm trying not to be defensive now but I had to weigh not moving with the fact Mal and Libby were scared shitless. Excuse my language. They were freezing and wanted to get out of the wind as fast as possible. It was disorienting in the whiteout and they were pleading with me to get off the top. I tried like heck to figure out which way you'd gone. They were so panicky. It was a split-second choice. I'm sorry. By the time we were at tree line we would have missed you even if we tried to go back up. And we'd be right back where we started, not knowing which way was right until the storm lifted."

No one noticed Rambler had left, crawling toward nearby bushes to lie down out of the wind. Hamish and Pete interrogated Tracy further about his decisions on the way down and how he had missed the Indian Pass trail crossing. It was difficult for Tracy to handle the criticism from the two men responsible for his expertise in the wilderness. But when he explained his actions to pendulum Malcolm over to the ledge to relieve the strain on his torso and to keep Libby warm and secure on the ledge, the critique from his mentors dissolved.

"Where's the pup?" Hamish asked after concluding Tracy's briefing.

"There's her tracks," Tracy replied, scanning the snow with his headlamp. Distinct paw prints led to a stand of cripplebrush twenty feet away. Tracy walked over, crouched low, training his light beneath the scrub spruce. Curled up, Rambler lay motionless, cold to the touch. Alarmed, Tracy shouted for Hamish to join him and, together, they gently pulled the lifeless dog out of the bushes.

"Sweet Jesus," Hamish gasped. He stroked Rambler's head, rubbed her chest, trying to will her spirit back. Pete knelt, put his hands under Tracy's armpits and lifted him away.

"Let Hamish . . . have a moment," Pete choked.

Libby and Malcolm were whisked into Saranac Lake, touching down at the Adirondack Medical Center landing pad. Quickly dispatching its two patients on the healthcare tarmac, the aircraft lifted off for a second ride back to Wallface. But when they returned, the scene was not as they had left it. The two men and their young companion seemed oblivious to the strong beam of light that focused down on the snowy summit clearing. Their attention was completely absorbed by the lifeless body of a border collie golden retriever whose heart had finally given out. Hamish cradled her in his arms, his head buried in Rambler's furry neck. Pete held Tracy, whose tears came in torrents.

Ramon was less than a mile out from the trailhead at Heart Lake when he heard the sound of the K-9s. When the contingent of state troopers appeared, he made no attempt to evade them, calmly accepting the manacles on his wrists.

"Heard your partner took quite a header," one smirked.

"He got what he deserved."

"Is that a fact? You think you're a hero for saving those kids? You were a damn fool to break out when you did. Now you may have Murder One on your head."

"Libby? Is she okay?" Ramon asked, alarmed that things had gone awry after his departure.

"I bet you're praying for her," the officer sneered. "Don't have any news, but if she kicks, you'll get the maximum, buddy."

"I didn't hurt her, man. I need to know if she's going to make it."

"Don't hold your breath."

The posse chaperoning Ramon out to the trailhead treated him roughly. Time and again he was smacked on the back, usually at a precipitous spot on the trail already difficult to negotiate in the dark. Time and again he sprawled headfirst. With arms handcuffed in front of him and the weight of his pack assisting gravity, the falls left his cheeks and nose broken and bloodied. Despite the misery of that final mile out to the parking lot, he took it all in silence.

PART III

A step backward, after making a wrong turn, is a step in the right direction.

—KURT VONNEGUT

41

Picking Up the Pieces

It was almost too much for Bonnie to handle. When Hamish called from the hospital to tell her the news of the students she was elated. Then, shattered. Rambler may have been more Hamish's dog but she had been nearly as important to the family as a child would have been. Bonnie wept for the sweet puppy, who had grown into a profoundly vital member of the Glencoe School fabric over her twelve years of life. Hamish worried how she would deal with this loss, whether she would withdraw even farther from him, adding to the old burden he had been carrying for years. Rambler's unconditional love and allegiance to both of them had helped sustain whatever glue remained in their marriage, her presence an unshakable bond that put into context the petty irritants two people sharing a life inevitably confront over time.

"Hamish, don't worry about me," she sniffled. "Let me get a tissue. I'll fill a thermos with hot coffee and meet you as soon as I can. Oh, that poor dog. At least she went doing what she loved best, with the person she loved doing it with."

That was Bonnie. Selfless Bonnie. Always thinking of others. She deserved more than he had to give.

Just past ten a sleek gray limousine carrying Libby's parents rolled into the hospital parking lot. They were furious, looking to vent that anger as vigorously as possible. On their way up from New York City, Adam and Shelley Goldman had first stopped at Glencoe and found a light burning in the headmaster's outer office. Cathy Swenson was dozing on a couch in the reception area, curled up under a down comforter, the phone within arm's reach. Adam stormed in, his wife hovering behind him.

"Where is he?" Adam demanded, startling Hamish's secretary.

"Excuse me?" Cathy said, rubbing her face to wake up. "Do I know you?"

"You ought to. I'm Adam Goldman. I've got a daughter lost in the woods somewhere! Or have you better things to think about?"

"Sorry, Mr. Goldman, I don't think we've met. My name is Cathy Swenson."

"Where is MacLean?" Adam asked imperiously.

"He's been in the woods since early yesterday, Mr. Goldman," Cathy answered, stifling a yawn and trying to maintain her civility. "And I have some good news for you. They've been found and were evacuated to the local hospital in Saranac Lake."

"Oh?" Adam was taken aback.

"Yes. Libby's at the Adirondack Medical Center. Would you like directions?"

"I'll find it," Adam grumbled, turned on his heel and stomped out.

"Bastard," she muttered under her breath.

At the nurse's station the Goldmans learned that Libby had suffered several lacerations to her face, body bruises, early-stage hypothermia, and frost nip on her cheeks and ears. Across the waiting room, as yet unseen and steeling himself for the onslaught he knew was coming, Hamish gave his wife's hand a strong squeeze when the Goldmans stormed in. He waited until Adam had finished grilling the nurse, stood, and approached both parents.

"Sorry to see you under such circumstances, but I'm glad you made the trip," Hamish said, offering Adam Goldman his hand.

"Excuse me, ma'am," Adam said, turning away from the nurse to confront the Scotsman, letting the extended hand remain unshaken. "Let me cut to the chase, MacLean. I've rarely encountered such professional incompetence as you people have demonstrated," he barked. "If I have my way, no child will ever have to suffer the indignities Libby has. The damages we'll seek will make your head spin." Hamish absorbed his words without flinching, turning to look at Shelley, to gauge the reaction from a mother. She looked decidedly uncomfortable as she used her husband as a human shield.

"Now might be a fine time to look into your daughter's . . . *indignities*," Hamish said, directing his words toward Shelley. "Perhaps your husband could check his anger at the door and ask Libby how she's doing and what you can possibly do to make her life a bit more comfortable. If she were *my* daughter, and I'd be proud to have a daughter like her, Mrs. Goldman, that's what my priority would be." Then, turning to Adam, Hamish finished, "I'm too tired to worry about your legal threats tonight, sir."

Libby was weak but conscious when her parents opened the door to her room. She smiled wanly at the familiar faces from home.

"You got here so fast!" she said, struggling to a sitting position. She grimaced in pain and slid back down again. Her father hesitantly pulled a chair beside her bed, reached for her hand and kissed her on the forehead. Shelley walked to the other side of the bed and took her other hand. Her lip trembled as she struggled to hold back tears.

"I can't believe these people could be so irresponsible," Adam countered.

"Don't be dramatic, I'm okay, really," Libby lied. "I'm just tired. And sore." She glanced up at the IV drip that was restoring her electrolytes, making her feel better by the minute. "I'm sorry you had to come all this way to see me like this. Have you guys been in Lake Placid the whole time we were lost?"

"Uh . . . no, dear. We just arrived," Adam admitted.

Libby looked puzzled. "I think we were lost for two days, or was it three? I forget already."

"We came as quickly as we could," her mother added.

"Could I have some water, Mom? I'm so dry." Shelley rushed to fill a cup with water from a pitcher by her bedside and helped prop her into a more upright position.

"Now that you're safe, Libby, I can focus on how such a disaster was allowed to happen in the first place," Adam said, stepping to the window. He parted the blinds and peered out into the darkness. "I'm horrified that the school we entrusted you to could let this happen. It's unconscionable. Even criminal."

"What are you talking about?"

"These people have to be stopped. You don't have to worry about . . ."

"Daddy, are you nuts?"

"I beg your pardon! I don't expect you to understand, but someone has to take a stand here. Glencoe needs to be shut down as quickly as possible before someone else gets hurt."

"Wait just a minute," Libby interrupted, wincing as painful spasms coursed through her body as if generated by an electric prod. "This place is more home to me than anywhere else on earth. These people are like family to me."

"You've just been through a terrible ordeal and you need to recuperate," soothed her mother. "Dad's right. You aren't in any position to appreciate how poorly you've been cared for."

"You can't be serious. If you do anything to Glencoe you'll freakin' never see me again!" Libby shrieked.

Out in the hall it was impossible not to hear the commotion. Hamish looked over to the nurse's station. The hospital staff looked embarrassed, their heads bent over computer screens.

Taken aback by the vehemence of his daughter's reaction, Adam backed off. "Maybe in time you'll understand, Libby," he sighed, shaking his head and fumbling with the zipper of his burgundy, ultra-suede jacket. "Your mom and I only want the best for you. I admit you've had an unorthodox upbringing but . . . it's worked for you. You're so strong."

"Yes Daddy, I *am* strong, even if I feel like crap right this second. But I'm not strong from what you've given me. It's in *spite* of what you've given me. You send me from place to place so I can never get close to people. Is that supposed to make me strong? For what? Living by myself?"

Adam Goldman had no answer for his daughter.

"The past few days were the hardest I've ever had," she continued. "I don't think anyone who wasn't there would ever really know what it was like, but what kept me going was the strength of my friends," she said, realizing the irony of her statement. A week ago, she would never have thought of Tracy and Malcolm as people she cared about in the least. "They mean more to me right now than . . . anyone."

Adam kept his head down through Libby's tirade, maintaining no eye contact with her. Shelley came to his side and gripped his arm.

"One of them chose to save my life, even though it meant he would be going back to prison," Libby continued. "If you want to do something to help, let your lawyer figure out how to save Ramon. His mother is Eva Ortiz. I think you know who she is."

Her parents looked at each other uncomprehendingly. "Eva?" Shelley stammered. "Our Eva? How can that be?"

"Oh, now she's *your Eva*. Unbelievable," Libby added. She lay back against the pillow and closed her eyes. "If you really love me and want to help me, tell Hamish you're going to donate some money to Glencoe for all it's done for me. As soon as I'm better, I want to go back to school, not home. Is that clear?" She turned away from him. The conversation was over. Shelley stepped forward placed a hand on her shoulder, leaned over to give her a light kiss on the top of her head and led her husband out into the hall.

"Maybe I was a bit short with you before, Mr. MacLean," Adam mumbled, bringing his wife across the room to Hamish and Bonnie.

"I'm glad you saw that she's going to be okay," Hamish said, changing the subject while thinking how much he would enjoy giving the man a punch in the nose.

"Clearly, our Libby has been through a lot in the last few days. I must say, she sounded so clearheaded. After what she's gone through, it's hard to process. Apparently, the fellow you met . . . his name was Ramon. Right, Shell?" She nodded. "Ramon's mother has worked for us for some time."

"What?!" Hamish gasped. "How can that be?"

"I know. Remarkable. We are quite fond of her," Adam said.

"And we are quite fond of your lovely daughter," Bonnie said. "It is an enormous relief to all of us that she, and the others, seem to have come through this ordeal so well. We can't wait to have them back at school where they belong."

"She says she's eager to go back as well," Adam responded. "But I'm not sure she's thinking straight right now. Shelley and I are very troubled that such a thing could have happened and the buck has to stop with you," he said, regaining his composure and pugnacity.

"Let's focus on her health, shall we?" Hamish asked. "There's plenty of time for recriminations. Rest assured I take my responsibility to keep our students safe most seriously. They're not coddled, Dr. Goldman, but they're not purposely placed in risky situations. What happened was highly unusual, but we'll look at the decisions that were made that allowed this to occur. I hope we can undergo that investigation without a lawsuit, but you obviously will do what you must do."

"Libby has given us a lot to think about," Adam said. "No decisions will be made in anger, but you must appreciate how upsetting it is for a parent to see his child in this state."

"On that, we agree," Hamish said. "I hope you two will have more time to spend with her before you head home."

Just after dawn, Ron Handy walked in to the hospital. Bonnie beamed with pleasure as Hamish and Ron embraced. "I hope there's at least someone who might need a ride back to Glencoe," Ron said. "I'm not just here to bring you guys coffee."

Late that morning, Tracy and Malcolm were discharged, the former sporting an ace bandage on his injured ankle. While the nightly routine at the hospital had not been conducive to the good night's sleep they craved, the hours attached to an intravenous line had done wonders for both boys' dehydration. When they saw Ron, their faces lit up, and on the ride back to school, the drama teacher was dumbfounded at the way the two boys chatted amiably in the back seat.

It was nearly lunchtime as Ron pulled into the school. A crowd was waiting to greet them in the parking lot. Tracy's eyes filled with tears as he remembered how it felt to hold Libby on the ledge for those interminable hours, fearing they would never see Glencoe again. He recalled the touch of her hand on the back of his neck as he had laid bare his secret by the campfire the night before. By all rights he should feel elated to be back, but instead he felt hollow. He saw Jake plowing through the throng to be the first to greet him. How could he face Jake, once the truth of what he had done to Malcolm on Balanced Rocks was out? How long, and in how many still-unknown ways, would he pay for that misdeed?

Following his recapture, Ramon was held overnight at the Lake Placid police station. His first request, which drew a quizzical look from the sergeant at the desk, was not to make a phone call home, which eventually he did ask to do, but to have a doctor check him out for rabies. When the corrections van came for him the next morning, it did not head back to the Adirondack Corrections Facility in Ray Brook. Ramon would not be returning to the place from which he had escaped. Instead, the van headed east out of town, in the opposite direction. As an escaped felon, he was "off the list" at the Ray Brook Facility. He was driven to the Essex County Jail in Elizabethtown, the county seat, to await possible indictment by a grand jury.

Hours of sitting at Libby's bedside enabled Adam and Shelley Goldman to reconsider their initial response to start legal action against Glencoe. There was no way to dismiss Libby's ardor for the school as the rant of a feverish child. They sat spellbound as Libby recounted the events of the previous days. Afterwards, her father phoned Alice Hawkins, the Austro-Lab's attorney, and asked if she could find good defense counsel for Ramon and make it clear that he, Adam, would cover all legal costs. Alice possessed no experience in criminal litigation, beyond what little she had absorbed in law school. She was no more prepared to navigate Ramon through the dangerous legal shoals of a grand jury investigation and likely trial to follow than a small-town electrician would be if handed a nuclear submarine to rewire. Mr. Goldman instructed Alice to "get the thing taken care of, whatever it costs," as though Ramon's legal problem was just another bureaucratic speed bump.

Several attorneys she knew gave her referrals but all were dead ends. Alice finally reached Garrett Pearson in his office at Georgetown Law School in Washington. Pearson had carved out a career integrating academic instruction and high-profile litigation regarding prisoners' rights. He interrupted Alice after a few introductory sentences. His current workload precluded him from taking on Ramon's case, he said. But he agreed to hear the salient details of the case in order to send Alice to a more likely candidate.

Alice outlined the story, careful to play up the emotional value of Ramon's heroism in helping to save the lives of the Glencoe students and causing the death of the main perpetrator. From the tapping of a keyboard at the other end of the phone, it sounded as if Pearson was barely paying attention. Occasionally he asked a question; mostly he just said, "Uh huh." Several times he cut her off with an order to his secretary regarding a totally unrelated matter. The instant she uttered the words *Glencoe School* the typing abruptly stopped.

"Glencoe? Did you say Glencoe School? Who is running that place?"

"Umm," she hesitated, buying time to do a quick search of the Glencoe website to find the name. "I believe the headmaster's name is MacLean. Is that relevant?"

"Well, if Hamish is in on this, so am I!" said Garrett Pearson.

"Excuse me? I thought you were booked."

"Old news. I'll always find time for that man."

"Oh! Really! You know MacLean?" She balled up her list of other attorneys to call and tossed it into the trash can beneath her desk.

Pearson laughed. "I've spent many hours clinging to the sides of huge mountains with Hamish MacLean. If he's mixed up in this and needs help, I'll be there. Let my secretary know how to reach you." Click.

There was no funeral for Garth LeGrange, and no one came to claim the body. The coroner signed the death certificate and directed the corpse to be cremated. Fire had been such a part of Garth's life it seemed only fitting it should be part of his death. From the traumatic burning of his father's trailer when he was seven, to the serial automobile torching that resulted in his initial incarceration, Garth's time on earth had been punctuated by flames.

Adam and Shelley Goldman were at her bedside when Libby awoke on her second morning at the hospital. They stayed with her until she fell into a deep sleep just after lunch. The reality of nearly losing their daughter prompted a good deal of soul-searching between the two parents while she slept. Their all-consuming energies on behalf of Austro-Lab had crowded out any other thoughts about how their educational project had impacted their only child. In a sense, they had abdicated parental responsibilities to a series of institutions, Glencoe being simply the latest, with Kibbutz Harduf presumably next in line. It was a difficult reckoning for these two adults who had seen so clearly that their baby was now a force to be reckoned with.

. . .

"Ma! The phone's ringing. You got it?" Pablo called. "Miguel and me are doing a puzzle."

"Hello," Eva said, reaching for the wall phone in their kitchen. Her sons watched her eyes widen and her jaw drop as the robotic voice on the other end asked her to accept a collect call from the Elizabethtown jail. The ensuing conversation became an emotional roller coaster for both mother and son. She could barely speak as Ramon explained he had not perished in the wilderness but that his recapture would mean even more jail time.

"I'll come right away. To see you," she exclaimed. "Dios mio. It's a miracle! And it's a tragedy! What will happen to you?"

She asked the Goldmans for some time off so she could travel north. She arranged for Consuela to look after the other children. But her anxiety brought on another cardiac episode, and another brief visit to the hospital. A mild episode, the doctors said, but they cautioned her against leaving the city in such a fragile physical condition. Several days later, Adam Goldman called to see how she was feeling, to assure her that her job was secure, and to inform her that he would personally be paying her son's legal expenses. Libby learned of this during an evening phone call that had none of the impatience or formality she had come to expect from her parents.

"Are you crying?" her father asked. "Aren't you happy we're going to help Ramon try to beat this new charge?"

"Yes, Daddy. Yes. It's the first time in forever that I feel heard. Thank you."

42

Shouldering Responsibility

After breakfast the morning following Tracy's return, Jake asked the kitchen staff to prepare a tray loaded with blueberry pancakes, sausage, and Glencoe's maple syrup, which he carried up to Tracy, who had been given permission to sleep in. "Hey, lazybones, you hungry?" Jake grinned, opening the door to their room.

"Jake! Why aren't you in class?" Tracy yawned, luxuriating in the security of his warm bed.

"Payton gave me permission to see you for a few minutes. I thought you could use some decent food."

"Thanks, man. Sorry I couldn't talk to you last night, but I was wasted. Running on fumes for so long, I crashed pretty hard. Man, do I have a wicked headache." Tracy rubbed his temples. "Is it true that Pete's gone?"

"Seems so. I saw Christine this morning, and she looks crushed. I couldn't bring myself to say anything to her."

"That's really tough. I always thought Hamish considered Pete like a son. I can't imagine how totally pissed Pete feels."

"I guess Hamish has been under a ton of pressure over this and maybe he threw Pete under the bus," Jake surmised. "It's a real loss." He handed Tracy a glass of juice from the tray. "You looked like death yesterday. When do I get the details?"

Tracy drained the glass. "Soon as I feel up to it. Sorry I screwed up the trip for you guys, but it was a hell of a couple of days. Here's a piece you won't believe. We ran into those escaped convicts from back in the fall, remember?"

"No way! No way! That's sick."

"Yeah, and the other thing is, Malcolm stepped up big-time. I'm rethinking the whole thing with him."

Jake whistled softly, shaking his head in wonder.

"And you heard we lost Rambler?"

"Yeah. Must be tough on Hamish and Bonnie. She was like a daughter to them."

"It was so strange. One minute she was peering at me over the ledge, puzzled as to why me and Mal and Libby were hanging out down there, next thing I remember, after the copter hauled Mal and Libby off to the hospital, Rambler disappeared. We tracked her paw prints and found her lying under some cripplebrush. Hamish, Pete, and I were so focused on the rescue we never noticed her slinking off to die. I think Hamish was so numbed out he didn't know how to react. He just sat there in the snow with Rambler in his lap. I was crying on Pete's shoulder like a baby."

"Hamish won't show us nothing," Jake added. "We'd see more emotion from a frog. But Bonnie, that's a different story. This has gotta be killing her. Maybe that explains why she hasn't been down to Dewey the last day or so. That was some helluva dog. Wish I could stay," he added, getting to his feet. "But Payton's gonna be all over my ass if I don't get back to class. Catch you later, bro. Great to have you back."

Sustained by nearly twenty-four hours of sleep, Tracy finally left his bed at dinnertime and ventured to Dewey Hall. He was overjoyed to see Malcolm in the atrium by the entrance to the dining hall. His schoolmate was happily telling all who asked what heroic deeds they had performed on the mountain. Tracy gave Malcolm a hug, noting how strange it felt, given their history, and the reality that the Balanced Rocks episode would inevitably see the light of day, with uncertain consequences. The three days in the woods had bonded them in ways no one else would ever understand.

As with every meal, the community paused for a moment of silence before sitting down to eat. Steaming plates of spaghetti tossed with pungent pesto sauce were passed down each table as Hamish walked to the front of the room and tinkled the little bell to bring the room to attention.

"By now, most of you know much of what has happened during the last eventful few days. What could have been a tragic accident has been averted, thanks to the strength and courage of three of you. Welcome home." The room erupted with unrestrained, enthusiastic hoots and applause. "We expect Libby will also be back with us soon. When she does return, please remember she's been under a great deal of stress, so try to give her some space." Hamish paused, then, with voice cracking, he added, "and, as perhaps you have heard, our beloved Rambler passed away on the mountain. She will . . . be missed . . . by all of us." Hamish sat down; the normal mealtime chatter resumed only after a long, respectful, silence.

From his seat, Tracy felt sidelong glances from other students awed by the presence of a hero in their midst. Though he relished the adulation, he knew the lie he was carrying must soon be revealed and he dreaded how everyone would regard him then.

At noon the following day, Libby could scarcely contain her excitement as the Goldman limousine drove past the barn and the lower pasture. As soon as the driver slowed to a reasonable speed, she hopped out at the entrance to Dewey Hall. "Thanks for coming to see me," she said, leaning in to the backseat window, "and for helping Ramon. I really, really appreciate it. Can you drop my things at Phelps House? I need to see my friends. Talk soon." She waved goodbye and disappeared into the building.

"We've got quite a strong young lady," Shelley Goldman said to her husband. "Maybe sending her here wasn't such a bad idea after all. We wanted to see some independence in that girl, and looks like we got what we paid for." Through welling tears, Adam watched his daughter bounce into Dewey and nodded.

As she stepped into the noisy atrium, Libby was immediately enveloped, much as Tracy had been. Standing at the periphery, Tracy watched with joy and more than a twinge of anxiety. Now that she was back, would she go back to thinking of him as a jerk? He couldn't bear that, considering he'd told her everything . . . and had kept her from freezing to death on that precarious ledge. That must count for something, he hoped.

Libby patiently acknowledged the attention, then scanned the room for the people she missed most. Catching Tracy's eye, she began to wade through the sea of people when Tina, who had just walked in, shrieked in delight. "You're back!!" Tina hugged her aggressively, then retreated as she remembered Libby's fragile state.

"It's okay," Libby laughed. "I'm sore, but you won't break me."

"You've *got* to tell me everything. Right *now*, before lunch. I just *have* to know all the gory details," she gushed.

"Later, Tina," Libby smiled. "We've got all night." She squeezed Tina's hand and searched again for Tracy, moving against the crowd that now waited for the table setters to finish their preparations for the midday meal. Reaching his side, she shyly threw an arm around his waist. From across the atrium, Tina's jaw dropped as she watched how affectionately her two housemates greeted each other.

"How's it going?" Tracy asked, feeling his face flush.

"That's a pretty casual greeting," she grinned. "I'll live. But I'm not leaving the art room until spring."

"Heard anything about Ramon?"

"My father's handling all the legal stuff. I'm petrified what will happen to him. If I had died Ramon would be facing a murder charge."

"He saved our lives," Tracy said. "They better consider that."

"And you saved mine."

Tracy looked down and shrugged. "You probably haven't heard about Rambler," Tracy said.

"What about Rambler?"

"She died after you were airlifted. Just crawled away."

"Oh, no! That's horrible! Hamish must be destroyed!" said Libby, looking stunned. At that moment Hamish approached and put an arm around each of them.

"It's the best feeling in the world to see you both up and about," he said with an avuncular smile.

"Hamish! I'm so sorry I just heard about Rambler. I don't know what to say. She was the most awesome dog."

"We're very sad to have lost her," he said, voice catching in his throat. Tracy saw he was not about to display in front of the kids how devastated he was. "But so glad we didn't lose you!"

Libby gave Tracy the *You haven't told him yet, have you?* look. Tracy's lips tightened and his far-off gaze gave her the answer. *I will* he promised silently.

The buzz in the dining room was extraordinary until Hamish rang the bell and asked everyone to settle down. "The nest is now complete," he chuckled, setting off another eruption of applause. Hamish let it float in the air for a long moment, allowing Libby to soak in the feeling. He tapped the bell again. "We have so much to be thankful for, and much to learn from the events of this week. Certainly, it will take time for us to absorb all that has happened and to see to it that this never happens again. I congratulate Libby, Malcolm, and Tracy for demonstrating the will and, God knows, the strength to persevere. Well done." Though he appeared to have finished his comments he continued to stand there, uncomfortably, at the front of the room, as though there was something more on his mind. But he did not elaborate, finally taking his seat and the semi-controlled din resumed. Normally, Hamish would have remonstrated the students for such noise, but this time he let it pass. There was just too much energy in the room to expect that the meal could be eaten sedately.

Libby caught up to Tracy standing by his locker after lunch.

"When are you going to say something?"

"Libby, that's all I think about. You think this is easy?"

"'Course not. But you've got no choice. Not if you ever want to put this behind you."

"How do I go about telling the whole world I nearly killed a kid?"

"You better figure it out. Maybe you should talk to Mal about it. He may have an opinion." They stopped talking as three other students passed on their way to class. Libby realized how much they both had changed. She couldn't have imagined having such a conversation with him before their trip, but now she felt an entanglement she couldn't fully understand. "Think of what it must have been like for Ramon to walk down the trail into the arms of all those cops," she said. "He made the right decision when it counted. You will, too."

"Easier said than done, Libby. I'm not sure I've got the guts."

"You are incredibly strong. I know you can handle this," she said. Tracy looked grateful. "I guess . . . I guess you could say something at Silent Meeting," she suggested. "I'm not saying it'll be easy but you just finished doing something a lot harder."

His first thought was, Silent Meeting is still a few days off, a few more days of avoidance. His next thought was, it made a lot of sense. Students respected the ritual and honored those who had the courage to stand up and reveal something of themselves. Jake had been among the first, early in the fall, to stand up and talk. There was no way anyone would make fun of Jake, especially after he showed the guts to publicly share the pain of losing a baby sister to cystic fibrosis. After Jake spoke about his personal struggles, it was somehow easier for others to find the inner strength to follow suit. Tracy decided Libby was right. That was how he would do it.

43

Plea for a Pardon

It was Christine's afternoon off. With no obligations in the art room or supervising an outdoors activity, she would typically have driven into Lake Placid to do errands, or simply steal a few hours before supper to continue whatever romance novel was on her bedside table. But this was not a normal afternoon. Since Pete had left, no days had been normal, and she decided that she owed it to both of them to try to reverse the decision Hamish had made. Hoping the headmaster was busy in his office, which was a reasonable assumption given that was where he usually spent his afternoons, Christine walked up the road to the MacLean farmhouse.

Bonnie was staring at a crossword puzzle that didn't seem to be filling itself in, a poor distraction from her grief, when Christine knocked. She folded a corner of the page in the book of puzzles, closed it, and walked to the door to let Christine in, wiping her nose with a tissue. Christine could see the headmaster's wife had been crying.

"Is this a bad time?" Christine asked.

"There've been better times, dear," she sighed. "But I can't keep feeling sorry for myself. What brings you here?"

"I don't know who else to turn to, Bonnie. I need to vent and you're the only person I feel comfortable doing that with."

"Would some tea help?"

"Yes, please. Whatever you have is fine."

Bonnie put on a kettle, selected a couple of herbal options and placed them on the kitchen table beside two mugs. She found it difficult talking with anyone since Rambler had died, but knew she had to put on a good face now. It was part of her job. She had an inkling as to what Christine wanted to talk about and anticipated there might be a difficult *ask* at the end of Christine's expected plea.

"Perhaps a cookie too?" Bonnie said, forcing a smile. "I shouldn't eat all of these oatmeal raisin things myself."

"Thank you, Bonnie. I don't want to take up too much of your time and I am so sorry for your loss. I will get to the point," Christine said, taking a deep breath. She had rehearsed the speech on her walk to the farmhouse but the words that tumbled out were totally scattered. "I'm hoping to persuade you to speak to your husband about Pete. I know I am probably overstepping here but I don't know what else to do." Christine kept her eyes on her tea, not wanting to see Bonnie's reaction. She forged ahead. "If anyone is at fault it's me. Pete assumed I would pick up the rear and keep the kids in front of me as we've been trained. I panicked in the storm, and I'm just heartsick over what has happened to him. He only had a minute or two to speak to me before he was forced to leave the other morning, but I know he is shattered. Did Hamish really have to do this?"

"I'm sorry about this, Christine. I truly am. Hamish and I have not discussed this at length, but I am pretty certain it came from the board, so he probably felt his hands were tied. Pete means the world to Hamish; this sort of decision is not typical of him. He usually bends over backward to keep people, whether it's a student or a faculty member. I don't know what I can do, Christine. He'll listen to me about some things. Others, not so much. I am so fond of Pete, and he's been wonderful here. This is not a matter of Hamish being persuaded that Pete is worth keeping. This is a matter of politics, I'm afraid. Even little schools like Glencoe are infected by politics. Know that you have support in this house. I can't imagine how hard this has been for you, too."

"Bonnie. I have a lot of survivor's guilt. I'm the one who should be going, not him. I feel like everyone's looking at me funny. I can't make it go away. As for our future, mine and Pete's, I just don't know . . ."

"Christine, I know you two have tried to be as discreet as possible about your relationship but some things can't be hidden. You two seem perfect for each other. You need to carry on. I can't help but see a beautiful wedding on the hill overlooking our lake."

Christine held it together until that last comment. The entire idea of speaking about a wedding at this place, at this moment, made it nearly impossible to breathe. "That's getting way ahead of where I am." Tears flowed and she did nothing to stop their descent. "If I ever dreamed of anything like that, well, that's not happening now. But that's not your problem."

They sat in awkward silence, each focused on lost love. For Christine, it felt like a golden future had been dashed by panic in a storm. Events beyond their control had extinguished what should have been a beautiful love story. Christine's passion reminded Bonnie that, in her own heart, Hamish had been gone a long time.

"I've got to go. I don't know what else to say." Christine got up from her chair and put on her coat. "Thank you for listening. If there's anything you can do, I would be forever grateful. I totally understand I may be way out of line. But I've got nothing to lose. My dignity, my boyfriend— they're gone. I'm humiliated." She placed a hand over Bonnie's. "Thank you for the tea."

"We don't talk much these days," Bonnie said, wistfully, walking her to the door. "But I will try."

44

Truth and Consequences

THE FINAL SILENT MEETING OF THE FALL SEMESTER, DECEMBER 15, found Tracy, Jake, Libby, and Tina sitting together in the last row. Predictably, Malcolm showed up late, and the only empty seat was in the second row with the fifth graders. Tracy noticed what was about to transpire, including the possible disruptions that might inevitably follow. He poked an elbow into the side of a sixth-grade boy next to him and said, "Hey, Brett, I think you'd be more comfortable up there, okay?" he asked pointing to the second row. "Now!" Brett rubbed his ribs and reluctantly moved. Tracy caught Malcolm's eye and motioned him over to the newly vacant seat next to him. Malcolm nodded appreciatively.

The musicians concluded their recital on the stage, set their instruments aside and took seats with their classmates. Quiet settled over the room. Libby noticed the difference from the first Sunday Meeting of the year, when distracting giggles and restlessness had precluded an atmosphere of contemplation and personal reflection. Now, even the youngest and newest in their midst had come to respect, if not necessarily appreciate, this time.

Libby gazed about the room. She had just endured an epic adventure and then come to a new understanding with her parents. She should have felt more content. But now, just as she began to feel better about herself, she couldn't enjoy it. Rather, she was absorbed with the troubles of others who just a few days before, were either unknown to her or unimportant.

"I can't stop thinking about what Ramon's going through right now," she whispered to Tracy. "I wish I could talk to his mom. Tell her how grateful we are for what her son did for us."

"Me too. Do you think we'll ever talk to him again? It's pretty weird to go through what we did with him and then never to meet him again. In your life and out of your life. Boom," Tracy said.

"Shush," a teacher remonstrated, turning to scold the whispering pair.

Libby nodded an apology but as soon as the teacher's head was turned, she continued, "And you? I'm worried about you more than anything." She reached for his hand and squeezed it. Tracy bit his lip and smiled weakly, his heart racing.

After fifteen minutes of a silence broken only by coughs, Christine Mason stood up. "You can't imagine how difficult this past week has been for me," she stammered, pausing to compose herself. "One of the most important things we do at this school is to offer to those of you who are interested a chance to test yourselves, to push yourselves beyond what you dreamed you could accomplish." Christine punched out the next words with some difficulty. "But it is also our responsibility not to place you in harm's way.

"On a mountain we're meant to teach you that when weather is bad and visibility is limited, we must always stay together as a group, with one leader at the front and one at the rear. On Algonquin, Pete and I were so intent on getting everyone off the summit quickly that we broke our own rules. We should have known better. I should have acted differently. Thank heaven it didn't end tragically. In the short while that I have worked here, I have learned so much from Hamish, from Pete, from all of you," she said, her lip quivering, "To climb in these hills is a rare and special privilege, and I hope my error will not cause you to think twice about hiking with us in the future, with me or any other teacher here.

"It's never easy to admit your failings and doubly hard to do so in front of an audience," she continued. "But we, as adults, have to set an example if we expect all of you to trust us. I sincerely apologize." Christine sat down and glanced over at Hamish, but his gaze and his thoughts seemed to be elsewhere.

Tracy knew his moment had arrived. All he had to do was stand up and pour it out. Silence cloaked the room as everyone considered Christine's repentance, as well as the unspoken absence of Pete Hedges. Tracy breathed deeply, steadying his nerves, rehearsing his opening words for the millionth time. Libby saw him shifting in his seat, trying to find the courage to rise. "Go for it," she whispered.

"I'm sorry, too." All eyes swiveled to the speaker at the front of the room. Sixth-grader Lauren Chang began an earnest confession of her own. It seemed she had teased Blinkers, one of two donkeys in the barn, by offering him juicy carrots just picked from the garden, only to pull them out of reach when the poor animal stretched out his nose for them. Then, feeling sorry for having "embarrassed" Blinkers in front of the other donkey, Lauren swiped sugar cubes from the coffee cart in the teachers' lounge, strictly off-limits to students, and fed them to Blinkers as a peace offering. As she stumbled through her story, obviously mortified at what she had done, many in the audience covered their mouths to muffle the guffaws. No one wanted to discomfit the plucky little girl, who had squirreled up the courage to confess before the entire community.

When Lauren sat down, tears in her eyes, Tracy knew his opportunity had passed. There were only a few minutes remaining in Silent Meeting and he could no longer summon the strength. Hamish stood and dismissed the assembly. As the orderly exit began, Libby whispered in his ear, "You were going to do it when Lauren started, weren't you?"

He nodded. "This is hard enough as it is, without having to follow that story. Maybe I can catch Hamish. I'll lose my nerve if I don't do it now."

The room was almost empty now.

"Hey, Tracy, you coming?" Jake beckoned from the hall.

"Better go on without me," he called. The headmaster was folding chairs and stacking them against one wall, readying the space for a dance class in the morning.

"Uh, Hamish, can I talk to you for a minute?"

"Grab a chair, Trace. You can talk while you work," he said with a twinkle.

"Can we talk somewhere else? In private?"

Hamish glanced at his watch and motioned to several teachers chatting in the hall to finish the job for him. "Let's talk in the kitchen." Tracy reached for Libby's sleeve and dragged her along as Hamish led them into the now-empty school kitchen and guided them over to a small table in an alcove where the staff often sat to have coffee. Immense pots and pans hung from hooks above an industrial-strength wooden chopping block, concave from years of slicing and dicing. Rows of six-grain bread sat cooling on racks in the corner, filling the room with a yeasty aroma. It was a comforting space.

"What's on your mind?"

Tracy hesitated and looked at Libby. She smiled and raised her eyebrows as if to say *You can do this, and I'm right there with you.* "It . . . It's about Malcolm."

"What about Malcolm? He's come a long way, hasn't he?"

Tracy squirmed in his chair. "I don't know how to say this," he mumbled.

"Maybe whatever you have to say should be just the two of us?" Hamish asked, not at all sure what was coming. "Libby, maybe you ought to leave us alone for a bit."

"Please, no!" Tracy interrupted. "I don't think I can go through with this if she's not here, Hamish." The Scotsman pulled at his beard.

"She knows what you want to discuss?"

He nodded. Under the table she felt for his hand. "During our last night in the woods when Garth was breaking trail toward Wallface, when Ramon told us that he thought Garth planned to kill us the next day, I figured it might be my last chance to get something off my chest." He looked up at Hamish, eyes moist.

"Get what?"

"The truth about what happened on Balanced Rocks."

Hamish whistled softly.

"What I mean is, we weren't just out there for fun. I was trying to scare him, to get back at him for stuff he'd been doing to me."

"Let's start at the beginning, shall we?" Hamish urged. "There's more I need to understand. Did you cook up this idea of climbing Balanced Rocks on your own, like you originally claimed?"

"Yes."

"And you took him up the back way for some reason?"

Tracy nodded.

"As I recall, you and Mal had quite a few issues back then."

Tracy nodded again.

"In fact, I think it's safe to say you two hated each other. Was this some sort of a dare?"

"Sort of. I . . . I just meant to scare him. He was driving everyone crazy with his stunts and I wanted to teach him a lesson so he'd stop. Putting the chicken shit . . . sorry, manure . . . in my boots was the last straw. I tried to think of something that would make him see we weren't going to take his garbage anymore. I know I sometimes used to tease people, too . . . "

"Just a bit," Libby interjected, kicking him affectionately under the table in an attempt to reduce the tension. Tracy smiled ruefully.

"Anyhow, I found out Malcolm was scared of snakes, so I came up with this plan where I could spring some garter snakes on him while he was on the rocks and . . . shake him up. Maybe make him realize how much we hated his bullying.

"So . . . I led him up that way . . . well . . . dared him into climbing the slabs of Balanced Rocks, so I could get ahead of him and then scare him with the snakes. I mean, they're not poisonous or anything. I carried them up there in a jar and . . . all I wanted to do was shake him up, Hamish." Tracy buried his head in his hands.

Hamish sat rigid. "Do you know what comes to my mind right now?" he asked.

"No sir," Tracy whispered.

"The vision of Malcolm sprawled in the rocks up there that night, Tracy. That was a tough evening. I've had enough experiences with injured climbers . . . " he paused, "and didn't need to be reminded of that again."

"It was awful for me, too," Tracy nodded. "Especially when I knew it was my fault. He was climbing up to me. I could see it was hard for him . . . but all I wanted was to . . . He panicked, lost his footing and peeled off. I scrambled down to him but it looked like he was dead. I was so scared. I never meant for him to get hurt, you gotta believe that." Tracy let go a sob, took a deep breath, and continued. "I knew he needed help bad so I tore outta there and . . . you know the rest. I couldn't bring myself to tell the whole story. I wanted to. I tried to. I just couldn't. And then when he made it through and didn't remember anything I just figured I'd leave it alone."

"Tracy, what happened there was unforgivable."

"Yes sir. I know that."

"Does Malcolm know all this from your campfire confession?"

"He does," Tracy said softly. "Actually, he hadn't forgotten. He understood what drove me to do that and he has an honor code all his own that prevented him from squealing about it. He is a complex guy. And he is now my friend, if you can believe that. I'd do anything to live that day over," Tracy sniffled. "It's eaten me alive."

Hamish heaved a deep sigh. "You've given me a lot to think about, lad. It wouldn't be fair for me to give you my response now, because it likely would be the wrong one. I may not be sure what this means for your future, Tracy, but it's clear to me that you owe the school an apology and you owe Malcolm's aunt an explanation. What she does with it, I cannae predict."

"Yes sir."

"Honestly, I don't know whether to comfort you or wring your neck. I'd like to do both," he sighed after a moment of silence. "I will contact Malcolm's aunt tomorrow and tell her that you will be calling. Are your parents aware of this?"

"No, sir . . . not yet. They told me they expect to be here in the morning."

"Good. Please see to it that the Barcomb family is in my office sometime during the next two days to discuss this."

Tracy nodded. "Can I go now?"

Hamish pursed his lips, thinking if there was anything else that had to be said. "You're sure getting more than fifteen minutes of fame this week, aren't you?"

"I'd rather have skipped it."

Oversized downy flakes licked their cheeks as Libby and Tracy walked up the gravel road to the residence halls on the hill, holding hands.

"You did great in there, Tracy. I'm proud of you."

Tracy shook his head in wonderment. "This whole thing is like a bad dream that won't end. I'm kind of glad it's out there now. I couldn't go on keeping it inside. At least I feel better about that."

"Think he's going to kick you out?"

"He may not have to. When my dad hears about this, he may kill me on the spot."

They paused where the road divided to each residence. Set above them in a rough semi-circle, the Glencoe dorms glowed cheerily in the icy Adirondack night.

"I'm really glad you finally did it."

"Thanks for being there. I kept remembering how it felt to tell you guys around the fire the other night. And Mal. It's amazing how he took it."

She looked at him for a moment, then stepped forward, brought her gloved hands up to cup his face and gave him a quick kiss. "You were there for me, too . . . on that ledge. Kept me warm and feeling as safe as I could be. I'll never forget that."

Tracy recalled that indelible feeling of her clutching his hand to her chest, willing the warmth from his body to hers. It was the most intense moment he had ever experienced with another human being. No phoniness. No kid stuff. His heart felt like bursting and he was nearly certain the feeling was mutual.

"Please do that again," he said, risking humiliation.

Libby smiled, lifted her face to his and kissed him again, long and deep. She stepped back, a sly smile creasing her face. "Was that as good as Tina's?"

Tracy's eyes widened. He struggled for an excuse but she didn't give him a chance to respond. She turned around and ran the rest of the way to Phelps House. Absently, he touched his face as if to locate some remnant of her.

"Oh, there you are," Payton Henderson said, looking up from the holiday cards he was addressing at the kitchen table. Libby stepped out of her barn boots, leaving them by the door, and hung up her coat in her mudroom cubby.

"Sorry, I'm late. Hamish kept Tracy and me after the meeting. He's right behind me." She walked over to the table to admire the cards that pictured Payton, Jane, and Nicky atop one of the Balanced Rocks, with Algonquin rising up in the distance. It was an attractive picture of a healthy, happy family, but it made her shudder. "That picture gives me the creeps, Payton."

"Excuse me? That's my family you're talking about!"

"The background. Don't you see?"

"Ahh," Payton said after a moment. "The two mountains of misadventure this fall, eh? We took this picture last summer, Libby. Pure coincidence. By the way, your dad just called. He said you could reach him in his car for another half hour. The number's on the blackboard in the mudroom if you don't have it memorized."

"Did he say what he wanted?" She eyed him warily.

"Call him and find out."

Reluctantly, she dialed the chalked number, steeling herself for the next surprise. Tracy walked in, hung up his coat, and gave her a hug on his way up the stairs.

"Adam here." The crackling connection indicated his car was between cells.

"Hello, Dad."

"Ahh, Libby . . . just a minute 'til I get better reception down the road . . ." She sat in her cubby, listening to the sounds of life in the house. At the top of the stairs, children readied themselves for bed, their banter garbled by toothbrushes and running water. In a few days they would be going their separate ways to join their families for winter break. As usual, she had no clue as to what her family had planned for the holidays. Tina was not available; her parents were meeting her in Montreal.

"Sorry, Libby. How are you feeling, honey?" Adam asked.

"Getting stronger. Is this about the holidays?" she asked guardedly.

"Did Payton tell you?"

"No. But I figured it's about time to tell me what hotel you've parked me into."

"How about Stowe, Vermont, for a few days of skiing. Are you up to it?"

"By myself?"

"Of course not. We have a retreat planned between winter break and New Year's and we thought it would be nice to combine it with a little family time. But if you've had your fill of mountains or would prefer to stay with a friend, we'll understand. What do you say?"

"Sounds good, I guess."

"The schedule calls for us to be free about half the time each day. We'll have to take turns with you, but neither one of us can keep up with you on the slopes for a whole day, anyhow." *Taking turns*, she thought. *Business as usual.*

"Okay." Then, under her breath, "Taking turns . . . business as usual."

"Sorry? Can you speak a little louder?"

"I said 'Thanks.'"

"I'm afraid your mother and I have to go out to the West Coast for a few days beforehand, so we've asked Eva Ortiz to stay uptown with you while we're gone."

"Great. She and I have a lot to talk about. But how can she look after her kids if she's at our place?"

"Her children are going down to Puerto Rico to visit their grandparents."

"You're joking. Did they win the lottery or something?"

"Sort of. It's our present to Ramon and his family. It's the least we can do for them."

Libby was stunned. "That's amazing, Dad. That's a really neat thing to do. How come Eva's not going with them?"

"She could have. I extended the offer to all of them, but she thought her children should see their father's family alone this time. She also wants to be available when Ramon comes before the grand jury." The volume of static increased, causing her father's voice to become almost unintelligible. "The connection is breaking up, Libby . . . We'll send a car to pick you up and bring you to Vermont. Don't forget to . . ." The line went dead.

"How'd it go?" Payton asked from the other room, concerned that she had hung up without saying goodbye. She walked into the kitchen and sat down beside him.

"Not too bad," she admitted, fingering one of the holiday cards. "Can I have one?"

"If you can't wait for the one in the mail," he smiled indulgently.

"You mean I'm on your list?"

"I'm afraid you're slated to get these sappy pictures from us as long as we know where you're living, Libby. We're not going to drop you just because you're graduating. This is a long-term commitment." He tousled her hair.

"That's really sweet, Payton. I guess one difference between kids and grownups is, we rarely think ahead more than one day at a time. We can't imagine the future being any different than the present. Maybe that sounds dopey, I don't know."

"It's developmental, not dopey. There are other differences you will come to appreciate. But let's get back to your family for a minute. Looks to me like there's been a change for the better, don't you think?"

"I guess. Talking to my dad is never easy. But at least he talks. Mom, I rarely hear from unless he's there. No matter how good it sounds on the surface, it always ends up being something they're doing because they have to, for some other reason. They're taking me skiing at Stowe, but it turns out they have to be there anyway! Stupid retreat or something. He's conned me so many times in the past, I'm suspicious. Or paranoid."

"And here's the latest, Payton. I forgot to tell you and Jane when I got back after Thanksgiving. They want to send me to school in Israel next year. On a kibbutz. So I won't have to do prep school applications or have my parents take me to visit places like everyone else is doing. I'm always the odd one."

"Hmmm. That's a different take. Say more."

"It's a kibbutz based on the Rudolf Steiner philosophy, like Austro-Lab that my parents started. But it's a whole community. Organic farming, Waldorf education. The whole bit. It's in the Galilee, northern part of Israel near the Lebanese border. Not as mountainous as here but my folks think it's a natural next step after Glencoe."

"What do you think, Libby? Sounds pretty exciting. And can't hurt your college application when it comes time for that. I know you don't exhibit a lot of your Jewish culture here, and I know you aren't interested in Friday-night trips to the synagogue in Lake Placid. But Israel could be a cool place to get in touch with who you are. I remember the essay you did on your great-granddad's escape from France and Africa. Family pride came through unmistakably. I learned a lot from that essay."

Libby looked at her hands. "I did enjoy that. Researching the history of it, talking to Bubby—my grandmother—on the phone about her recollections of her parents' adventure. It was probably the best writing I've ever done."

"Because it came from your heart."

"I guess so. It's just . . . I mean . . . I wish I hadn't learned about it from the Israeli visitors. They knew what the plan was before I did. It was embarrassing. Why couldn't my parents have shared it with me? It's *my* life they're messing with."

"You've got an unusual family, Libby, and I know it hasn't been easy figuring out where you fit in. It's not for me to sit in judgment of your parents, but I don't think Janey and I have hidden our feelings all that well. We choose to bring up our family in a different way and we sometimes share your exasperation. But they are your parents, blemishes and all, and they *do* love you. Although it's asking a lot of a fifteen-year-old, you don't have much choice but to accept them for who they are and stop beating yourself up about it. It's not your fault and it's not your responsibility to change them. It *is* your obligation to make it clear to them how you feel, but in ways that enable you to keep communicating."

"It's funny. I love my parents. . . . But I don't like them much. Isn't that a terrible thing to say?"

"Not necessarily. Feelings about parents can be pretty complicated. Everybody's are. As you get older, you're becoming more aware of how you've been brought up and how that may differ from the experiences of your friends. You may need some help figuring out what it means. I'm not suggesting you start therapy, Libby, and I don't mean to imply there's something wrong with you that needs fixing. But there's something to be said for having someone you can talk to about these things, someone you trust and who can help you clarify your feelings and communicate them in ways your parents will understand and respond to. There are times when life can get a little overwhelming. It happens to everyone."

"Did you ever see a shrink?" Libby asked shyly.

"That's kind of personal, young lady," Payton answered sternly, though his eyes twinkled. "But, yes, I have, upon occasion. To help me make things a little less confused. It's nothing to be ashamed of. I think this episode in the mountains may have shaken your parents more than you realize," he continued. "Don't dismiss their offer of a ski vacation. It seems like a pretty positive sign."

"Nicky sure is lucky to have you and Jane."

Payton smiled. "And we're grateful to have good role models like you and Tina living with us. You have no idea how tough life is with Nicky when you guys are on vacation," he laughed. "It's always *When is Libby coming back? I want Tina to read to me, not you.*" Libby smiled appreciatively. "Enough philosophizing," Payton said with a smile. "Time to get upstairs and do your homework before we shut off the electricity."

Tracy told his parents the whole story of both ordeals during a long walk to the barn. Emily Barcomb wept a great deal. Wendell kicked a lot of stones, hands clasped behind his back as though that might prevent him from using them in anger. When he had completed his story, Tracy looked to each parent like a puppy seeking clemency.

"This is a lot to absorb, Tracy," his dad said, clearing his throat. His mother threw her arms around him as if to protect him from any possible assaults. Wendell continued, choosing his words carefully, "I can't imagine what you must have felt, that last night in the woods. You certainly acted heroically under great stress and, for that, I am intensely proud of you." Tracy looked at his boots. So far, it was going better than he had predicted, but he guessed he was not yet out of trouble.

"Wendell, please," she interjected, hugging her son ever closer. "I know he feels terrible."

"Emily. Didn't I just say how impressed I am with our son's performance under fire?"

"Yes, you did," she responded. "But that's not all, is it?"

"No."

"I just don't want you to inflict any more pain. These past few weeks must have been nightmarish for him," she said.

Tracy was having difficulty breathing with her arms wrapped around his neck and embarrassed that someone might come along and see him in his mother's clutches.

"Trust me, Emily, I am not going to crucify our son. He has made it crystal clear to us that he understands his responsibility to Malcolm's family. I admit to being ashamed that it took so long for him to come forward, and I hope he is, too, but at least he finally did. Son?" He looked sternly at Tracy.

"Yes, Dad?"

"You have a call to make."

45

Seeking Counsel

Winter break proved a welcome interlude for students and faculty alike. The campus was quiet for nearly three weeks, with only a handful of the faculty, mostly the married couples, remaining to help the farm staff handle barn chores and decompress with occasional evening parties together. Much of the chatter when they gathered was whether Hamish would decide to expel Tracy or give him another chance. A few wagers were made.

More than one quiet evening at the MacLean farmhouse found Bonnie and Hamish discussing that very issue before the fire, tea in hand, so aware of the empty hooked rug at the foot of their chairs. Rambler was desperately missed, adding to the chasm between them. Hamish knew the decision on Tracy needed to be prompt, and conveyed to the Barcomb family before the winter term commenced. Plans had to be made, a family would have to move on, if he chose to punish Tracy with expulsion. Given his propensity to seek alternative solutions to the obvious, as well as his deep fondness for the boy, Hamish agonized over this one. Given Tracy's heroism on Wallface, it was as tough a call as he had encountered during his time as Head of school. At Bonnie's urging, to hear another voice, Hamish reached out to Ron Handy for counsel before a New Year's Eve party the Hendersons were throwing for faculty still on campus over the winter break.

He was already into his second scotch when Ron strolled into the Maple Leaf Inn and spotted the headmaster tucked into a corner booth. Hamish realized it was the first time he'd been back to his favorite haunt since that fateful night two months earlier on the day the convicts flew the coop. Over the years, he and Ron had shared many meals and expensive spirits in this cozy corner of the Adirondacks. It had always been an ideal setting for tough decision-making.

"Evening, Hamish," Ron said, sliding into the booth across from his friend. "Is this a crisis we can solve before Jane and Peyton expect us up the hill at their shindig?"

"Shindig? You *are* old, aren't you?"

"Do you prefer soirée?"

"God help me, you are impossible."

"What are you drinking?"

"Fourteen-year-old Caribbean cask Balvenie. It's a comfort to me."

"You're due for some comfort, Hamish. How can I help?"

"Ron, I'm really struggling with what to do with Barcomb and hoped to have your input before I call his parents. It's only fair they know what we've decided so they can make plans, if necessary."

"Plans? Sounds like you've made your decision."

"I feel Connaughton staring at me whenever I think about this boy. Sir Philip," Hamish added snippily, "is not a nuanced fellow. He sees blight and demands its surgical eradication."

"Blight? A fifteen-year-old who made one terrible decision and many more heroic ones? That's a terrible word to describe a child," Ron said.

"Agreed. I don't know how widely the story of Tracy's horrific plan to scare Malcolm will become known to school consultants, parents, and the press. But Connaughton worries about a threat to admissions and has made it clear to me he wants Tracy separated from Glencoe immediately. But, Ron, that young man is one of my all-time favorites. I can't stand groveling before that English dandy."

"I already had him penciled in for a lead role in the graduation show. He's a natural on stage. And I know how at home he is in the mountains. He's so looking forward to finishing his forty-six peaks as a Glencoe student."

"Ron, I never told you this, but when I was grilling him after the weaving got scissored back in September, he came up with a line to explain his behavior that came right out of your *Henry IV* show last year.

Last year. Totally appropriate to the moment, brought me up short, made me remember I was dealing with a very unusual lad. And we can take some credit for his growth. It kills me to think we could take the graduation ceremony away from him after all he's accomplished here."

"Take Connaughton out of it," Ron said. "He's a cold fish and from where I sit, his eminence, the patrician Brit, has treated you shabbily from the outset. I've always suspected the core reason is no more complicated than you're a Scotsman. If you weren't so damn good at this job, he'd have swayed the board to can you a long time ago. It's class prejudice, plain and simple."

"I'm paying for your drinks anyway. You don't have to kiss my ass," Hamish chuckled. "But you're damn right. Phil may be a hell of a fundraiser and has saved our bacon more than once, but Jesus, Mary, and Joseph, he is a flaming asshole. To Sir Philip," he said, raising his glass in a toast. Ron laughed and took a sip of scotch.

"Seriously, what do you think I should do? You helped me with such a creative solution when Scotty Morrison pulled those stunts a few years ago. Is there any way I can justify defying Connaughton and let Tracy finish out his time here?"

"I anticipated we might be having this conversation and have given it a lot of thought. Tracy is near and dear to me, too, but fundamentally quite different from our old friend Morrison. I worried then that expelling Scotty might destroy him. He did not possess nearly the intestinal fortitude I see in Tracy. I have a feeling Tracy has already baked in the inevitability that he must move on. He knows that causing the accident on Balanced Rocks, compounded by his lack of truthfulness at the time, and hoping Mal would not recall what really happened, must result in consequences. The piper must be paid. Also, having a mother who is passionate about environmental equity, fairness, and wilderness ethics influences Tracy's sense of what's right. It's quite a lesson he has learned and I am certain he expects to be held accountable.

"Hamish, I honestly believe we do him a disservice if we deny him that accountability. He will be just fine. Tracy's days here are done. We've given him all he needs. At least that's my advice. This may deep-six any thoughts he had of moving on to a leading prep school but if I read him right, he is destined for great things regardless of where he attends high school. That fellow is learning quickly who he is, and has a brilliant future, once that brain of his is fully developed. But if we are complicit in his evading accountability through some creative solution, like the one I cooked up for Scotty Morrison, we will compromise his entire future. That is not fair to him, or us."

As Hamish digested the words of his trusted friend, the Balvenie in his glass, like amber truth serum, dissolved defenses he had clung to for many years. There was much he could learn from a fifteen-year-old in terms of accepting responsibility and being accountable for his actions. Andy Boarder had no idea his crippling injuries were caused by a self-centered climbing partner whose cowardice prevented the facts from being shared. He knew in his core that until he stopped dodging personal accountability, he would continue to suffer self-inflicted physical and emotional punishment, with Bonnie an additional, innocent, victim. It would haunt him until he could face it, as Tracy was now doing rather gracefully, he had to admit.

Separating Tracy from Glencoe would be a tough, but ironic, gift, permitting the boy to resolve his transgressions, pay an appropriate price, and put it behind him. Hamish envied Tracy. He could only wish for the day when the trauma of his treatment of Andy Boarder could come to an end, would no longer haunt him. His dependence on opioids to make the pain go away was a penitence he, and the woman he loved, had suffered long enough. How to retrieve his moral compass and finally move on? That remained an elusive mystery.

Ron was not yet done with his friend and boss. "Though you did not ask me, Hamish, I think you made a terrible decision with Pete."

"No, I dinnae ask," Hamish grumbled. He knew he was about to be taken to the proverbial woodshed by the only person, besides his wife, who could get away with it.

"I'd put this year's salary on the fact this decision to fire one of our most valuable staff members also has Connaughton's fingerprints all over it. Hamish, he may be right about Tracy for all the wrong reasons, by the way. But being pressured to fire Pete is one decision you should not take lying down. Connaughton has no clue about life here. Why we have a board chair who is so disconnected from who we are and what we stand for is an abomination, and a discussion for another time—I'm getting too old to help you fight that battle.

"And I'll wager next year's salary as well, that Connaughton doesn't have the balls to fire you for standing up to him on Pete. If you don't, or can't put your foot down with that man, and I understand this is hard stuff, then Glencoe is no longer what Glenn and Susan had in mind when they blessed your hiring."

"Crivens, you must have been conspiring with my wife. She's given me more than one talking to on that one."

"A wise woman. Listen to her if you know what's good for you," Ron smiled, rising to get his coat.

"I'll sleep on it, my friend. Thank you for your candor. On both topics. This is the most miserable job in the world but nothing makes me happier." The two men laughed and clinked glasses.

After mulling over the advice he'd just been given, and nursing his scotch for a few more minutes after Ron had departed, Hamish gathered his coat, nodded thanks to his old friend behind the bar, and drove carefully up the hill to his farmhouse, conscientiously observing the speed limit. Though it was late, past ten, the kitchen light still burned bright. His wife was baking again.

"Smells yummy, dear," he said, kissing her on the back of her neck. The smell of banana bread filled the cozy kitchen. Bonnie did not look up to greet him and he felt the chill. "We're expected at the Hendersons shortly. Are you nearly done with the baking?"

"Sit down, Hamish. We need to talk."

"Uh oh. Not you, too."

"I'm not sure what that means, but no one else that I know of talks to you like I do." She placed a hot cup of tea in front of him, warming her hands with a cup of her own. "Since the rescue we've barely spoken, except to share our daily schedules. You've nearly no idea what I've been going through. I believe you don't want to know."

"Now, hang on, Bonnie. I've . . ."

"Don't with the *Hang on, Bonnie* stuff," she interrupted. "I'm grieving something terrible, Hamish. For our sweet Rambler. For Pete. For us.

Something's got to change. I feel like we're eroding like your precious Adirondack trails. We're down near bedrock and there's little fertile soil left. I'm not sure I know who you are anymore. I barely know who I am. And I don't like what I see in the mirror. Do you?"

"Bonnie, Bonnie, Bonnie," he said, choking up. "Where do I start?"

"Start with acknowledging I'm right. Where did we lose it, Hamish? What are you prepared to do to change?"

"We both have our demons," he said quietly. "I can tell you I've learned a lot from a fifteen-year-old boy about how to face the darkness. I know I can't medicate away my shadows and I see that it has infected you as well. That is a tragedy."

"Hamish, I know that I have not ever really accepted that we could not have the family I dreamed of. My ways of coping were no healthier than yours. I need to own that and be thankful for what we've managed to build. But it is so hard for me. So hard. And I wish I felt you shared that pain with me. I need it to be shared. It's too heavy for one Scottish lass to carry." She put her head into her hands and began to cry.

Hamish stood, walked around the table, and enveloped her in his arms. "You have always been my guiding light, Bonnie. Even when I dinnae deserve it or show you that I felt it. I cannae promise you I know the way back, but my focus will change. Must change. Ron gave me a talking-to, as well, just now. He cannae help me do what's right by you. But he will always be a North Star for me when it comes to running this place. For as long as they'll have me . . . and you'll have me."

"Well, thank you for listening, even if you're totally foutered," she said, finally returning the kiss she had been given when he first walked in.

"I am *not* drunk," he said, gratefully accepting the peck on his cheek. "Just got the rough edges sanded off, that's all."

"Then you can bloody well get your friend Pete Hedges back here before he finds a better job that pays him what he's worth!" she said, wiping her nose with a tissue.

"Oh, God. Not again."

"Christine was by the other day. She's taking this pretty hard, too. She sees her future with that fellow going up in smoke and feels it was her fault anyway. And she's right, Hamish. Pete doesn't deserve what he got."

"You can thank our chairman for that one."

"No, Hamish. We can thank *you* for that one. Stand up for what's right. If it means we go back to Edinburgh . . . there could be worse things."

The following day Hamish solicited opinions from both Malcolm and his aunt on their feelings for Tracy's actions. Both felt that the past need not be revisited and encouraged Hamish to let bygones be bygones. But the advice from Ron won the day. Hamish reluctantly concluded that Tracy and Glencoe must part ways. He called the Barcomb family on January 2nd, not wanting to ruin their New Year's. They supported his decision without objection, thanking him for taking care of their son for two and a half years.

Softening the blow, Tracy accepted an invitation from Malcolm's Aunt Mathilda to spend the final week of the break with her and Malcolm at their condo on St. Thomas in the Virgin Islands. It was the first time Tracy had been out of the Northeast, let alone the country. It was bittersweet in light of the decision to end his time at Glencoe. Given the tough economic situation he had grown up in, it was more than a shock to enjoy the trappings of wealth that Malcolm had inherited.

Tracy endlessly expressed his appreciation for the invitation and, at dinner one evening, Malcolm could take it no longer. "Enough with the thank-yous, Tracy. Just enjoy it," he erupted.

"Malcolm, you could learn a little humility from your friend, and maybe not take so much for granted," Mathilda scolded.

The boys spent their days getting certified in scuba diving and their evenings trying to get served in the bars of Charlotte Amalie; on only one occasion were they successful. The alcohol lubricated their ability to talk at length about the day on Balanced Rocks, the events that led up to it, and how weird it would be that Malcolm would be the one returning to Glencoe. Tracy promised to be there for Malcolm and Libby's graduation, unless Hamish banned him.

The week in Vermont turned out to be positive, even therapeutic, for Libby and her parents. For the first time in years, she was granted *quantity* as well as *quality* time. She slept late each morning while her parents pursued their professional duties, then joined them for ski runs in the afternoons and private dinners in the evenings, apart from the other retreat participants. It gave them a chance to rediscover one another. Nevertheless, she was eager to return for her final semester at Glencoe, and excited about how her relationship with Tracy might evolve. When she heard the bad news from Tracy, it felt like getting lost all over again.

"I may be in Vermont, but you're going to be in Israel. Who's abandoning who?" Tracy teased during one of many phone calls they had over the break.

"Whom. Who's abandoning whom. You better write," Libby said, sniffling. They both understood it would be difficult to nurture such a tenuous relationship from a distance, but the pain they shared now proved how intense their brief relationship had been.

"What else have I got to do? Of course, I'll write. Libby, you're the most important person in the world to me now."

Though the ache would not soon disappear, she was grateful that Tina would be there to help her heal the hole in her heart.

46

Fighting an Indictment

ATTORNEY GARRETT PEARSON DEVOTED WHAT LITTLE TIME HE HAD in his overly booked schedule to creating a sympathetic client in Ramon. With gentle arm-twisting and other persuasions, he extracted commitments from a number of media people with whom he had long-standing friendships, or for whom he'd done some service over the years. He called a squash buddy who worked at CNN in Atlanta, a golfing partner who was also vice president of public relations at NBC in New York, and, lastly, a senior editor at *USA Today*. Timing was critical, he told them. Pearson's NBC friend pulled some strings with the network affiliate in Burlington, Vermont, and was promised a full five minutes on the dramatic rescue that would run on the six o'clock news, then again at eleven. That story, including helicopter shots of the summit of Wallface, mug shots of Garth LeGrange, and a favorable description of Ramon's battle with the lumberjack, would be seen by prospective grand jurors in Essex County, New York. The CNN contact set up phone interviews with Libby, Tracy, and Malcolm, and met with Eva Ortiz in New York City. The piece ran nationwide every thirty minutes on Headline News for much of the Saturday prior to the first day the grand jury was presented with the facts of Ramon's case. The public's fascination with the story turned viral on social media as well.

By the first day of grand jury proceedings, much of the country knew of the mountaintop drama and the people involved. On the first business day of 2003, twenty-three citizens from towns and villages throughout

Essex County arrived in Elizabethtown to consider the most celebrated case the county had seen in years.

District Attorney Marcus Webster orchestrated the proceedings, for no judge presides at a grand jury hearing. Originally designed in the twelfth century to protect the average citizen from summary arrest and prosecution by the King of England, the grand jury is something of an anachronism in modern times. While England abolished it in 1933, in the United States, it remains a secret proceeding, during which the prosecuting attorney presents evidence and questions witnesses who are compelled to appear by subpoena. The grand jury ultimately decides whether or not there is probable cause to indict defendants and hold them for trial. Ramon was permitted, but not obligated, to testify. Pearson felt it was their only shot to sway the jurors, so he advised Webster that Ramon wished to participate. As the target of this inquiry, Ramon was permitted to have the assistance of a lawyer only while he was physically present in the grand jury room, but the process did not allow for cross-examination by his lawyer, who also could not address the jurors directly. Both sides understand the process is weighted heavily in the prosecutor's favor—it is a rare outcome, indeed, when the jurors opt not to indict, given the way the cards are stacked, for they need only decide there is probable cause that a crime was committed, a much lower bar than the *beyond a reasonable doubt* threshold that is required in an actual trial. It was hard to dispute the facts that Ramon had not left prison with permission.

Webster launched into a summary of the events leading up to Ramon's recapture. At a time of such widespread lawlessness and permissiveness in society, he argued, it was incumbent upon the grand jury to send a strong message that prison breaks had to be punished, no matter the extenuating circumstances, or how exemplary an escapee's behavior might appear. He was doing his job, but Pearson felt there was no passion in the DA's performance. Was it just overconfidence that this was an open-and-shut case? Or was his heart not in it?

Ramon sat impassively through the preamble, but inside his stomach was churning. This was not how the little boy who had ridden beside his father in the tobacco fields of Puerto Rico had envisioned his future—a common criminal ping-ponging through the US legal system. His conscience was clear; he had done right by his young friends and, with his mother under the protective wing of Libby's family, he would accept the final result.

Hank Cassidy, the Ray Brook Corrections Officer whose life had been turned upside down since the prison break, followed the ACF warden to the witness stand. Webster led him through the day of the escape, how he had tried to break up the fight, placing himself in great personal danger. Bitterly, Cassidy told the jury how the escape had changed his life; how he'd been forced to apply for welfare after losing his job at the prison; how his wife was humiliated and his children were bullied in school because of the bad publicity surrounding his dismissal. It was convincing testimony that seemed to resonate with many of the jurors.

When Cassidy stepped down, Marcus Webster informed the grand jury that Ramon Ortiz wished to testify. Alice Hawkins, second chair to Garrett Pearson, squeezed Ramon's knee in a sign of support.

"It's showtime, Ramon," whispered Pearson. "Just be yourself." Ramon nodded weakly, took a deep breath, and rose to approach the witness stand. He turned to face the jury, took the oath, and answered every pointed question clearly and humbly.

"I made a foolish mistake," he said, looking at each juror in turn as he spoke, challenging them to make eye contact. "Every day I curse myself for that decision. You must understand, Garth LeGrange came to me the day after I learned that my mother had had a heart attack and my brother was attacked by a gang. I was desperate to help in any way I could, so I said, 'Yes' when he asked me to run." Ramon bit his lip.

"Too obvious," whispered Garrett Pearson to Alice Hawkins. "Too melodramatic. I wish we'd had more time with him."

"Living in the woods was very difficult for me," Ramon continued. "Many times, I thought of giving myself up. I even tried to escape him, but nearly froze to death. When Garth told me that night of his plans to kill the kids, I knew I had to try to stop him." He paused for a moment to take a sip of water. There was not a sound from the jury, no coughs, no rustling of papers. "I didn't really believe he would do it, but when he grabbed Libby to throw her over the edge and she started screaming, that's when it really hit me. I couldn't let that happen." The jury could see from the faraway look that Ramon was back atop Wallface. They saw sweat bead up on his forehead as he recalled the moment. District Attorney Webster, saw it too. Rather than pound Ramon with a follow-up, which is what all his training demanded that he do, Webster allowed Ramon a moment to collect himself. "You gotta understand," Ramon said softly, wiping the sweat with his sleeve. "Those kids became family to me around that campfire."

After the prosecutor finished his questioning, Ramon walked back to the defense table and sat down beside his attorneys. He had told the truth and there was nothing more he could do. The next day the jury heard, in turn, from Libby, Tracy, and Malcolm. Winter break was not yet over but the three classmates had cut short their vacations to make the trip to Elizabethtown to support the man who had saved their lives. For Tracy, it was bittersweet being together with his friends, knowing he would not be joining them at Glencoe to finish their senior year together.

After the three had finished their testimony, the jury retired to deliberate. Four hours later the jury members asked that dinner be brought in. At eight o'clock, they sent word to Marcus Webster's office that a decision had been reached.

"We vote to present a *true bill*, Mr. District Attorney," the jury foreman announced. Webster let out a deep breath. He hadn't been certain the jury would vote to indict, so pervasive had the sympathy been for Ramon in the press and on the street. He could count on one hand the number of *no bills* he'd heard in his career, those rare decisions by grand juries not to indict a defendant despite the prosecutor's request. Apparently, the jury felt the facts of the escape held more weight than the intense media coverage sympathetic to the defense, the compelling accounts of three persuasive teenagers, and, above all, the authentic testimony from the defendant himself. Ramon had fled, and that was, in the end, all that the jury needed to know. So why, Webster wondered, was he feeling no satisfaction?

Garrett Pearson reached Ramon by phone at the Elizabethtown jail the next morning.

"Sorry, man. You did the best you could. I'm really proud of you."

There was silence on the other end. Then, a sigh. "What's next?"

"A judge will be selected and the date of the trial will be set. I suspect it will all happen pretty quickly. I wish the outcome had been different, Ramon, but I'm afraid that's not the way it turned out. We're not going away, though. If you want us, we'll defend you at trial and, maybe we can beat it then. If you get convicted at trial, we'll argue that any new sentence should run concurrent with your existing one, not just tacked on at the end."

"I understand," Ramon said, disconsolately. "Thank you for sticking with me."

"It's a bummer, but you did an extraordinary thing on Wallface, and we'll make that case to the jury. Yes, you broke out of prison. Yes, you humiliated the guard. You have to understand, you're not Mr. Popularity with law enforcement people right now. But given all that was against you, when the shit hit the fan, you stood up for the kids and for what was right. We'll make the case as best we can."

"Thanks," Ramon mumbled. "It was pretty scary getting all those questions fired at me. Hard not to lose my head or get angry."

"I know. It's a terrible thing to go through. You may have to do it all over again at trial. We don't have much of a case without you. By the way, I spoke to Mr. MacLean last night. You know, the headmaster at Glencoe?"

"Yes sir. I met him in the woods."

"Right. Of course. He's got a job waiting for you at Glencoe when you get out. However long that takes."

"Waiting for me?"

"On the maintenance staff. You'll be able to help repair buildings, keep the place running, that sort of thing. It's something to hang on to while we fight this."

"Huh. That's the program I was taking at Ray Brook before I got myself sucked into that escape. Never figured it would lead to a job."

"Let's hope it's not too far down the road. One step at a time. For now, keep out of trouble. No drama, okay?"

At ten o'clock the next morning Ramon was summoned to the visitors' room at the county lockup. He couldn't imagine who would be interested in seeing him.

"Surprised to see me?" Libby asked, smiling.

"I sure am. Thank you so much for testifying for me," Ramon said. "And thank your parents for getting me a great lawyer. But I won't lie. I hoped the result would be better."

"I know. We tried."

Ramon nodded sadly.

"I wanted to see how you were doing before school starts," she said. Ramon could see she was nervous. *Got to be her first prison visit*, he thought. The last time they had spoken, the only time, really, had been around a campfire by Lost Pond; before the forced march and the struggle atop Wallface. Intense events compressed into a tiny slice of time. Is this beautiful girl, so put together now, the same screaming child I saw hurled over the edge? He remembered how that heave had galvanized him into action.

"I'm so sorry the vote didn't go your way," Libby said. "But I wanted you to know we've all been worrying about you. And I needed to see you again."

"I don't know what to say," Ramon said, clearly appreciative.

Libby looked around the room, taking it all in—the drab institutional colors, the harsh lighting, intimidating guards near the door. She shuddered. "This place scares me."

"Me, too. It's taken me a while to get used to it." He hesitated. "That's not true. I'm not used to it. I know how to survive here a lot better than I did out there," Ramon said, waving his arm in the theoretical direction of the mountains. "But when I get out of here, whenever that is, I damn sure hope to never see the inside of a place like this again. I've had a lot of time to think about what got me into this mess. It gets to be home for a lot of people. Eventually, they don't know how to live on the outside, so they just keep coming back. That can't be me."

"How did you manage, living with that crazy person in that miserable spot? I was lost for two days and was sure I was going to die out there."

"That would take a whole lot more time to explain than we've got today," Ramon said. "I've asked myself the same question."

"We're both city kids," Libby said, immediately regretting the implication that their upbringings were equivalent. "I mean, did you ever get used to life at Lost Pond? Weren't you kind of just as trapped as you are in here?"

Ramon was silent for a moment. He steepled his fingers, stared at the table between them. He had wrestled with that since the night he had been recaptured. "It was pretty tough at first. I had no idea what I was getting myself into. And I knew it was a mistake right away. All I could think about was how my mom and brother were doing. And I wasn't doing shit to help them. So, I ran to a place that was even scarier than prison. It's funny, though. After a couple of weeks, when I felt less scared Garth was going to kill me, I realized he actually needed me . . . to help keep us both going. I got more comfortable. I gave up hating myself. Don't get me wrong. The food sucked, what there was of it. You never really got warm. And the fear of getting caught didn't just disappear. But the daily routines helped. I kind of liked controlling my own life.

"When I had a chance to just be on my own, to get away from that monster, I saw how beautiful the place was. Clean. Quiet. Peaceful. Even the storms got to be okay. The wind was something else; I was sure our shelter would just blow away; so many different kinds of snow. I never noticed snow before, back in the city. Sometimes soft and gentle, sometimes swirling sideways, sometimes like needles. Piling up around us like blankets. I sort of felt protected by all that snow. Like the more snow there was, the safer we were. I never understood that thing about the Eskimos having so many different words for snow. Now I get it. If you're living with it day after day, you see that it's not just one thing."

In his faraway look Ramon was clearly back there, reliving it. Libby did not interrupt.

"I never really thought about the weather before, or paid attention to it, or had my life controlled by it. It's a complicated place, the wilderness. I understand now why Garth liked it so much. It grew on me, even though I never stopped wanting to get out of there and get home.

"So . . . to answer your question . . . yes, it was a kind of prison . . . but I could one day see myself going out there again. Under the right conditions," he smiled. "And I sure as shit don't want to spend any more days in a place like this. Yeah, the wilderness is different. Better."

"You could have just run away after you left us up there," Libby said. Ramon recalled the horror of seeing her on that precarious ledge, of seeing Malcolm dangling. It was a nightmare that still dominated his dreams.

"I thought about it. Tracy gave me good instructions about how to get down to a trail, but I wasn't sure what I was going to do once I got there. Libby, you're probably the main reason I didn't run again. After our talk, when I found out you knew my mom and all, that we had some crazy connection, and then after Garth threw you off the top, all I could think of was to get you help so you didn't die up there.

"I won't lie. I wasn't happy getting recaptured. They beat me up pretty bad on the way out. I figured I'd probably bought myself a lot more years behind bars. But I knew it meant you weren't going to be up there another night. It's amazing that you came to visit today. I don't know what to say. It's really sweet."

"Hah! Sweet is not an adjective most of my friends would use to describe me," Libby chuckled. "But, from you? I'll take it.

"Ramon, that day, up there, we all grew up a lot. I wouldn't be here if you hadn't stepped up. I'll never forget that." She checked her watch, stood up, and walked around the table to embrace him. "I guess I'd better be going now," she said. "My dad is probably getting impatient. He's still in the parking lot."

"Thanks for coming, Libby. You have no idea how much it means."

Eva Ortiz and Consuela took advantage of the kids being in Puerto Rico to travel to Elizabethtown to see Ramon after the indictment. Ramon was relieved to see that his mom was not about to die from a failed, or broken, heart. He was also elated to hear that Libby's family had made it possible for his siblings to visit their father's side of the family and get a few welcome days out of the frigid New York weather. The visit gave him the strength to handle whatever he still had to face.

Several days after the grand jury's decision, back in his Georgetown office, Garrett Pearson phoned District Attorney Marcus Webster to discuss the timetable for selecting a judge and setting a date for Ramon's trial. He expected to leave a message and was surprised when Webster got right on.

FIGHTING AN INDICTMENT

"Missing the North Country yet, Garrett?" Webster cracked.

"Don't miss driving in that wintry mess," Pearson rejoined. "In truth, I intend to be there again, regardless of your miserable weather, so the sooner we get this trial scheduled the better."

"I'm actually glad you called," Webster said, turning serious. "Your client has been weighing on me."

"Oh? How so?"

"Between you, me, and the lamppost, this is not a trial I am looking forward to. Not because I worry about losing. In fact, I'm pretty certain it's going to be easy getting a verdict I should be happy with. But it just doesn't sit right with me, to tell you the truth."

This was not at all what Pearson expected to hear. His mind was racing. Was there a way out?

"How familiar are you with New York law, counselor?" Webster asked. "Not to be dismissive, but you probably don't defend many folks up our way, do you?"

"That's right. Not many. I probably wouldn't have gotten involved if it hadn't been for my friendship with the head of Glencoe School. An old climbing buddy. But I keep up with New York law, and I'm not walking away from Ramon Ortiz any time soon. I'll see it through, and maybe our jury will be more sympathetic than the crew we just dealt with."

"I did what I had to do," Webster said. "But I didn't enjoy it one bit. Ortiz got himself in a pickle that maybe he didn't deserve and I've got a thought about how we might resolve it."

"I'm listening."

"Make a Clayton motion."

"Huh! Interesting. Especially coming from your side of the table."

"I know. Look, it's a straightforward and speedy way to get Ortiz out of that pickle and get me some sleep again."

"I don't think I've ever had the right case to make a Clayton motion. 1973 if memory serves, right?"

"On the money, Garrett. People versus Clayton. Poor fellow was indicted for murder but subsequently had his case dismissed, *in the interest of justice*, due to persuasive proof that his confession had been coerced. I think making this go away with a Clayton motion is a neat option."

465

"The Clayton dismissal was overturned on appeal, wasn't it?" Pearson asked, racking his brain for the background on this novel approach to Ramon's predicament.

"Bingo. But it did not erase the concept of this type of motion to the court as a mechanism to reconsider the value to society of pursuing a trial in certain circumstances."

"Ramon deserves a break," Garrett said.

"No argument here. You inform me that you wish the indictment the grand jury just handed up be dismissed in the interest of justice. I will choose not to oppose your Clayton. Representing the People, I don't see any value in keeping him locked up beyond his original sentence. Not after everything he did to save lives. He's been punished enough, in my view. I had to bring this to a grand jury for an indictment, and I did that. But that's enough for me. If we are both supportive of the motion, I don't know of any judge in this county who is going to insist we go to trial. Their workload is heavy enough."

"I'm not going to argue with you. It's a helluva needle-threading you've proposed. I'm pretty taken aback that the approach is coming from you. Can we execute this right away?"

"As soon as you get it on my desk, I'll present it to the judge. We can dispose of this in a matter of days, I think. I'll feel better knowing we took this case off the docket."

"You're a stand-up guy, Marcus. I appreciate it."

"My advice? Don't say anything to your client until we get this done, okay?"

"Agreed."

47

Grasping the Nettle

O N T H E M O R N I N G O F T H E F I R S T D A Y O F T H E N E W T E R M, H A M I S H
MacLean sat alone in his darkened study. In the stillness of predawn, the
world sat poised for a new day. Through the window beyond his desk, he
could barely make out wisps of smoke lifting from the chimney in Dewey
Hall as the sky grayed from black. Some good soul had already lit a fire
in the dining room fireplace. The plume of smoke rose without waver,
foretelling a placid morning.

Daybreak revealed a heavy quilt of clouds tinged with pink from
a winter sun struggling to burn through. The overcast blanketing the
Adirondack High Peaks suggested snow, probably before the day was out.
Muffled noises of dishes clinking and water running downstairs in the
kitchen reached his ears. The aroma of fresh-perked coffee wafted up the
stairs. He felt a pang of remorse. Bonnie deserved better.

It promised to be a good day—a morning devoted to plowing
through student evaluation letters, then an afternoon of cross-country
skiing with his rediscovered friend, Garrett Pearson, on the Olympic course at Mt. Van Hoevenberg. He wondered idly if he could
still keep up with Garrett, and made a mental note to bring his ski
wax kit to his office. He reached for a pile of mail that Cathy Swenson had been so kind to drop off at the farmhouse the previous
evening. In the middle was an envelope whose address was written
by an adolescent hand. He removed the letter and began to read.

Dear Hamish,

*I'm writing to you from the Virgin Islands! I'm staying with Malcolm and his aunt. They have been so kind to me. Crazy, right? I can't remember the last time I wrote a letter but something told me I would feel better about talking to you this way. Thank you for everything you've done for me these three years. I understand why you decided I can't come back even though I cried a couple of times thinking about not being able to finish what I started. Libby told me Pete isn't coming back. That's really terrible. I feel awful thinking it was because of me that he lost his job. Pete taught me a whole lot. You did too of course. I don't think it was fair that my mistake should ruin things for Pete. He was the best teacher I had. I've been thinking about my English class with him. Bet you never thought I could think about a class! I finished the book he assigned—*Endurance*—and the theme Pete kept talking about—the Hero's Journey. I couldn't get it out of my head. I feel like I understand that being a hero doesn't mean everything always works out. There's painful consequences even for a hero. That class helped me feel more ok about the stuff I did and didn't do. What happened to me—I'm not trying to say I'm a hero—but I did do some good stuff and maybe saved a life or two. But I also almost took a life. Malcolm's, I mean. I've had a lot of time to think about that. I'm really sorry about not telling you the truth about what happened on Balanced Rocks. If it happened tomorrow I would act differently now. At least I hope so. Living with that hanging over me was really tough and I do feel relieved that I finally was able to tell you about it, even if it meant I got kicked out. Mal and I have talked a lot about it too, and he's been telling me to stop beating myself up so much. I think I'm his best friend now. I never would have bet that could happen. He's different now. I think I am too. Anyway I just wanted to thank you and Glencoe for helping me grow up. I'm going to miss everyone a whole lot. I hope you will let me come back to see my friends graduate.*

STILL YOUR FRIEND,
TRACY BARCOMB

Hamish folded the letter and replaced it in its envelope. He swallowed hard and reached for a tissue, blowing his nose to stem his tears. He felt regret but no lesser amount of pride that this young man had honored the fellowship of the rope, and saved lives as a result. Glencoe had made a difference, even if he had decided, reluctantly, that Tracy must go. *Some people don't need forty years to exorcise a ghost*, he thought. Nor must they rely upon alcohol and pain pills. It had been an unusually stimulating, if not unsettling, fall and early winter, chock-full of new lessons for an aging leader perhaps not too old to learn from a protégé not too young to teach.

Hamish felt uncertain about his place at Glencoe and wondered whether this semester should be his last. The community under his care had grappled with tests of honesty, accountability, tolerance, the fragility of life. For a quarter century, Hamish had enjoyed the privilege of occupying the captain's chair, providing students and faculty alike with invaluable, life affirming experiences as they left this place and went their separate ways into the world. He was honored to be their steward, but not certain how worthy.

As he replayed the events of autumn, culminating in the letter he had just read, and considered the toll they had taken on his psyche and his marriage, it became indelibly clear he could not lead others until he put his own house in order. From the trustees there remained the persistent concern about enrollment and endowment, both vital to assure a future here. He knew from the grapevine that some on the board were concerned by the notoriety Glencoe had received in the press. Connaughton, for one, did not hide his criticism. It was not the kind of publicity that boosted admissions, nor bolstered reputations. If push came to shove, he wondered how many votes would go his way for a contract renewal, despite what he had done for this magnificent school.

More to the point, how could he teach others to face their fears, their insecurities and dark secrets if he refused to do the same? Was it right to refuse his wife her fervent wish that he confront his own demons? Oxycodone and alcohol would forever lay claim to him until he found the fortitude to face the root cause of his torment. Deal with the past or leave the tiller to a truer captain.

To address the first bit of unfinished business and honor the promise he had made to his sensible wife, and wise friend Handy, Hamish checked the contact list in his cell phone and clicked the entry for Pete Hedges. He recalled one of the early staff meetings of the year when, addressing the newcomers to the faculty, he had advised them to *get comfortable being uncomfortable. If you want to make a difference at Glencoe, you have to push yourselves just as we ask the students to do the same. We want them to learn what they are capable of, and the same applies to all of us.* Waiting for Pete to pick up certainly made him feel he was walking the walk, struggling to get comfortable with discomfort.

"G'morning, Hamish," said the familiar, though guarded voice. "I guess you'll be seeing the buses arrive in a few hours for the new term."

"Aye. I hope to ski a few kilometers first, Pete. Are you settled? Did you get away for New Years?" Hamish temporized.

"What's this about, Hamish?" Pete said. "I know you didn't call to chat and I think I've done all the exit stuff you asked."

"I'll nae hold you long, Peter. I made a mistake and I'm sorry. About the sacking. It dinnae help us find the kids and it dinnae make us a stronger school. If the board needs their pound of flesh, they'll have to take it out of me. I need you here, at least as long as they let me run the place. As far as I'm concerned, if you haven't a better offer yet, and you've got it in you to forgive a stubborn old man, this is an error I'd like to correct. The job's waiting for you if you'll have it." He knew this would be a board agenda item for sure. Would they line up behind Connaughton on this one? If so, Pete would probably not be the only one getting fired. So be it. At least his conscience would be clear.

Pete gave himself the luxury of a few seconds to think it through, and to extend the pain just a bit more for his friend and mentor. "I want it," he said finally. "It's what I know and what I'm good at."

"I appreciate it, Pete. Please hurry back. I'm so sorry for putting you through this."

Hamish hung up, feeling one weight lift from his shoulders. Two more scores to settle.

He pulled a blank sheet of Glencoe letterhead from his desk and began to write, in longhand. *Dear Chairman Connaughton . . .*

He had never written a letter of resignation before. He took his time. Were he most interested in ease of editing he would have used his laptop, but this exercise was a cathartic effort to get those long pent-up frustrations out of his brain and into the fresh air. He would decide later whether this letter would find its way to an envelope and a mailbox, or the trash, but exorcising ghosts was necessary, even if this letter never saw the light of day. Something about committing his truth to paper made him feel he was taking an important step—perhaps another lesson Tracy had inadvertently taught him. If his tenure at Glencoe School was about to end, let it be on his own terms—through resignation, not a firing. But he would follow advice he had given others—wait a day, sleep on it— don't put a stamp on a letter written under stress.

Hamish desperately missed Rambler who should have been curled up by his feet. He rose from his chair, walked to the bookcases that lined one wall of his study and ran his finger across his prize possessions: books of adventure, first ascents, memorable moments of mountaineering, a world-class collection of Heroic Journeys he had meticulously and lovingly accumulated over the decades. His finger lingered upon a well-worn notebook and unconsciously began to hum a familiar Scottish tune. With a slight tremble he selected the journal and opened it. Dated entries in his familiar hand revealed themselves as he scanned the yellowing pages. Toward the end of the notebook, he came upon several empty sheets, then a list of names and addresses, the way contacts were maintained before the days of electronic devices. Some were faded almost beyond recognition but . . . there it was . . . probably no longer accurate, but a place to start . . . *In care of Mrs. Catherine Boarder, 241 Willow Crescent, St. Albans, Hertfordshire, United Kingdom.* And a phone number. Was it possible Andy's mother was still alive? If not, where could he find someone who might know what had become of Andy? Hamish imagined him a renowned doctor, despite the disabilities he'd suffered on Zero Gully. Maybe some British medical society would have a record of him. With luck, that trail had not grown cold, for Hamish was now compelled to walk it. He hoped at the end of that trail he would find Andy Boarder. He would look into the man's eyes and tell him the truth of what had happened during that ferocious night. He would admit that by striking out for the summit on his own he had failed the fellowship of the rope. He, alone, was responsible for Andy's grievous injuries. He would ask the man he had abandoned for forgiveness and in that long-delayed conversation he hoped to find peace.

What are you waiting for? he thought. *Have you learned nothing?* With more than a bit of trepidation Hamish's fingers tapped in the number from those faded pages. An unfamiliar set of beeps signaled he was connecting to a distant phone in a faraway world.

"Hello," intoned a deep male voice.

"Good day. This is Hamish MacLean, calling from the United States. I'm trying to reach Mrs. Boarder," Hamish said, hesitantly. She would be in her eighties at least, Hamish calculated. Would this be a caregiver? There was a pregnant pause.

"This is her son. Dr. Boarder. Do you know my mother?"

Hamish took a deep breath. "Hello, Andy. . . . It's been a while, hasn't it?"

Acknowledgments

This novel would not have been possible without the willingness of several folks to ensure poetic license did not stray too far, converting unassailable facts into credible fiction. Thanks go to Jeff Smith for his close reading, Roger Schwarz for his advice on legal issues, Laura Waterman for her wise counsel and setting me straight on some flora issues, Ron Konowitz for ensuring search and rescue depictions were true to life, and to my agent, Craig Kayser, who helped in numerous ways to make this a richer brew. Tip of the hat to my children—Ben, Daniel, Josh, and Rachel—who gave sound advice on some arguably questionable choices I made, and assured me the work was worthy, even if I didn't always believe them. I am so grateful that Jake Bonar believed in the story and sold the concept that North Country Books / Globe Pequot should dip a toe in the fiction pool. Lastly, huge thanks to my life partner, Laura, my most ardent supporter.